Peach Retreat at Turtle Cove

THE MIGHTY APHRODITE WRITING SOCIETY

DARCI BALOGH

KNOWHERE MEDIA

For Dad and Carolyn

Thank you for your unwavering support of me going after my dreams. Because of you I was able to shift my life and pursue my writing career and I will be forever grateful. With all my love!

Darci

$O_{n\varepsilon}$

Phoebe

Before her 35th birthday, Phoebe Collins was determined to change her life.

She had made that pact with herself while staring into a roaring fire in a beautiful room at a romantic B&B on February 14th. Alone.

After her long distance boyfriend, Giovanni, disappeared into thin air. After paying for his plane ticket from Italy. After paying for a lot of things, actually. Phoebe had come to realize that the man she had met online, fell in love with, but never seen in person, was gone forever.

Without saying a word. No goodbye. No 'I just want to be friends'. Not even a thank you for her tireless emotional, and financial, support of his dreams of being an artist.

Giovanni, if that was even his name, had never arrived on his flight from Italy on Valentine's Day for the *vacanza romantica* she had planned for him. For them.

The last text she received from him said he was boarding the plane. That, too, must have been a lie. He had never gotten on the plane, never planned on coming to see her, and perhaps never even existed. Not in the way she believed he did at least.

The first few hours after he failed to show up at passenger pickup had been full of panic on her end. Then the panic melted slowly, painfully, into humiliation and, finally, shame. She had been duped. Her dreams of romance twisted by the words of a charlatan and turned into a joke. An expensive joke at that.

"You will never be made a fool of again, Phoebe. You need to focus on yourself, follow your dreams, change your life," she had said to the empty B&B room.

Easier said than done.

While she was still nursing her broken heart and recovering from all of the money transfers she had made to Giovanni over their months of online courtship, the company she worked for began to fall apart.

A merger didn't happen. A company move to a new location in another state became necessary. And Phoebe's job disappeared. Just like Giovanni.

That was when she had hatched the plan for a writing retreat at a beach house in Turtle Cove, a place she had never been, but had heard wonderful things about from her mother's youngest sister, Aunt Scarlet.

Inspired and ready to build a new future for herself, the Mighty Aphrodite Writing Society Beach Retreat had been formed. When Phoebe was at her lowest, she had turned her eyes to her future and said 'Yes'.

With Giovanni in her rear view mirror, her job over, her apartment lease up, and her belongings stuffed into a storage unit, she left her old life behind and took off on a two day road trip to Turtle Cove. Destiny awaited and Phoebe was ready.

Of course, if she had known there were no street lights at the beach house she would have planned her arrival during daylight hours. She didn't like not knowing where she was going. It wasn't her natural feel good place.

"You wanted a change," she chided herself as she leaned forward and squinted through the windshield at the dark road, trying to determine if she was even headed in the right direction.

The steering wheel pressed uncomfortably into her belly, making it difficult to hold the position.

She frowned.

Yet another reason she should lose weight, so she could maneuver while driving through the pitch black night down an unfamiliar street in a neighborhood, city, and state she had never been to before–reason number gazillion.

"You have arrived at your destination," the annoying GPS announced...again.

"Where?!" Phoebe threw her hands into the air. "There's nothing here!"

Again she squinted into the darkness. All she could see was directly in front of her car, the gravel road edged by thick vegetation illuminated by her headlights. She punched the button to end the computer directions.

When she had planned this whole little adventure she had thought everything through completely.

The cost of the rental and other expenses for a three month stay, the size of the beach house – they needed enough room for three unrelated adults to live comfortably together – the quality of the beach, nearby amenities, and supplies like food and toiletries. She had planned everything out to a 't' on her spreadsheet.

No street lights. How could she have planned for that?

"Ugh," Phoebe got out of the car, leaving it running with the high beams on just in case. Were there panthers or some kind of horrific night snakes lurking in the vegetation? That was another detail she had missed. "Note to self," she said to the dark night. "Double check for man-eating animals in the surrounding area next time you book a writing retreat."

The sound of her voice dissipated into the night and was quickly washed out by a low rhythmic rushing noise. It took a few moments for Phoebe to realize what she was hearing – the ocean.

A vibration moved through her body. Adrenaline. She was here.

Well, she was close anyway.

Phoebe took a deep breath and fresh ocean air filled her lungs. It was delightful. Inspiring. So different from the stale scent of concrete and car exhaust she was used to smelling.

"I can write here," she said with renewed confidence. Glancing around at the dark she added, "If I can find the house."

Reinvigorated, Phoebe began a careful inspection of the edges of the gravel road, holding her cell phone out for light. Her GPS couldn't be that far off, could it?

Within a few minutes she found what appeared to be the entrance to a driveway. There was no number or mailbox or anything that might indicate she had found the right place, but it was all she had to go on.

Back in her car she turned carefully onto the gravel driveway. "321 Barracuda Lane, I hope this is you."

The house at the end of the drive fit the image she had downloaded from the rental site. At least what she could see of it.

Two stories. Blue with white trim. A wide railed porch on each level and a spiral staircase from the second porch that looked like it led to the rooftop. All of it fit Phoebe's expectation.

Plus it was completely dark. Not a light on in the entire place. Either nobody was inside or they had all gone to sleep and Phoebe was about to give them a rude awakening.

With some relief she saw the numbers 321 attached just above the door. She knew for sure she had found their vacation rental when she spied a wooden plaque on the door that read 'Sol Mate'. One of the reasons she had chosen this rental was because of the pun.

The key was exactly where the owner, William Dvorak, had told her she would find it. Under a pelican statue, the middle of three, that sat next to a palm tree in the front yard.

Curious, she went inside to inspect the place she would be staying for the entire summer. Where the Mighty Aphrodites would be staying for three full months to focus on writing their books and, with any luck, be published–or at least ready to publish–by fall. Right before she turned 35-years old.

The interior of Sol Mate was perfect, absolutely perfect. Phoebe had steered away from the ultra modern chic rentals not only for monetary reasons, but because she was going for a particular style on this retreat.

Original with updates. Worn, but not worn out. Classic beach vibe with something...*intelligent* about it. A place where words would flow.

"Beautiful," she said under her breath as she looked out the French doors that opened onto the wide back deck looking out at the beach.

Phoebe unlocked the French doors. She pulled on both of them at the same time so they would open dramatically. The sound and smell of the ocean wrapped around her as she stepped out onto the deck.

Every difficult moment since February seemed worth it.

Losing Giovanni. Losing her job. The anxiety of trying to decide what she should do next. Admitting that she couldn't face getting another secretarial job and wanted to use her severance pay for something more. Admitting that she wanted to *be* something more.

Chills shimmied down her neck and spine. Not because she was cold, but because she knew this summer was going to be the biggest, best summer of her life. It was the beginning of her career as a romance author. Regency romance to be exact.

Phoebe's heart swelled at the idea. Obsessed with Jane Austen, Charlotte Bronte, and their peers since she was a child, pining for the politeness and decorum of times long ago, seeking–yet never finding–the kind of old fashioned relationship she dreamed of, she had decided that channeling all of her love of the written word into becoming a Regency romance author made perfect sense.

Her writing had always been a hobby until last year when she started the online writing group. She had grown in confidence after getting positive feedback and finally opened up to the idea that she could write for a living.

The upheaval in her life since February had pushed her toward that goal like never before. After her job concluded, Phoebe spent the following weeks diving into research so she could get every detail correct in her first novel, Lady Everton and the Duke.

A meticulous outline of each chapter including specific notes about what the characters were wearing, eating, and doing, was saved in a spreadsheet on her laptop. All she had left to do was write the words.

"And that's why we're here," she said to the night air.

Well, not exactly *we*. Not yet.

She had purposefully arranged to arrive the night before the other two Mighty Aphrodite writers so she could have some alone time and, if truth be told, inspect the bedrooms to see which of them she preferred.

The largest bedroom at the front of the house had a spa style ensuite and a small private balcony, but it did not have an ocean view, so that was out.

Of the two with ocean views, Phoebe preferred the one on the North side. The furniture in that room was dark stained wood instead of the whitewashed look of the other bedrooms. Plus it had a four poster bed. She liked visualizing herself retiring to a four poster bed every night.

Worn out by her long drive to get to Turtle Cove, Phoebe was suddenly exhausted. She was barely able to get all of her belongings out of the car and into her chosen bedroom before collapsing into the four poster bed and falling asleep.

When she awoke in the morning she was full of the kind of vibrant energy that only comes when starting a new adventure.

She hopped out of bed and put on a navy blue cotton sundress she had purchased as part of her new author wardrobe. Nothing was going to stop her from diving into the writing retreat, especially not her work clothes. She had tossed nearly all of them out when she packed up her apartment and put everything into storage, hoping to never return to those clothes or that life again.

"New clothes, new life," Aunt Scarlet had advised her during one long phone conversation. Phoebe believed there was something to that philosophy.

She made a pot of coffee in the spacious kitchen, humming as she pulled a large mug the color of sea coral out of the cupboard and searched for sugar and cream. As the smell of coffee filled the room she remembered the sign.

Retrieving a thumbtack and a small poster board sign that she had decorated with drawings of fish and seashells and mermaids from her laptop bag, Phoebe opened the front door and attached the sign just underneath the Sol Mate plaque that was already there.

The Mighty Aphrodite Writing Society Summer Retreat!
The sign looked good. She liked it.

Pleased with her little effort at making a warm welcome to Violet and Nicole, she went back to the kitchen. She was ready to begin her first day as a full time writer. Phoebe poured a cup of coffee, grabbed her laptop and went to the back deck to write.

By the time she found the outlet, rearranged a deck chair and low table so she could keep her laptop plugged in, and gotten her spreadsheet and writing software open, her coffee was cold. Carefully climbing out of the deck chair in her flowing sundress, she took the coffee to the kitchen for a quick microwaving.

"There, that's better," she said as she settled back into place with her steaming coffee. She took a sip, scalding her tongue.

Fifteen minutes later her coffee was cold again and she had only managed to write the first sentence of her novel.

Lady Elizabeth Everton's life, like the untended walls of her estate, was crumbling before her eyes.

Though Phoebe's fingers hovered over the keyboard, they were hesitant to type. Every thought, phrase, or word that popped into her mind didn't seem right. All she could think about was the fact that her coffee needed warming up.

"Just a small case of writer's block," Phoebe said. Only the low rumble of the waves answered.

Perhaps if she moved around. Often if she acted out a scene it helped the words start flowing.

Extricating herself once more from the deck chair, Phoebe adjusted her sundress that had gone into a twist and went to the edge of the deck to gather her thoughts.

The view off the deck wasn't just the ocean. The ocean was there, for sure, but it was a little further out with plenty of sandy beach between.

A wood plank walkway started at Sol Mate's deck, went through two low rises of sand and reeds that lifted up on either side of it, then ended at the more pristine sand of the actual beach. The low rises of sand added to the privacy of the deck as it blocked the view of almost everyone on the beach to see straight into the house.

With that visual barrier and the early morning hour, Phoebe felt completely unseen.

She leaned against the railing, letting her hands slide seductively along the smooth surface, sinking into the mind of Lady Everton, a young widow who was about to meet the powerful dashing Duke, the man who would be her one and only true love.

Phoebe sighed dramatically, imagining the tall, dark, and handsome Duke stepping up onto the deck of the beach house.

"And who are you?" she asked in Lady Everton's haughty tone.

"I'm the man who is going to make your dreams come true, Lady Everton." The Duke's deep, sultry voice was clear as could be in Phoebe's mind.

She gasped. The Duke's familiarity with her before being properly introduced was scandalous. "Please, sir," she said angrily to the imaginary Duke. "I demand that you leave these premises at once. This behavior is insulting, outrageous, and offensive!"

"I'll leave when I decide to leave, Lady Everton," the Duke's one good eye raked over her bodice.

"I never!" Phoebe cried out. "Don't you dare lay a hand on me, sir. I am a lady!"

"Hello?" a man's voice–a real man's voice–came to Phoebe from the direction of the beach.

She whirled around, her imaginary scene with the lascivious Duke forgotten.

A tall, blonde man wearing the red swimming trunks of a life-guard stood at the end of the wooden walkway where it met the beach.

"Are you all right?" he asked.

Blood rushed to Phoebe's cheeks and she dropped her hands, which had been dramatically gesturing at the imaginary Duke.

"Yes, yes I'm fine."

He scanned what he could see of the deck, looking suspicious. "I thought I heard an argument."

"Oh, no, no!" She laughed and waved her hand around behind her. "That was the television."

The lifeguard was muscular in the way swimmers get, long and lean. He was tan and his blonde hair looked like it might be brown normally, but was bleached from long days in the sun.

"You sure you're okay?" he asked.

"Oh, yes, thank you. Thank you for checking," Phoebe tried to sound normal, as if she wasn't an adult who had been caught playing pretend like a five-year-old.

The lifeguard walked backward, still looking at her curiously. He was seriously attractive. Another reason she continued to blush madly.

"Well, let me know if you need any help. I'm out here at the station." He pointed to his left at a lifeguard station she couldn't see, the view of it being blocked by the sand mound.

"Thank you, I will." She waved at him. "But I won't because I'm fine," she added awkwardly.

When the lifeguard turned and left, Phoebe grabbed her cold cup of coffee and took it inside to heat it up again.

"Note to self," she muttered. "You're not actually alone on this beach...and sound travels."

Two

Violet

Violet could not figure out how to operate the music stations on her rental SUV.

She had never been technically savvy. Nor car savvy. Her world was one of words and books, beautifully written stories and poems that tugged at the heart and fed the soul. Good books and serene gardens. That's where she found solace and joy. Not hurdling down the highway in a monstrosity while trying to figure out all of the buttons and gizmos on the dashboard.

The controls were futuristic even if the gas guzzling engine of the oversized vehicle was set firmly in the past. She had requested a compact fuel efficient model from the rental place, but there was not one available at the airport lot.

She had explained in vain to the clerk at the counter that she had no need for a four wheel drive vehicle that could comfortably seat eight adults, but arguing was not one of her strengths and she had driven away in the SUV in the end.

Not only was she stuck driving the hideous thing through unfamiliar traffic on her way to Turtle Cove, but the music had been left on a country station.

A baritone voice with a southern accent crooned - *I kissed her under the walnut tree, but when I kissed her she didn't kiss me.*

Country music was not her favorite. At one time she had sung along with all of country music greats, when she and Toby had been together. He had loved country music and could easily have been classified as a redneck. Her first real relationship, which had formed when she was in college and turned her life upside down.

She had been so young, so naive. Toby had been charming in his own way. Different from her quiet and subdued family. A wild country boy who pulled over to help her change her tire and swept her off of her feet with his undivided attention. Unfortunately, that attention had grown into controlling, and then violent, behavior. It had taken her years to get away from him and move on with her education and life. Needless to say, country music left a bad taste in her mouth ever since.

Violet's frustration with the music controls mounted.

"Go around," she muttered under her breath as another car raced up to her rear bumper and didn't back off.

She was driving the speed limit and remained in the slow lane. She knew that every other driver felt the need to go twenty miles an hour over the speed limit, but there was no reason for the excessive tailing and nasty looks she had endured all morning.

A frustrated grumble of borderline curse words escaped her lips, "Frickity fracking chicken looper."

The whole trip had been a series of confrontations and misunderstandings so far. Why shouldn't she expect problems on the highway?

First her flight had been delayed. Then canceled. The airline offered another flight to replace it, but had given her and the other passengers a mere fifteen minutes to get to the gate on the other side of the airport to make that flight.

Then there was the overly friendly businessman seated next to her with his alcohol breath and roaming hands. And *then* the airline had lost her luggage due to the flight change.

Violet had only the items in her purse and laptop bag—and a promise from the airline to send her bags as soon as they were located—to start her beach vacation.

Thank goodness she always packed emergency clothing into her purse when she checked luggage, just in case. One swimsuit, an oversized T-shirt to sleep in, a change of underwear, and a floppy folding hat she had picked up just for this trip, was all she had until her luggage arrived.

Exit 129 was next and Violet dutifully used her blinker to indicate she was leaving the highway. Hopefully all of the speed demons would be pleased to have her out of the way.

The car that had been tailing her sped past as she veered onto the exit. The driver was a woman and there were two kids in the back seat. The woman flipped her off.

"Wow," Violet muttered. Shocked, but not shocked, she focused on maneuvering the giant SUV around the tight loop of the exit ramp.

People could be really awful. A woman with kids acting like that! No wonder the students in Violet's classroom were so unruly. Most likely they learned their behavior from their parents.

A pang of anxiety shot through her stomach and her hands shook as she turned the wheel of the SUV.

"Everything is okay. You're okay. You're in control," she spoke the affirmative words out loud, but they were drowned out by another country singer.

Your cheatin' heart don't get me down. My love for you don't make me frown.

Violet scowled at the radio controls as she turned onto the county road that would take her to Turtle Cove. She located the volume button and turned it to zero. It would be better to drive in silence.

Finally off the main highway and headed to her summer vacation, she took a few deep calming breaths.

This would be the first true summer vacation she had taken since she started teaching junior high English years ago. In previous summers she had been forced to work part-time jobs to supplement her low teacher salary, but this year was going to be different.

Violet had scrimped and saved enough to splurge a little bit and she was finally going to take the whole summer break off. When Phoebe had suggested to the Mighty Aphrodite Writing Society group that they spend the summer on a beach and write their masterpieces, Violet had jumped at the chance.

A road sign appeared just ahead... *Turtle Cove - 47 miles.*

Her anxiety morphed into low level excitement.

"This is going to be great," she told herself. "Just put everything behind you and focus on the present."

Violet pressed the down button on her window and let the fresh air rush into the interior of the vehicle. Wet and salty. Invigorating.

Her fine blonde hair tossed around in the wind as she released all thoughts of the dramas in her classroom, her worries about money, and her anxieties about dealing with people in general.

"For the rest of the summer I'm a writer," she said into the rushing wind.

Her love of literature had been the main reason she chose English as her major in college. Though between her struggles with being in an abusive relationship and the harsh reality of dealing with critiques of her writing, the major hadn't been for her.

Dreams of becoming the next Virginia Woolf or Margaret Atwood had quickly fallen apart in the critical world of English Lit. Between professor's sometimes scathing comments and the other students turning their noses up at her work, Violet had decided being a great writer might be too much for her gentle personality. She switched her focus to teaching the greats to young, bright eyed students as an English teacher.

Little had she known that the youth of today were not all

bookworms wanting to know everything there was to know about great writing, like she had when she was young.

It turned out most of them cared very little for writing and even less for reading. Most of them wanted to play video games or stare at their phones all day.

To add to the problem, her natural aversion to conflict made it hard for her to inspire the middle schoolers and even harder for her to deal with their parents. The whole experience had taught Violet another disappointing thing about herself, she probably wasn't cut out to be a teacher.

That realization along with her acknowledgement that she wasn't good enough to be a great writer of literature had left her in a terrible funk.

Until she found the Mighty Aphrodite Writing Society.

As a virtual writing group they had fluctuated in size, varying between three to eight members. The core three were always the same. Herself, Phoebe, and Nicole. They were the three Mighty Aphrodites who had stuck with the group through thick and thin. They had bonded.

Phoebe and Nicole had encouraged Violet to write despite her insecurities and guided her into the possibility of writing genre fiction, romance specifically, instead of a great literary work.

They had filled her small one bedroom condo with laughter and good conversation when they video chatted. They had been her friends. And now they were all getting together for a writing retreat.

Violet smiled. She had a lot to look forward to this summer.

In less than hour she would arrive for a summer of writing, sunshine, and friendship. What could be better than that?

Three

Bronwyn...

"Calm down, Nicole," Ryan, said as she put the key in the ignition.

"Oh, trust me, Ryan, I am calm. Deadly calm!" Nicole glared at him as she slammed her foot on the clutch and put the BMW convertible into neutral. She turned the key and the engine roared.

"Where are you going?" he asked.

"I'm going to my writing retreat," she informed her husband, glancing in the rearview mirror at the closed garage door.

An overwhelming urge to slam the car into reverse and crash through the garage door came over her. Nicole suppressed it and reached up, squeezing the button on the garage door remote that was clipped to the sun visor.

"In my BMW?" he asked, incredulous.

As the garage door ground its way open she leveled her gaze at him. "I thought you bought this car for us." Nicole put extra annunciation on the word 'us'.

Ryan, receding hairline, purple plaid golf shorts, her husband of 20 years, father of her two young sons, admitted adulterer, rolled his eyes and let out an exasperated sigh.

"We should work out who is getting what before you run off for weeks on end," he said.

"Should we?" Nicole's hazel eyes, normally one of her best features, narrowed as she gave him a scathing look. "Okay, how's this? I'll take the BMW. You can have the other cars." She waved her hand at the other two cars parked in their three car garage. One was an older two door sedan and the other a minivan they had purchased brand new last year. "There. All worked out."

She ground the gears as she put the BMW into reverse. Ryan winced at the sound.

"Nicole, be reasonable," he called out to her as she backed out of the garage.

She slammed on the brakes. All of the BMW was in the driveway except for the hood.

Nicole calmly pushed the button Ryan had specially programmed to open and close the convertible's roof. She waited for the car trunk to automatically open, the roof to fold up and store itself neatly into the trunk, and the trunk to close, all the while shooting daggers at her cheating husband with her eyes.

Free from the encumbrances of a car roof, Nicole felt like the whole world was opening up. The world she had left behind to get married, support her husband through law school, have children, and keep a perfect upper middle class suburban home. The world of the artist that had always existed just outside of her reach.

She pulled her prescription sunglasses out of her metallic Balenciaga bag and methodically switched them with the frames she was already wearing. When she was done she spoke clearly so Ryan wouldn't misunderstand.

"My mother will bring the boys back tomorrow night. Carol is going to watch them during the week. If something happens and she can't then my sister can watch them while you're at work. You have their numbers."

Ryan walked to the front of the car with a disapproving frown. "I have important meetings next week. I can't be worrying about the boys."

The stunning shock of learning that her husband was in love with another woman just that morning suddenly went away. Or maybe the reality finally hit her full in the face. She couldn't be sure. Whichever it was, she was unable to keep her cool any longer.

Rage boiled up from deep inside of her belly and made her voice shake as she responded, first spitting the words at him then screaming them to the rooftops of their HOA controlled community.

"Maybe you should have thought of that before you slept with Melinda...or Melissa...or whatever her name is. Maybe you should have thought about your sons before you did that, Ryan! Maybe you should have thought about our WEDDING VOWS, Ryan! Before you had an AFFAIR and *RUINED EVERYTHING*!!"

Halfway to the main stoplight that led out of their neighborhood, Nicole still wasn't sure if she had run over Ryan's foot when she backed wildly out of the driveway. If she had, she wasn't sorry.

The thought of him hopping up and down on one foot in their driveway as she cruised away made her laugh. A loud guffaw of a laugh that quickly turned into a choked sob.

Mrs. Chesterfield was at her mailbox at the end of her drive and gave Nicole a wave and a queer look as she drove past.

"Hello!" Nicole tried to smile and wave like a normal person, a person whose life hadn't just shattered into a thousand pieces, but she could tell by Mrs. Chesterfield's reaction that her smile leaned more toward the grotesque than the friendly.

Maybe having the top down while she left her husband wasn't the best idea.

"Screw 'em," she said and punched on the gas. The sooner she got out of Lilywood Estates and on the open highway, the sooner she would be at the Mighty Aphrodite writing retreat.

She needed the retreat.

She had needed the retreat before Ryan's confession, needed to have something in her life that was her own, something that wasn't connected to being a stay-at-home wife and mother. Now that she knew about his affair, she needed it even more.

Half of her suspected that he had chosen to tell her right before she left because he thought she would stay home to try and save their marriage. If she stayed home all summer he wouldn't need to take care of Jeremiah and Nathanial.

Her initial reaction to his confession had been annoyance. "Why are you telling me this now?"

"Why now?" Ryan had not expected this reaction. He had expected hurt and crying, maybe despair, but definitely not annoyance.

"Yes, Ryan, why now? I am about to leave for several weeks. I have my bags packed already for God's sake." Tremors of emotion had already started rippling through her body, but her terseness had remained strong.

"I–uh...I thought you would want to know."

Nicole's heart iced over. She knew him like the back of her own hand. Ryan never did anything that wasn't motivated by his own selfish reasons. The only reason he wanted her to know was so she would handle the situation for him.

She had looked at him, her lips pinched together, and said, "That depends."

"Depends on what?"

"Are you telling me you're in love with another woman because you're leaving me or because you want to save our marriage?"

The skin on his face turned a milky white, making the tired crows feet at the corners of his eyes stand out even more. His lawyer training was not kicking in. He'd never been a good trial lawyer anyway, more of the behind the scenes, paper pushing, cut a deal early kind of lawyer.

Nicole had felt the power of the moment shifting in her favor, so she continued, "Which is it? Are we getting a divorce or are we saving our marriage?"

Ryan swallowed. She could almost see his mind twitching behind his eyes, trying to remember what he had promised Megan or Michelle or whatever her name was.

"Divorced," he had said quietly.

Nicole punched the gas pedal of the convertible and maneuvered into the fast lane on the highway. The BMW responded quickly...60...68...74...83 miles per hour. Pieces of her long dark braid, which she had plaited last minute in the downstairs powder room once she decided to take the BMW, broke free and whipped around her face.

"If he wants a divorce I will give him a divorce," she said out loud, her words lost in the roaring wind.

Adrenaline, both from driving fast and free down the highway, and from her emotional morning, pumped through her veins. She was invincible, unafraid, barreling into her new life as a single woman with abandon.

No longer would she be an average, every day, suburban mom. She was going to write her first book and become an author. A famous author. She had already chosen her pen name, Bronwyn Beck.

"Nicole Speer is dead," she shouted into the screaming wind.

Long live Bronwyn Beck.

Four

Phoebe

P hoebe had only ever seen Violet during their virtual writing group meetings, so it wasn't that she didn't know what to expect. But Violet online compared to Violet in person was a surprise.

Pale silky blonde hair in a weak perm, medium height, Violet was thin to the point of being flat, and not just in her bust. When Phoebe looked at her from the side she was so narrow she appeared to be a living, breathing board. Phoebe wondered how all of her organs fit inside of her body.

Even more than her frail appearance, Phoebe found Violet's whole demeanor to be meek. Her voice was weak without the magnification of the computer microphone and she kept averting her eyes shyly when Phoebe looked in her direction.

In short, Phoebe hadn't expected Violet to be quite as nerdy as she turned out to be in real life.

"I chose this room, if that's all right," Phoebe said as she showed Violet around the beach house. Though they were splitting the cost of the vacation rental, Phoebe couldn't help but feel a sense of proprietorship. She had been the main organizer and arrived first, after all.

"That's fine," Violet said. "This one is beautiful," she peeked her head into the second ocean view room. "Do you think Nicole will like having the larger room if I take this one?"

"She'll have to, since she's the last one here. Didn't we agree, first come first serve?"

Violet relaxed a little bit as she answered happily, "Then I'll take this room."

"Great! Do you need help with your luggage?"

Violet made an exasperated sound. "The airline lost it. They'll deliver it when they find it."

"That's too bad. Are you hungry? I have some makings for sandwiches."

"I'm starving."

Soon they were sitting on the back deck looking at the view and munching on turkey and avocado sandwiches.

"Phoebe, this is great," Violet gushed. She wore a crooked wide brimmed hat and sunglasses that hid most of her face, but her voice was unmistakably excited. "I am so glad you came up with this idea. I've never done anything so...so..."

"Decadent?"

Violet chuckled. "Yes! It feels decadent, doesn't it? A whole summer to ourselves on the beach with nothing to do but write...I already feel like an author."

"You are an author," Phoebe reminded her. "And soon you'll be a published author." She grinned.

"Have you gotten any writing done yet?" Violet took a sip of iced tea.

Phoebe had not. Not directly.

She had walked through the first scene a little in her mind, looked up some details of the kind of jewelry Lady Everton would be wearing during her time period and added those details to her spreadsheet, but she hadn't exactly written any words on the page just yet.

"A little," she fibbed.

"How exciting!"

"Yes," Phoebe agreed before taking a huge bite of her sandwich.

"I came up with a few good ideas on the drive here," Violet said.

"Oh?" Phoebe tried to sound supportive as she chewed, but she was afraid Violet's ideas would have more to do with the animals in her novel than the two love interests.

Violet put a lot of unimportant, random information about her main character's animals into her work. It was something they had critiqued her on quite a bit in the Mighty Aphrodite Writing Society online meetings.

"I think I'm going to add a chapter where the guy's dog gets hurt and he has to take it to the vet."

Phoebe nodded and swallowed. "Do they meet up there? At the vet's office?"

"Who?"

"The guy and the girl. The two main love interests?"

"No, this chapter would be about him taking his dog to the vet. You know, show a sweet side of him to the reader."

Phoebe tried not to sigh. "Isn't it a romance?"

Violet hesitated, then answered, "Yes...I just thought–"

"No, no, I think it's a good idea to show that he loves his dog. I just wonder if you might want to throw the girl in there with him somehow. You know, build up tension."

Violet stayed quiet. Phoebe hoped she hadn't hurt her feelings first thing on their retreat.

"I see your point," Violet said, though she did sound wounded.

"Well, I'm sure you'll figure it all out. We'll have all kinds of time to work on every single chapter in our books, won't we?"

Violet perked up. "That's right, that's what we're here for."

Phoebe felt the need to change the subject. "I wonder when Nicole will get here. I found a really great steak place I think we should go for dinner tonight. To celebrate, you know?"

"A night out to celebrate sounds good," Violet agreed.

As if on cue, the sound of music blaring from a car pulling up came to them from the front of the beach house. All the Single Ladies by Beyonce was the tune.

Phoebe and Violet looked at each other and said at the same time, "Nicole."

Five

Bronwyn

When the other Mighty Aphrodites met her at the door, Nicole was taken aback by their in person appearances. Not that she had expected super models, but real life Phoebe and Violet looked very different than computer screen Phoebe and Violet. Plus they were complete opposites of each other.

Violet was blonde, pale, and slender...quite slender...skinny, actually. While Phoebe was brunette, pale, and round...tubby, actually. Correction, they did have paleness in common.

Compared to them Nicole felt like she was the super model arriving at the party. Not that she minded that feeling, but being the oldest one of the group and the only one with children, it was a surprise.

"Hello!" Phoebe greeted her with a hug. Violet followed suit.

"Hello ladies!" Nicole was overjoyed to see them. Her summer of transformation was officially underway. She paused at the front door to admire the homemade sign. "The Mighty Aphrodite Writing Society Summer Retreat." She smiled widely at the other two women. "That feels good to say, doesn't it?"

"It does," Violet agreed. "Do you want some help getting your luggage to your room?"

"We've chosen rooms already?" Nicole asked.

Phoebe and Violet looked at each other, but it was Violet who spoke. "Well, yes...let's get your stuff upstairs and you can see."

Nicole wasn't pleased with the bedroom set up. Or, rather, Bronwyn Beck wasn't pleased. Her old self, the suburban housewife who had a cheating husband, would have been satisfied with not having an ocean view on her summer vacation. But Bronwyn Beck, world famous author, did not settle for sub-par accommodations.

"I would have thought you might like the larger room with the balcony," she said to Violet. "So you could look out over the lawn and see into the trees. There's bound to be more wildlife on that side of the house. All you can see from this smaller room is sand and tourists."

Violet pressed her lips together. She glanced at Phoebe, who was pretending to read the Emergency Exit map that was hanging in the hall.

"I hadn't thought of that..." Violet answered meekly.

Nicole's alter ego, Bronwyn, pounced on the indecision in her voice. "I wouldn't mind sacrificing the balcony for you, Violet. If you would rather have the larger room."

Violet glanced sadly at the ocean view room then smiled politely. "That's nice of you to offer, Nicole–"

"It's Bronwyn," Nicole, now Bronwyn, interrupted.

Phoebe and Violet gave her an odd look.

"I decided not to go by Nicole this summer. I want to embrace my pen name. Embody it," Bronwyn explained.

"Oh," Violet raised her eyebrows in surprise, though it was difficult to tell how high because they were so fair.

"And what was your pen name again?" Phoebe asked.

"Bronwyn Beck."

"Bronwyn," Phoebe repeated. She smiled supportively. "That might be a really good idea. That's what this whole trip is about, embodying our inner writers."

"Exactly," Bronwyn replied as she ignored Violet's hurt expression and pulled her rolling suitcases into the ocean view room. She turned and gave the other Aphrodite's her best future famous author smile. "Who wants to go for a dip in the ocean with me?"

Ocean water filled her up in a mysterious almost mythological way. Bronwyn liked to imagine she was secretly a mermaid awaiting love's first kiss to bring her out of the sea and onto dry land.

Maybe that would be the topic of her novel, a love story between a man and a mermaid. Maybe the man would cheat on the mermaid, invoking her wrath.

She dove under a wave and let the pressure of the ancient ocean water cover her entire body. Holding her breath for as long as possible, she stayed underwater, willing thoughts of Ryan and his mistress to leave her mind. They had no business here on her retreat. She had a book to write. Her book, not a rehash of her marriage.

When Bronwyn came up for air, Phoebe and Violet were scanning the water anxiously. Their concern for her was sweet and amusing. Bronwyn giggled.

"I'm over here!" She waved at them and swam to where they were standing waist deep in the water.

"We were about to call the lifeguard," Violet said, only half joking.

"Oh, I'm fine. I'm a strong swimmer. Always have been," Bronwyn bragged. She looked up and down the beach. "I didn't know they had lifeguards on these smaller beaches."

"They do, I saw one earlier today," Phoebe volunteered. She had her hand up to shield her eyes from the sun as she sought out the rickety looking lifeguard station and pointed to it. A tall delicious blonde in red swim trunks was manning the station.

"I can see why you took notice," Bronwyn teased. Bronwyn had a raunchier sense of humor than Nicole ever had, she had decided. And as a super wealthy and successful author, she wasn't afraid to use it.

There was an awkward pause as Bronwyn did underwater ab exercises. Violet and Phoebe watched. Silenced, no doubt, by her athleticism.

"Well, this is fun, but I need to get out of the sun," Violet inspected her pale arms. "I don't want to get burned on the first day."

"You put a whole bottle of sunscreen on before you came out here," Bronwyn pointed out.

"And I'll still get pink," Violet answered with a self-conscious laugh. "Besides, I need to shower before we go out."

"Me too," Phoebe added.

"Where are we going for dinner again?" Bronwyn asked.

"I found a great steak restaurant in town. It looks like a good place to have a Mighty Aphrodite writing retreat kick-off celebration," Phoebe said with some measure of excitement.

Bronwyn thought it was a little cliche that the plumpest of them had been hunting down good restaurants in the area.

She frowned. "Steak? Do they have seafood? If we're going to kick off a beach retreat we must have seafood. I must insist on it."

"Yes, of course there's seafood," Phoebe answered, irritation in her voice.

In Bronwyn's opinion, Phoebe was being overly sensitive. No need for her to get snappy. Bronwyn was only offering her opinion, an opinion that would soon be highly sought after by her adoring fans and the public at large.

Phoebe and Violet were lucky to have her here with them to ensure they had an excellent experience on their summer writing retreat.

Was it too much to ask that they show a little appreciation?

Six

Phoebe

Phoebe was already on her second glass of wine, but trying to pace herself.

She had imagined the first day of the writing retreat for months. The Mighty Aphrodites would finally get together at their beautiful beach house and creativity would flow. Their first day would be fun, a celebration, joyful even.

Alas, that had not been the case.

Aphrodite tensions were high. Not in a face-to-face arguing way, more of a heavy, difficult to ignore, undercurrent of strained emotions way. Things had only been slightly awkward when Violet arrived, but after Nicole–or Bronwyn, as she wanted to be called–showed up, everything had gotten pretty weird.

First there was Nicole changing her name. Not that Phoebe was opposed to the idea, it might be helpful to take on a pen name personality to get the creative juices flowing, but somehow the name switch felt off, almost aggressive.

Then there was her hijacking of Violet's chosen bedroom.

They had agreed during one of their online meetings that it would be first come, first serve, to avoid any hard feelings. But Bronwyn had walked in and literally swiped Violet's room right out from under her in broad daylight.

Her actions had been so assertive, so rude, that Phoebe hadn't known what to do and grown unnaturally quiet, unable to remind Bronwyn of the rules. Confrontation wasn't her strong point and she had left Violet to unsuccessfully fend off the room coup all on her own. Guilt for that abandonment weighed heavy on her mood.

Phoebe had expected mutual politeness and respect from all writing group participants at their retreat. She had not been prepared to police anyone on common courtesy.

"And then there was James," Bronwyn was in the middle of giving her and Violet a rundown of every sexual conquest she had experienced in college.

Normally the Mighty Aphrodites were pretty open with each other, but most of their online interactions had been about what they were writing, rarely straying into intimate personal details. For instance, Phoebe had never shared much about Giovanni with Violet or Bronwyn, wanting to wait until she had met him in person and solidified their relationship before she bragged about her super hot Italian boyfriend with anyone.

However, tonight Bronwyn was being especially open after finishing an extra large strawberry Pina Colada and starting a second. "But he was a real disappointment, if you know what I mean." Bronwyn laughed...loud.

Violet looked at Phoebe with wide eyes as Bronwyn collapsed onto her bread plate, laughing.

Phoebe was at a loss for words. She glanced around the restaurant, hoping to spy the waiter bringing their main course. They needed to get some food in their stomachs before Bronwyn started swinging from the chandeliers.

Her eyes fell on a couple seated a few tables away. They were striking, both attractive, slender, and well dressed for a night on the town.

What caught her attention was what seemed to be a heated conversation between them. A scene in the making. A big scene. Big enough to distract her from Bronwyn's drunken antics, which was saying something.

Phoebe had a good view of the girl's face. She was beautiful. High cheekbones, almond shaped eyes done up with fashionable makeup, long straight brown hair, lips that were so well shaped and full that Phoebe took special note of them. She would have to remember those lips and put them on Lady Everton.

She watched discreetly, trying to interpret what the girl was saying to her date, ready to turn away quickly if she looked in her direction.

The girl leaned forward, her eyes flashing with anger, and said something that looked like, "You never listen to me...*something, something.*"

The guy's voice was deep and tinged with pleading, but he was facing away from her and Phoebe couldn't make out the words. All she could see of him were his wide shoulders and blonde hair.

The girl laughed, but there was no humor in her expression. She pushed her plate of surf and turf away scornfully, then looked up and turned the same scorn on her date. "This? This is nothing. I want...*something, something.*"

"Ugh," Phoebe couldn't make out the argument and she was dying to know. People watching helped immensely in her writing and this interaction looked like something she might want to include in a book someday.

"...but Barry was horrible, too!" Bronwyn was still carrying on about her pre-marriage sex life. Violet looked miserable.

"I'll be right back. Gonna run to the powder room," Phoebe announced to her friends, ignoring Violet's look of despair.

She stood and pretended to look around for the restrooms, but she had already located them in the far corner of the room. She could easily walk past the arguing couple and, if she moved slowly enough, catch more of their conversation.

"Layla, I *do* care about you," the guy said as he leaned toward his date and stretched his hand across the table.

Phoebe slowed her walk to a snail's pace as she approached, thrilled that she could make out what he was saying without even seeing his face. She kept her eyes on the floor in front of her, but could still see the girl, Layla, in her peripheral vision.

Layla pulled her hands off the table and shoved them in her lap. A mean little pout came across her beautiful lips and she whined, "Then why don't you do something really romantic for me? Dinner? Really? And jewelry?" She lifted one hand where a beautiful bracelet sparkled on her wrist. "It's so predictable. You're so predictable, Tanner," Layla added with disgust.

The woman's critique of her date was harsh. Absorbed with hearing the whole conversation, Phoebe continued slowly moving toward the restroom. She was taken by surprise when Layla suddenly shoved her chair back dramatically and stood.

The chair almost hit Phoebe's hip, she was that close to their table. She side stepped and looked up, unable to keep her eyes averted from the drama happening right next to her.

Tanner stood up from his chair and said, "Don't leave. I'll try harder. I promise."

"I need something more, Tanner. I want an amazing life and I don't think you're capable of giving it to me." Layla grabbed her small clutch purse off the table and turned, shooting an annoyed glare at Phoebe who was directly in her way.

"Excuse me," Phoebe said, trying to act like she hadn't seen the whole thing.

Layla responded with a derivative snort and pushed past her, knocking her a little off center as she did.

Tanner was quick on his feet. He grabbed Phoebe's elbow as

his date, the demanding Layla, stormed out the front door of the restaurant.

"Sorry about that," he said.

Phoebe looked up, embarrassed she had involved herself in their lover's quarrel, embarrassed for Tanner being abandoned at his table, embarrassed that her round body had been too big for the gorgeous svelte Layla to get past without bumping into her.

"Are you all right?" Tanner asked.

Phoebe blinked up at him. There was something familiar about his voice and his face. Recognition made her face and ears hot. He was the lifeguard from her beach.

He looked down into her eyes, concerned that she had been knocked off kilter by the enraged Layla. Phoebe found it difficult to speak.

He was quite handsome up close. Strong jaw with the tiniest cleft in his chin, a well shaped nose, a good natured and good looking face all around. He had warm brown eyes, which she wouldn't have expected to go along with his blonde hair.

"I'm sorry for all of that," he said, glancing around at the disrupted patrons nearby.

"Oh, no, no, don't worry about it. I'm fine," she finally found her voice, wanting to ease his public humiliation.

He smiled, and it was a genuinely warm and comforting smile. Remarkable given that he was the one who had just gotten dumped. "Good. At least one of us is okay."

Phoebe laughed, charmed at his self-deprecating comment. She wanted to tell him she was sorry his evening had been ruined, tell him something encouraging.

She opened her mouth to do just that, but was interrupted by Bronwyn shouting her name.

"Phoebe! Phoebe! Put the cute man down and come back here right now, the shrimp cocktails have arrived!"

Phoebe's face grew even hotter and she knew she must be beet red. "Excuse me," she said hurriedly, returning to her table without looking back.

"These are delicious," Bronwyn exclaimed sloppily, her mouth half full of shrimp.

Violet looked as mortified as Phoebe felt.

It was a full five minutes before Phoebe remembered she hadn't even gotten to use the powder room. When she glanced back in its direction, Tanner was gone.

Seven

Violet

Violet woke up early and depressed.

Her first day on the Mighty Aphrodite retreat had been a real bummer.

Overcoming her initial shyness with Phoebe had been a little challenging, but she had managed. Then Nicole had arrived – or Bronwyn as she requested they call her – and everything had gone downhill from there.

How strange was the whole *Bronwyn* thing anyway? Violet wondered. Very strange, that's how strange.

Not only because they had to get used to calling Nicole by a completely different name, but she was acting differently, too. Nicole had always been a smidge overpowering in their online meetings, and maybe a little full of herself, but Bronwyn? Bronwyn was a real snot.

Violet had been willing to overlook the whole name change

thing as just an odd creative quirk, but then Bronwyn had basically kicked her out of her ocean view room. Not to mention Bronwyn's brash, embarrassing behavior at the restaurant.

Add in the loud break up scene Phoebe had accidentally stumbled upon, which had been truly mortifying to watch, and the whole night had been awful. Violet had never wanted to leave a restaurant so badly in her life.

She sat up on the side of the bed.

It was a King mattress compared to the Queen in the other room. Feeling a little spiteful, Violet was glad to know that Bronwyn had chosen the smaller bed. This larger room had so much extra space it even had a small coffee and tea bar set up on a dresser against one wall. Plus there was the private balcony.

Though she would never admit it to Bronwyn, Violet did enjoy having sole access to the balcony. Given the events of her first day at the beach house, she figured she might need more privacy on her summer getaway than she had originally anticipated.

The sun was not yet up and neither, from the sound of silence in the house, were her roommates. She would make some tea and sit on her balcony until she felt up to facing Bronwyn again.

The view of the sunrise from her balcony was lovely, only broken up by a few palm trees, which she thought added a little interest to the scene. She could still hear the ocean and smell the fresh, moist air, which was nice. There were birds, too, flitting in and out of the tropical flowers and shrubs below her balcony in the yard.

"Peace," she said quietly and relaxed into the comfy patio chair with a cup of Mango Tango tea.

She realized this would be the perfect time to write. Retrieving her laptop, Violet settled back into the chair with it perched on a pillow in her lap.

"I'll just start on that vet scene," she murmured to herself.

A bird trilled from a Bougainvillea covered in hot pink blooms that climbed up the corner of the beach house. Violet had never heard that particular bird call. Both of her parents were bird watchers and Violet had picked up a lot of what they knew over the years. The bird trilled again. She wondered what it was.

"That's why you brought binoculars," she chided herself.

Violet got up, thinking she could rummage through her large suitcase and get the binoculars she had packed just in case she had some extra time to go on a nature walk. Halfway back into her room she remembered that her luggage was still lost. Her binoculars were flying around in the belly of an airplane somewhere.

"Perfect," she sighed, and went back to the balcony, her laptop, and her tea.

Curious, Violet did a quick online search on birds that were normally found in the area. From there, she found an article on bird migration, then one on how migrating birds were being negatively affected by human population growth.

There was a soft knock on her bedroom door.

Violet looked up from her computer. The sunrise was over and her Mango Tango tea was cold. She went to the door to find Phoebe, fully dressed in a navy blue T-shirt dress.

"Do you want some breakfast?" Phoebe asked in a whisper.

Violet glanced at Nicole's– Bronwyn's–door, which was closed.

"She's still sleeping it off," Phoebe said. "I don't think she'll be up for a long while. I made coffee downstairs."

"Okay, I'll get dressed and be down."

Getting dressed consisted only of changing into her fresh underwear and the clothes she had been wearing when she arrived. She washed her other pair of undies in the bathroom sink and hung them to dry next to her swimsuit. She really hoped her luggage would arrive soon. She couldn't afford to buy a brand new wardrobe for the summer.

Downstairs smelled delicious, like someone had been baking.

"Ta-da!" Phoebe pulled a cinnamon and sugar crusted coffee cake out of the oven, raising it up for Violet to see.

"That looks good. You made it from scratch?"

Phoebe carried the piping hot coffee cake out to the table on the deck. "Yes, I love to bake. It's my second favorite pastime."

They each got a cup of coffee and sat down to breakfast outside.

"We'll have to go to the grocery store today to stock up on supplies," Phoebe said. "And I think we should come up with some kind of a Mighty Aphrodite schedule, you know?"

Violet nodded in agreement, her mouth full of coffee cake.

"We could set aside blocks of time to write and maybe do an in person critique meeting once or twice a week?" Phoebe suggested.

"Sure," Violet agreed, but inside she was cringing.

"What's the matter?" Phoebe asked, her round eyes watching Violet carefully.

Violet didn't want to say anything against anyone and cause problems right away on their retreat. "It's nothing. Not a big deal." Phoebe continued to watch her, knowing that she was lying. Violet tried to ignore her pointed stare, but couldn't take it. "Nothing's the matter, Phoebe."

Phoebe sighed and put her fork down. She wiped the crumbs off the corners of her mouth with a napkin and looked out toward the ocean.

"Do you think Nicole's acting a little..." Phoebe paused, looking for the word.

"Weird?"

"Yes, weird, *really weird*," Phoebe leaned toward her and whispered the words.

Relieved that she wasn't the only one, Violet whispered back, "I'm glad you think so, too. I hoped I wasn't just being angry at her about the bedroom thing."

Phoebe's round eyes got rounder, not whispering, but still speaking softly in case Nicole woke up, "Right! I didn't know what to do, she just kind of took everything over."

"I know!" Violet glanced behind them at the wide open door

leading to the kitchen and living room area. "And making us call her Bronwyn...what is that about?"

Phoebe leaned back in her chair shaking her head. "I don't know, it's so odd. It's like she thinks if we call her by a different name she doesn't have to act like the Nicole we know."

"Like it gives her license to act like a *bitch*," Violet whispered the curse word so quietly she was almost mouthing it.

Phoebe snorted out a laugh, which made Violet giggle, which put them both into a fit of laughter over the whole bizarre situation.

"I don't want to be mean," Violet said when their laughter slowed down.

"You're not being mean, not at all," Phoebe answered. She wiped tears of laughter from her eyes. "I'm glad you see it, too. Maybe she will calm down once we start writing."

"Hopefully," Violet said.

Violet turned her attention toward the ocean and noticed the same tall blonde lifeguard they had seen yesterday walking midway between them and the waves. He was looking in their direction and when Phoebe's gaze followed hers and found him, he lifted one arm and gave them a quick wave.

Phoebe let out an almost inaudible gasp, drawing Violet's attention. Phoebe's cheeks burned red.

"Isn't that the same lifeguard that was here yesterday?" Violet asked.

Phoebe nodded and took a nonchalant sip of her coffee. "He was at the restaurant last night, too."

"Oh, really?" Violet put two-and-two together. "Wait, was he the guy who's date ran out on him?"

Phoebe nodded again, avoiding Violet's look by keeping her eyes trained on the table.

"Hmm, small world," Violet said, amused at the blush that lingered on Phoebe's cheeks.

"It is, isn't it?" Phoebe replied.

Before Violet could ask if she had a little crush on the lifeguard, Phoebe expertly changed the subject and they spent the rest of their breakfast working on a Mighty Aphrodite writing schedule.

Eight

Phoebe

Positioned underneath a bright red beach umbrella looking out over the lazy ocean waves, Phoebe was finally relaxed.

She and Violet had spent the morning at the local grocery store buying supplies, having convinced Bronwyn that they would be fine going on their own since she wasn't feeling well.

"Not feeling well?" Violet had complained in the short car ride to Turtle Cove. "Hung over is more like it." Bronwyn had rubbed Phoebe the wrong way since she arrived, but she had really gotten under Violet's skin.

Phoebe spent their time grocery shopping trying to smooth things over, hoping to reduce tensions between her fellow Aphrodites at the Sol Mate beach house. In a fit of optimism she insisted they stop at the liquor store to pick up a few bottles of wine. Maybe Bronwyn could hold her wine better than she held Pina Coladas.

Turtle Cove was an adorable beach town. There was a definite pandering to the tourist crowd in its cute whitewashed boho look with a lot of white and turquoise buildings, and driftwood and seashells decor. The overall look of the town did, however, seem to be rooted in truth. Turtle Cove was a beach haven for surfers, naturalists, and sun worshipers.

They had only come to the edge of town the night before to eat at the steak house, but there were several restaurants of all varieties including a well renowned gourmet place called Cobalt Edge, which sat at the end of a pier used for strolling and fishing.

Phoebe would like to dine at Cobalt Edge before the end of the summer, though she wondered about taking Bronwyn someplace really nice. Maybe she would wait and see how the next few weeks went before she brought it up or made a reservation.

"Do you want some more iced tea?" Violet asked, interrupting Phoebe's concentration.

She was doing some pencil sketches of Lady Everton's evening wear. She didn't want to bring her laptop out to the beach and risk getting sand in it, but she hadn't wanted to waste time in the sun doing nothing.

"Yes, thank you," she handed Violet her insulated cup.

Violet's umbrella was set up to Phoebe's right and Bronwyn's was set up to her left, where she lay fast asleep. Bronwyn had been awake when they returned from getting groceries and anxious to get in some beach time.

Phoebe had agreed, though she was getting a little anxious herself. They had yet to solidify the writing schedule for the duration of the retreat. Time could easily start slipping through their fingers if they spent too much time relaxing. They risked coming to the end of the retreat and not having their books completed if they procrastinated too much.

"Hmm?" Bronwyn murmured then startled awake, wiping a little drool from the corner of her mouth.

"That was Violet going to get some more iced tea. Did you want anything?" Phoebe asked.

Bronwyn dismissed the question with a floppy wave and went

back to sleep. Probably for the best. Phoebe got the feeling that even though Violet was considerate to Bronwyn, she may tire quickly of waiting on her.

She sighed. She had made such careful plans for this trip, but had failed to consider the possibility that they wouldn't all get along. They had always had such fun in online meetings.

"Note to self," she said under her breath. "Online is not the same as real life. You should know that one, Phoebe."

"Hello," a man's voice interrupted her thoughts.

"Hello?" Phoebe answered, she squinted into the sunshine outside of her umbrella to see the unmistakeable ripped abs and red swim trunks of their friendly local lifeguard, Tanner.

"Remember me?" He ducked his head down and leaned underneath the shade of her umbrella, pushing his sunglasses up onto his head so she could see his face.

"Oh, yes, hello," she answered, trying not to sound giddy, but not sure she did a good job of it. "I do remember you. You're the lifeguard...and you were at the restaurant–" she stopped short, not wanting to bring up the whole embarrassing Layla incident.

He smiled a little sheepishly and nodded. "Yeah, that's me, the guy that was dumped at the restaurant."

Phoebe felt sorry for him, but a giggle escaped her despite of it. She covered her mouth discreetly and regained control.

He glanced at Bronwyn, who was snoring. Then he looked up toward the beach house before turning his friendly brown eyes back to Phoebe. "All of you ladies are staying at Bill's?"

"Bill's?" Phoebe didn't recognize the name, or maybe she had forgotten it. She was having a hard time thinking straight while conversing with Tanner.

He wasn't the normal teenage boy lifeguard she had always encountered at her local pool. He was a full grown man lifeguard. She would guess he was in his late twenties, and he was gorgeous.

"Bill Dvorak...he calls the place Sol Mate," he said.

"Oh, yes, right, *William* Dvorak. That's how he has his name on the rental agreement," she answered.

"Ah, right, William. He goes by Bill, too."

She nodded, a flurry of nerves going off inside of her as she tried to hold up her side of the conversation. Filled with the urge to seem more interesting than just an average tourist on vacation, she said, "We're renting it from him for the summer...for a writing retreat."

Tanner raised his eyebrows, impressed. "You're authors?"

Surprised at being called an author by a total stranger, Phoebe almost denied the question. But they were authors, technically. They just hadn't been published yet.

"Yes, we are," she said.

"Nice, well, I'm here every day for the most part, except for Tuesdays and Thursdays. Bill and I go way back. If you need anything let me know."

"Thank you, that's very nice of you," Phoebe said. The details of his life should not have mattered to her, but her brain automatically filed the information about his scheduled days off for future reference.

He backed away, moving in the direction of the guard station before adding suddenly, "I'm Tanner, by the way."

"Yes, I know," Phoebe answered. Tanner's smile faltered and she realized there was no reason she should know his name. "I mean, yes, thank you, I'm Phoebe." Heat rose in her cheeks. She could only hope the shade under the umbrella hid some of the red on her face from him.

His smile returned and he pulled his sunglasses back down over his eyes. "Nice to meet you, Phoebe."

"You too!" she called out after him, noting too late that she was fluttering her hand up and down in a kind of frantic old lady wave.

Phoebe dropped her hand back into her lap, willing herself not to watch him walk away just in case he looked back and caught her ogling him. She picked up her pencil and stared meaningfully at her half-finished sketch.

"Tanner..." Bronwyn groaned from underneath her umbrella.

Though she still had her eyes closed, apparently she hadn't been asleep during the whole interaction. She opened one eye carefully, trying to focus it onto Phoebe before closing it again. In a voice thick from too much liquor followed by too much sleep she added, "He's a doll, isn't he?"

"Mm-hmm," Phoebe murmured noncommittally.

"Why is Violet taking so long?" Bronwyn asked.

Phoebe shrugged, not answering.

"I'm back," Violet announced as she appeared and handed Phoebe her drink. "What did the lifeguard want?"

"He was saying 'hi' to Phoebe," Bronwyn said. "He's friends with the guy who owns the beach house."

"I thought you were asleep all that time," Phoebe said, surprised Bronwyn had heard and retained that much of the interaction. Apparently Bronwyn had mastered the skill of looking like she was asleep without actually being asleep.

"I was only half asleep."

"You were snoring."

Bronwyn grinned slyly. "It's a skill I picked up after having children. Sometimes it's better if everyone thinks you're asleep." She sat up slowly and readjusted her bikini top.

It was ironic that the only woman out of the three of them who had given birth was also the only one wearing a bikini. Not that Phoebe was jealous, much. Violet wore a dark pink tankini that did a decent job of adding a little weight to her super thin frame and Phoebe was in a tasteful navy blue full piece suit. She would never even consider wearing the skin baring black bikini that Bronwyn sported so casually.

"How are you feeling?" Violet asked Bronwyn.

As much as she had been annoyed at Bronwyn's behavior the previous day, Violet certainly did act concerned for her well being. Phoebe would tag Violet as a helper type, the kind of personality that cannot stop giving to others.

"I've been better," Bronwyn admitted. "Thank you for dragging me home last night. I honestly don't remember much about dinner."

Violet looked at Phoebe then back to Bronwyn. "It was..."

"Interesting," Phoebe interjected.

"Yes, it was an interesting night," Violet agreed.

Bronwyn brushed their responses aside, she had thought of something else she wanted to talk about. "I need to get the owner's phone number from you," she said to Phoebe. "Bill was it?"

"William...or Bill, I guess."

"Whatever. I need him to fix the window in my bedroom. It doesn't open all the way."

Phoebe agreed, though she felt a prick of concern that Bronwyn might come across a little harsh and demanding to their summer landlord, maybe cause some unnecessary problems. She decided not to get involved if she didn't have to and turned her attention back to her sketch.

"What did you pick up for dinner tonight?" Bronwyn asked.

"We thought we would try out the grill. We got some chicken and salmon and vegetables," Violet answered.

"Sounds healthy. Did you get any wine?" Bronwyn asked.

Violet cringed, but Phoebe kept her cool. "Yes, we got some wine."

What Phoebe wanted to do was suggest that Bronwyn not drink as much during dinner, but stopped herself just in time. She wasn't anyone's mother and maybe if they simply tried to have a relaxing time and get to know one another Bronwyn's rambunctious behavior would mellow out.

Phoebe focused harder on her sketch of Lady Everton, but her mind was running in too many directions. She couldn't decide how to shape Lady Everton's full skirts or how elaborate she wanted to make her hairstyle.

In frustration she flipped the page and started her sketch of the Duke. The calming sound of ocean waves and silence of her two companions allowed her to finish his general outline, positioning, and his head and face. With a few quick strokes she created a pair of trousers.

Her pencil froze, however, when she started to draw in the Duke's jacket and waistcoat. The image she normally held in her mind so easily of regency era clothing had all but disappeared.

The only visual Phoebe could bring into her thoughts as she tried to sketch out the dashing Duke, the hero of her novel, was the tan lean torso and six pack abs of Tanner the lifeguard.

Nine

Bronwyn

Bronwyn was bored.

She had agreed to the writing schedule. She couldn't deny that. Phoebe and Violet had presented their suggested schedule the night before, after they grilled on the deck and after they had consumed quite a bit of wine.

That being what it was, actually being forced to sit still and do nothing but write wasn't working out very well for her. Bronwyn realized the whole idea might be a mistake. Rigid structure wasn't how she worked best.

Not when there was sunshine and an ocean just a few steps away.

Not when there were unopened bottles of wine in the house.

She sighed, ignoring how the sound made Phoebe's shoulders stiffen. They had decided to try their first writing sprint in the living room, working separately and quietly, but still near one another. Phoebe had already shushed her twice when she had tried to make relevant comments or ask questions about the music.

Violet had chosen the music, a kind of ambient piano tune that wasn't loud enough to drown out the sound of the ocean outside. Bronwyn had tried to suggest something more upbeat, but the other two hadn't liked her suggestions. Phoebe thought writing together for a set amount of time with those ambient sounds would increase their creative flow.

It wasn't increasing Bronwyn's creative flow. Not at all. She was about to fall asleep.

She had given it the old college try, too. Really focused, really dug in with her laptop and a giant mug of coffee. She had been staring at her computer screen for at least 20 minutes.

Nothing.

No words popped into her head. No witty banter. No description of the location of her story. Nothing. Nada. Zilch.

The novel she had decided to write over their summer retreat was a story she had outlined weeks ago. It was a contemporary romance, one of the easiest genres to write in her opinion. But whenever she tried to envision any interaction between the lovers in her story she came up completely blank.

Bronwyn realized she was about to sigh again and suppressed it for Phoebe's sake, which made her yawn instead. How was she ever going to make it through the rest of the two hour window they had set aside to write together? She was either going to fall asleep or scream out of frustration.

A loud knock on the door interrupted the ambient flow in the room, startling all three of them.

"I'll get it!" Bronwyn said, desperate to get up and at least stretch her legs.

When she opened the door she found a good looking man she guesstimated to be in his late-40's. He wasn't good looking like a model might be, more like an attractive contractor that showed up to remodel a kitchen.

A little taller than Bronwyn, thick, but not fat. He had the body of a mature male of the species, strong and sturdy, like a silver back gorilla except for the dirty blonde hair and blue eyes.

"Mrs. Speer?" he asked.

Speer was her married name, Nicole Speer. A spark of fear that Ryan was serving her with divorce papers on her writing retreat sent her into an internal panic. Then she remembered she wasn't Nicole Speer. Not while she was in Turtle Cove.

"Bronwyn. Bronwyn Beck." She offered him her hand and gave him a flirtatious smile.

He looked down at her extended hand, uncertain how to respond. Then he looked up, his blue eyes seeming even bluer if that was possible, and took hold of her hand, giving it a firm shake.

"I'm William, William Dvorak. I own this place."

Relieved, she smiled. She was enjoying her little charade as well as the warm rough skin of his hand holding hers. She tilted her head coyly. "Bill! Of course, it's wonderful of you to come so quickly."

Bill let go of her hand and stepped into the foyer. "I got a message from a Nicole Speer, or that's the name that came up on my phone. She's one of your group renting the house for the summer?"

"Yes, yes, that's right. I know exactly what you're here for, the window that won't open."

"That's right, ma'am."

"Now, now, Bill, *ma'am* makes me feel like my grandmother."

He smiled politely. "Sorry, what did you say your name was again?"

"Bronwyn Beck...the author."

"I see. Nice to meet you...Bronwyn."

"You, too."

He paused, waiting for her to do something besides smile at him. When she didn't he cleared his throat and asked, "Is Nicole here? I'd like to take care of that win–"

Bronwyn held up her finger to stop him from talking. "I know exactly what window needs fixing. Follow me."

There was something decidedly wicked about leading a strange man upstairs to her bedroom under an assumed name. He was only there to fix the window, but Bronwyn couldn't help but wonder what Ryan would think of the situation. Ryan didn't know what Bronwyn Beck was capable of – neither did Bronwyn for that matter.

She led Bill into her room and to the problem window. He tried it a few times, his muscled arms flexing as he pulled up hard on the window to no avail.

Bronwyn appreciated Bill's capable presence. Ryan had never been good about fixing things around the house. He had always hired those tasks out to blue collar types.

Bill stopped pulling up on the window and said, "Yep, it's stuck all right."

A man of direct communication. What an attractive quality.

Bronwyn dipped her head slightly and lowered her eyes, considering trying a seductive look on the unsuspecting handy man, just to see if she still had it after being married for over 20 years.

Bill moved in even closer to the window, squinting at the sealant between the glass and the wood. Thrusting the ridge of his palm against the top frame, he grunted. He pulled a pen from his pocket to poke at the corner of the window, which seemed to be the area that wouldn't budge.

"I'm gonna need some tools to get this fixed. I may have to take it apart first." He glanced back over his shoulder. "That will mean making a mess up here. Are you sure you want that? This can wait until the end of the summer when you've all gone home. It's not what I would call an emergency."

Memories of spats with Ryan over the years came rushing back her. He had always rolled his eyes when she requested money to fix something around the house, which used to drive her crazy. His disregard for the upkeep necessary to maintain a beautiful home was sickeningly similar to his disregard for the work it took to strengthen their relationship. To save their marriage.

"No, it can't wait," she annunciated the words slowly and carefully. Annoyance at Bill's flippant dismissal of her concerns combined with her memories of Ryan and rolled into a giant ball of anger at men in general. "I think we should have a fully functioning rental unit for the summer, don't you?"

Bill gave her a long look, choosing his words carefully after insulting her with the suggestion that her simple maintenance request be intentionally overlooked, no doubt.

"Sure, no problem," Bill said. "I'll pick up what I need and be back later this afternoon or tomorrow morning."

"See that you are," Bronwyn said haughtily.

"Is everything all right?" Phoebe asked from the bedroom doorway. Her nose, cheeks, and the tops of her arms were already sunburned from their brief time on the beach.

Bill turned his attention to her and asked, "Are you Nicole?"

Phoebe looked between Bill and Bronwyn a few times, confused into silence.

Bronwyn spoke up before Phoebe could answer, "This is Phoebe Collins...another author."

"Nice to meet you," he said, giving her a nod of his head in greeting. "Well, if you ladies will excuse me, I have some supplies to pick up." Phoebe, still a bit baffled, stepped into the room so he could get out the door. Right before he disappeared he turned back and spoke to both of them, "If you could let Nicole know, I would appreciate it."

"We will!" Bronwyn smiled hard and ignored Phoebe's bewildered expression.

Ten

Phoebe

Phoebe's feet ached as she trudged through the sand. She remembered reading somewhere that walking on a beach was exceptionally good for butt muscles, but probably should have factored in her low fitness level before starting off on a barefoot sunrise outing.

She hadn't thought about much besides wanting to get away from her summer roommates and maybe get some exercise. Phoebe tried to include exercise in her daily plans, even if those plans fizzled out a lot of the time.

Pink and orange filled the sky and beautiful blue waves lapped gently on the sand. The gorgeous setting helped her ignore the cramps in her feet. Maybe if she had worn workout shoes it would have been easier. Next time.

Phoebe took a deep breath. Next time. It was nice to know that she had a few months here, time enough to get her beach exercise regimen in order as well as write her book.

A knot of anxiety twisted in her stomach at the thought of

her book. She hadn't gotten any new words written in the actual story over the past several days. She blamed Nicole...wait, not Nicole, *Bronwyn*, Nicole's annoying alternate personality.

Bronwyn had been impossible during their writing sprint, unable to keep quiet or hold still for more than just a few minutes. And the way she had acted with the landlord, like a lusty desperate housewife. It was positively unpropitious.

Nicole might want to change her name, but she was still a married woman. Even if her husband wasn't with her on the retreat, Phoebe would expect a spouse to uphold their marital vows regardless. Not that the over the top Bronwyn had actually done anything untoward with Bill, especially after Phoebe went upstairs to see what was going on, but her wild flirting had been, well, embarrassing to watch.

Phoebe took in a deep breath of fresh ocean air. She needed to calm down. Her own feelings about what was acceptable and not acceptable in intimate relations between a man and a woman had always been a little old fashioned.

More than a little old fashioned, if truth be told.

That's why regency romance had always appealed to her. The idea of someone having an affair while married, or having intimate relations before marriage, didn't fit her view of romance at all.

She winced, guilt poking at her stomach. She had been willing to throw all of her high ideals aside when Giovanni had told her he would come to America to see her. She had no room to judge Bronwyn when her own love life, or lack of, was so full of contradictions.

"And that is why you're alone," she said into the morning air, huffing and puffing as she did. "That and you're out of shape."

She paused to catch her breath and look out over the water. The sad condition of her dating life notwithstanding, the view was epic. Gazing at the glistening water while listening to the methodical waves and the occasional call of a lonely sea bird could be romance enough to give her inspiration to write.

Another sound came from behind. A voice. A voice calling her name.

"Phoebe, wait up," the voice said.

She turned to see the silhouette of a man jogging up to greet her. The morning light soon brought out his features and she could see it was Tanner, gorgeous Tanner, calling out her name.

"Good morning," he said, stopping to talk. "It's a beautiful one."

"Hi, yes it is...it is," she looked back to the water, trying to control the butterflies in her stomach at the sight of him. "Where are you headed this morning?"

"To the guard station, getting a little jog in first," he answered.

Phoebe couldn't imagine how difficult it would be to actually jog on the sand. No wonder he was in such good shape.

"Are you going back to Sol Mate?" he asked. She nodded. "Want some company?"

She swallowed. "Sure, yes, that would be nice. I'm not jogging though, just walking." The thought of trying to jog and keep up with Tanner filled her with dread.

"That's okay, I'd like to walk and cool down a little anyway," he answered.

They fell into step next to each other and Phoebe almost pinched herself.

The whole scenario was completely opposite to her life just a week ago. No job, sad one bedroom apartment, no boyfriend. Not that Tanner was her boyfriend, but walking next to him on the beach as the sun came up had a pretty boyfriendy vibe.

"Are you enjoying your visit so far?" he asked.

"Yes, it's been very nice."

Tanner scanned the water as they walked. Most likely a lifeguard habit. Then he continued, "So, all three of you are writers?"

"Yes," Phoebe smiled, pleased that he remembered.

"What kind of books do you write?"

"Romance, we all write romance."

"Oh, romance," he smiled knowingly.

"I actually write regency romance, clean and wholesome regency."

"Clean and wholesome would mean, what, no sex scenes?"

She nodded, expecting him to be weirded out like most people when they found that little detail out.

"Kinda like Jane Austen?" he asked.

Surprised that he knew about Jane Austen at all, Phoebe answered, "Yes, a little like Jane Austen." Then, because she didn't want him to think she was bragging. "Not that I would suggest my work is as good as Jane Austen's..."

"I'm sure you're very good."

"You're very kind, but I know I'm not Jane Austen good."

They continued on for a little while without talking. Waves rolled. Sea birds called out. Phoebe tried not to breathe too hard from the exertion of walking.

"Have you read a lot of Jane Austen?" she asked, still curious about his knowledge of her favorite author.

"Naw, I've seen a few of the movies. My Mom loves them and I have an aunt that works in publishing...Miss Austen's work has come up a time or two between them."

A tiny thrill rippled through Phoebe at his choice of words. He was verbose for a lifeguard.

"You have an aunt in publishing?"

"You sound surprised."

Phoebe glanced at his well formed physique, his height, his obvious genetic predisposition to being a prime physical specimen. "I would have imagined the family of someone as physically fit as you to be full of people in health or sports professions. Like football."

He chuckled. "No, my aunt isn't a football player."

"Right, of course. Sorry, I didn't mean that as an insult or anything."

He shrugged, accepting her apology. "I get it. People assume you're a lifeguard because you have to be."

"I didn't mean..." she was at a loss of words to explain,

because he was right. She had assumed lifeguarding was a job for high schoolers, not a career.

He noticed her struggling and smiled. "It's okay, I'm not offended. I like being a lifeguard. It's good for now."

"Oh? You have other plans for the future?" Phoebe cringed at her own question. What was she trying to be, his career counselor?

"Right now I'm taking EMT classes on Tuesdays and Thursdays. And I'm a volunteer fireman. That's what I want to do."

"Be a fireman?"

"Yeah, it will take a few years probably. Not a lot of openings come up in the fire departments nearby."

"That's a noble career. And you want to stay in Turtle Cove?"

He looked at her like she had asked him if he was planning on keeping his head attached to his body. "Yes, definitely. It's my home."

The sun was higher on the horizon and had burned away the pink and orange colors in the sky. What remained was a beautiful golden light that fell over the sand and sea, and created a glow on Tanner's skin that was almost ethereal.

"I don't blame you for that," she said. "This is a beautiful place to live." Looking up into his smiling brown eyes with the sunlight glistening gold across his blonde hair, she had to stop herself from saying the next thing that came into her mind, that he was as beautiful as the place he called home.

"It's fun, too. Nice people," he added. "Which reminds me, Turtle Cove has a summer festival that's a pretty good time. You should come. All of you. It's this Saturday."

They had arrived at the end of the walkway leading to Sol Mate, his lifeguard station was several yards further on. Phoebe knew the only thing to do was for her to go back to the beach house and she fought the urge to linger. It wasn't very often she got to stroll along the beach at sunrise with a gorgeous man. In fact, it had happened zero times in her entire life.

She forced herself to say something normal, neighborly, not

like a gushing virgin who didn't know how to handle a little friendly attention from a man. "That sounds fun, Tanner. Thank you. We'll be sure to check it out."

"Great," he smiled and it brightened her soul. "I'll see you later," he said and turned with a wave.

Phoebe waved back and wondered what it might be like to be rescued from a fire by Tanner as she walked back to the beach house. She hadn't even noticed that her feet no longer hurt.

Eleven

Bronwyn

The second writing sprint was worse than the first.

Bronwyn could barely pretend she was even looking at her laptop screen. She was bored and she was too busy texting her sister.

Trouble with the boys. Ryan wasn't communicating. She would have to call him and smooth things out, maybe call her mother to take the boys for a few days.

She had planned to stay through the first weekend at the beach house and return home for the second weekend before the boys went to summer camp. Bronwyn really wanted to stick to that plan. She didn't know if she could face Ryan only one week after his big confession.

Bronwyn sighed. Was her whole life going to be split into two sections from now on? Before finding out about Ryan's adultery and after?

She felt Phoebe's look before she saw it. The disappointed stare.

Phoebe was taking this writing time way too seriously, which was a little judgmental considering neither her nor Violet had been typing much either. Maybe Phoebe should worry more about her own writing and less trying to keep Bronwyn quiet, treating her like a kindergartner.

Bronwyn put her phone down and turned her attention back to her laptop. She would type like a mad woman if that's what it took to get Phoebe off of her back. It wasn't like anyone could see what she was typing. She could fill a page with complete gibberish and nobody would be the wiser.

Just as Bronwyn finished typing out *flibberty gibbet* there was a firm rapping on the front door.

"I'll get it," Bronwyn jumped at the chance to abandon writing time for a while. "Bill!" she said excitedly when she opened the door.

"Morning," Bill said, with far less enthusiasm. "I'll get to the window now if that works."

"Of course, of course, come in," Bronwyn cooed.

Bill was looking masculine in a pair of old jeans, a faded green T-shirt, and a tool belt hitched around his hips. Despite her overt flirtations, Bronwyn hadn't really thought of him as a man she would ever take seriously. In this get up, however, she was having second thoughts.

Bill carried an armful of supplies up the stairs and Bronwyn followed, admiring his muscular backside as she did. When they reached her bedroom she remembered that she had left some of her clothes strewn about.

One of the luxuries she was allowing herself over the summer was to be messy. Years of picking up after Ryan and the boys had turned her into a robot, constantly cleaning to try and keep the perfect home. The perfect home was off the table now, so she had decided not to care.

Still, she hadn't thought about Bill seeing her underthings. There was no reason to allow him to think she was a slob, or that Nicole was either.

Bronwyn darted around him before he could enter the bedroom and went in first. "Let me tidy up really quick," she said, her temperature rising ever so slightly as she swept past his muscled arm, almost grazing it with her torso.

He paused politely just outside the bedroom door and she did a swift pickup of her clothes, tossing them onto the floor of the closet, then pulling the comforter up hastily so the bed was technically, if not beautifully, made.

"All clear," she said with a smile, sitting down on the edge of the bed. May as well stay and visit with Bill a while. Anything was better than going back to the forced silence and unproductive writing sprint downstairs.

Bill entered the room, noticing Bronwyn's position on the bed, but not saying a word. He went to the window and unloaded his supplies on the floor so he could get started.

Bronwyn kicked her feet back and forth, feeling youthful and frisky. Bill didn't seem to notice and after a long moment she felt the need to fill the quiet with conversation. "Didn't mean to have the room so messy when you arrived."

Bill eyed her without turning away from the window and said, "That's all right. I'm used to it being messy in this room."

Bronwyn was baffled by his statement. "What do you mean by that?"

"It was my daughter's room," he said, glancing more directly at her than before, but still focusing mainly on the window.

"You used to live here?" The news was unexpected, tossing her out of of her flirty summer renter mood.

"Yes, I used to live here...until it got too expensive I had to move out and turn it into a rental."

Bronwyn stared at him as he used a screwdriver to take out a piece of the upper window frame. He had only been a fun distraction up until now, but there was more to him. It wasn't surprising that he owned Sol Mate, but she certainly hadn't thought about him living and raising his family in the beach house.

"Where do you and your family live now?" she asked.

His arms were raised up high to work on the window frame, his triceps flexing as he turned the screwdriver. He paused and looked back over his shoulder. Bronwyn saw the glint of an emotion in his deep blue eyes. She couldn't tell if it was pain or annoyance.

"My daughter's grown up now. Going to college. So I live by myself. Got a condo in town."

"Oh," Bronwyn was disappointed at the sad description of his life. A sudden sense of grief overcame her and she almost asked what had happened to his wife. But no, that would be too forward.

"I'm divorced," he added, as if reading her mind. Then, more bitterly, "That didn't help the finances."

She remained on the side of the bed, but had stopped kicking her feet. She felt like she was sinking into the mattress, weighted down by thoughts of her failing marriage, the future of her children coming from a broken home, the pathetic life stretching out in front of her, renting some crummy run down condo.

"What about you?" Bill asked.

"Me?"

He put down the screwdriver and worked his fingers into the stuck corner of the window. "Married? Divorced? Kids?" He tugged gently on the wood as he asked each one word question.

The answer stuck in her throat. She hadn't prepared any words to state the condition of her marriage to anyone yet. She wasn't divorced, for sure. But she didn't know if she was technically separated either, since this writing retreat had already been planned before the confession.

Still married, but miserable and lost. Was that an appropriate answer?

"That was too personal," Bill said, noticing her hesitation. "You don't have to tell me anything."

"I have two sons," she said quickly. "Six and eight."

He smiled and nodded in approval.

Bronwyn looked around, suddenly conscious that her boys

weren't with her to take to the beach. "They're at home...since this is supposed to be a writing retreat for me."

More silent approval from Bill as he used what looked like a chisel to chip away at some offending bump in the upper corner of the window that was making it stick.

The longer she sat stewing in her situation, the more she wanted to explain her life to Bill. Inexplicable as the urge was, Bronwyn couldn't help herself.

"I may be divorced...soon," she said.

He paused what he was doing and turned thoughtful eyes to her, truly looking at her, perhaps wondering if she presenting an awkward come on.

She looked down at her feet and blinked hard. Crying would not be cool in this situation.

"You'll be fine," he said.

Bronwyn looked up and coughed out a laugh. "You think?"

He eyed her with kind amusement, flicked his eyes down her body to her toes and back up again quickly as if sizing her up, and shrugged noncommittally. "Yes, I do. You're a nice looking lady."

"Am I?" Another humorless laugh escaped. The irony of him flirting with her when she was no longer interested was too much.

He nodded, standing behind his statement. "And you seem pretty spunky."

"Spunky?"

They locked eyes for a moment. Bronwyn not sure if she was offended or flattered. Bill's expression saying he wondered the same.

Suddenly, his unusual descriptor broke through the gloom that had settled in her mind and she laughed again, real laughter this time. Bill smiled, revealing laugh lines at the corners of his eyes.

"Spunky," she repeated, shaking her head.

"Spunky's a good thing," he added with a wink and went back to mending the window.

Bronwyn wasn't sure if she felt better or worse after their

conversation, but it was nice to talk to someone who had been through the dreaded 'D' and come out on the other side at least somewhat intact.

Twelve

Violet

If Violet were to grade the first week of the writing retreat she would give it a C...possibly a C-minus.

The location was amazing. Beautiful beach, a sweet little town to visit, a classic beach house with everything they needed except a chef to cook their meals. These facts alone should have been grounds for an A-minus, minimum, but not on this retreat.

The poor preliminary grade wasn't because of the location or accommodations, it had more to do with the lack of connection with her fellow Aphrodites. Not to mention the loss of focus on her writing.

Violet hadn't felt a natural chumminess with Phoebe or the newly named Bronwyn and she wasn't sure why. Plus her luggage continued to elude the airline and she was sick and tired of wearing the same shorts and top she had worn on the plane and continuing to wash her underthings in the bathroom sink.

Phoebe had finally convinced her to borrow one of her short dresses, a gold cotton T-shirt dress with a white star print. Violet took the offer with appreciation, but she and Phoebe were not at all the same size.

Violet swam in the abundance of gold starred fabric. Her legs and arms appeared comically skinny sticking out of the dress. Her appearance was marred in other ways too. Her hair was frizzed out from not having her normal conditioning treatment, her skin was bright pink from too much time on the beach the first week. Violet knew she looked more like a cartoon character than a serious writer.

Not that she had been writing well anyway. Focus during their scheduled writing times wasn't a challenge for Violet, unlike Bronwyn, but coming up with anything interesting to write was a problem.

She had spent most of her time working on the chapter where her protagonist's love interest takes his dog to the vet. Even though she had managed to finish the chapter, after reviewing it she knew that it fell flat and didn't add much to her story.

"Who wants to go first?" Phoebe asked.

Being the founder of the Mighty Aphrodite Writing Society, Phoebe was the leader by default. She naturally took control at meetings. They had all settled around the kitchen table for their first writing critique of the retreat. Despite having attended countless critique meetings online with the same women, Violet felt oddly nervous.

On her second glass of Pinot Grigio, Bronwyn did not offer to go. She looked at Violet to volunteer.

"I guess I'll go," Violet said. She had her laptop open on the table in front of her. "I don't think you're going to like it much."

"Don't be like that, Violet," Phoebe said encouragingly. "You know what we say, you can't edit a blank page."

"That's right," Bronwyn raised her glass. "There's no such thing as bad writing in critique group. Read on!"

Violet pulled the front of the T-shirt dress up where it was sagging heavily down her chest and took a deep breath before reading the pages of text about her hero and his sick dog. When she was done she looked up to see Phoebe and Bronwyn's reactions. Bronwyn was nodding slowly, staring at her wine glass, which was significantly more empty than when Violet had began. Phoebe was scribbling notes on a pad of paper.

"Boring, isn't it?" Violet asked, knowing it was true, but holding out a sliver of hope that she was mistaken.

Phoebe scrunched her mouth up and tilted her head before answering, "It's not that it's boring exactly."

Bronwyn's brow pinched into a wince, obviously disagreeing with Phoebe's statement.

"I think it's well written. The wording is pleasant to listen to, but there's not much conflict," Phoebe said.

"Right," Bronwyn latched onto that idea. "Like, what if the dog was hit by a car or something? Add urgency to it. Drama."

"Hit by a car?" Violet tried to imagine her hero's beloved golden retriever bleeding and yelping in pain. She didn't want to write that scene. She didn't like life or death situations or gore in her stories. Her shoulders slumped, which allowed the T-shirt dress to slip over one shoulder as she stared glumly at the words on her computer screen. "I was expecting to do better work while I was here."

Phoebe gasped and put her hand on her heart, making an empathetic sad face. "Me too!"

Violet laughed, "You were expecting me to do better work?"

"No, no, not you...me! I have been in such a slump this week. I thought being here on the retreat would feel...different," Phoebe sighed.

Bronwyn nodded in understanding as she topped off the wine in her glass. "This week has kind of sucked for writing." Violet and Phoebe both laughed, which encouraged her to top their wine off as well.

"Maybe it's because everything is new and exciting. It's not our normal routine?" Phoebe wondered.

"Could be," Violet said. "Most people are creatures of habit and this place is definitely outside of my normal day-to-day life."

Bronwyn picked up her wine glass and urged them to do the same. Then she called out a toast. "To a new normal...of beaches and suntans and being the brilliant writers we know we are!"

"Here! Here!" Phoebe and Violet said in unison.

Violet added, "And so what if we aren't tan yet."

They all laughed together, Phoebe hardest of all.

Bronwyn took a hefty swig of wine, swallowed, and said, "So what if we've written some real crap this week? As long as we don't quit!"

Phoebe agreed, "That's the important thing."

Violet closed her laptop, glad to be done with her portion of the sharing and feeling a little more relaxed.

"I mean, we have all summer. We should enjoy ourselves as well as write. This first week has just been an adjustment time," Phoebe added.

"Do you have anything to share for Lady Everton?" Violet asked.

Phoebe's cheeks turned a shade darker than the sunburned pink they already were. "I didn't get much done either. I got some outlining done, and research..."

"Oh, let's forget the sharing part of the night," Bronwyn suggested. "We need to cut ourselves a break. It's not easy to uproot and go away for the summer." Violet noted that Bronwyn's words were a little slurred as she gestured with her wine glass, making the wine slosh sloppily. "We can be brilliant tomorrow. Tonight we celebrate!"

Bronwyn took her glass and the open wine bottle and teetered out to the deck where she flopped into one of the deck chairs.

Violet looked at Phoebe and shrugged 'why not?'

As Violet sank into her own deck chair she relished the reds and golds in the sky over the ocean, the sun making its final showing of the night. The breeze coming off the water was invigorating and relaxing at the same time. Sipping her wine, its warmth spreading through her body, Violet listened to Bronwyn and Phoebe chatter and laugh and let her tension slip away.

She felt better about the whole retreat after this meeting, even though they had gotten basically nothing done on their novels. It was good to know that the other two Aphrodites weren't faring much better than she was.

"Misery loves company," she murmured.

A series of rapid knocks sounded from the front of the house and they all perked up.

"Who could that be?" Phoebe wondered.

"I'll get it," Violet offered, she figured she was the least tipsy of all of them.

As she went back into the house to answer the front door, Bronwyn called out, "If it's Bill, tell him I'm busy!"

Violet could hear Bronwyn laughing and snorting at her own joke all the way to the front door. When she opened the door it wasn't Bill at all.

"Ms. Brown?" The delivery man asked.

"Yes, that's me," Violet answered.

"I've got your luggage for you." He gestured to her bags that he had placed next to the door.

"More good news!" Violet exclaimed.

She took the arrival of her luggage, finally, as a good omen. Maybe after their initial adjustment time things were going to get better and better on the Mighty Aphrodite Writing Society retreat.

She reminded herself it had only been a week. They had all summer, and you never know what might happen over a summer.

Thirteen

Phoebe

P hoebe had already bought too much seashell jewelry and they were only halfway through the artisan's booths.

The small surf town of Turtle Cove had been transformed into a party. Part open air market full of canvas booths where local artisans displayed their wares, part carnival where children and adults alike played games for prizes and rode rickety rides, and part beer garden where local bands played live music and spirits flowed.

"What do you think of this?" Violet held up a necklace made of leather strung with small turtles carved from white seashells.

"That's really pretty and it goes with your dress," Phoebe said.

Now that she had access to her own clothes, Violet's mood and look had improved dramatically. Her natural style, it seemed, was Boho. Phoebe could see the turtle necklace would go nicely with the dark orange short sleeved gauze dress Violet wore. The dress added a little bit of weight to her slight frame and color to her cheeks, and the necklace was a good finishing touch.

"Do you think?" Violet held the necklace up and checked her reflection in the small mirror provided.

"I do," Phoebe said.

It was nice being out in Turtle Cove with the other Aphrodites. Bronwyn had slipped away to take a call from her boys, but before that they had enjoyed a delicious breakfast at the cutest restaurant called Honey Lime. Phoebe had already spent too much money according to her budget, but she was drawn to a booth selling sun hats. She left Violet to purchase her turtle necklace and started trying on hats.

"Oh, that's a nice one," the lady running the booth said as Phoebe tried on a super wide brimmed straw hat in bright red.

"I don't know if red is the right color," Phoebe checked out her reflection in the mirror.

"It looks good with what you have on," the lady said.

She had chosen a black sundress because it was flattering to her figure and the material was light. Phoebe wore a lot of navy and black, mostly because those colors were slimming. Maybe she did need to add a splash of color here and there.

"Nice hat," a man's voice commented just moments before Tanner's reflection joined hers in the mirror.

"Oh!" Phoebe's delighted surprise on seeing his handsome smile in the mirror made her blush. She was glad she had the giant hat to mask at least some of her reaction. "Tanner...hi!"

When she turned toward him the hat's wide red brim bumped into his chest, nearly knocking the hat off her head.

"Whoops," he stepped back, but not before she caught the scent of his cologne, which was inviting.

Tanner wore a pair of long shorts in olive green, a black short sleeved shirt, and what looked like a new pair of leather sandals strapped on his well formed feet. Even the man's feet were handsome.

"You look so nice with your clothes on," Phoebe said, realizing too late that she could have chosen better wording. Tanner laughed, luckily, so she did, too. "I mean...it's just I don't normally see you dressed...I mean dressed up!"

Tanner threw his head back and laughed again. Phoebe's blush intensified, though she couldn't help but laugh with him.

Seeing that she was bordering on mortified, Tanner said, "I know what you mean. Sometimes I forget that I have other clothes besides red swim trunks."

Glad he had smoothed over her embarrassment, Phoebe tried again. "Well, you look nice in black."

"Thanks." He grinned. Flicking his gaze up to her hat then back down so she could see the smile in his eyes, he added, "And you look nice in red."

"Oh, I was just trying this on," she said, flattered.

"It suits you, makes you look regal."

Phoebe's heart skipped a beat at the compliment. She couldn't think of a way to respond that wouldn't make her look like a gushing teenager so she found a more neutral subject.

"Thank you for letting me know about this party. It's been nice," she said.

"I'm glad you made it." He glanced around the area, "Did your friends come, too?"

"Yes, they're here somewhere," she pretended to look around for Violet and Bronwyn, but she was actually busy admiring him. Standing next to Tanner was invigorating.

"Hi!" Tanner waved to someone who Phoebe couldn't see. He turned his attention back to her, but only for a moment. "It was good to see you. I've gotta run. Hot date," he said, but before he left he leaned down so she could hear him speak more quietly. "I convinced my girlfriend to give me another shot. Wish me luck," he winked conspiratorially and disappeared.

Phoebe was left a little out of breath and extremely disappointed. Peering into the crowd where he had headed, she caught a glimpse of him greeting none other than Layla, his beautiful, demanding, fit throwing girlfriend. Phoebe was let down, but she knew she was being ridiculous. Tanner had only been being polite to her, he hadn't been seriously flirting with her.

She sighed and turned back to the mirror.

"Oooh, I love that on you," Bronwyn joined her at the hat booth. Her eyes were red and she was sniffling. "Do they have any in yellow?"

"Are you okay?" Phoebe asked.

Bronwyn waved her hand and refused to look Phoebe in the eye. "I'm fine."

Phoebe didn't believe her at all. She lowered her voice, "You've been crying. Is everything all right at home?"

"Home?" Bronwyn let out a caustic laugh then clamped her mouth shut. She turned her back on Phoebe and started picking up random yellow hats out of the selection. She plunked one on her head and turned around to face Phoebe. "What about this one?"

"Nicole, what's the matter?"

Bronwyn's face crumpled and her shoulders slumped. She complained in a thin high voice, "I want to be Bronwyn."

"Okay, yes, I'm sorry. Bronwyn, is everything okay?"

Bronwyn lifted one shoulder and let it drop in a defeated shrug.

"Are your kids all right?"

Bronwyn let out a shuddering sigh and sniffed again. "The boys are fine. I don't need to go back home, not right now. Everything's a mess at home. "

Phoebe was relieved to hear the children were okay, though she could tell Bronwyn needed to get something off of her chest. She smiled kindly and straightened Bronwyn's hat. "This one's pretty. It's just like mine, but yellow."

Bronwyn managed a smile. "We should get matching hats. All of us."

"Yes, Mighty Aphrodite hats," Phoebe agreed.

"Mighty Aphrodite hats?" Violet had found them in the booth. She wore the turtle necklace and was carrying a handful of brochures. "We're getting hats?" She noticed Bronwyn's red eyes and nose and was immediately concerned. "What happened?"

Phoebe jumped in, "What happened is we need to buy each of us a gorgeous hat then go find lunch somewhere, preferably a place with outside seating and a solid margarita. Does that sound good?" She looked at Bronwyn for her approval.

Bronwyn agreed. "I'll get our hats, my treat."

"What color do you want Violet?" Phoebe asked.

Violet looked back and forth between the other two women and their hats. "Since we're going with primary colors, I'll take a blue one."

* * *

Once they were comfortably arranged on the outdoor patio of the beer garden munching on warm tortilla chips and salsa, frozen margaritas in hand, proudly donning their Mighty Aphrodite hats, Bronwyn finally loosened up.

"Things haven't been great with my husband," she confessed, her yellow hat dipping slightly as she took a sip of her margarita.

"Oh no," Violet said, shooting Phoebe a 'we-knew-there-was-something-wrong' look.

Phoebe asked, "Do you want to talk about it? We're here to listen."

Bronwyn sighed and leaned back in her chair. Her glum mood didn't quite fit into their festive surroundings. Mariachi music was playing, apparently the Turtle Cove beer garden was sponsored by the local Mexican restaurant, El Tio.

"I can talk about it unless I start to cry...then I don't want to talk anymore," Bronwyn said.

"Deal," Phoebe smiled with encouragement and took a sip of her margarita.

With the slightest tremor in her voice Bronwyn confessed, "My husband has been cheating on me." Phoebe and Violet both gasped in surprise. "He told me right before I came here. The morning I left in fact."

"That's awful," Violet said.

Bronwyn picked up a chip and dunked it angrily into the bowl of salsa. "I think he only told me to keep me from coming to the retreat. He doesn't like having to be responsible for the boys."

"What a jerk!" Phoebe declared. She leaned back in her chair and shook her head, her mind clicking through Bronwyn's weird behavior since arriving at the retreat. Everything began to make sense.

"I'm realizing how much of a jerk he is," Bronwyn said before popping the chip into her mouth and chewing on it miserably.

"How long have you been married?" Violet asked. Bronwyn's eyes teared up as she chewed and Violet hurriedly reversed her question. "Never mind. That's not important." Violet looked at Phoebe for help.

The problem with trying to comfort Bronwyn, Phoebe thought, was that she had never been married. Neither had Violet. They had no children either. Both of them were at a a loss of what to say or do.

"The weird thing is I don't feel bad about losing Ryan, not really. I don't even know if we like each other anymore, let alone love each other." She traced the bottom of her margarita glass thoughtfully. "It's more like I'm upset about my life blowing up, you know?"

"I think so," Phoebe offered.

"I mean I thought my life was going to be one way and now it's going to be something else. Probably a different house, different friends, my boys won't be with me all the time anymore..." Her eyes filled with tears again.

Violet reached over and took Bronwyn's hand. "Is there anything we can do?"

Bronwyn smiled at Violet with the most genuine smile Phoebe had seen from her since the beginning of the retreat. No wonder. The poor thing had been covering up all of her emotions from day one.

"Yes," Phoebe said. "We want to help. Do you need to back out of the retreat?" A ball of dread sank in Phoebe's stomach. Covering another third of the beach house rental for the summer would push her already strained finances, but she would do it if that's what Bronwyn needed.

"No!" Bronwyn's eyes got big and she shook her head so hard that her yellow hat flopped a little madly. "I need this. It's better not to be right there in the middle of it. I think I would go crazy if I had to see Ryan every day."

Phoebe thought maybe Bronwyn had been going a little bit crazy on the retreat, too, but decided not to bring that up.

"I know it's been a little...weird...with the whole Bronwyn and Nicole thing," Bronwyn said sheepishly. "I guess I wanted to be somebody else for a while."

Phoebe and Violet shared a pained look.

"I like the name Bronwyn," Phoebe said helpfully. "It sounds old fashioned."

"And mysterious," Violet added.

"I think you should be whoever you want to be," Phoebe told Bronwyn, reaching out and patting her on the shoulder.

"Me too," Violet agreed.

Bronwyn smiled, her eyes shining with tears again. "Thanks, girls."

"We writers stand up for each other," Phoebe said. She raised her margarita in a toast and the other two joined her. "To the Mighty Aphrodite Writing Society!"

They all laughed and sipped their margaritas and it was good to see Bronwyn truly relax. The beer garden was filling up with the lunch crowd and Phoebe recognized Bill as he maneuvered past their table. He caught her eye and hesitated.

"Hello Bill," she said with a smile.

He stopped at their table, a red plastic cup Phoebe assumed was full of beer in his hand.

"Hello ladies," he said politely. His eyes went to their matching hats as they greeted him in return.

Bronwyn, eyes red and puffy, nose still running, sniffled as she looked up at him from underneath her yellow hat. Bill's back stiffened. Phoebe sensed he wanted to say something, but was holding it back. He watched with concern as Bronwyn ducked her head and hid under the wide brim of her hat.

Their brief, silent interaction was over in a matter of seconds. To an outsider who wasn't familiar with the nuances of body language between star crossed lovers during regency times, when people weren't allowed to touch each other or even speak about their attraction, there was nothing to see.

But to Phoebe, who was familiar with body language, both writing it and reading it in other people, there was an important development happening right under their noses at the beer garden. Bill liked Bronwyn and his hackles were up at the sight of her being so upset.

Phoebe took an innocent sip of her margarita and pretended to watch the Mariachi band as Bill made his way to a different table. What she had just witnessed between Bill and Bronwyn may have been completely innocent, but it was also interesting. Very interesting.

Fourteen

Phoebe

Phoebe had gone on her sunrise walk several days in a row, which in her mind made it a routine. The muscles in her legs already showed significant tightening and she was excited. There was a good possibility that by the end of the summer she could be in much better shape – if she kept up the routine.

This newfound healthy habit put her in a good mood as she trudged along the sand enjoying the beautiful colors of the sunrise over the water. Her mind wandered to the attraction she had noticed between Bill and Bronwyn. The trouble an affair between them would create if they ended up falling in love was intriguing.

Not that it was completely unheard of for a woman in the midst of a divorce to have a relationship with another man. Not in this day and age. But in regency times such behavior would constitute a scandal...in fact there would probably not be a divorce at all, just an affair, or the tragedy of lovers forever kept apart by the cruel, cruel world.

The whole situation had turbo charged Phoebe's imagination and the ideas of different romantic scenarios for her Lady Everton story kept flowing.

After all, that was part of the fun of writing romance. Phoebe was free to live out a variety of love affair scenarios in her mind with her characters, and she could include happy endings, which almost never happened in real life. Certainly not in her life.

"Good morning," Tanner said, jogging up behind her like he had the other morning.

Speaking of imaginary love lives.

Phoebe had been plagued with visions of Tanner in his black shirt and olive green shorts, dressed up and smelling wonderful, since she saw him at the Turtle Cove town party.

"Good morning," she said calmly. She wanted him to think she took their random meeting in stride, no butterflies or anything weird on her part.

He slowed to a walk next to her, a sly grin on his face. "Fancy meeting you here."

She laughed. Probably too hard, but Tanner's presence put her into giddy schoolgirl mode.

"How are you today?" she asked.

"Oh, you know, getting by," he said.

Phoebe heard a hint of dissatisfaction, but wasn't sure. "How did your date go?" she asked politely.

Instead of the upbeat answer she was expecting, Tanner made a drawn out growling sound then said, "Not great."

"No?" Her interest was piqued.

Tanner avoided eye contact by surveying the ocean as they walked and he answered, "Yeah, we broke up...again."

"That's too bad."

"It wasn't quite as ugly as last time," he confided, remembering Phoebe witnessed their last breakup. "We never actually made it into the Coastline this time."

Surprised at the mention of the steak place, she asked, "You took her to the same restaurant? Where she broke up with you last time?"

"Yes," he admitted. "In retrospect I can see how that might have been a bad idea."

Phoebe felt a little sorry for him. It was quite a blunder to make with a woman who had explicitly said she wasn't happy being taken to the Coastline Inn. She tried to make him feel better. "It's not bad per se, it's just...didn't she express her displeasure with that place last time?"

He sighed. "Yes, she did. She said I don't put enough thought into our relationship." He lifted one shoulder in a defeated shrug. "I didn't know where else to take her."

Phoebe thought about the nice place they had seen on the dock. "What about the Cobalt Edge? That looks pretty impressive."

"It's booked out for weeks. I didn't have time to wait."

They walked a little while without talking. Tanner in gloomy silence. Phoebe's mind going strong.

"Maybe you could do something different for her that doesn't require making a reservation," Phoebe said.

"Like what?"

"A picnic on the beach? That would be romantic and totally unique."

He wagged his finger at her. "You see, that would have been a good idea."

"Aren't there horseback rides on the beach you can rent?"

"I don't know, those are kind of for tourists."

Phoebe couldn't stop her suggestions. She had so many unused romantic date ideas swimming around in her mind. Words kept spilling out of her mouth. "Maybe she wants to be pampered like a tourist. Maybe she wants her life to be different, you know? Bigger, better, more than the same things she sees every day around her."

Tanner looked at her thoughtfully. "I never thought about it that way."

Phoebe took a breath to calm down. This wasn't her business, really, she wasn't sure why she was getting so worked up.

"Sorry, my brain just really latches onto *romantic scenarios*," she used her fingers to air quote the last two words.

He smiled and the sweetness in his eyes melted a small piece of her heart.

"I do wish I would have talked to you about it before I took her to the Coastline Inn again," he said.

"Yes, bad timing I guess."

They were nearing the beach house and Phoebe knew he would be stepping away to the guardhouse. She wanted to keep walking and talking with him instead of going inside and opening her laptop for the day. Staying outside in the early morning sunshine, with waves gently lapping on the shore, conversing with a shirtless Tanner, sounded much more appealing.

"I could help," she blurted out.

He gave her a questioning look. "Help with what?"

"Next time, if there is a next time," the words caught as she spoke and Phoebe had to clear her throat to keep explaining. "I mean, if you could convince her to go out with you again I could help you plan things...make it really romantic."

Tanner stopped walking and turned to her, a smile widening on his handsome face. "You'd do that for me?"

Basking in the direct glow of his happy attention Phoebe's heart fluttered in her chest. "Of course."

"Really? Wow, that would be great!"

Phoebe blushed, thrilled to be involved with him in some way. "You would need to convince her to go on another date with you," she cautioned.

"I can do that, I can do that," he repeated, trying to convince himself as well as her. He grabbed her hand and squeezed it warmly. "I really appreciate your offer."

"I'll get started on the planning," she said, a little breathless from his touch.

"Thank you so much," he continued, dropping her hand and

walking backward toward the guard station. "I'll try to convince her today!"

"Good luck," Phoebe waved at him with her still tingling hand and went into the beach house, a giant smile on her face that she could not contain.

Fifteen

Violet

Violet sipped her morning coffee and read through the brochures she had grabbed in Turtle Cove at their Marine Life Rescue booth.

According to the brochures, Turtle Cove had been aptly named. The quaint little town was nestled in a cove that was also a sea turtle nesting beach. Conservation efforts had long been underway to protect all marine life in the area, especially the turtles.

Violet gazed at the bright images of ancient sea turtles swimming in blue waters and baby sea turtles making their way over the sand to the ocean after hatching. Intrigued, she flipped the brochures open to find depressing pictures that tugged at her heart.

Sea turtles with fishing nets wrapped tightly around their necks and flippers, cutting into their flesh and creating open wounds. Dead baby sea turtles in broken shells that had been disrupted on the beach as they incubated.

Sad. Shocking. Violet abhorred mistreatment of animals, especially vulnerable, adorable, baby animals.

The address of Marine Life Rescue wasn't too far from Sol Mate. Maybe she could do some volunteering while she was here, help make a small difference.

"Isn't it a beautiful morning?" Phoebe asked as she practically waltzed into the kitchen.

"Been on another walk this morning?"

"Yes, another one!"

Her answer was so bright and happy Violet took notice. These early morning walks were doing wonders for Phoebe, she looked invigorated.

"Nothing like a walk along a beach, is there?" Violet asked.

Phoebe nodded in agreement, humming as she grabbed one of her many notepads and a pen, poured herself a cup of coffee and sat down at the table with Violet.

"Did you get some ideas on your walk?" Violet asked.

"You could say that," Phoebe smiled. She glanced down at the brochures. "Are those the brochures you got in Turtle Cove?"

"Yes, they're for a conservation group in town. They help all marine life and especially the sea turtles that nest here."

"Oh?" Phoebe raised her eyebrows in interest as she took a sip of coffee.

"I was thinking about going over there and seeing if they are taking volunteers. You know, something to do to clear my head after writing."

"That's a great idea, Violet."

"Do you want to join me?"

Phoebe looked at the blank notepad in front of her. "I don't think so, not this morning. I have a lot of ideas I need to get down on paper."

With Phoebe busy and Bronwyn still asleep, Violet decided to visit Marine Life Rescue on her own. When she stepped out the front door of the beach house, she remembered that her car was a gas guzzling SUV rental, not her eco-friendly economy car back home.

Giving the monstrosity a look of disgust, she murmured, "I can't drive up in that thing." Pulling the brochure out of her purse she found the map on the very back that showed the conservatory's location. It wasn't too far. Just on this side of Turtle Cove. Only a few miles. "I'll walk," she decided. It would do her good to get some exercise, just like Phoebe's morning walks had been doing her good.

By the time she found the shabby building that housed the Marine Life Rescue of Turtle Cove, Violet was parched. She hadn't thought to bring water and the morning had heated up considerably since she left the beach house. Pushing on the door she was glad to find it open.

"Hopefully they have public bathrooms and a vending machine with bottled water," she mumbled.

Marine Life Rescue had none of those things. Barely more than a shack set up on the back edge of the beach, the conservatory was quite unimpressive. Inside there was one long counter that looked like it had been rehabbed from a demolition site, several rickety windows propped open with sticks to allow the sea breeze in, and two mismatched tables with several mismatched chairs set up around them in the main area, all of which held stacks of the same bright blue brochures Violet had in her purse.

Despite all of the unusual decor, it was the walls of the building that captured Violet's eye. Every wall was nothing but shelves from floor to ceiling. Each shelf was packed full of books, jars, boxes, and bags. Some of them looked brand new and some looked ratty with age. Some looked empty and some looked like they were in use. All of them were jammed tightly together on the shelves giving the place a disheveled appearance.

Tying the whole vibe of the room together was the man sitting at the center table with a floppy black dog laying at his feet. The man had short dark hair and a five o'clock shadow that was at least twelve hours old. He had a heavy jaw and long legs that stretched under the table and stuck out from underneath on the other side. His ankles were crossed and he dangled one of his flip flops from his big toe.

The dog raised its head and perked its floppy ears up at Violet when she entered. Its fur was so black she could not see where the fur ended and the dog's dark eyes and nose began.

"Bear, no," the man said, but it was too late, the floppy dog was headed right toward her. Lucky for Violet, Bear was only about a foot and a half tall and seemed more interested in licking her to death than biting, despite his tough name.

"Hello, Bear," Violet leaned down to pet the dog's soft fur. "Is Bear a 'he'?" she asked.

"Yes," the man extricated himself from his unique sitting position at the table and stood. She had not been wrong in thinking his legs were long. He had to be at least six foot four. "Sorry, he's pretty pushy when he wants attention." In two strides he was in front of Violet, taking hold of Bear's collar and holding him back.

"That's okay, I love dogs. He's so cute! What kind is he?"

"A Le'Mutt," the man said, grinning.

Violet laughed, "I see. Well, he's an adorable mutt."

Bear wagged his tail in agreement and trotted back to his spot at the table, plopping down so he looked like a pile of black fur on the ground.

"How can I help you?" the tall man asked, a smile in his dark green eyes.

"Well," Violet looked around the room for a second, gathering her thoughts. "I got your brochure this past weekend and I was wondering if you were looking for any volunteers for the summer."

"You want to volunteer?" he seemed pleased.

"I was thinking about it, if you need anyone."

"Yes, yes, yes, we always need people, especially people who've been personally approved by Bear." He ushered her toward the table where he had been sitting, then remembered that he hadn't introduced himself and stuck his hand out to shake hers. "My name's Ben, by the way."

"I'm Violet," Violet took his hand and noticed how small her hand was in comparison.

"Violet, that's not a name you hear every day."

"No, my parents were what you might call hippies."

He seemed delighted at that possibility. "Nothing wrong with hippies. They're my kind of people."

Violet glanced around at the untidy shelves as she sat down. Bear moved his head so he could snuggle it up against her foot. Definite hippy vibe in the place. Violet felt right at home.

Ben sat across from her and leaned his elbows on the table. "I haven't seen you in Turtle Cove, are you new here?"

"Yes, I'm here for the summer."

"You're at a rental?"

She nodded. "A beach house named Sol Mate."

"Bill's place?"

Surprised that he would know then immediately not surprised given the size of Turtle Cove, she answered, "Yes, Bill's place. You know him?"

Ben laughed at the idea that he wouldn't know him. His laugh was deep and mellow. "Absolutely. He's kind of famous around here."

"He is?"

Ben leaned toward her as if he was about to impart some heavy duty wisdom. "He's a hardcore surfer. World class, actually. One of the founders of Turtle Cove."

"Oh? I didn't know that."

He looked fondly around at the overstuffed shelves surrounding them. "He started this place to try to make a difference."

"I didn't know that either." Violet followed Ben's gaze as it swept the room, trying to appreciate it as much as he was appreciating it.

"And he built that beach house where you're staying by hand from the ground up."

Violet was impressed. "Really?" Ben looked back to her, nodding. When his eyes caught hers something stirred in her heart and she forgot what they were talking about. He held her gaze for a long moment, the whole time his deep green eyes were smiling. Finally, she thought of something to say, "How long have you been here? This place, I mean. How long has this place been here?"

Casually leaning back in his chair, Ben stretched his legs out again, to the side this time so he wouldn't kick Violet or disturb Bear. "We're going on ten years this July."

"And you've been here the whole time?"

"Yeah, I started out volunteering at first, like you," he gave her an approving nod, which only sent ripples of attraction through her body. "It worked with my degree so when Bill offered me a job I took it. Then when Bill–" The smile in Ben's eyes faded and he seemed to catch himself, remembering that he and Violet had just met. "Bill couldn't keep managing the place so I took over for him."

Violet sensed they should move on to another topic so she shifted gears. "I would love to do some part-time volunteering while I'm here for the summer."

Ben's smile returned. "That would be awesome. We have our yearly fundraiser coming up and we always need help with that. What would you like to do?"

That was an unexpected question. She didn't know she could pick what she wanted. "I'm not sure..."

"Well, what are you good at? What do you like to do in your normal life?"

"I like to write," Violet confessed, pretty sure that wasn't going to be much help.

Ben's face brightened. "You're a writer?"

"Yes, I write. I'm also a teacher. So I'm pretty good with words. But that's probably not what you need help with."

"Au contraire mon cher, we haven't had a good writer around since we put together these brochures a few years ago." He sat up and leaned on the table again, excited at the possibilities. "Might you be interested in writing some blog posts?"

Violet could barely contain her enthusiasm. "Interested? I would love to do that if you think it would help."

He cocked his head and considered her happily, then asked, "Can I get you something to drink? Then I can tell you all the ways that it would help."

Her conversation with Ben was extraordinary. He was funny, passionate about saving the environment, intelligent, thoughtful, and it didn't hurt that he was so cute.

By the time they were done she had outlined two blog posts for the Marine Life Rescue website. The first on how fishing nets were one of the biggest threats to sea turtles and other marine life and what could be done about it. The second was a review of all of the ways Marine Life Rescue had made significant changes in the wildlife and community of Turtle Cove.

"It'll be kind of a warm up blog post to prepare everyone for the big ten year fundraiser in July," Ben said. "Is that all you need to get started?" He glanced down at the notepad she had borrowed to scribble down the outlines.

"I think this will be good."

"Here," Ben pulled his cell phone out of his pocket. "What's your number? If you're okay with me having it."

Violet had no recent memory of a time when she wanted someone to have her number more than she wanted Ben to have it. She told him and he punched the number in then called her so his was on her phone.

He grinned. "Now you'll know how annoying the director of a nonprofit can be when you've said you want to volunteer."

Violet laughed, "I doubt you're annoying."

"We'll see," he chuckled. "I've taken up too much of your time already today." He glanced outside. "It looks like it's gonna rain. I've got to get a few things done outside before the monsoon."

Violet stood. If there was going to be a monsoon she needed to get going. She had a few miles to hoof it back to the beach house. She bid a hasty and slightly awkward goodbye to Ben and Bear and started back.

Giddy with her new involvement at the conservatory, not to mention the fact that she had Ben's number in her phone and would be seeing him more over the summer, Violet barely noticed the clouds building quickly above her head. The soft breeze of the ocean turned cooler and harsher as she walked, but she was busy putting together words in her head for the sea turtle blog post.

It wasn't until the first few fat drops of cold rain fell on her bare arms that Violet took note of the deepening storm. By that time it was too late to find cover.

She had made it halfway back to Sol Mate and was alone on the long stretch of desolate road that led to the private beach houses. The rain came sudden and fast and there was nothing around Violet except for the gravel road, sand and scrub brush.

Within a few minutes she was soaking wet, her T-shirt and shorts soggy and bagging down. She thought about calling Phoebe to see if she would drive down and get her, but she was honestly afraid the rain would douse her phone and ruin it. So she trudged on, trying to keep her feet from slipping out of her wet sandals and cursing her decision to leave the SUV parked at the beach house.

A car horn honked behind her and Violet turned to find a small green pick up truck with the now familiar logo for Marine Life Rescue painted on the side door slowing down to a stop beside her. The driver window rolled down and Ben stuck his head out.

"Can I give you a lift?" he shouted above the sound of pouring rain and wind.

Heart pounding, Violet shouted back, "Yes!"

Sixteen

Phoebe

The rain put Phoebe into a dreamy mood. Wrapped in a light blue throw blanket and curled up on the reading chair in the living room, her thoughts were far away. Ever since she was a child the sound of rain on the roof had sparked her imagination.

No longer, however, were her daydreams those of a young girl.

After she told Tanner she was going to plan a truly romantic date for him she had not been able to get her gorgeous lifeguard acquaintance out of her head.

Tanner in a tuxedo pulling up in a limousine ready for an expensive night on the town. Tanner dressed like Shakespeare's Romeo reading poetry up to the balcony of his love under a glowing full moon. Tanner shirtless and riding a glistening black stallion along the shore of the beach. Tanner in his olive green shorts and black shirt sitting on a beach blanket with a picnic basket and a bottle of wine.

Phoebe sighed, "If only."

The front door opened with a bang then shut again. A few seconds later a sopping wet Violet entered the living room.

"Violet! What were you doing out in the rain?"

"I walked home!" Violet said, seemingly exhilarated by the experience. Her hair was stringy wet and clung to her head and neck, her shorts and shirt hung wet and loose on her thin frame, they dripped onto the floor creating a pool of rain water around her feet.

"Didn't you have your car?"

Violet shook her head 'no' and kicked her sandals off her feet. Her brown eyes looked bigger without her glasses and there was something rather beautiful about her wet and wild appearance. If Phoebe had to describe it, she would say that Violet was glowing.

"I walked to the conservatory, but got caught in the rain on the way back."

"You should have called me!"

"It's okay, I got a ride about halfway here." Violet paused for a second before adding, "Ben from the conservatory. He gave me a ride."

Phoebe noted a playful smile on Violet's lips when she mentioned this Ben person, and a flicker of excitement in her eyes. Phoebe unwrapped from the soft throw blanket and stood up.

"Why don't I make us some tea and you can tell me about it? Do you want this blanket?" Phoebe asked.

"I think I need to take a hot shower and then I'll come down for some tea," Violet answered.

"Of course," Phoebe smiled knowingly as she watched Violet practically flit up the stairs like a happy soggy bird. She went to the kitchen and put the kettle on.

"I think the rain is affecting us all," Bronwyn announced as she came into the kitchen.

"Why's that?" Phoebe asked.

"It made me so drowsy I zonked out for a while and now I can hear Violet singing in her room."

Phoebe couldn't contain herself. "I have a hunch she met a man today."

Bronwyn pulled the tea tray into the center of the kitchen island so they could choose a flavor. "Do tell!"

"I don't know for sure, but she certainly was in a good mood for nearly getting drowned in the rain while she walked home from the conservatory."

"What was she doing at a conservatory?"

"She wants to do some volunteer work."

"That's nice," Bronwyn said, pulling a bag of mini chocolate chip cookies out of the cupboard. "Why didn't she drive there?"

"I'm not sure, but she mentioned that someone named Ben picked her up in the rain and drove her the rest of the way home...and she's got that look."

"What look?" Bronwyn asked, crunching on a mini cookie.

"The look someone gets when they're...*twitterpated.*"

Bronwyn stopped chewing and stared at Phoebe for a second before cracking up laughing. "You're too much, Phoebe."

"What?"

"Twitterpated," Bronwyn shook her head and shoved her hand back into the cookie bag. "That's not a word you hear every day."

"What's not a word you hear every day?" Violet asked. Freshly showered she had changed into leggings and an oversized sweatshirt.

"Twitterpated," Bronwyn said with her mouth half-full of cookie.

"Like from Bambi?" Violet giggled.

"Yes, exactly," Phoebe said.

"Who's twitterpated?" Violet asked.

"You are, according to Phoebe," Bronwyn teased, tilting her bag of cookies toward Violet so she could take some.

Violet's mouth dropped open in surprise. "Me?" She tried to look innocent as she stuck her hand in the bag, but the immediate reddening of her cheeks gave her away.

Phoebe pulled three mugs out of the cupboard and placed them on the island. "I was just saying that from the way you looked when you came home I would bet this Ben guy is pretty cute." Violet blushed furiously and wouldn't stop smiling. "See what I mean? If that's not twitterpated I don't know what is," Phoebe said, happily vindicated by Violet's reaction to Ben's name.

"So, tell us about this Ben guy," Bronwyn said.

With her bright pink face betraying her true emotions, Violet tried to act nonchalant. She picked an orange spice tea from the tray and got her mug ready for hot water as she explained. "He runs the Marine Life Rescue for Turtle Cove. They save sea turtles."

Phoebe and Bronwyn waited for more, but Violet busied herself with carefully pouring honey into her waiting mug.

Bronwyn looked at Phoebe. "He saves sea turtles."

"A noble cause, indeed," Phoebe said.

"Anything else we should know about Ben?" Bronwyn asked.

Violet kept her eyes on her tea, but she couldn't keep from smiling. "Oh, I don't know. He's tall."

"Tall is nice," Phoebe said.

"And he has a dog named Bear."

Bronwyn let out a hoot of laughter. "A dog?"

"Oh no!" Phoebe cracked up laughing, too.

"What?" Violet asked.

The tea kettle whistled on the stove and Phoebe grabbed it to pour. "If this Ben guy is tall, gallant enough to save you from the rain *and* he has a dog, you don't stand a chance, Violet."

"I don't?"

"It sounds like he's one of your characters," Bronwyn added.

Violet smiled a little coyly. "I hadn't thought about it that way."

"And you with your lifeguard," Bronwyn said to Phoebe.

"What's this?" Violet turned the teasing back on Phoebe.

"My lifeguard? I don't have a lifeguard," Phoebe said, but she felt her cheeks burning.

"Don't think we haven't noticed you chatting up Mr. Gorgeous Redtrunks," Bronwyn said.

"I wasn't chatting him up," Phoebe tried to argue, but she giggled nervously, which damaged her credibility immediately.

"What were you two talking about this morning? He seemed pretty into it," Bronwyn asked.

"You weren't even awake yet. Were you spying out your window?" Phoebe asked.

"I told you, life is more interesting if everyone thinks you're asleep." Bronwyn gave her an exaggerated wink, which only increased Phoebe's giggles.

"What's his name again?" Violet was pretty eager to get the spotlight onto someone else.

"Tanner," Phoebe answered. The other two repeated his name in unison like a couple of teenage girls. "It's not like that," Phoebe said. "I was just giving him advice."

"Advice on what?" Bronwyn wanted to know.

Phoebe hesitated before answering, "Romantic date ideas."

Bronwyn and Violet both hooted in laughter, which made Phoebe laugh, too. They had to compose themselves to finish fixing their tea and settle in the living room.

The rain poured and wind whipped the cold sheets of water against the tall double pane windows. Phoebe pulled two more throw blankets out of the large wicker basket that doubled as a coffee table and handed them to the others.

"Maybe this weather is making us silly," she said.

Wiping tears of laughter from her eyes, Bronwyn said, "I'm glad you two are having a little fun at least. I think I'm going to swear off men forever."

Phoebe and Violet started to make sympathetic sounds, but they were interrupted by a loud banging on the front door.

"Who could that be?" Phoebe asked.

"Maybe it's Ben stopping by to make sure you're all right," Bronwyn teased.

Violet dismissed the comment with a wave of her hand and they all went to the door, throw blankets wrapped around their shoulders to fend off the damp cold.

"Bill!" Phoebe said when she swung the door open to reveal their soaked landlord.

"Sorry for interrupting, but I'm gonna need to check on that window repair in this rain," he said.

"Of course, come in," Phoebe said.

They all stepped back and let Bill pass them to get to the stairway. With their blankets wrapped around them Phoebe realized they looked like grown women holding a slumber party.

"I'll just be a few minutes," he said. He glanced at the three of them, his eyes lingering for a millisecond longer on Bronwyn. "Is everything okay in the house? With the rain?"

"We haven't noticed any problems," Violet volunteered. "Do you want a towel or something?"

Bill, who looked like he'd been doused with buckets of water between his car and the front door, brushed the offer away. "I'm fine, thank you. I'll just check on that window. Is there anyone in the bedroom?" he directed the question at Bronwyn.

"No, it's empty," she answered.

They all watched Bill's strong masculine form bound up the stairs two at a time. His light grey T-shirt was wet, practically see through and clinging to his muscled back. Phoebe looked at the other two, amused at his sudden appearance when they were talking about men.

Bronwyn sucked in her breath.

"What is it?" Violet asked.

"I may or may not have left some underthings out," she said.

Phoebe giggled again. "I'm sure Bill has seen an underthing or two in his lifetime."

"True," Bronwyn didn't turn away from the stairs as Phoebe

and Violet went back to the living room. "I'm just gonna go make sure," she said quickly and hurried up the steps.

Violet looked at Phoebe with wide eyes. "Should we go up after her?"

"I don't think so. They'll be fine," Phoebe said with partial confidence.

"What kind of romantic date ideas were you advising Tanner on?" Violet asked.

Excitement at all of the Tanner date possibilities rushed back to Phoebe and she listed them for Violet. She had just finished explaining the elaborate beach picnic idea and was complaining that she didn't have the perfect old fashioned picnic basket available when Bronwyn came back down the stairs. She was carrying a wet grey T-shirt in her hand.

"I'm gonna toss this in the dryer for a few minutes," she told them before disappearing into the utility room off of the kitchen.

Phoebe and Violet looked at each other with surprise.

Violet whispered, "She got his shirt off."

Phoebe laughed out loud at the comment just as a shirtless Bill appeared at the top of the stairs. Though several years older than them, maybe even a decade older, his age did not stop them from admiring his physique.

"I've gotta wait a few minutes to see if this leaks again. Is there anything else you ladies need done around here?" Bill asked.

Phoebe had to bite her tongue to not say something outrageous in response. Sometimes flirtatious wit was better left for her writing.

"You don't happen to have a picnic basket that we could borrow do you?" Violet asked, smiling helpfully at Phoebe.

"A picnic basket?" he asked.

Violet nudged Phoebe.

"Yes, an old fashioned picnic basket. The kind with two flaps that lift up and down?" Phoebe explained.

Bill looked at them silently, his brow furrowed. Phoebe was a little worried they had offended him somehow. He was a busy man after all, he probably didn't want to be bothered with helping them find a picnic basket.

Bronwyn emerged from the utility room just in time to watch Bill reach toward the upstairs hallway ceiling. He pulled down a hatch door revealing an opening to the attic. He yanked on something and a ladder slid out of the hole, stopping short about halfway to the floor.

"Damned thing," he muttered, jerking on the ladder. It didn't budge. Apparently it was stuck.

Before Phoebe could tell him not to worry about it, she didn't want to put him out if he couldn't get into the attic, Bill grabbed the highest rung he could reach and pulled himself up. An impressive show of athleticism, which Phoebe found attractive and imagined the other two, especially Bronwyn, did as well. Within a few moments he had disappeared into the hole in the ceiling.

Sounds of movement came from the attic and the flash of Bill's cell phone flashlight swept past the opening once or twice. The three women looked at each other then back up into the hole.

Suddenly a large brown picnic basket with flap lids that lifted on each side dropped out of the hole and landed on the hall rug.

Bill's head popped out of the hole, upside down. "Is that what you're looking for?"

Phoebe hurried up the stairs and picked up the basket. "This is perfect!"

Bill's head disappeared and a moment later he was lowering himself gracefully from the attic opening. She could tell the man did a lot of pull ups.

"Thank you," she said.

"We aim to please," he answered.

He closed the hatch door and gave them all a quick nod before going back into the bedroom. When Phoebe looked down at Violet and Bronwyn they were both pretending to swoon.

Seventeen

Bronwyn

Bronwyn had pre-rehearsed every possible chaos that might greet her when she returned home for the weekend.

After almost two weeks away, her imagination ran wild with scenarios ranging from a house utterly destroyed by two little boys left to fend for themselves to walking in on Ryan and what's-her-name in bed.

When she did walk into her home she encountered something wholly unexpected. A quiet, clean, empty house.

The smell of it stopped her in her tracks. It smelled like home. Her home.

She had entered the house through the garage where she had parked the convertible carefully, dutifully, in its normal spot. An action that felt strangely domestic considering how she had left.

The spot had not been filled with what's-her-name's car. Not yet.

Bronwyn remained still, standing in the kitchen she had

remodeled four years ago to create the perfect place for her family to cook and eat and be together.

"The perfect kitchen for us," she had told Ryan when the last contractor finished and went home with a healthy check in his pocket.

"It's nice," Ryan had said.

Nice.

Bronwyn went to the island and put her keys and purse on the white marble countertop, marveling at how clean it was, as if no children had sat on the stools next to the counter and eaten their cereal that morning. She glanced around and saw no evidence that anyone had used the kitchen...ever.

She took a deep breath.

The air felt thick around her body, pressing against her as she moved through it. The feeling was similar to coming home after a normal, everyday fight with Ryan, but much heavier.

She was returning home after an ending. A grand let down. She had spent two weeks on a beach pretending to be someone else. A writer.

Coming back to this place was like walking through a model home, a staged set of a play which she had no desire to act in. The show was over. The curtain had dropped.

Melancholy fell over her, the way it did when she was done watching a movie, when the credits started rolling and the lights came up. Nothing to do but clean up popcorn and spilled soda.

Here in this shining kitchen there wasn't even that to do.

She took her suitcase upstairs. It was stuffed to the gills and heavy. She had brought all of her dirty clothes thinking she could get her laundry done while she was home.

She didn't turn on any lights or music or the TV as she moved through the house. The quiet suited her mood better in this moment.

In the upstairs hallway, halfway to the master bedroom, she stopped cold. What if, despite being warned of her plans to return to see the boys for the weekend, Ryan had forgotten? What if he and his mistress actually were in bed together and hadn't heard her come in?

Her stomach clenched. She preferred the silent empty house to that scenario.

Bronwyn ducked into Nathanial's room and sat on the dinosaur comforter on his bed, pulling his stuffed Tyrannosaurus Rex into her lap. Something to hold onto. His lizard, Barney, sat under the heat lamp in his terrarium. At least there was some form of life in this room.

Noise filtered up from downstairs. Her children's voices. Ryan's voice.

She knew their sounds so well it almost came as a surprise. Going away to the beach house had been a convenient escape. She had taken on her new identity as a successful romance writer easily, like pulling a long elegant cape over the sad and pathetic Nicole, the stay-at-home mom whose husband was a cheater. Now that she was home, the Bronwyn cape was slipping off, but the old Nicole was no longer underneath.

As if she had two identities that were only specters. Neither of them real.

The voices grew louder. Small footsteps running up the steps. Her heart raced in her chest and involuntary tears welled up in her eyes, making her vision blur.

"Mommy, are you home?" Nathanial's sweet voice called out from the hallway.

"I–I'm in here," she called back, her voice cracked and broken. Not the clear strong voice of Bronwyn...but the weaker troubled voice of Nicole.

Nathanial, excited and breathless, spied her through the open door to his room. He ran to her and climbed into her lap, displacing the stuffed dinosaur.

She wrapped her arms around her youngest son, breathing him in. He smelled like sunshine and grape juice. Sticky and warm and light in her lap. A memory of bringing him home as a baby to this very room flashed through her mind, bringing more tears.

Her oldest, Jeremiah, stood in the doorway. At eight he was already too cool to run to her, she knew. He leaned on the door-frame awkwardly and shifted on his feet like his father did when he wasn't sure what to do.

"Hi honey," she patted the spot on the bed next to her.

Jeremiah shuffled over and sat. She put her arm around his shoulder and pulled him in. He let her. Neither she nor Ryan had told him any specifics about the troubles in their marriage, but he was old enough to notice something wasn't right. That thought broke her heart.

Bronwyn mustered her strength. She didn't want to ruin her time over the weekend being morose. "My boys! You've gotten taller while I was away."

"We've been playing baseball with Grandpa," Nathanial explained.

"Oh, well, that's probably what did it. Baseball is good exercise."

"I ate all my breakfast burrito, too," Nathanial said. "Jeremiah didn't."

Jeremiah scoffed at his little brother. "You had a kiddie breakfast. Anyone could eat all of that."

"You went out to eat for breakfast?" No wonder the kitchen was spotless.

"Dad said we were gonna try all the new restaurants in town while you were gone," Jeremiah said.

"That sounds fun," she said.

"Some of them aren't very good, are they Dad?" Jeremiah asked Ryan who had appeared in the bedroom doorway.

Her heart wrenched in her chest, but she managed an almost serene expression as she looked up at her cheating spouse.

"Hi," he said.

He was dressed for the weekend. Khaki pants, yellow polo shirt. He looked older. She wondered if she looked older, too.

"Hi," she said, a little too cheerfully.

He shifted on his feet. Their family, alone together in their house, had never felt this way. Like strangers.

"How's the writing retreat going?" he asked.

"Great! Really, really well." That was a lie. Or, at least, half of a lie.

The retreat was going just fine. She loved Sol Mate and her room overlooking the ocean. She was feeling more and more comfortable with the other Aphrodites. They had enjoyed some really fun times together this past week.

Her writing, on the other hand, was non-existent.

During their daily writing sprints she could barely sit still let alone type. Even when she did type, because she knew the others would notice if she did nothing, only nonsense came out. There was no story. She couldn't hold a story in her head.

"That's good. I'm glad," Ryan said.

Anger rose hot into her throat. She didn't want his opinion on her writing retreat. If he wanted to be concerned about what was happening in her life maybe he should stop sleeping with another woman. That would be a good place to start.

She bit her tongue and didn't respond. After another drawn out pause where she felt Jeremiah begin to squirm under her arm, Ryan spoke again.

"I thought I would take off for a while, run some errands. Give you some time here with the boys."

The anger she had felt just moments before disappeared and was immediately replaced with despair. He was going to see *her*, the girlfriend. She was certain.

"Mommy, will you make beefy macaroni for dinner?" Nathanial asked.

She looked down at him, distracted, and said, "Sure, honey." When she lifted her gaze from her son's, Ryan was gone.

Ryan was true to his word and stayed away from the house all day while Bronwyn caught up with her children. They went to the neighborhood swimming pool, played giant Jenga and giant tic-tac-toe in the back yard, read books and made beefy macaroni for dinner. The boys had chosen a movie to watch together when Ryan came home and were busy building nests of blankets on the sectional sofa when he called.

"I'm going to be late," he said.

She was angry again. Incensed. "You've been gone all day." She almost asked him what exactly he had been doing, but stopped.

"I know...I think it'll be better if I'm not there. We don't want to fight in front of the kids, do we?"

"No, of course not..." her seething turned to nausea in an instant. Is that what they did when he was home – fight?

"Don't be mad," he said.

That sounded very much like a command. Her hackles went up.

"I came home to see my boys...and do laundry...not to see you." Bronwyn was immediately irritated at herself for mentioning the laundry. It sounded like something a dull old housewife would do over the weekend.

Silence on the other end of the phone. Silence in the bedroom later after she put the boys to bed. Silence echoing through her heart keeping her awake.

At nearly eleven o'clock her cheating husband had still not returned.

He said he would be late, not that he wouldn't come home at all. She wanted to text him, call him, demand that he show her some respect and leave the woman who wasn't his wife and come home, come to bed.

No, that would be too much like begging.

Better that he should come home so she could go back to the beach house. He was the one who wanted a divorce, why should she be the one that tossed and turned all night worrying about where he was and what he was doing. It should be him that wondered what she was doing with her friends...what she might be doing with some other man.

Her thoughts shot instantly to Bill. His gruff exterior, his weathered good looks, the way he had finally given in and took off his shirt for her to dry when she insisted he was going to catch cold.

"Thanks, you didn't have to," he had said, taking his dry T-shirt from her without a smile on his lips, but a small one in his eyes.

"The least we could do for you stopping by to take care of us...take care of the window," she had answered, unable to tear her eyes away as he slipped his shirt back on.

Ryan wasn't athletic. He wasn't chivalrous. His shirts didn't smell as good as Bill's T-shirt had smelled when she got it out of the dryer for him. How was it possible she had been married for so long to someone who didn't smell good?

Bronwyn sighed. "I'm never going to get to sleep," she mumbled, sitting up in bed and turning on her reading lamp.

Ignoring Ryan's side of the bed – the empty side – she pulled out the bottom drawer of her night stand. It was stuffed with books. She rummaged through them, looking for something that would entertain her enough to keep her mind off of her miserable life and also let her get some sleep.

At the bottom of the stack was a an old paperback she had bought at an estate sale the previous summer. A romantic adventure novel that looked like it had been printed in the 1970's. A muscled man and busty woman both in elaborate medieval costumes with the title, "Ladies of Paradise - Knights of Fortune".

"Must be a bodice ripper," she said grimly. Maybe a bodice-ripper was exactly what she needed.

Eighteen

Phoebe

Tanner pored over the drawing Phoebe had handed him moments before, his handsome brow pensive as he tried to take it all in.

"So this is where the picnic will be set up?" He pointed to the spot on the rough map where Phoebe had drawn a big heart.

"Yes, I guess I should have put an 'X' there to make it more obvious."

He grinned, glancing up at her from the page, putting her own heart into palpitations. "I like the heart. It's symbolic."

"Right," Phoebe answered, trying to remember that she was not sitting at a picnic table near the beach with Tanner to plan their perfect date, but to help him set up the perfect date to win his girlfriend back.

Even though she knew this was the plan and had always been the plan, it was still difficult to squelch her feelings. Tanner wasn't just handsome. He was kind and funny and willing to go out of his comfort zone to please the difficult to please Layla. Phoebe couldn't help but fall a little bit in love with him.

"So, I set up the picnic before I pick her up and take her to the stable to get the horses?" Tanner pointed to the small square labeled STABLE on the map.

"Yes, though I would suggest you have someone set up the picnic for you and kind of stand guard over it until you arrive. You wouldn't want to go to all this trouble and have the picnic stolen or ruined by seagulls."

"Good point." He tapped his finger on the map, thinking. "I have a few people I could trust with that job. I'll have to check around and see what everyone's work schedules are."

"I could do it," Phoebe blurted out, immediately sorry to volunteer, yet mysteriously unable to keep herself from being Tanner's right hand in the saving of his love life.

"Oh, no, I couldn't ask you–"

"I don't mind, really," she lied. "I'm not working so that won't be a problem. Besides, you won't have to explain anything to me!"

Tanner tilted his head and peered at her. "You're such a sweetie. I don't want to impose, though. You've already done so much." He swept his hand over the map, the stable brochure with their hours and prices for renting horses, the picnic food suggestions, the list of ingredients for those suggestions, and the wine list she had created giving him options for his date.

Phoebe looked miserably at all of the paperwork, evidence that she didn't have much of a life, certainly not a love life, and gave him a weak smile. "I'm kind of invested in the success of this date. Anyway, I can use it as research for my book." That wasn't a complete lie.

"Oh, that's a good idea." He continued watching her thoughtfully. "I suppose a lot of what you do is research for your book?"

She nodded and took a sip of the iced latte she had brought to their meeting.

Tanner straightened from where he had been hunched over the picnic preparation paperwork and stretched. Tight muscles twisted in his forearms, sunshine glinted off of his blonde hair. His arms reached higher into the air making his shirt lift ever so slightly up his muscled abdomen.

Phoebe wished she could look away.

He put his elbows on the picnic table and leaned toward her. "If you help me set up this picnic I will owe you a big one. Anything you want, you name it."

She laughed, pretty sure he wouldn't be interested in doing what she truly wanted to do, but appreciating his offer just the same.

"Deal," she said, sealing her fate for another day spent basking in the glow of the man, even if it was all to help him get back together with Layla.

He was still watching her and Phoebe melted a little under his steady gaze. A few more moments and he didn't look away, causing her self consciousness to swell. She blushed. "What?"

"I was just thinking."

"What about?"

"Whoever you end up with will be a lucky guy. You'll have a handle on all of this," again he swept his hand over the picnic paperwork. "And you won't be afraid to get in and do some of it yourself. A lot of us men aren't too good at that part, you know."

She did know. Phoebe had lamented the inability of men to think romantically for most of her adult life. She didn't hold much hope that any future partner of hers would share her obsession with romance.

The most recent man in her life had seemed to know a lot about the art of love, but had turned out to be nothing more than a conman. Her stomach twisted at the thought of Giovanni. Determined to keep her mood positive, she pushed the thought out of her mind.

Tanner's deep brown eyes were still smiling at her, making it difficult to concentrate.

"Let's make some decisions then," she said. "We need to get down to business if we want to pull this off any time soon."

Tanner chose well from the picnic meal suggestions. Shrimp, mango salad, vegetables crudite and a fine bottle of white wine, a Muscadet from the Loire Valley region in France.

"Just one bottle?" Phoebe asked.

He grinned. "Well, maybe two. If everything goes well it would be nice to have and if everything doesn't go well...I might need an extra bottle for myself."

"That's no way to think. You have to be positive and move forward with confidence," she said brightly.

"All right, all right, Coach," he laughed.

Phoebe's enthusiasm dimmed. Coach. That wasn't the word she wanted him to associate with her. She looked down and away from Tanner, the fun of their interaction fading.

No matter how much she would like to think all of these plans could somehow truly involve her instead of girls like Layla, she couldn't deny her role was one of a Coach. She was destined to be on the sidelines looking on as the real players played the game.

She thought about that analogy later as she tapped away at her laptop during the Mighty Aphrodite writing sprint of the day. Before she knew what her fingers were doing, Phoebe had written several paragraphs about a female coach of an all male soccer team who was in love with one of her players.

Phoebe scowled and hit the delete button. None of this had anything to do with her Duke and Lady Everton story. She needed to get her head in the game.

She had hoped writing everything down for Tanner and meeting with him to hand off romantic date ideas would clear all of the extra thoughts that kept invading her writing space out of her head. Thoughts about Tanner. But all it seemed to have done was create new modern day romance scenarios, which pushed out the regency stories she needed to write for her novel.

"Ugh," she muttered, making sure to delete each and every syllable of the offending storyline. "Back to the Duke."

In her mind's eye she could see Lady Everton pacing in one of the elegant rooms of her worn down manor, wringing her hands about what could be done to save her family's legacy. There was a knock on the door and the housekeeper showed in an unexpected visitor. Not the Duke. Somebody new. Perhaps a rogue or a vagabond. A tall blonde messenger boy who had beautiful dark brown dancing eyes and a lean muscled body. A modern thinking military man in a dashing red coat.

Phoebe's breath caught in her throat. That was it.

A handsome Colonel who didn't care about the hierarchy of Lady Everton's life.

The conversation between Lady Everton and the Colonel flowed through her fingers onto the keyboard. Funny. Flirty. Saucy. Completely inappropriate.

A giggle escaped her lips. Violet and Bronwyn both stopped typing and looked at her in surprise.

"Going well, is it?" Bronwyn asked, a smile curling on her lips.

"Very well," Phoebe answered, though she felt like she wasn't being completely honest.

The story was flowing. The characters of Lady Everton and the tall blonde Colonel were talking and moving around the scene almost faster than she could get down onto the page, but it wasn't a scene from the novel she intended to write. The words came so quickly that she wasn't even sure if it was good writing. All she knew was that the words were flowing. For that she was grateful.

After the writing sprints were over, they all came together to cook a nice dinner on the grill. Chicken that had been marinating in the fridge and some zucchini and cherry tomatoes on skewers, brushed with olive oil and sprinkled with kosher salt and coarse ground pepper.

"You were having fun writing Lady Everton today," Bronwyn said, popping open a bottle of Muscadet.

Phoebe noticed the wine was the same Tanner had chosen and

smiled to herself. She had managed to keep her little coaching session with him off the radar of the other Aphrodites. Not that she was ashamed, exactly. She simply felt like they may not understand and would read more into her and Tanner's relationship, which was not a relationship at all.

"Yes, it was a fun scene," she answered, deciding to leave out the part of the rebellious Colonel being introduced because the Duke seemed to have gone AWOL from her imagination. "The characters are really coming into their own."

"I'm jealous," Violet said, accepting the glass of wine Bronwyn offered her. "I've been really struggling with my story. It's not coming very easily. Sometimes I have to write about something completely different just to get my brain into writing mode."

"Do you?" Phoebe took heart in Violet's confession. She wasn't the only one having problems focusing on her novel.

"Yes, today I kept thinking more about fishing nets in sea turtle habitats than my hero and heroine in my romance. So I had to write about that instead."

"You wrote about sea turtles?" Bronwyn asked with a laugh.

"Don't tease," Phoebe said. "Whatever it takes to get the writing juices going, right?"

"I feel like I need some of this to get the writing juices going during sprints sometimes." Bronwyn took a big swig of her wine.

Phoebe had noticed Bronwyn's slow pace during their sprints and asked, "Is there anything we can do to help? This is our writing retreat after all. We're here to support each other on our journey to becoming authors."

Bronwyn was mid-swig of another gulp of wine and shook her head 'no' as she swallowed. "I've been getting quite a bit done in my room late at night. Not necessarily during the sprints."

"That's a good idea," Violet answered thoughtfully. "I might try working in some time in the evening when I'm alone as well."

"Me too," Phoebe agreed. Even as they stood around drinking wine and grilling dinner, new ideas involving the dashing Colonel bombarded her thoughts. She would have to write them down after dinner or risk losing them forever.

Not that she would really write a whole book about the Colonel. She had a better plan. She would use her obsessive thoughts about the Colonel, who looked exactly like Tanner in her mind's eye, to get herself into the habit of writing more fluidly. Then she would turn her focus back to the Duke just as she had originally planned.

"We do whatever we have to do for our art," Phoebe said.

The other two Aphrodites readily agreed.

Nineteen

Violet

"These are great, Violet, really great," Ben said, looking up from his laptop.

Violet's cheeks flushed and she wished she could hide from his admiring smile. There was nowhere to go in the small Marine Life Rescue headquarters, however, so she had to sit in full view of the man and allow him to watch her cheeks turn bright red.

"I don't know what to say," she finally admitted.

"You could just say thank you," Ben said with a smile. "But I think I should be the one saying thank you. These posts are really excellent. They're interesting and informative. The way you lay it all out it's like reading a story instead of a blog post."

"You think?"

Ben nodded emphatically and sat forward. "I think they're really going to pull people in."

Violet couldn't help but be pleased. She had been focusing all of her writing time on creating blog posts for the big fundraiser and it was nice to know her work was appreciated. Phoebe and Bronwyn didn't quite understand why she was getting so distracted writing for ecological awareness, but then they hadn't met Ben.

Over the past weeks Violet had spent several afternoons at the conservatory with Ben. He was funny, encouraging, and truly motivated to do what he could to change the fate of the marine animals he loved. Most of her energy while volunteering in person had gone into organizing the place and cleaning it up. Ben had responded in the most adorable way.

As the shelves, counter, and table tops had been rearranged and set up more neatly, his daily attire had progressively gotten nicer and nicer. Gone were the flip-flops he donned when she first met him, replaced with beach sandals. She also noticed him wearing newer, crisper, cargo shorts and T-shirts as time went on. He still had a laid back hippy vibe, but he and his nonprofit were both a little less shabby since she had joined the team.

Today he wore a light blue short-sleeved honest to goodness button up shirt, which was almost formal wear in Turtle Cove.

"In fact," Ben tapped the table top with one long finger, emphasizing his words. "I think we should send some of these to the newspaper instead of posting them online."

Violet was sincerely surprised at this suggestion. "Really?"

Ben's voice rose with building excitement at his idea. So much so that Bear woke from his nap underneath the table.

"Absolutely! Maybe three of them? Definitely the one on the fundraiser. We could submit them as separate articles. The first two to get people informed about some of the threats our marine life face and the fundraiser article as an announcement to get people interested in coming. It would be nice to get more locals involved."

Bear stretched and pushed his soft furry side against Violet's leg, begging for a good pet. She obliged, still processing what Ben was suggesting.

"I've never thought about publishing anything in a newspaper," she said.

"Don't you think it would be good to get this information in front of everyone? Not everybody reads blogs or even knows that we have a blog, but a lot of people still read our newspaper."

"I do think it's a good idea for exposure...I'm just not sure it's written well enough for a newspaper."

Ben screwed his face into a funny scowl and waved away her insecurity with his hand. "I'm betting this is some of the best writing the Cove Gazette has ever seen."

Violet blushed again, certain he was wrong but flattered nonetheless. "Maybe I should look up the proper format for journalism and make some changes."

"Or, maybe you just let me send three of the posts down to my friend, Nanette, who works at the paper and see what she says. I don't want you doing any more work if you don't have to." He scanned the room with a humble expression. "You've already done so much for the place."

Violet's heart sank at the mention of Nanette. It sounded like the name of a young, pretty woman. Someone Ben knew well enough to call in a favor from. Maybe someone he would ask to the fundraiser as his date. A position she had dared to think she might have been in for the upcoming event.

Bear nuzzled his black muzzle into her hand and she stroked his head to soothe her disappointment.

"What is it?" Ben asked, tuning into her mood with remarkable precision.

Violet managed an upbeat smile. "Nothing, really." Ben continued to watch her, waiting for more of an explanation. She couldn't very well tell him that she was jealous of his friend Nanette, so she opted for the next point of unease on her mind. "I'm nervous to send my writing out to professionals. To send it out at all, actually. It's nerve wracking."

Ben considered her problem for a moment then asked, "But you were okay letting me read your work?"

Violet nodded.

"These are all going to go up online for everyone to see, and you're okay with that?"

"I am. I know it's contradictory, but posting something online is basically anonymous. And it's not asking for acceptance. You just post it and if someone comes by to read it then no big deal," she tried to make it make sense.

"But sending it to a newspaper...?"

"Well, you're asking it to be approved by someone. Someone with authority." Violet didn't feel like she was explaining it well.

"Kind of like getting a grade?" Ben asked with a grin.

Violet smiled. They had shared a lot about themselves over the past severals week and he knew she was a school teacher.

"Yes, it is a lot like the nervousness of wanting a good grade," she admitted.

Ben closed his laptop and leaned back in his chair. "We don't have to submit anything to the newspaper if you don't want to, but I think your writing is at least as good as anything else I've ever read in the Gazette. Especially the post on sea otters and everything you have here on sea turtles." He stopped himself from going on and on. "But it's up to you. No pressure."

Tension she didn't realize had balled up in her stomach suddenly released and she relaxed. Leaning back in her chair, mimicking Ben unconsciously, she studied him in his button up shirt, the tidied up Marine Life Rescue headquarters surrounding him. She had been helping him, yes, but he had also been putting in more than his fair share of work on the place over the past few weeks. Not to mention all of the work he had put in for years and years before she even knew this nonprofit existed.

Who was she to deny him an attempt to get more interest in the fundraiser if it would help the end goal, protecting and enriching the marine life of the area and beyond?

Ben tapped his fingertips lightly on his closed laptop, a kind smile in his big green eyes.

She sighed.

"What's that?" he asked, raising his eyebrows in delight.

"Fine."

"Fine?"

"You can send some of the posts to the newspaper if you think it will help."

"I can?" He feigned surprise.

Violet laughed. "For the turtles."

"For the turtles!" Ben called out, jumping to his feet and raising fisted hands into the air as if he had just scored a touch down on a football field.

Violet laughed again, her heart light even though anxiety pinched at her stomach. Bear barked and hopped around Ben's feet, joining the celebration.

"Just don't be surprised if the newspaper doesn't want to print it," she warned.

Ben reached out his hand and pulled her up from her chair, twirling her in an impromptu dance move. "That's not going to happen. Nanette knows good writing when she sees it."

Again with the Nanette person. Another twinge of jealousy.

Ben's hand dwarfed hers as he twirled her once more, slower this time. She let him because she enjoyed the feeling that they were dancing together even if there was no music. When the second twirl ended they were standing quite close, Violet's eyes on the same level as his shoulders.

She looked up at him. He looked down at her. Bear sat down with a shake of his head and looked at both of them curiously.

The air between seemed hot and Violet suddenly couldn't take a breath. Captured by his gaze she couldn't think of anything to say or how to move away from him without coming across prudish.

Not that she wanted to move away.

"Thank you–" his voice cracked and he stepped back, dropping her hand gently while he cleared his throat. "Thank you for this, Violet. It means a lot to–to the conservatory."

Warmth filled her heart. Seeing Ben so excited was worth a little anxiety about getting rejected from the newspaper.

"I'm happy to help where I can," she said. And she meant it.

Later that afternoon when the Aphrodites were settling into their writing sprints she explained some of what was happening to them.

"Is the fundraiser a formal affair?" Bronwyn wanted to know.

"It's kind of a dress up if you want, but not technically formal. It's on the beach," Violet explained.

"It would be nice to be published in the newspaper," Phoebe said.

"I don't know if they will publish it. I didn't really think it would be submitted to a journalist for review." Violet decided not to tell the others about Nanette. She wasn't sure if she could talk about it without sounding like she had a crush on Ben.

Bronwyn snorted. "Small town journalists. They'll be blown away by your writing. Good for you."

"Well, they're just articles, not fiction," Violet said.

"Hey, being published is being published. It's an interesting development," Phoebe said. "And we get to go to a fun party on the beach to raise money for sea turtles. Sounds like a win-win."

Violet smiled in agreement and they settled into their respective sitting areas with their laptops to write. Staring at the document she had open on her laptop Violet couldn't focus. Her mind was still considering all of the possibilities of having her name in print in the newspaper and her heart was still twirling slowly round and round with Ben.

Twenty

Bronwyn

It was the little things that ruined a relationship. All the small moments filled with hurt or anger...all of the disappointments. Every moment ignored or allowed to dissipate into the ether. Never confronting, never resolving, never building anything. Just drifting away from each other.

"Slowly drifting..." Bronwyn said, staring at the blank page on her laptop screen. Thoughts of those lost moments in her marriage kept crawling across her mind, distracting her from the task at hand.

She lifted the wine bottle that rested on the small table in the corner of her bedroom. It was heavy. She poured. The deep red wine sloshed into her glass, spilling drops onto the shining wood surface.

"Whoops! Can't have that," she said to the empty room, sloppily sopping up the droplets with the sleeve of her shirt. It was black. It wouldn't stain.

She was in a dark mood.

Alone in her beach house bedroom instead of at home with her husband and children. Guilt pinched her heart. She couldn't bear the thought of her boys alone with Ryan.

"They're not alone," she reminded herself, taking another drink of the wine, closing her eyes as its heat moved down her throat and into her stomach.

Jeremiah and Nathan were fine. They were spending their days at camp and staying with her parents and her sister more than they were with Ryan anyway. He was at work most of the time. Or worse.

A jolt of hot envy shot through her heart. What if Ryan was bringing his slutty little mistress around the house when the boys were there? Were they playing happy family while she was at her writing retreat?

She shut her eyes tight against that image. No. That wasn't happening. Ryan wouldn't dare.

"He dared to sleep with her in the first place," Bronwyn whispered.

Her voice caught in her throat and a knot of heat swelled at the back of her throat. She wasn't sure if she was going to cry or throw up.

"Neither," she said between clenched teeth.

She took another deep swallow of wine and forced the knot in her throat back down into her belly. Into her soul.

"This is the pits."

She stood and went to the open window. From her second story vantage point she could see moonlight reflecting off the ocean. The sound of waves came to her on the cool breeze that moved off the water and through the night.

She was overcome by a sudden urge to run into the night, into the dark water where the moonlight glistened and none of these problems existed. To disappear there.

Fear bristled up her spine.

Can't have that either. She turned briskly back to face the comfortable bedroom.

It was late. Phoebe and Violet were already asleep. There was nobody to talk to. Maybe she should call her sister.

She sighed. A conversation with her sister would only expand into a conversation about Ryan and the boys and how her sister thought she should be home working through her marital problems.

Her sister thought that. Her parents agreed. Even Ryan had made it clear he would rather her not be out of town, probably because he wanted to hurry up on divorce proceedings.

But Bronwyn needed to be here. She knew it deep down in her bones.

Here was the only place in the world that didn't make her want to scream out loud.

Here was where she could be a writer.

Not a wife. Not a mother. Not a sister or a daughter or a pathetic divorced suburban woman. A writer.

But the words didn't come. Weren't coming. No words. No story. All she had was a blank laptop screen and a full glass of wine.

Bronwyn went back to the table and sat down. She took another swig of wine.

"Almost full," she smirked. She put the glass down clumsily and leaned her elbows on the table. Pressing her palms against her forehead she muttered, "God, that's not even funny."

Nothing good was coming out of her mind. No wit. No play on words. Nothing presentable to the world.

She wasn't presentable.

Bronwyn sniffed. Drinking too much wine made her nose run. Another beautiful and sexy trait she had developed over the years. When she was young and naturally fit she could drink all night long and not even suffer with a mild hangover the next morning. Nowadays she started falling apart before her second glass of wine was finished.

She snatched some tissue out of the tissue box on the table and blew her nose angrily. Her eyes paused on the copy of Ladies of Paradise - Knights of Fortune she had brought from home and read. Twice.

It was a good book. Well written, dramatic, fraught with peril and sex. Lots of sex.

Bronwyn wouldn't mind writing a book like Ladies of Paradise - Knights of Fortune. She had actually been using it as a writing tool, transcribing it onto her laptop at night in her room when she couldn't come up with her own words. Transcribing another writer's work was supposed to give the transcriber automatic insight into their style and use of pacing.

Of course, she had fibbed a little to the other Aphrodites about how much actual writing she was getting done while alone in her room. Most of it had been transcribing. Okay, all of it.

Tonight, however, she had promised herself she would work on her own story. No matter what.

Bronwyn tossed her tissue into the wastebasket and ran her hands over her face. Time to focus.

She pulled her shoulders back straight and held her hands poised over the keyboard, squinting her eyes as she tried to think of an interesting way a man and a woman could meet then fall in love. She had done enough procrastinating and transcribing. It was time she got down to business.

She stared at the screen. Fingers held perfectly still.

Anytime.

Bronwyn's eyes slid to Ladies of Pleasure - Knights of Fortune.

"No." She shook it off and focused back on her laptop.

But the book was too much of a distraction. She couldn't stop glancing at it. Bronwyn grabbed it and tossed it behind her onto her bed.

"Good, okay, got it."

She posed her fingers over the keyboard again. Her eyes flicked to her wine. She sighed, dropping her hands and letting her arms fall to her side.

There was no forcing it. She wasn't in a flow. She didn't have any ideas.

She stood again and went to her bed, taking her wine. Sipping, slowly this time, she considered the man and woman on the cover of the paperback. In love. In lust was more like it, but she supposed love was part of that.

Reaching down, she ran her fingertips along the spine of the book, admiring the font. The title and author's name, Lacy Spencer, in shining gothic raised font. She wanted her name in print like that some day. Silvery white, forever stamped on the thick cover paper, on the hearts and minds of her readers.

Screw it.

Grabbing the book she plopped back down at the table. She would continue transcribing for practice. Let the words of Lacy Spencer be her guide and inspiration.

There was no reason to feel guilty. She would get her inspiration back. This was a rough patch and if the best she could do was transcribe the words of another author then that was what she would do.

It wasn't like she was going to publish it or anything.

With that decided, Bronwyn took another sip of wine and dove into the trials and tribulations of the Ladies of Pleasure and their Knights of Fortune with abandon. Her fingers flew over the keyboard. Her troubles floating away with every word.

Twenty-One

Phoebe

Phoebe glanced around. It was a beautiful morning. Sun shining, a nice breeze coming off the ocean, the sounds of sea birds and distant voices of vacationers on the beach floating through the air.

She sighed.

Sitting outside on the deck so she could enjoy the morning might have been a mistake. She was distracted by the beach and her attention was constantly pulled in the direction of the lifeguard station.

Tanner wasn't there today. It was his day off. He had told her he didn't have class so he was planning on working on his beach picnic date.

Bronwyn was still asleep, having stayed up most of the night writing. Phoebe had been jealous listening to the faint sounds of typing coming from Bronwyn's room in the wee hours of the morning. Bronwyn was really making headway on her novel. Phoebe not so much.

Violet had left the beach house early. Something to do with her volunteering at the Marine Life Rescue place. Despite being happy that Violet had found a cause she was so interested in, Phoebe felt a twinge of jealousy at the idea of her friend possibly getting published in the local newspaper.

Phoebe certainly was spending a lot of time feeling jealous and not enough time writing. She shifted in her lounge chair, adjusted her lap desk and trained her eyes on her laptop screen.

"It doesn't matter what anyone else is doing, Phoebe. Focus," she muttered.

She closed her eyes, trying to imagine Lady Everton strolling through her gardens, dismayed at the weeds that were overtaking her great-grandmother's rose bushes and kneeling down in the dirt to pull them herself. She had let most of the servants go due to lack of funds and was terrified that her family's estate would continue to sink into disarray and she would be left with a lonely life, drifting through the house and grounds like a ghost.

To Phoebe's surprise, the Colonel appeared in her mind's eye. Blonde tousled hair, his fine red coat hanging open as if he had not been expecting to see anyone, especially not a lady.

Phoebe's imagination allowed her to apply details to the image of the Colonel, filling in his face, body, and mannerisms with Tanner's. This was her indulgence. One nobody would ever see, thank goodness, but it allowed her to explore her slight obsession with Tanner. Perhaps it wasn't the most emotionally healthy way of dealing with it, but at least it kept her writing.

She opened her eyes, full of the scene she had just created. The Colonel accidentally coming across Lady Everton kneeling in the roses. He had slept outside the night before because he was so poor and friendless that he didn't have a roof over his head. Lady Everton's breathless surprise. The titillating exchange between them as he buttoned up his coat and knelt down next to her offering to help in the garden. These were the most exhilarating words she had written in days.

Phoebe's fingers flew over the keyboard. She wanted to get every detail of the scene down as quickly as possible before it slipped away.

The buzzing ring of her cell phone interrupted her flow.

"For heaven's sake," she threw her hands up in the air, annoyed. "Why now?"

She strained to see her cell phone, which she had left next to her coffee on the small side table. Her annoyance disappeared, flipping immediately into uncontrolled excitement when she saw who was calling. Tanner.

"Hello?" Phoebe answered quickly, practically losing her balance as she twisted to grab her phone and get it up to her ear without accidentally hitting the wrong button and hanging up on him.

"Hey, Phoebe, sorry to bother you," his beautiful deep voice melted into her ear causing a delicious shiver to zip across her body.

"No bother, no bother at all," she said brightly. Too brightly.

"I'm kind of having an emergency and you're the only one who can help," he explained.

Phoebe sat up, her sun hat tilting off center and flopping sideways on her head as she threw her feet off the chaise lounge onto the deck. Overwhelmed by him choosing to call her with a problem, she was ready to stand up and race to wherever Tanner needed her to be.

"Of course, I'm happy to help. What's the emergency?" she answered, trying not to sound out of breath as she discarded her lap desk and laptop onto the chaise and stood up.

The emergency, it turned out, was picnic date related. Even though Phoebe was mildly disappointed to find out Tanner wasn't using her as his Emergency Contact for an actual emergency, she still hurried over to his apartment to assist.

By the time she arrived she had calmed down. At least outwardly. But when Tanner answered the door in a worn pair of shorts and faded coral T-shirt that only set off his great tan, a fresh surge of butterflies flew through her stomach.

"Hi," he said with a sigh of relief. "Thanks for coming." He opened the door wide and ushered her into a small bright apartment. "I've been trying to follow your directions and, well, nothing is turning out right." There was a hint of desperation in his voice and the acrid smell of burned garlic in the air.

She stepped into his place and was charmed by its casual style. Overlooking the surfboard propped up in the corner of the dining room and the pile of what appeared to be EMT equipment next to it, Tanner obviously had a particular taste in design. Beach Bachelor Boho, if that was a thing.

"I'm sure we can figure it out," she reassured him, attempting to remain a calm and supportive presence and not turn into a giggly schoolgirl just because she was alone in his apartment with him.

"I put the Shrimp Scampi on to cook and thought I'd pick out my clothes, like you suggested," Tanner swept his arm toward the open door of his bedroom where Phoebe, if she leaned forward just a little, could see clothes strewn across his bed. She felt a blush coming on and turned her attention to the source of the smell. The kitchen.

"Is that what I smell? The Hawaiian Garlic Shrimp Scampi?"

"I got a little distracted trying to find the right clothes and forgot about the food." He led her to the galley style kitchen as he spoke. Phoebe gave the doorway to his bedroom a wistful glance as they passed.

Tanner held up a pan so she could inspect it. She wrinkled her nose. The pan was full of blackened blobs of shrimp covered with tar-like garlic sauce. She picked up the wooden spoon in the pan and poked at the burned remains of food.

"Are you supposed to cook the sauce with the shrimp?" she asked, searching her memory for the details of the recipe she had suggested to him.

"That's what I'm saying. I don't think burning it was the only thing that went wrong. It was just the last straw." His eyes flicked to a pot of steaming mush sitting on top of the stove. "I messed up the rice, too."

Tanner's shoulders slumped as he watched her grimace at the smelly remains. Phoebe's heart went out to him.

"Do you have more ingredients to try again? I could help you with it," she offered. She couldn't stop herself. He was worried and overwhelmed and so adorably incapable in the kitchen. Phoebe wasn't sure she had ever seen anyone so appealing as Tanner scanning the mess of pots and pans and running his hand through his hair.

"Would you? Really?"

She nodded. Her decision strengthened by the relief in his voice. "I would," she smiled then turned her attention to the pan full of black, smelly shrimp scampi. "And I think the first thing we should do is clean this up. Then we can start fresh."

Tanner, to nobody's surprise, least of all Phoebe's, was an absolute delight to wash dishes with. As he filled the sink with soapy water he playfully gathered all of the dirty dishes and plopped them in while Phoebe went to work scrubbing them clean.

The proximity of his incredibly fit body was impossible to ignore. Every time she turned around she was confronted with his muscled chest or his long sinewy arm or, if he was facing away from her, his perfectly formed back.

Luckily, after a while, she grew more accustomed to being close to him. So much so that when they did accidentally bump into each other she didn't become a stammering ninny. In fact, Phoebe realized that Tanner's cramped kitchen was the perfect setup for a romantic moment. Too bad she was only there so he could romance somebody else.

"How about some music?" he asked, practically bouncing over to a stereo system with large square speakers that sat on top of his refrigerator.

"That's kind of an old fashioned setup," she noticed.

"Yeah, I know," he said with a shrug. "I've got a whole collection of cassette tapes. My Dad was into it and I kinda caught the bug from him."

"Cassette tapes?" Phoebe turned to watch as he selected a tape out of a kitchen drawer and popped it in. "Where do you find them?"

"My Dad, for one. He gave me a lot when my Mom made him clean out their garage. And now he gives them to me every now and then. I think he finds them at garage sales." He grinned at her, his finger pressing the heavy PLAY button until it clicked into position. "Do you know this song?"

A few moments went by as the tape began turning in the machine and then the intro played, very familiar guitar strum with rhythmic drums. Still, Phoebe wasn't exactly sure who the band was until the singing began.

"Oh, it's CCR!"

Pleased she recognized the song he laughed, "Yes, ma'am, Creedence Clearwater Revival. Do you like them?"

"I love them. I haven't heard them in forever."

Soon the familiar chorus of Have You Ever Seen the Rain filled the kitchen and they both sang along. Tanner moved with the music as he wiped off the top of the stove, dancing in small, controlled steps. Absolutely sexy.

A sudden fantasy popped into her mind's eye. Tanner dancing up behind her as she washed dishes, wrapping his arms around her waist and swaying with her to the music. The idea was entirely too intense for her to concentrate on cooking.

Pushing that impossible scenario aside, she swayed to the music on her own, determined to enjoy what was really happening in Tanner's kitchen rather than losing the moment in her imagination.

They sang along to Fortunate Son, Bad Moon Risin' and Up Around the Bend as they cleaned and prepared the ingredients for a fresh batch of Hawaiian Garlic Shrimp Scampi. Moving to the music with Tanner and going through the familiar act of cooking lifted Phoebe into a buzz, almost like she had been drinking.

Normally keeping such close company with someone like him would send her into fits of nervous behavior. But with Tanner it felt almost like she was floating outside of her body, watching what was happening from a different perspective. All of her fears and insecurities drifting away.

Even though she was warm and overwhelmingly happy just being near him, she was also calm, complete...normal. Not like a fantasy at all. Just her and Tanner cooking and singing in his kitchen. As if they had done this many times before.

"Like this?" Tanner lifted the cutting board so she could see how small he had chopped the garlic.

"Yes, that looks good. I think the only big mistake you made was cooking the garlic and butter with the shrimp instead of separately."

He nodded. "Right, and leaving it on the stove to burn while I was looking through my closet." He shook his head in disgust.

"This time will be fine," she reassured him. "And I'm sure you'll figure out what to wear." She looked him in the eye and smiled knowingly. "I think any girl would be thrilled with how much effort you're putting into this date."

Tanner didn't look convinced. "You don't know Layla."

Phoebe's mood sank.

Tanner didn't notice, he was distracted by the song that had begun spilling out of the refrigerator speakers.

"Oh, man, this song," he reached up and turned the volume dial so the sound of Heard it Through the Grapevine filled the space around them and vibrated through Phoebe's chest.

Dancing, Tanner turned to face her and picked up her free hand, the other one still holding a raw shrimp which she had been about to devein. He pulled her to the center of the tiny kitchen and ignored her protests about dropping the shrimp. Instead, he held her eyes with his, which twinkled with fun, and expertly pulled her to and from him, twirling her slowly to the funky rhythm of the song, singing the whole time.

Phoebe wasn't sure if her heart would ever fully recuperate from that moment, for she found a piece of it missing when the moment was over.

But she was sure of one thing. She would write about it.

Twenty-Two

Phoebe

"We did it!" Tanner beamed at Phoebe from across the table on his cozy balcony.

On the table were two plates, each holding Hawaiian Garlic Shrimp Scampi, Mango Salad, and vegetable crudite that they had prepared together, practicing for his picnic date.

Across the table was her heart. Her whole being wrapped up in Tanner's smile. Her future as miserable as the burned shrimp blobs they had thrown away earlier.

Thrilled that the food had turned out well, Tanner had insisted she eat with him.

"I couldn't have done this without you and I won't eat it without you either," he said, guiding Phoebe to a sweet little bistro table he had set up on his balcony.

She had thought about resisting, but what was the point?

Phoebe knew she had already fallen for Tanner. By the end of their cooking spree, most likely during the dancing, she had silently given over her entire heart. There was no reason to deny the obvious, at least to herself.

How much more pathetic would it be to eat his practice date dinner with him than it was to plan and cook it with him? Zero percent more, she had decided, and flopped miserably into the chair he pulled out for her.

"The wine," Tanner said, hopping up from his seat and going back inside to the kitchen.

"No, no wine," Phoebe said, so low he would never be able to hear her. She continued, pretending that she had a spine and would be leaving before sharing this meal, driving the final nail into her lovelorn coffin, "None for me, thanks."

Tanner returned with a bottle of Muscedet. "What was that?"

Phoebe looked away, directing her gaze at the sunset over the ocean. Of course he had a view of the ocean from his balcony. Of course they were dining at sunset. It was perfect. He was perfect. And none of this was meant for her.

"Nothing," she answered quietly.

Tanner poured a generous amount into her wine glass then sat down and filled his own.

"A toast," he said, lifting his glass.

Phoebe raised hers weakly into the air to meet his.

"To good friends," Tanner said.

They clinked glasses and Phoebe drank a slug of the wine.

The old friend toast. Perfect.

"You don't want to save this for Layla?" she asked. Not sarcastically, but with a hint of quiet despair.

"I've got another bottle and I can pick another one up before Saturday," he said happily. His merry eyes took in the food on their plates, delighted at what they had accomplished. He looked back up at her and Phoebe's heart twisted at the shine in his eyes. "Dig in!"

She took a few feeble bites to appease him. Then a few more. Delectable sweet garlic shrimp scampi melted in her mouth. It was really quite delicious and before she knew it she had gobbled up almost everything on her plate. Shoving food into her mouth to fill the hole in her heart.

Phoebe paused, hoping Tanner hadn't noticed how fast her food was disappearing. But he was also intent on eating, making soft grunting noises of satisfaction as he enjoyed the dinner.

She picked up her wine and sat back in her chair, a dieting tip she had learned a long time ago and rarely used. She took a sip of wine and let the flavors roll over her tongue as she admired the sunset.

"Great view," she said.

Tanner swallowed and wiped his mouth on his napkin. "Thank you, it's the reason I picked this place. Not much elbow room inside, but the view is worth it." He picked up his own wine, mirroring Phoebe's move. "I don't spend a lot of time indoors anyway."

Phoebe's eyes moved from him to the surfboard and EMT equipment in the dining room just inside of the balcony door. "Is that your stuff for school?" She nodded at the bright orange and red stack of emergency items, none of which were anything she recognized.

Tanner followed her gaze and nodded. "Yep, everything I need for my class. I don't have enough closet space to store it, besides I need to take it back and forth with me to school so it doesn't make much sense to put it all away."

"Oh, right. Besides you have it ready if there's ever an emergency," she added.

He winked at her, "Bingo."

Her heart flipped inside of her chest.

This was bad. It was really bad. She should have seen it coming, but she had ignored the obvious. How could she be expected to spend any amount of time with this gorgeous, kind, fun man and not fall in love with him? How could she let this happen...again!?

"Do you want more music?" he asked, but was already up and going back inside to pick a new cassette tape before she had time to form an answer.

Phoebe took another drink of wine. It was good. Strong. She needed strong wine at the moment.

She glanced at her plate. She had managed to snarf down almost her entire meal in a matter of minutes. No wonder she was overweight. No wonder she wasn't attractive to someone like Tanner. No wonder she was forever in the friend zone.

Phoebe sighed.

She didn't want to be rude and she wanted even less to leave Tanner's company. His adorable bachelor apartment. His old style cassette music. His beautiful view. But she had to remove herself.

Sooner rather than later.

She couldn't allow her heart to continue stitching itself to Tanner's presence when she knew there was no future in it. What had she been thinking getting involved like this with him? What kind of glutton for punishment was she?

The smooth sound of 70's R&B music floated out of the balcony door and Tanner called out to her, "Ever heard of Al Green?"

She let out a tragic groan and picked up the last remaining shrimp on her plate, throwing it into her mouth whole. She would absolutely be eating her pain away tonight.

The shrimp skimmed over her tongue and hit the back of her throat triggering her gag reflex. But her gag reflex was in direct conflict with her attempt to swallow and somehow, between the two opposite actions, the shrimp lodged itself firmly in place, plugging her windpipe.

In shock, Phoebe sucked in air, or tried to, but no air would move. Her eyes flew open and she opened her mouth trying to breathe, but to no avail. Like a fish gasping for oxygen on land, she gaped in silence, unable to call out for help.

She stood up. Her chair clattered to the floor of the balcony.

Clutching her throat she turned in terror to face the balcony door. Just in time to see Tanner pausing mid-stride on his way back to the balcony. At the sight of her panicked face, his happy smile melted into concern and then, sudden understanding.

Twenty-Three

Violet

Violet stopped by the local bakery, Shore Is Sweet, on her way home from Marine Life Rescue. High on the news that her blog posts were going to be published in the newspaper, she felt like celebrating.

Shore Is Sweet was a little crowded for being late morning, but smelled delicious so she didn't mind waiting. She couldn't wait to break the news to Phoebe and Bronwyn over a cup of coffee and chocolate croissant. Being published in the newspaper wasn't nearly as thrilling as publishing a fiction novel, but it was still something.

"The Gazette loved your articles," Ben had told her at their early morning planning meeting. He had met her at the door, grinning ear-to-ear, Bear jumping excitedly around his feet.

"They did?" An exhilarating rush had gone through her body and she had to sit down to process the information.

"I told you they were good," Ben said, bringing her a cup off coffee from the old coffee machine he kept behind the counter.

"All three of them?" she asked, taking the coffee.

"All three. And they would love to look at more if you have time," Ben informed her, happily folding his long limbs into the chair opposite her at the table. "They gave me this for you." He pulled a folded piece of paper out of his shirt pocket and handed it to Violet.

When she took it she noticed that her fingers were trembling ever so slightly. She placed the paper carefully on the table and unfolded it, revealing a statement of payment with a check stapled to the upper left hand side.

The check was from The Cove Gazette and made out to her, Violet Brown, in the amount of $75.00. The statement verified that they were purchasing three articles from her at $25.00 each. It was all very official.

"I get paid?" The thought had never crossed her mind that she might get paid for her work.

Ben laughed his deep pleasant laugh. "Sure, I mean it's not a huge amount, is it? But people will pay for good writing."

Violet had stared at the check, her stomach trembling. When she looked up at Ben, her eyes bright with the thrill of it all, he held her gaze for a long moment.

The phone had rang, interrupting...something...Violet couldn't be sure what.

At the bakery she stood contentedly at the back of the line, breathing in the delicious smells of doughnuts and other goodies, humming softly. She couldn't wait to show the other Aphrodites the check. It was a small check, she knew that, but it was symbolic of something bigger to her. To be paid for her writing was a dream she had long held and it wouldn't have happened without the Mighty Aphrodite Writing Society.

Her celebration would have to wait. When Violet arrived back at Sol Mate mid-morning, she found the beach house empty. Phoebe's car was gone and the whole place was so dead silent that

Violet determined she and Bronwyn had gone somewhere together.

"I'll have to eat you by myself I guess," she said, addressing the box of chocolate croissants as she placed them on the kitchen counter.

"Eat who?" A voice asked abruptly from the living room.

Violet jumped at the sound then peeked around the corner to see Bronwyn wrapped up in a ball of blankets and sort of crumpled into a pile at the end of the couch. She was bleary eyed and had a bad case of bed head. Violet was pretty certain she was also hung over, which seemed to be par for the course with Bronwyn.

"Do you want a chocolate croissant?" Violet asked perkily.

Bronwyn grunted and began disentangling herself from her blankets. "And coffee," she said in a thick voice.

"Got it," Violet stepped back into the kitchen and started a pot of strong coffee. "Where's Phoebe?" she called over her shoulder.

"Not so loud, please," Bronwyn answered from the kitchen island. Not expecting her to enter the kitchen so fast, Violet startled at seeing her there. "Jeez, you're awful jumpy this morning," Bronwyn said, opening the bakery box and reaching inside for a croissant. "Where have you been?"

"At the conservatory," Violet said, barely able to contain her sunshiny attitude even in the face of Bronwyn's hangover. "And I'm not jumpy, I'm excited!"

Bronwyn still had one of the blankets draped over her shoulders. She chewed on a big bite of her croissant as she surveyed Violet with droopy eyes. An idea struck her and her eyes grew wider. "You haven't...?"

"Haven't what?"

Bronwyn chewed mischievously. "You know..."

"Oh!" Violet swatted away that idea with a swift flick of her hand. "No! What makes you think that?"

Her mouth full, Bronwyn explained, "I don't know, you're all happy and *glowy*."

Violet, fighting a blush, turned to pour them both a cup of coffee. "Glowy's not a word."

"Okay, okay, so if it's not *that* then what's got you all pepped up?"

"I'll show you!" She set the coffee down on the island and pulled the check from the Cove Gazette out of her purse, placing it in front of Bronwyn.

Bronwyn took another bite of croissant and leaned down to get a better look. She lifted her eyes sharply back to Violet. "Is this for your turtle blogs?"

Violet nodded, beaming.

Bronwyn sat down on the nearest kitchen island stool, the blanket slipping off of her shoulders and falling to the floor. Holding her croissant in her mouth she wiped her hands off on her pajama bottoms and picked up the check to admire it.

"I didn't know they were going to pay me," Violet couldn't contain her excitement. "I wanted to show you two. I know it's not like selling a book to a publisher, but it's kind of a Mighty Aphrodite win, isn't it?"

Bronwyn's response was unintelligible through the croissant in her mouth. She handed the check carefully back to Violet and removed the pastry so she could speak.

"Absolutely! This definitely merits chocolate croissants. Maybe even mimosas!"

Violet brushed the suggestion for more liquor aside. She wasn't sure Bronwyn needed any more alcohol today or anytime soon.

"Where's Phoebe?"

"I don't know. She was gone when I got up. Both of you were. I decided to slip into a catatonic state until you returned." Bronwyn tipped her coffee cup at Violet. "But now we have something to celebrate." She watched Violet thoughtfully for a moment. "How about we finish our coffee then go for a swim? Surely Phoebe will be back by then and we can decide what to do."

"Hey, we could get pizza for dinner. I'll buy!" Violet suggested.

They finished their bakery treats and coffee then got ready for the beach. Violet noticed that their regular lifeguard, Tanner, wasn't at the lifeguard station as she and Bronwyn made their way across the sand to stake out a place for their umbrellas amongst the tourists. For a brief moment Violet wondered if his absence had anything to do with Phoebe's absence, but that didn't make any sense. Phoebe had probably left to run some errands and would be back soon.

But she didn't return. Not while they were swimming. Not while they were showering afterward. And not as they waited through the late afternoon growing more and more worried.

"Text her again," Bronwyn said.

"I've texted her twice. She should answer when she sees one of those."

"If she's able to answer."

Violet tried not to let Bronwyn's doom and gloom attitude rub off. "I'm sure she's fine. She's a grown woman. Maybe she had something to do." Again, the lifeguard station passed through Violet's mind. She didn't know why she was associating Phoebe's absence with the absence of the handsome blonde lifeguard, but she hoped whatever was keeping their friend it was something as pleasant as a gorgeous guy.

"Well, I'm starving. We can't go out to eat without her, can we?" Bronwyn looked like she hoped Violet might allow it, which she wouldn't.

"No, let's not do that. How about I order pizza? We can eat in," she suggested.

Bronwyn shrugged, miffed that her grand ideas of going out for the night were derailed by Phoebe's MIA status. "At least we won't die of hunger."

Violet ignored Bronwyn's drama and set about ordering two large pizzas, one with pepperoni and black olives and one vegetarian. It was fun to splurge a little using her newspaper paycheck.

Her small teacher's salary had made her used to being on edge over finances ever since she could remember. Having even a small bonus was a treat.

Plus the money had come from her writing. Her very own thoughts that she had put down on paper and sold. Unreal.

They were done eating the pizza and about to wrap it up to save it for later when Phoebe's car finally pulled into the drive.

"Thank goodness," Violet breathed a sigh of relief. As much as she had been trying to put forth a calm demeanor, she had begun to really worry about Phoebe's whereabouts hours ago. She and Bronwyn looked at each other then hurried to the entryway to grill Phoebe as she entered the front door.

"Where have you be–" Bronwyn's best Mom voice fell away when they caught sight of Tanner helping Phoebe through the door.

Violet was stunned at the sight of him. So was Bronwyn. They stood motionless in the entryway gawking at the handsome lifeguard.

"Good evening, ladies," he said, his hand protectively under Phoebe's elbow.

Violet stared mutely at Tanner. Her earlier thoughts about Phoebe being with him confirmed, she wondered if she had experienced an actual premonition. Then she wondered why they were together. What had they been doing? Had they been on a date?

Violet turned her attention to Phoebe who, to her surprise, looked miserable. Not what Violet would have expected the way Phoebe always lit up whenever Tanner was nearby. She was dying to know what was going on, but Bronwyn was the only one willing to openly ask.

"What happened?" she asked Phoebe, shooting a suspicious look at Tanner.

Tanner started to answer, but Phoebe interrupted before he had a chance to speak.

"I'm fine," she said, pulling her arm out of Tanner's

supportive grip and pushing past Violet and Bronwyn. "Nothing happened."

With Phoebe's exit from the entryway, the mood reached peak awkward levels at the front door. Violet switched a curious gaze between Tanner's handsome face creased with concern and Bronwyn who was watching him with an accusatory glare.

The beep of a car horn in the driveway broke the tension.

"There's my ride," Tanner said, mostly calling out the words to Phoebe, who had already disappeared down the hallway and into the kitchen.

"Okay, thanks Tanner," Phoebe's voice rang out from the kitchen in a light sing-song way, strange and inappropriate for the tension Violet sensed in the entryway.

"No, thank you...again," Tanner said to the empty hallway. Then he smiled at both Violet and Bronwyn, his dimples flashing, "Good night, ladies."

As soon as the door clicked shut behind him, Violet and Bronwyn shared a look, then turned and rushed to the kitchen to find out what in the world was going on.

Twenty-Four

Phoebe

P hoebe wanted to disappear. Just melt into nothing. Lay down on the beautiful tile floor of the beach house kitchen and give up her life as she knew it. She was pathetic. Her life was pathetic. No reason to keep trying.

Even as these thoughts crossed her mind she knew she couldn't lay down on the kitchen floor and give up or do anything else on the floor, not without a tremendous amount of grunting and groaning and pain in her ribs. When Tanner had done the Heimlich maneuver on her and saved her life he had bruised her ribs, at least that's what the emergency room doctor had told them.

But more than her ribs had been bruised.

Her ego. Her femininity. Whatever grace and sense of self worth she had possessed had been bruised as well. She was nothing but a blue and purple squishy pulpy mess. Yuck.

Instead of laying on the floor she pushed aside open pizza boxes so she could flop onto the kitchen island. Leaning her elbows on the island, Phoebe covered her face with her hands. The little romantic fantasy she had allowed herself in Tanner's apartment, the one where he moved in behind her, wrapped his arms around her waist and they swayed to the music, had partially come true anyway.

Except she had been red-faced with bulging eyes and clutching at her neck, because she was unable to breathe. And he had wrapped his arms around her from behind in order to force-fully jam his fists up into her ribcage until the Hawaiian Garlic Shrimp she had tried to swallow whole flew out of her mouth and hit the sliding glass doors to his balcony with a soft thunk.

Phoebe groaned. It was all so awful that it was almost funny. She might be able to laugh if laughing didn't hurt so much.

"What in the heck is going on?" Bronwyn demanded, bursting into the kitchen with Violet on her heels.

"Are you all right?" Violet asked, the same worried look creasing her brow as Bronwyn's.

Phoebe groaned again. "I'm fine." She forced herself to stand and try to appear as normal as possible, but couldn't help wincing as she did.

Bronwyn's eyes narrowed. "What did he do to you?"

The sharp question surprised Phoebe. "Tanner?"

Bronwyn nodded.

"No, Tanner didn't do anything to me. Well, technically I guess he did do something. He saved my life."

Violet let out a gasp and moved to Phoebe's side. "What happened? Why are you in pain?"

There was no getting around explaining the situation to them, so Phoebe tried to be short and sweet. "He gave me the Heimlich maneuver because I was choking."

Surprised understanding registered on their faces. Perhaps they would let her go to bed and she could forget about this terrible day.

Violet glanced down where Phoebe was gingerly holding her side. "Did he break your rib?"

"No, just bruised them." Phoebe tried to make her way around the island to get a drink of water. Her mouth was suddenly very dry.

Bronwyn watched her skeptically as she moved carefully, holding her side gingerly. "Are you sure they're not broken?"

"The ER doctor said they were just bruised," Phoebe answered.

"The ER doctor?" Violet's concern mounted. "You need to sit down." She pulled one of the stools by the island out then reconsidered and put it back. "In the living room. On a comfortable chair. Do you want something to drink?"

Phoebe allowed Violet to lead her to the fat comfy chair in the living room and bring her a drink of water.

"Are you hungry? Violet bought pizza," Bronwyn offered.

"No, thank you. I don't think I'm ever going to eat again."

"So you choked on something?" Violet asked, trying to get the story straight.

Phoebe nodded and took a sip of her water. "Shrimp."

Bronwyn and Violet both sat down on the couch opposite her, completely confused.

"And Tanner the lifeguard happened to be there to save you?" Bronwyn asked.

"I was at his apartment."

Eyebrows raised in surprise, Violet and Bronwyn exchanged a look.

"It was nothing. I was helping him out."

"And how, exactly, were you helping him out?" Bronwyn asked.

Phoebe gave in. She was too tired and deeply mortified by the whole experience to try and pretend that she had it under control. She spilled her guts. Starting from the beginning.

Violet and Bronwyn listened to her story about offering to help Tanner win over Layla, about planning out a romantic picnic date for them, and about ending up at his apartment all day. She left out the part about falling head over heels for him. She didn't want to talk about that at all.

After she finished telling her tale, Violet and Bronwyn sat in silence, digesting the information.

"Why didn't you tell us what was going on before?" Violet asked.

Phoebe shrugged, her lower lip trembled. "I don't know. I felt kind of silly getting involved with him like that. Like..." she searched for the word.

"Like Cyrano de Bergerac," Violet offered.

Phoebe choked out a laugh. "Sort of."

"You've fallen for him, haven't you?" Bronwyn asked bluntly.

Phoebe's mouth dropped open and she stammered her answer, "Wh-wha-? No, no, not at all."

Bronwyn snorted. "Of course you have. Look at your face."

Phoebe touched her cheeks with her hands. Was it that obvious? If it was obvious to them was it obvious to Tanner?

Violet gave Bronwyn a disapproving look then smiled at Phoebe. "It wouldn't be difficult to fall for someone like Tanner. He seems very nice...and he saved your life."

"And he's totally hot!" Bronwyn declared with a laugh that ended in another snort. Ignoring Phoebe's discomfort about the subject, she kept on, "You need some wine. And some pizza. So we can figure all of this out." She stood up and went into the kitchen.

Phoebe turned to Violet, hoping for some gentle direction. "What needs to be figured out?" she asked weakly.

"I'm not sure what she means, but I do think it might be good for you to talk about it. You're upset."

"She's more than upset," Bronwyn said, carrying both pizza boxes with three wine glasses balanced on top in one hand and a wine opener and bottle in the other. "She needs some good old fashioned girl talk to figure out how to snatch that lifeguard right out of his girlfriend's clutches."

Twenty-Five

Bronwyn

"Men," Bronwyn scoffed the word into the wind that whipped around the convertible. The same wind drew her hair out of its loose bun and sucked away the sound of her voice.

She was driving. Fast. On her way home at the break of dawn instead of last night like she had planned. She'd been delayed by Phoebe's disastrous dilemma. Being the oldest and wisest of the Aphrodites, Bronwyn felt compelled to stay and give Phoebe the best advice possible to deal with her predicament.

Advice Phoebe had not liked.

"I'm not going to try to steal Tanner from his girlfriend," Phoebe had said.

"You're not technically stealing him from his girlfriend if he's trying to get *back* with his girlfriend. She's not his girlfriend right now!" Bronwyn had argued. "You're literally helping him win her over again. Just sabotage their little picnic date and be there to pick up the pieces, that's all I'm saying."

Offended at the suggestion, Phoebe said, "That's hardly the kind of person I am or want to be. I wouldn't want a relationship built on deception."

"All's fair in love and war," Bronwyn reminded her.

"Phoebe's right," Violet had agreed. "That sounds like a recipe for disaster."

Violet. Ugh. She was such a mealy mouse of a woman. Typing up a bunch of blog posts trying to save sea turtles instead of working on her own project. Always being so damned nice about everything. Violet was too wishy-washy to give good relationship advice, if anyone asked Bronwyn's opinion. Which they didn't.

"Nope," she said to the wind again. "Everybody just wants a bunch of affirmations, nobody wants the truth." Again, her words were stolen by the wind. She shouted in defiance, "Nobody wants the truth!"

And what was the truth, exactly?

Men suck. That was the truth.

She stepped on the gas. Faster was better. More speed, more wind, more noise to drown out the sound of her reality.

"Men suck!!" she screamed.

The wind took it all, but didn't hide her from a passing truck, whose driver gave her a second look when he saw her screaming. Bronwyn flipped him off and pushed harder on the gas. He was a man. She didn't care what he thought.

Leaving the trucker in the dust made her feel better so she kept her foot on the gas and overtook several more cars and trucks that were also cruising the highway on their way to who knew where.

She was on her way home to see the boys. And Ryan, possibly. He had texted that he thought it would be good to spend some time with the boys together. She had agreed, a kernel of mistrust forming in the pit of her stomach as she sent the text.

Now that she was driving back, within an hour of seeing Ryan and the boys, the mistrust had turned into good old fashioned anger. Or fear. Sometimes these days she didn't know the difference.

Bronwyn glanced down at her speedometer – 98. She let her foot off the gas. That was too fast, even for her. She was a mom after all.

What about Jeremiah and Nathaniel? Her boys. They would be men someday. How was she ever going to keep them from growing into the hateful bunch of males she believed existed in the world. Most of them were cheaters. Liars. Or, in Tanner's case, *users*.

She let her foot up even more. Jeremiah and Nathaniel needed her to guide them into becoming decent human beings. She couldn't guide anybody if she was smeared across the side of the highway, the victim of some horrific car accident.

78 miles per hour, that was better. Safer. The wind wasn't howling in her ears anymore, though it was still strong enough to take her words.

The blast of a horn startled her and she looked just in time to see the truck she had flipped off roar past, the trucker's middle finger jutting up into the air in her direction.

Bronwyn moved to the slow lane and ignored him. Inspiring a road rage incident was not on her list of things to do today.

What was on her list?

Getting home before the boys were up so she could have breakfast with them. Keeping up a brave face with Ryan while they spent time together as a family. Trying to forget that he had been sleeping with another woman.

Once again the anger flared. Men did suck, no matter how hard she tried to overlook it.

When she pulled into her driveway the sun was already up, her hair was a mess, and the boys were watching for her at the front door. They raced out the door to greet her as she parked and got out.

"Mommy!"

"Mom!"

"My darlings!" Bronwyn said, grabbing them both up in one huge hug.

"Daddy says we're going to go the museum today!" Nathaniel said.

"We are?" Bronwyn asked.

That had always been one of her favorite excursions with the boys. Take a picnic lunch to the Museum of Natural History, look at all of the dinosaur bones and stuffed wild animals from around the world that they could handle then sit in the park behind the museum to eat. There was a fountain built for children to run through to cool off in the park and a place to rent buggy cycles that four people could sit in and pedal up and down the paths.

"Is that all right with you?" Ryan asked.

He was leaning in the doorway watching her and the boys. Bronwyn's heart felt choppy when she laid eyes on him. As if it was grinding to a halt.

Same polo shirt she would expect. Same dad shorts. Same old Ryan. But different somehow.

"Can we, Mom?" Jeremiah asked.

"Sure, that sounds fun," Bronwyn answered, trying not to sound too stunned.

"Boy's bring in Mom's suitcases and get your stuff. We can get breakfast on the way?" He posed the question to Bronwyn, asking her permission to make plans.

A little overcome at his attention to detail and the way he was instructing the boys, which was the way she would normally instruct them, she nodded. "Yes, that will work."

Energized by the plans for their day, the boys hurriedly pulled her luggage up the front walkway and inside the house. Bronwyn followed, not sure what to think about the way Ryan was watching her every move.

"You want to freshen up before we get going?" Ryan asked when she reached the front step.

She nodded, "Yes, I would." She hadn't said yes so many times in a row to anything Ryan had suggested in years.

He smiled, genuinely smiled, and stepped back into the entryway, ushering her into her own home. Bronwyn found herself smiling in return, an unexpected shy smile. She brushed past him as she entered, breathing in his familiar scent.

He touched her elbow. "Nicole."

She stopped abruptly.

Ryan ducked his head a little as he spoke. Not a move she was used to seeing on him. "I want you to know that I've gained a new perspective on everything you do around here, everything you do for the boys."

She stared at him.

He smiled and the smile actually reached his eyes. "I just wanted to say that I appreciate it all." He let go of her arm and directed his attention to the commotion upstairs. "Come on guys, let's get a move on. Don't want to waste the morning."

She blinked, dazed. Not sure which was more jarring, when he told her she was appreciated or when he called her 'Nicole'.

Twenty-Six

Phoebe

Phoebe was glad Bronwyn had gone home for the weekend. The onslaught of advice she had dished out after Phoebe returned from the ER had been hard to hear. But none of Bronwyn's complaints about Tanner had changed Phoebe's mind about wanting to help him. Though Phoebe's mind had changed about Bronwyn.

While it was true that Bronwyn had more experience with men than Phoebe, she was married after all–albeit to a cheating husband - her life experience seemed to have left her bitter and suspicious. Neither of which Phoebe wanted to be. Not with Tanner. Not with anybody.

So, despite the fact that it hurt her heart and her ego, she hadn't changed her plans to help Tanner with his picnic date. In fact, she had decided to dress up for the occasion, picking out a fun sundress with wide navy and white stripes along with her big brimmed red hat as her picnic set up outfit.

"You look smart," Tanner had told her when she dropped by his apartment to pick up the food and wine.

"Thank you," Phoebe managed to reply. He was in the middle of getting ready and was still shirtless. Not that Phoebe had never seen him without his shirt, she saw him constantly on the lifeguard stand with no shirt. But this was different. This was in his apartment.

Utilizing massive willpower she managed to leave his place without too much mumbling and fumbling around. She even arrived at the picnic site earlier than they had discussed so she could clean it up a bit before setting up the food. Nothing very romantic about random bits of dried kelp and dead palm fronds sticking out of the sand or, worse, trash that had washed up or blown onto the site.

"There," Phoebe looked around, satisfied at the pristine surroundings. The sand was white and free of debris, the nearby palm trees cast the perfect amount of shade on the area, and the ocean continued to do its job in the near distance, which was to be blue and beautiful.

She checked the time on her cell phone and noticed a text from Tanner.

Leaving to pick her up now. Wish me luck!

The text made her all gushy. He was so sweet. She needed to figure out a way to get over her feelings so perhaps they could be friends after all of this.

And if Phoebe wasn't the woman on the date, she would try to find happiness in setting up the picnic as beautifully as possible, then write about it later. She mused about how this picnic experience would play out between Lady Everton and the Colonel.

She would write about how the Colonel slaved in one of the townspeople's kitchens to get the seafood pie perfect. She would write about how he failed miserably at cooking and a kind matronly woman stepped in to help him. She tried not to linger on the fact that the woman she was choosing to represent her role in the story would be described as matronly.

Then she would write about the picnic itself. How the blue in the picnic blanket matched the blue of the ocean. How the picnic basket held delectable treats, including a dessert of coconut macaroons. Those Phoebe had picked up at Shore Is Sweet on the way there after realizing that she and Tanner had forgotten to plan a dessert.

She would write about the fresh breeze, the brilliant sunshine, the feeling of endless possibilities when someone went out of their way to create a beautiful experience for a woman. Lady Everton would be surprised, then gush a little bit, then bask in the adoration of the young Colonel.

The Colonel would be dashing. His red coat as vibrant as his yearning for Lady Everton. Blonde hair kissed by the rays of the sun, blue ocean backdropping his dimpled smile. He would cut a bold, handsome figure riding on his horse across the sand.

The horse! Phoebe was roused out of her reverie by the sound of a horse whinnying.

She whirled around from where she had been admiring her set up of the picnic to see two horses galloping in her direction. One golden palomino horse with flowing blonde mane and tail carrying a woman wearing a floral dress whose arms flailed about from the horse's fast pace. There was also a larger, all white steed with the Colonel–er, Tanner–astride its impressive muscled back.

How long had it taken her to set up the picnic? She didn't know exactly, but it had taken her too long. Tanner and Layla were almost upon her. She had to get out of there. But if they were close enough for her to see them clearly on the backs of their horses, they would certainly be able to see her running away from the picnic.

Cursing her choice to wear bold striped clothing and bright red hat, Phoebe zeroed in on the only cover nearby. The group of palm trees that shaded the picnic. It might be possible to make it there without being seen.

Ducking low with one hand on her hat to keep it from falling off, she ran through the sand as fast as she could, which was not fast, and made it to a secluded space behind the base of the trees. The ground near the trees was surrounded by mounds of short shrubs, thank goodness. Phoebe sank down into the sand to hide.

As soon as they were seated and distracted by the food, she could crawl through the remaining grove of palm trees and and make her way to the parking lot. Squinting in that direction, she could just see the glint of sunlight reflecting off of her car's windshield through the trees.

Out of habit, her hand went to her sundress pocket to check for her keys.

And found them empty.

Peeking around the tree she spied her keys laying in the sand halfway between the picnic and where she was hiding.

"Oh, no!" Phoebe wanted to curse, but the sound of horse hooves thudded close. She flipped back behind the tree and covered her mouth with her hands, closing her eyes like a child who thought if they couldn't see anything then they were invisible.

"Tanner! Tanner!" Layla's voice was panicked.

More hoof beats, even closer. A high pitched squeal. Tanner's soothing voice, though Phoebe couldn't tell what he was saying. She pressed her back against the base of the palm tree, praying they wouldn't see her.

"Oh my God! I could have died!" Layla came in loud and clear from somewhere very close.

"I've got you," Tanner said.

"I told you," Layla whined.

"You're fine, you did good," he answered.

Phoebe's heart was beating fast. How embarrassing it would be if they discovered her hiding nearby during their date. Though by the sound of Layla's voice the date wasn't going so hot at the moment anyway.

"I know I did good. It's this stupid horse. It just started running!"

"She got a little excited when you were yelling is all."

"I wasn't yelling and they should have given me a better horse," Layla told him.

"Here, let me help you down. We can rest here a while," Tanner suggested.

There was a pause, then, "Ugh. Now my dress smells like horse."

"You smell fine. Come with me. I have something to show you."

Another pause. Phoebe knew Tanner was bringing her around the short rise in sand into the shade of the palm trees. Any moment she would know if they could see her or not.

If they could see her she would have to go through the mortification of explaining why she was there to Layla. If they could not see her she would have to go through the heartbreak of listening to them on their romantic date. The date she had planned and helped execute. The date that was one of her dream dates.

Phoebe didn't know which would be worse.

Twenty-Seven

Phoebe

Five minutes into listening to Tanner and Layla's date, Phoebe knew she was in the worse case scenario. Much worse than if she had been caught trying to leave the scene of the picnic.

Why had she been so embarrassed to be seen?

It wasn't shameful to help Tanner set up a picnic. For all Layla knew she was some woman he had hired from a restaurant. Nothing more than a caterer.

Why had she been overcome with the need to hide?

Phoebe knew why, but she didn't want to think about it. She squeezed her eyes closed and wished she could stop sweating. Stop hearing every little moment between the two of them.

But there was no escaping Tanner and Layla's date and no escaping her feelings. Feelings she was loathe to admit, even to herself.

She had been embarrassed to be caught at the picnic site by

the woman Tanner loved, because she wished she was the woman Tanner loved. It was as simple as that.

The shame pulsing through her body was from her secret feelings, not the situation. A neutral party would look at the situation from the outside and see that it was all in good fun. Nothing to feel weird about at all. Just a friend helping a friend.

But Phoebe wasn't a neutral party. And shame seemed to be baked into her DNA.

She was nothing more than a miserable party of one hiding in the sand behind a palm tree.

Listening to the two lovebirds enjoy their picnic turned her stomach. The way Tanner spoke so sweetly to Layla, helping her get comfortable on the blanket, offering her sparkling water or wine. The sound of him in love with someone else echoed through Phoebe's lonely soul.

She wondered how weird it would be if she showed herself now. Pretty weird, she guessed. There was no way she could stand up without being seen and she had to stand up to brush all of the sand off of her dress so she didn't look like she had been crawling around on the ground.

Besides, what would she say? *Excuse me, hello, I'm just walking by, don't mind me.* Or maybe *Oh my, I didn't know anybody else was here. I'll just be on my way.* Or *Sorry to interrupt, I'm the picnic catering assistant and I seem to have dropped my keys.*

Actually, that last one wasn't too bad. Maybe she could pretend to be a bumbling picnic catering assistant and get out of this mess.

Phoebe rolled onto her stomach so she remained low to the ground and raised her head to take a peek at what was going on. At the last moment, she remembered her bright red hat and pulled it off, poking her bare head up just far enough to see the picnic blanket.

What she witnessed sent her already sickened stomach reeling.

Tanner and Layla sat close together holding wine glasses and gazing into each other's eyes. Tanner reached up and brushed a tendril of Layla's hair away from her face. He let his fingers trace down her cheek and leaned in closer, going for the kiss.

Phoebe sucked in her breath and lowered her head back to the ground muttering under her breath, "No, no, no, no."

"What is that?" Layla asked.

Phoebe clamped her mouth shut and closed her eyes as tight as she could.

"What?" Tanner asked.

"That!"

Phoebe didn't move, envisioning Layla pointing at her navy and white striped form in the palm trees. She prayed Layla was hearing something else other than her whispers and her heart pounding in her chest.

"I don't–" Tanner started to say.

Layla shrieked and there was the sound of shattering glass. "A spider! A spider!" Another shriek of terror.

"Watch out," Tanner's voice was loud so Layla could hear him over all of the commotion she was making. "Don't step on the glass."

"Get it off me!" Layla screamed.

"Okay, okay, hold still."

Phoebe detected a hint of amusement in his voice. Since the couple was distracted with some kind of horrifying spider she took the opportunity to peek at them through the grass.

Layla stood in front of Tanner holding her hair up off of her neck with both hands and grimacing, tears streaming down her cheeks. Tanner was leaning over plucking something off of her bare shoulder.

"Hurry! I can feel it crawling on me!"

"Don't move...and...got it," Tanner said as he calmly held something between his thumb and forefinger. He kept it at an arm's length, as far away from him and Layla as he could, but Phoebe had been right, there was a twitch of a smile on his lips.

Layla turned to see what he had in his hand and immediately

began shrieking. The horses, who were untethered and standing several yards away from the picnic area, moved restlessly away from Layla's piercing voice.

"Shhh," Tanner said.

Layla stopped shrieking and glared at him. "Did you just shush me?"

The horses continued to step nervously side-to-side.

"Layla, please," Tanner moved slowly toward the horses, still holding the spider away from his body. "Keep your voice down. You're spooking the horses."

Layla was not backing down. She wasn't shrieking, but she was still yelling, "You bring me out to this spider infested sand pit then tell me to be quiet? *Shush* me!?"

Phoebe could only see Tanner's back, but something about the way it stiffened told her he was getting annoyed. Though she couldn't be sure, there was nothing in his tone that gave him away.

"I'm just gonna get the horses calmed down and we can eat," he said.

It was then that he did it. Something perfectly natural, but nothing Phoebe could have foreseen. Something so innocent that nobody could blame him for what happened afterward. Phoebe, anyone really, would have probably done the same thing if they were in his shoes. After all, he didn't know anyone was hiding in the shrubs. And he had not way of knowing the consequences of his actions.

In order to free up both hands, Tanner made a move to discard the spider. With a flick of his wrist he tossed the horrifying creature he had saved Layla from high into the air in the opposite direction of the picnic and the horses. Directly at Phoebe's hiding place.

The detested spider, brown and wriggling, flew head over heels as if in slow motion, right at Phoebe's face.

Phoebe's mouth became a surprised 'O'. She scrambled clumsily in the sand, trying to get up off the ground. All thoughts of keeping hidden were overshadowed by the tiny disgusting creature tumbling toward her through the air.

Layla saw her emerging from the shrubs, which set her off on a new round of shrieking.

Tanner jumped at the sound and at Phoebe's sudden appearance.

That was the final straw for the horses.

Hooves pounded on sand as the great beasts reared up, landing hard, their powerful muscles flexing as they bolted and galloped away down the beach, picking up speed when they realized nobody had hold of their reins.

Layla, Tanner, and Phoebe all watched them with dismay. Phoebe wishing with all of her heart that she could have escaped with them.

Twenty-Eight

Violet

Violet couldn't concentrate.

She was worried about Phoebe. She was also worried about Bronwyn.

Phoebe because she was helping Tanner on his big date when she had feelings for him, which Violet was afraid would end up a heartbreaking experience. And Bronwyn because she had grown more and more hostile toward men in general, Tanner more specifically, when they had stayed up late trying to support Phoebe through her dilemma.

"Can't you see that he's using you, Phoebe?" Bronwyn had asked, unconcerned her words might be too blunt for Phoebe to appreciate the meaning.

Frowning, Phoebe argued, "He's not using me. I offered to help him. This was all my idea."

Bronwyn wasn't cutting Tanner, or any man, any slack. "He should know better. He should be paying attention to what he's doing to you. It's not your job to take care of him or his stupid love life."

Violet had found a nugget of truth in the thought, but she didn't dare agree. Her two friends were locked in a battle, which she didn't think was going to be won that night. Before either of them said something they might have regretted, she had managed to get them off to bed.

Mothering people wasn't her specialty, exactly, but Violet had channelled her teacher training to get them to do what she wanted. It was for their own good.

Phoebe, because she had had an awful day and nearly choked to death. Bronwyn, because she was suffering through her own marital problem, and she had drunk way too much wine. Again.

Violet was concerned about Bronwyn's drinking. And about Phoebe's emotional involvement with a guy who was interested in somebody else.

"What's up?" Ben asked.

Violet looked up from her laptop. "What?"

Ben gave her a curious smile. "I was just wondering why you were sighing. Is something bothering you?"

"Did I sigh? I didn't mean to."

"Anything I can do to help? Is it Marine Life Rescue related?"

"No, nothing here is the problem," Violet said, looking around at the the slightly shabby room that she had grown so fond of over the past weeks. Ben looked concerned. "Nothing for you to be worried about either," she reassured him.

"Is there anything wrong at the beach house? I'm sure Bill would be happy to fix any issues you're having with the place."

"I don't think Bill could fix this problem," she confided.

"So there is a problem."

Violet purposefully did not sigh. Instead, she nodded. "It's the other Aphrodites."

"The other who?" Ben was even more curious.

Realizing her slip, Violet explained. "That's the name of our writing group, The Mighty Aphrodite Writing Society."

"Wow, that's quite a name," Ben chuckled. "I like it. So...there's trouble amongst the goddesses of writing?"

"I'm just worried about them. They're not getting along that great." Violet didn't know how much of their personal lives Phoebe and Bronwyn would want her to share, besides what if Ben knew Tanner like he knew Bill? She couldn't spell everything out for him the way it was. But it would be nice to talk to someone. Choosing her words carefully, she explained, "Phoebe has been a little preoccupied and Bronwyn, well, she is having some problems at home...with her husband...and she's been drinking quite a bit of wine lately."

"Oh, I see," Ben watched her with his green eyes. "And you're kind of stuck in between them, worrying?"

Violet smiled weakly. "I guess you could say that."

"Well, if you need to take off to go sort things out, I totally understand."

Violet shrugged. "There's not much I can do right now, they're both gone all day." She stared cheerlessly at her laptop.

"Oh," Ben said, unable to come up with another suitable suggestion. After several moments of watching her out of the corner of his eye and fiddling with a pen he was holding, he abruptly smacked the pen on the table. "I've got it!"

"Got what?"

"How I can help," Ben answered with a broad smile.

Puzzled, Violet asked, "Help?"

"With your Aphrodite problem."

"Oh," she smiled, a little confused. "I don't know what you could do to help with Phoebe and Bronwyn."

"You're right," Ben pointed his finger at her jokingly. "I can't do anything for Phoebe or Bronwyn. But it seems to me I do have one of the Aphrodites right here in my office." He swept his arms out from his sides, encompassing the entire room, his smile growing wider. "You!"

Violet blushed slightly. She wasn't sure what he meant to do for her, but appreciated his effort to cheer her up.

"I'm going to get you outside and help you get your mind off of all of your troubles."

"You are? Where?"

"Snorkeling."

Surprised, Violet could only repeat what he had said. "Snorkeling."

"Why not? We're Marine Life Rescue, if we can't use marine life to rescue an Aphrodite from her troubles, what good are we?"

Violet shook her head, laughing. "That logic is completely skewed."

Ben disappeared into the back room and returned with two pairs of fins and two snorkels.

"Have you ever been snorkeling before?" he asked.

"Once, a long time ago, but you don't have to do this," Violet said.

"Come on, come on, get up, I'm not taking no for an answer."

"But I have work to do!"

Ben pointed at her with one of the snorkels. "Don't make me fire you from you unpaid volunteer job, Miss Aphrodite."

Violet blushed deeply this time, but she couldn't refuse. Ben was a skilled snorkeler, scuba diver, and surfer. She would be hard pressed to find anyone more qualified to escort her on her second time snorkeling in the ocean. Or anyone more adorable.

It turned out that Ben was right. Snorkeling was just the thing to take her mind off of her problems with Phoebe and Bronwyn. It took her mind off of any problem she had ever had for practically her entire life, in fact.

Floating on the the gentle waves of blue water along a quiet rocky shore with coral and fish and all kinds of vibrant marine life underneath was the most at peace Violet could remember feeling in a very long time. Peering through her mask, she watched in awe as the almost alien looking plant life undulated to the rhythm of the waves and schools of bright fish swam nearby.

"Over here," Ben called out, beckoning to her with his long, lean arm.

Violet swam to him. Between moments of awe from seeing all of the underwater beauty, she was also experiencing intense moments of attraction to Ben. Appreciating his height and good looks anew in his swim trunks. Deep down, she hoped he was feeling the same way about her in her new bikini.

She had bought it on her credit card with the idea that she could pay it off with her check from the newspaper and, luckily, hadn't taken it out of her car yet. It was a beautiful poppy orange and had ruffles on the bust and behind. Now that she had been at the beach for a few weeks she wasn't quite so pale and looked pretty good in the bright color. The ruffles added much needed weight to her figure.

Having lived for years near the beach, Ben didn't need to work on his tan. And as far as she could see he didn't need any extra weight added to his frame nor taken off. Tall and sinewy strong, he was next to perfect in her eyes.

"Look who I found," he said when she finally made it over to where he was snorkeling.

Violet ducked her head underwater and gasped in delight, accidentally opening her mouth and letting sea water rush in. She didn't lift her head above water right away to spit it out, though, because she wanted to take in what Ben had called her over to see.

A sea turtle. Right below them. Swimming steadily, free and healthy, through the ocean waters. Violet's heart swelled with joy at the sight.

After snorkeling they stopped by a food shack on the beach called Mudcrab's and grabbed several fish tacos to eat back at the Marine Life Rescue office.

"That was...it was amazing," Violet gushed as they sat at their table eating lunch.

Ben smiled, lighting up the room with how pleased he was at making her happy. He ripped the end of one of his tacos off and tossed it to Bear, then took a big bite.

"Seeing a turtle in real life, it's inspiring isn't it?" she asked.

He nodded, swallowing. "Everything is better in real life, wouldn't you say?"

Violet tossed the end of her taco to Bear. "I would. I think we can get so attached to our screens, you know? When seeing something in reality, reaching out and touching it, gives it so much more meaning."

"Agreed," Ben answered. "We'll have to take snorkeling breaks more often."

She would like that, but she didn't answer right away. She was chewing and couldn't answer, but also something was niggling at the back of her brain. As she enjoyed the spicy fish taco a thought came to her mind. She looked at Ben with excited eyes.

"What?" he asked.

"I just thought of something."

"Yeah?"

"A way to help Phoebe and Bronwyn...and me, too, with our writing."

"What's your thought?" Ben took another bite of taco.

"Maybe if we could see our manuscripts in person. Hold them in our hand to read them. Maybe that would help the writing process."

"Print them?"

"Yes, I think that could really get us all focused better on what we're doing." Another thought struck her. "Do you know where I could print a few large document files out?"

Ben pointed at the printer in the corner behind the counter.

"Really? It will be quite a few pages. I don't want to use up your ink."

"Please, use it up. We get all of our brochures done at the printers, as you know. Everything else is online these days. If we don't use the ink it just dries up anyway. Do you have the files now?"

"I can pull them up on my phone. We've been using shared files for critiquing. I can access Phoebe and Bronwyn's and print from there. Are you sure it's okay with you?" Violet was thrilled at this idea. It could be the thing that got them all back on track again with their novels.

"Be my guest," Ben made a gallant sweep of his arm in the direction of the printer.

As the papers spit out of the printer with hers, Phoebe's and Bronwyn's unfinished manuscripts, Violet had an indescribable feeling that this was going to be a defining moment for the Mighty Aphrodites. That it was going to be the thing that put them over the edge. The beginning of their success as authors.

She couldn't wait to get the manuscripts back to Sol Mate and hand them over to the others. As she was fantasizing about their delighted faces, her phone buzzed with a text.

It was from Phoebe.

Going to be later than I thought getting back. At the Emergency Room.

Flabbergasted, Violet said, "Again!?"

Twenty-Nine

Phoebe

The ride back from the infamous picnic date was
miserable for Phoebe.

It didn't seem to be a bucket of sunshine for Tanner
or Layla either. At least not from what Phoebe could tell when
she stole looks at them. Tanner in her back seat and Layla next to
her in the passenger seat.

Since the date had been declared over in no uncertain terms
by Layla, and their mode of transportation had galloped away,
Phoebe felt the least she could do was offer them a ride.

"Would you take me home first?" Layla requested.

"She could take us to my car at the stable and I'll take you
home," Tanner said.

Layla set her jaw and shook her head curtly. "No, I would like
to be taken home right now."

"Layla," Tanner said, resistance in his tone.

He was going to argue that it made more sense for Phoebe to
take them back to the stable and Layla was going to argue back,

possibly yell at him, and the fight would go down while Phoebe was trying to drive. She didn't want to hear it. Everything was her fault anyway, if she had to drive a few extra minutes back and forth it only served her right.

"It's okay," she volunteered cheerily. "I don't mind. Just tell me where to go."

"Happy to," Layla said flatly.

Phoebe caught Tanner's eye in the rearview mirror. He mouthed 'I'm sorry', but he had nothing to be sorry about. Phoebe tried to convey that message with her eyes, but wasn't sure if it worked.

The rest of the ride to Layla's apartment was dead silent. Only the occasional instruction from Layla to turn left or right and the rather comical sound of Phoebe's turn signal, which seemed especially loud in the quiet car, as she followed those directions.

When they did arrive at Layla's address, Phoebe wasn't surprised to find that she lived in a luxury condo complex outside of Turtle Cove. Pristine white buildings with expensive landscaping complete with giant fountains, a golf course, and guards at the entry.

"Why don't you take the lunch with you?" Tanner suggested as he opened Layla's door for her to get out.

She turned up her pretty little nose at the idea, but Tanner was insistent.

"I'm not hungry," she sniffed.

"Yes you are, or you can eat it later. I made it for you, Layla."

That last part hit Phoebe hard. Tanner had put so much effort, time, and money into this date to impress Layla and Phoebe had botched it all up. He really loved Layla, Phoebe could hear it in his voice. He wanted nothing but her happiness.

"Fine," Layla gave in, snatching the picnic basket Bill had loaned Phoebe and Phoebe had loaned Tanner out of his hands, she hurried away.

No worries, Phoebe told herself, Tanner would be able to get that basket back sometime. She had more pressing concerns at the moment. Phoebe squeezed the steering wheel with both hands and bit at her lip when she realized she was about to drive Tanner, alone, back to the stables to pick up his car. She was not looking forward to it.

She didn't have much time to worry about it, though, because Layla refused to allow Tanner to walk her to her door. As soon as she disappeared into the corridor, floral dress flouncing perturbedly, picnic basket laden with goodies on her arm, Tanner returned to the car and climbed into the passenger seat.

Phoebe couldn't contain herself. He'd only just gotten his seatbelt on when she turned to him, teary eyed, and said, "I am so sorry, Tanner! I can't tell you how sorry I am."

He seemed surprised. "It's not your fault."

"Not my fault? I should have been long gone before you even got there. And then popping out like that and scaring her, that didn't help."

A smile ticked up at the corner of his mouth. "It didn't help, no, but things were already going south. And what were you going to do? You needed your keys. You didn't leave them behind on purpose."

Phoebe wasn't sure if that was completely true. After Bronwyn's lecture on sabotaging his date, maybe she had left her keys behind on purpose. Well, she knew that she hadn't left them behind *consciously*. "No, I guess I didn't do that on purpose."

Tanner nudged her. "Besides, without you there wouldn't have been an epic date to go epically wrong anyway."

She was suddenly keenly aware how close together they were sitting. And how good he looked...and how amazing his cologne smelled. He was dressed up for a romantic date, after all.

"I suppose so..." she murmured.

"I am still hungry though. Didn't get a chance to eat much before that spider came along."

"Right, that spider," Phoebe shuddered at the memory of it landing in her hair.

Tanner's smile grew. "If we're gonna lay blame on anyone let's lay it at the feet of that spider."

Phoebe chuckled. "Yeah, all eight of its creepy little feet."

Tanner let out a short laugh. "You should have seen your face when it landed on your head."

The ridiculousness of the hysterics caused by the stupid spider hit them both at the same time and they cracked up laughing. It was several minutes before Phoebe could breathe.

She wiped tears of laughter from her eyes and put the car in gear, pulling out of the parking space. "We should get back to the stable and let them know the horses ran off, shouldn't we?"

Tanner, still chuckling, waved away her concern. "I already texted them. The horses got back on their own. They went straight home. I guess that's what horses do."

"Oh good, then I'll take you to your car," she said. Tanner snorted out another short laugh. "What?" she asked, not sure what was funny now.

"You should have seen Layla riding on the beach." He found the memory almost too funny to explain.

Phoebe was laughing again even though she didn't know exactly why he was laughing. Her question came out a little choppy, "Wh-why? What happened?"

Tanner could barely get the words out. "Sh-sh-she almost fell off!"

On one hand Phoebe empathized with Layla in her beautiful dress trying to ride on the back of a horse that so obviously made her uncomfortable. On the other hand, the idea of her falling off the horse on the oh so romantic date was too funny.

They both laughed so hard Phoebe had to pull the car over to the side of the road because she couldn't see through the tears of laughter. Tanner was doubled over in the passenger seat.

"That would have been terrible," Phoebe managed to say, trying to empathize between peals of laughter.

"Yes, terrible!" Tanner howled.

"My side hurts," Phoebe added after catching her breath. This only made Tanner laugh more.

When they did finally settle down they had only gotten a few minutes away from Layla's condo.

"I'm starving," Tanner announced. "Do you want to get a burger or something?"

Phoebe was hungry, but even if she wasn't she would not have refused.

"Sure, I'd love a burger."

"And maybe a beer," Tanner added. Then more to himself, "I need a beer." He looked at her and smiled. Phoebe couldn't believe how well he was taking the picnic date fiasco. "There's a great burger place nearby."

Sitting across the table from him at the Sunset Grill was surreal. Dark wood tables with benches for seats, a long bar down the center of the main dining room, neon signs of different beers along the walls. There was a stage for live music, which sat empty now, but probably packed in a lot of people when it was occupied.

Phoebe was surprised. She had expected to be excited or nervous to eat with Tanner, but she wasn't either of those things.

She was serene, almost tranquil. Maybe she was in shock.

Not necessarily. They shared a comfortable familiarity. She supposed it was from the time they had spent planning the date and then cooking at his house. The small piece of her that never gave up on romantic ideals hoped it came from somewhere else...like shared destiny, perhaps?

"Thanks," Tanner told the waitress who had placed frothy beers in front of them. He picked up his and waited for Phoebe to pick up hers. "Here's to the most memorable date I've ever been on."

She clinked her glass to his and smiled. Knowing he would remember this day, as crazy messed up as it had been, eased the pain in her heart, if only a little. Perhaps that meant he would remember her after she left at the end of the summer. Probably not exactly the way she would remember him, but it was something.

"You've been here a lot?" Phoebe asked, taking in the red and white checkered table cloths.

"Yeah, Layla and I've come here a lot. It's so close to her house."

She didn't know how to respond so Phoebe took a sip of beer. It was ice cold and the foam stuck to her upper lip.

Tanner scanned the room, thinking. "I don't think she liked it very much."

"No?"

He shrugged. "Maybe we weren't really ever on the same page. Maybe she couldn't really be happy with a guy like me."

Phoebe could not imagine.

A cell phone beep interrupted Tanner's thoughts. He pulled his phone out of his pocket and his shoulders slumped.

"Speak of the devil. She texted me," he said to Phoebe then looked back at his phone.

Phoebe waited as patiently as she could, but she was extremely curious about what Layla had said in her text.

"Uh-oh," Tanner's brow furrowed.

"Uh-oh, what?"

"She's having an allergic reaction." He flipped his phone around to show her a picture. It was of Layla, but she was changed. Her normally beautiful full lips were bloated into a grotesque blob. Her eyes, eyes Phoebe thought were nearly perfect, were puffy and swollen shut.

"Oh no!" Phoebe said.

Tanner pulled out his wallet and threw a twenty on the table. "Can we go back to her place? Do you mind?"

No, Phoebe didn't mind.

Of course, later, after they figured out what had happened with Layla and her allergies, Phoebe wished she hadn't gone back to the apartment with him and was even more sorry for ever getting involved with Tanner trying to woo his ex.

Thirty

Bronwyn

Bronwyn's face hurt from smiling. Not from the authentic kind of smiling. From the inauthentic kind. The fake kind.

She didn't think it was possible for an authentic smile to cause your cheeks and jaw to ache. A fake smile, now, that was a different story.

"Mommy, watch!" Nathaniel shouted to her as he readied himself to run through the children's play fountain again. He was already soaking wet, hair dripping, shorts and T-shirt hanging off his small, thin body, but he was having a good time, which was all that mattered.

She wished she could say the same.

"I'm watching, honey," she waved to reassure her youngest that she would not look away as he ran full speed into the flying drops of water. She was grateful to have the excuse to keep her eyes trained somewhere, anywhere, except on Ryan.

Ryan had spent all morning glued to her side, making sure

they packed her favorite lunch, ushering her through all of her favorite exhibits at the museum, finding her favorite spot in the park to watch the boys play in the fountain.

He was getting on her nerves.

"How are you doing?" he had asked in the car ride to the museum, his expression remarkably genuine.

Bronwyn hadn't answered him, just stared out the window and pretended she didn't hear the question. She managed to remain politely distant for the rest of the ride, through the tour of the museum and during their lunch in the park. But it had been hours and hours and her fake smile was beginning to give her a headache.

"You seem tired," Ryan said from his side of the blanket they had laid out on the grass. Bronwyn had begun to think of everything they owned as having 'his' and 'her' sides.

"I'm not tired," she turned her radiantly perfect smile on him for a few moments so he could see how not tired she definitely was before shifting her attention back to her boys.

A few minutes went by. Ryan pulled out a bag of cheesy Goldfish crackers from the picnic tote bag, the boy's favorite snack.

"You know, perpetual smiling is a sign of insanity," Ryan said. "That's why not all of these little guys have smiles. It makes people uncomfortable." He held out a hand full of Goldfish crackers for her to see.

Bronwyn was compelled to look at the crackers and see if he was right. When she looked back up at him, Ryan was watching her closely. She couldn't pull her gaze away from his. It was the longest she had looked at him since she left for her writing retreat at the beginning of the summer. Her fake smile faded.

"Are you all right?" he asked.

Again with the sincerity. She couldn't handle it. With a frustrated groan she dropped back on the blanket so she was flat on her back staring up into the sky.

"Nicole..." Ryan moved into her field of vision and peered down at her. "Seriously, I'm asking."

"I'm a little stressed, okay?" She didn't like him calling her Nicole, but she knew he wouldn't understand the whole Bronwyn thing. Throwing the word stress at him was a jab. Ryan always said the word was so overused it had become generic.

"That's such a meaningless word anymore," he complained.

She smirked at his answer. "Okay, I'm *tense*."

"Why?"

Bronwyn let out a caustic laugh. "Gosh, I wonder why I'm tense?!"

"That's what I want to know."

She looked at him, incredulous. "We're getting divorced, Ryan. Sorry if that stresses me out."

"I never said we were getting divorced."

"What!? You absolutely did say we were getting divorced!" Bronwyn's voice rose and Ryan looked around nervously. Taking his cue she slipped a look at Jeremiah and Nathaniel, who were still safely out of earshot. She sat up and spoke again, this time in a hissing whisper as she punched her finger at his chest. "I specifically asked you if we were going to work on our marriage or get divorced and you said...what!? You said *divorce*, Ryan. *You* said it."

He watched her placidly, waiting for her to stop emoting. It was one of his habits that drove her absolutely nuts.

Finally he said, "I thought that's what you wanted."

Bronwyn let out another joyless laugh. "You thought I wanted a divorce?" She flopped onto her back again, covering her eyes with the palm of one hand. "If you're gonna sleep with another woman, Ryan, then yeah, I'm gonna want a divorce. It's not rocket science."

"I'm not."

"You're not what?"

"Sleeping with another woman."

Bronwyn sat up again, watching him for any sign of lying. There was nothing but his normal, everyday, plain, boring face.

"What are you saying?" she asked.

Ryan squinted up into the sun then toward the fountain. Nathaniel had tripped and Jeremiah was helping him up.

"We broke up," he said quietly.

His use of 'we' made her cringe. She suddenly felt sick, the knot of stress or tension or anxiety or whatever it was that had sat in her belly all day transforming into nausea.

Her nausea made her angry. Her preferred reaction would have been to laugh. Loud and in his face. But she didn't. All she did was suck breath in and out, trying not to throw up all over the picnic blanket.

"Mommy, Mommy, did you see me crash and burn?" Nathaniel dropped onto the blanket between her and Ryan.

"Watch out, buddy, you're going to get Mommy all wet," Ryan reached out to their son.

"It's fine," she interjected, shooting a look at her husband. Her cheating then not cheating, wants a divorce then doesn't want a divorce, husband. "He's not bothering me."

She managed to quell her sick stomach and to avoid being alone with Ryan the rest of that day and night. Even though he was there, under foot, the entire time.

Bronwyn spent all of her energy focusing on the boys, playing whatever game they wanted to play and basically using them as a shield. Even sleeping in Nathaniel's indoor tent that was set up in his room as a kind of slumber party. As long as she kept one of the boys next to her Ryan didn't dare bring up any of their marital problems, which suited her just fine.

He did follow her out to the convertible when she was leaving the next day. The mid-afternoon sun beat down on their driveway and Bronwyn noticed the flower bed that circled their mailbox needed weeding.

"Nicole, we really need to talk," Ryan said, stubbornly holding onto the suitcase he was carrying instead of putting it in the car.

"Now's not the time," Bronwyn said, putting on her sunglasses to dull the glare coming off of his shiny forehead.

Suddenly, the memory of Bill lowering himself slowly down from the attic at Sol Mate, his muscled arms flexing, his intensely masculine frame impressing not only her, but Phoebe and Violet as well, flashed through Bronwyn's mind.

A smile twitched at the edges of her mouth. It had been good to see the boys and her heart hurt every time she drove away from them, but they seemed to be having a fine summer without her around all of the time and she was more than ready to get back to the beach.

"We have to talk about it sometime," Ryan argued.

Bronwyn reached down and took hold of her suitcase, pulling it not so gently out of his grip and tossing it into the back seat of the convertible as if it was weightless.

"Sometime," she let her lips part into a smile. "But not right now."

It wasn't until she returned to the beach house that she was able to process what he had said. She told Phoebe and Violet that her cheating husband had broken up with his girlfriend while they relaxed on the deck of Sol Mate.

"Wow," Violet responded. "That's huge, right?"

"Huge would cover it," Bronwyn answered.

They were sitting in the lounge chairs drinking a nice bottle of Pinot Grigio Bronwyn had bought on the way back.

"What did you say?" Phoebe asked.

"Nothing, the boys came back and we didn't have time to talk anymore. Thank God." Bronwyn stared at the sky, which was turning a brilliant pink as the sun prepared to set. The sound of the ocean waves made her feel steady. At least she wasn't nauseated anymore.

"What are you going to do?' Violet asked.

Bronwyn turned her head on the lounge cushion so she could see her two writing friends. They looked so concerned...and young. They hadn't yet realized what Bronwyn had, that men were secondary to one's life happiness and the sooner you knew that the better off you were.

She sighed. "I don't know. I'm gonna have some more wine and then sleep on it. That's all I can promise right now." She smiled at their worried faces then zeroed in on Phoebe. "What I want to know is how everything with your plans to help the lifeguard out with his date worked out."

Phoebe's cheeks turned pink. "I already told Violet last night when I got home."

Violet chuckled. "That's okay, I don't mind hearing it all again. It's pretty entertaining."

"Do tell. I need all of the distracting entertainment I can get," Bronwyn said.

Phoebe took a deep breath and told her dramatic, and quite comical tale. Starting at deciding what she was going to wear and ending with what Layla had looked like when she and Tanner took her to the Emergency Room.

All three of them were laughing like schoolgirls by the time she was done.

"What was she allergic to?" Bronwyn asked when the merriment had died down.

Phoebe smiled and Bronwyn was delighted to see a spark of mischief in her eyes. Perhaps Phoebe wasn't the type to lay down like a doormat and let everyone walk over her after all.

"Coconut," Phoebe answered.

"The coconut macaroons you bought on a whim?" Bronwyn asked.

Phoebe raised her eyebrows and averted her eyes in a look of faux innocence as she took a sip of her wine. She swallowed and said, "Who knew?"

They all fell into another fit of laughter.

"Bravo!" Bronwyn said. "May your random acts of kindness always vanquish your enemies through no fault of your own!"

Thirty-One

Violet

Violet opened her eyes the next morning to a whole new day. A clean slate. A fresh look on life.

They had all stayed up talking and laughing and, yes, drinking wine, but not to excess, which was a pleasant change. She had been surprised at Bronwyn's reaction to her husband's announcement. Violet would have expected Bronwyn to go off the deep end, but she hadn't. At least not yet.

That combined with Phoebe's wild weekend had postponed Violet's big announcement to her fellow Aphrodites. The manuscript printouts. That was okay. She planned on showing them during their first writing sprint of the day and kick off this week, the first in their second month at Sol Mate, with a bang.

Violet threw her covers off and went to her balcony, opening the doors wide to the brand new morning. The sun was just coming up and the others wouldn't be awake for a bit, so she fixed a brisk cup of tea at her tea and coffee bar, humming softly the entire time.

All three of the Aphrodite manuscripts were sitting neatly on her dresser. She picked up hers and took it with her tea out onto her balcony. In reality, hers wasn't a true manuscript since it contained the writing she had been doing for Marine Life Rescue. She flipped through the pages, reading through the weak beginnings of her romance novel, which had stalled out in a big way when she began writing blog posts.

"I have time to get back into it," she reassured herself quietly.

Filling just as many pages as her novel were her blog posts, including the three that had been published. Violet read through them, pride filling her chest. Not to get too puffed up, but they were pretty good. Plus she had loads of ideas for new posts. She wanted to write several on coral reefs and the different fish and wildlife that called them home. Then there were whales and dolphins and sharks. So many creatures in the ocean interested her, she didn't think she would ever run out of subjects.

Sadly, she would be returning home at the end of the summer to start another school year. There was no way she could write everything she wanted to write for the Marine Life Rescue blog before then. Maybe she could keep helping Ben out even after she left Turtle Cove.

A tiny thrill pinged her heart.

To have a reason to keep in touch with Ben, maybe even return to Turtle Cove someday, made her a little giddy.

Violet pushed the feeling aside. She didn't want to overthink her relationship with Ben. They had spent some time together, yes, but she didn't want to assume anything beyond that was possible. She was only there for the summer after all. And after watching Phoebe's strange involvement with Tanner, Violet was especially concerned about what crushing too hard on someone could do to a person.

She got dressed and went downstairs, carrying her laptop and the Aphrodite manuscripts. They had planned to start their writing sprints at 9:00am so she had time to make breakfast, maybe even go for a quick walk on the beach. May as well soak up as much beach life as possible before settling in to write.

As Violet stood in front of the refrigerator trying to decide if she wanted eggs or yogurt for breakfast, her phone rang.

"Hello?" she answered.

"Hi, this is Nanette from the Cove Gazette, is this Violet Brown?"

"Yes it is," Nanette? That was Ben's friend at the newspaper. She sounded pretty. Violet's stomach dropped slightly. She didn't want to think about Ben's pretty girl friends. Another negative thought popped into her mind. She hoped Nanette wasn't calling to tell her that the newspaper had paid her by mistake.

"Great, sorry to call so early," Nanette said.

"No problem, what can I do for you?" Please don't ask for your money back. Please, please, please.

"I got your contact information from Ben." Violet's heart saddened at that, but she tried to focus. "We would like to talk to you about your articles. We got some great feedback on them and want to commission more from you."

Violet froze with the refrigerator door still open.

"Ms. Brown?" Nanette asked.

"Yes, sorry, I'm not sure I heard you correctly?"

"We really liked your articles on the Marine Life Rescue organization and their work. We're interested in publishing more on climate change, marine animals, and anything to do with the environment here in Turtle Cove. And we'd like you to write them."

"Oh, I see," Violet answered. Her voice sounded so calm, but she had to bite her lip to keep from squealing *Really? Me?*

"Are you interested?" Nanette asked.

"Yes, yes, of course," Violet finally closed the refrigerator door. Her stomach was flipping back and forth and all over the place. She wouldn't be able to eat any breakfast anyway.

"We were hoping for ten articles in total. Eight smaller pieces like you sent us before. And two longer pieces for Sunday editions, at least 2000 words each on those."

"Oh, okay," Violet's head was spinning. "When do you need these by?"

"We would love to publish one small article per week starting this week."

"This week?"

"I can email you what we're looking for as far as deadlines and a copy of our normal reimbursement scale. You can get back to me on it," Nanette suggested.

"I can get back to you," Violet was so stunned all she could do was repeat Nanette's words.

"Could you let me know if you can meet the deadlines by tomorrow?"

"Let you know by tomorrow. I can do that," Violet managed to sound normal as they said goodbye, she hoped.

Feeling a little unsteady on her feet, Violet sat down at the kitchen table. Phoebe, still sleepy eyed, came in and went straight to the coffee maker.

"Good morning," she said through a yawn. "I slept hard. This weekend wore me out more than I thought it would."

"Yes," Violet answered, still chewing on what Nanette had said over the phone.

"What's the matter?" Phoebe asked, noticing her silence.

Violet laughed nervously. "The newspaper wants to commission me to write some more articles for them." She looked at Phoebe, her eyes wide. "Can you believe that?"

"That's wonderful, Violet," Phoebe joined her at the table. "Isn't it?"

"I'm not sure," Violet answered.

"Not sure about what?" Bronwyn, looking even sleepier than Phoebe, shuffled into the kitchen.

"The Cove Gazette wants to hire Violet to write more articles," Phoebe filled her in. She looked sharply at Violet. "They are going to pay you, right?"

Violet nodded.

"How much?" Bronwyn asked, pouring a big mug of coffee for herself.

"I'm not sure," Violet clicked on her phone to check her email. True to her word, Nanette had already sent the information. "She emailed me, hang on," Violet told the others.

Bronwyn joined them at the kitchen table. She and Phoebe sipped their coffee and waited for Violet to read the email.

Violet scanned the fee schedule, her excitement building. "For the short articles, like the ones they bought already, it's $25.00 each. But they want two bigger articles of more than 2000 words. Those are $100.00 each."

"Hey, that sounds pretty good," Phoebe said encouragingly.

"Can you get them done?" Bronwyn asked.

Violet's excitement got all twisted up with worry and she gave them a pained smile. "I guess?"

"Do you *want* to write the articles?" Phoebe asked.

"I like writing them. It's just...it's just going to take some time. And they want them over the next few months. That's the whole time we're here for the retreat."

A dull sense of doom settled in on Violet as she stared at the fee schedule. From what she could tell the Cove Gazette was offering to pay her $400.00 total for the articles. That was a nice chunk of extra money in her teacher's salary world.

"You're worried you won't write your novel?" Bronwyn asked, showing a surprising amount of insight so early in the morning.

Violet nodded, tears filling her eyes.

"Oh, honey, you don't have to write the articles if you don't want to," Phoebe said, patting her arm.

"But I do want to write the articles," Violet said, sniffling. "That's the problem. I want to do both."

Silence fell over them. If the others were thinking what she was thinking, it was a gloomy thought for a day that had started out so well. Being pulled in too many directions in writing, or anything else in life, put any dreams of writing a novel in peril.

Violet stood and retrieved the printed manuscripts from the counter where she had left them. She placed them down in front of their respective authors.

"What are these?" Phoebe asked.

"I had an idea that maybe it would help for us each to see what we've written so far on paper," Violet explained. "I printed out each of our shared files so we could all have a hard copy. You don't mind, do you?"

Phoebe picked her manuscript up and flipped through it, her eyes filling with delight. "Mind? I think that's a great idea."

Bronwyn, whose manuscript was the largest of all of them, did not seem as pleased. She didn't thumb through the pages like Phoebe, merely picked it up then let it drop with a thump back onto the table.

"You don't think it's a good idea?" Violet asked.

Bronwyn shook her head, "It's a little early in the morning for me to think, that's all."

Violet picked up her own manuscript, finding the place where she had stopped writing her novel and started writing blog posts. She split the papers at that point and placed each section on the table in front of her. Both stacks were almost identical in size.

"This is it in a nutshell," she said. "I've lost interest in my story." She placed one hand on the novel stack. "And I've gained interest in writing these, gotten paid for a few of them, and have a request to write more for money." She placed her other hand on the blog post stack. Looking back up at Phoebe and Bronwyn, she asked, "So...what, my fellow Aphrodites, should I do?"

Thirty-Two

Bronwyn

Her chest stung with humiliation as Bronwyn sat at the kitchen table and tried to listen to Violet go on and on about her non-issue. Her eyes kept drawing back to the manuscript printed out in front of her. Her manuscript. Or, in truth, Lacy Spencer's manuscript.

She hadn't told the others that she was copying Lacy Spencer's work as a writing exercise and now they both thought that every chapter she had transcribed was a chapter she had written in her own book. Bronwyn didn't know what she wanted to do about that misunderstanding.

She did know what she didn't want. She didn't want to hear any more about how Violet was torn between writing her novel and getting paid to write newspaper articles. That wasn't a problem. It was an opportunity. One that Bronwyn found especially grating when she thought about how little opportunities she had for anything good in her life right now.

"Don't you think?" Phoebe had turned to her and asked her to respond to their conversation.

Bronwyn hadn't been listening. All of the sound in the room had dimmed when she flipped the top page of her manuscript and saw Lacy Spencer's words. She looked up into Phoebe's eyes then Violet's, both of them waiting for her response.

"Yes, I do," Bronwyn answered. Better for them to think she agreed than have to admit she was distracted at the fact that the rather impressive looking stack of papers in front of her had nothing to do with her own writing abilities.

"See?" Phoebe turned back to Violet. "We both think you can do it."

God, they were still talking about Violet's successful foray into journalism. Bronwyn remembered feeling supportive when she first heard the news. She was glad Violet had gotten some positive feedback on her writing even if it wasn't fiction writing. And she was happy she had gotten paid a little something for her trouble. But Bronwyn's troubles had expanded since then. She didn't have the energy for anyone else's worries.

First and foremost, Bronwyn had a crumbling marriage and a husband that suddenly seemed interested in slapping it all back together again.

Second, there was the little issue of pawning off plagiarized work as her own. This was no way to start her brilliant career as a romance author. A beautiful, intelligent, sassy, and absolutely single, romance author.

Bronwyn scowled. She hadn't done it on purpose. She hadn't told Violet to go off and print anything. She never planned on plagiarizing anyone. And, technically, she reassured herself, she wasn't. She was merely getting over a little writer's block with Lacy Spencer's work. There was no Mighty Aphrodite rule book on what you could or could not type into the shared folder.

She scowled again, wishing she had kept everything on a document saved only to her laptop.

"You don't like that idea?" Violet asked.

Bronwyn looked up once more. Violet had caught her glaring at her manuscript and not listening again.

"Sorry, I was thinking about something," Bronwyn tapped the top of her stack of papers lightly, as if she had been lost in thought over her own novel. "What was the idea?"

Violet was smiling ear to ear, energized and youthful. Bronwyn filled with envy at the sight.

"I'm going to go for it. Do both!"

Bronwyn forced a smile. "That's great."

"The summer isn't over yet, right?" Violet asked, trying to pump herself up.

"Nope, it's not even close to over yet," Bronwyn agreed.

"Plus that gives you some extra money," Phoebe added.

"Right, which reminds me of something else I wanted to talk to you ladies about," Violet continued. "With the Marine Life Rescue fundraiser being kind of a big event, I was thinking maybe we could go shopping for something new to wear. If you want to."

"That would be fun. I didn't bring anything very formal for the summer. What do you think?" Phoebe asked, looking at Bronwyn for her response.

"Yes, shopping," Bronwyn answered. Anything to get her mind off of writing.

"There are a few boutiques in the downtown shopping area of Turtle Cove," Phoebe offered, excited at the prospect of going shopping.

"Eternal Summer is nice. I bought a lovely swimsuit when I was by there the other day," Violet told them.

"Eternal Summer. If only," Bronwyn repeated under her breath.

The boutique, Eternal Summer, it turned out, was darling. Chock full of an assortment of pretty things to catch the eye of tourists or locals. Exotic glass bowls and wine glasses with accents of brightly colored edges and swirls, sparkling one of a kind jewelry made by local artisans, shimmering scarves, and shining leather purses, shoes and sandals to name just a few.

If Bronwyn hadn't been feeling so dull she could have spent a large chunk of Ryan's money in the place. As it was, she merely walked alongside the beautiful knick-knacks and wondered if there would ever be a time in her life when she was happy. Truly happy.

"The clothing boutique is at the back." Violet led them to the back of the store, which was wider than the front and lined with large mirrors on one side and changing rooms on the other.

Bronwyn struggled to care about the items Phoebe and Violet found on the racks and held up for all to see. Dresses, light and flowing, prints and pastels, a few tropical colors, all of them appropriate for a fundraiser. None of them interesting enough to lift Bronwyn out of her gloomy mood.

Phoebe zeroed in on the only navy blue dress in the entire place and held it up. "What do you think about this one?"

"Why don't you wear a new color, Phoebe? You're always in navy," Bronwyn snapped.

Phoebe and Violet turned to her, surprised at her tone. Phoebe put the dress back on the rack, looking a little forlorn as she glanced down at the navy blouse and white shorts combo she was wearing.

"I thought that was pretty," Violet said, trying to be helpful.

Being helpful wasn't always what someone needed. Sometimes being helpful just kept them from knowing the truth. Still, Bronwyn saw that some of the fun had drained out of Phoebe's eyes and knew she should probably try to rectify the situation. Her own miserable existence didn't need to spread to her friends.

"It was pretty. I was just thinking for a big party on the beach maybe you'd want to wear some more color. Not be so dark. Something different," Bronwyn said.

Phoebe perked up, but cautiously. "I usually look better in navy and black," she confessed.

Seeing that her words could change Phoebe's outlook so

completely, Bronwyn decided she would go full in. If she put her mind to it perhaps she could get Phoebe to make the kind of fashion change that might bring her better luck with things. Things like men. Tanner to be exact.

"That's what I'm saying, Phoebe," Bronwyn said. "This isn't your usual life. You should do something *unusual*. Punch it up a little bit."

Just speaking the words to Phoebe and watching both her and Violet's faces sparkle with excitement made Bronwyn feel better. She didn't need to wallow in the problems of Nicole Speer, not while she was in Turtle Cove. Not while she was on a Mighty Aphrodite beach retreat.

"Don't they have a place in this town where you're not buying straight off the rack?" Bronwyn asked nobody in particular.

A snappily dressed older woman overheard and leaned in close to answer Bronwyn out of the earshot of Eternal Summer's staff. "Tropical Radiance, turn right outside this door and it's about two blocks away."

"Thank you," Bronwyn said with enthusiasm. When they entered Tropical Radiance she wished she would have thanked the kind woman even more. The store was exactly what she needed. "This is more like it," she proclaimed.

White tile floors, sleek white statues in the shape of slender palm trees lined an elegant walkway, which ended at a stage with several comfortable chairs set up to view models. Bronwyn decided Tropical Radiance would be the place they would find their dresses for the fundraiser. She turned around and beckoned Phoebe and Violet to follow her to the stage, laughing at their bewildered expressions.

"This, my fellow Aphrodites, is where we will be transformed," Bronwyn told them. Her mood lifted considerably with every step she took toward the elegant chairs.

"Where are the clothes?" Violet asked.

Bronwyn chuckled kindly at her naiveté. "They'll choose what suits us and have the models wear them out."

Violet and Phoebe both hesitated.

"I'm not sure I can afford a dress from a place like this," Violet said quietly.

"Oh, sweetie, it's on me," Bronwyn said with confidence. "Or, total disclosure, it's on my cheating lawyer husband." She laughed at this and the others followed suit, if with slightly less glee.

The attendants at Tropical Radiance were sublime and they had soon zeroed in on some gorgeous choices for Violet and Phoebe. After seeing several dresses, they each chose a few to try on and were thrilled to show off their favorites.

Violet picked a light and airy floor length halter dress. The skirt had layers of thin material that flowed around her as she moved. It had a vertical pattern of colors, blending softly from light orange to pastel teal to cream, that worked wonderfully with the tan she had developed since the start of the summer.

"Oh my, Violet, you're going to be a vision on the beach," Bronwyn said. Over her sour mood, and sipping on champagne that the Tropical Radiance staff provided, Bronwyn was dishing out compliments like mad.

Violet blushed and did a little twirl in her new ensemble. "Thank you, it's beautiful!"

Phoebe's dress was nothing less than a complete transformation. After much encouragement she managed to break out of her navy addiction and picked a V-neck, flutter sleeve, off the shoulder dress in light plum. The cut of the bodice accentuated Phoebe's full bosom and lovely shoulders while providing a slimming effect to her tummy before falling sensually around her legs.

"You look amazing in that color, Phoebe! Those lifeguards won't know what hit them, will they?" Bronwyn asked with a wink.

Phoebe smiled, flattered. She smoothed the front of her dress before giving Bronwyn a more serious look. "Are you sure you can buy these? They're a little pricey."

"Nonsense," Bronwyn argued. "I won't hear another word. Now help me pick out my show stopper."

Violet and Phoebe, thrilled with their dresses, set about assisting Bronwyn. But Bronwyn could not be pleased by any of the looks presented.

"Too girlish." "Too old." "Too vampy." "Too boring." Were just some of her many, many comments.

A while later they were all afraid it was a lost cause. It seemed that no dress in the inventory of Tropical Radiance was anything Bronwyn wanted.

Until. Something special happened.

"Perhaps madame would like to explore something a little more untraditional," the attendant suggested.

"Why not? We've looked at everything else, haven't we?" Bronwyn said.

The attendant snapped her fingers and a model stepped out onto the stage wearing a strapless white pantsuit with a deep green palm frond print. The pant legs were wide with ultra flare at the bottom. There was a diamond shaped opening showing off skin that started underneath the sternum and ended just above the naval. And, best of all, attached to the back of the bodice was a sweeping piece of white cloth that flowed behind the model like a cape.

Bronwyn was speechless for a few moments, as were the other Aphrodites. Bronwyn's heart fluttered and a tingle washed over her shoulders and arms.

Finally, she broke the silent gawking of her and her fellow Aphrodites. "If this isn't a Bronwyn Beck outfit then I don't know what is," she announced. Then, her voice raised in celebration, "And...it's a winner!" She laughed to a chorus of cheers from her two friends.

Bronwyn gazed at her beach fundraiser outfit. It was like something out of Kim Kardashians' wardrobe, and probably priced accordingly.

She didn't care. All she knew was if she was going to truly build a new life as Bronwyn Beck then it looked like she was going to have to invest in more pantsuits.

Thirty-Three

Phoebe

Phoebe watched out her bedroom window, waiting to see Tanner walk to the lifeguard station. She had done this every morning since the picnic, forgoing her normal early morning walk in fear of running into him.

After the fiasco that was Layla in the Emergency Room, she had decided enough was enough. Even though Layla's condition had turned out to be a non-life threatening situation, and Tanner had kept a great sense of humor about the whole thing, Phoebe needed to get her head in the game of writing. Not play nursemaid to a cute guy who couldn't get his romantic life together.

After she took some time to read through the printout of her manuscript, Phoebe had been both excited and mortified. Excited because the story was really coming together. Mortified because it would be obvious to anyone reading it who knew Tanner that she was writing about him. That she was in love with him.

She had decided to avoid him as much as possible. She needed to guard her heart and think about her future as an author. There was nothing to be gained by continuing an unfruitful friendship with...with...

There he was. Walking along the shoreline on his way to the lifeguard station. Was it her imagination or did he seem lonely?

"Don't be stupid, Phoebe," she whispered to herself. The dead quiet of her bedroom absorbed the sound.

Just like that, Tanner turned toward the beach house. Phoebe gasped and stepped back, ducking behind the wall, her heart pounding in her chest. Did he see her standing in the window? Did he see her back away?

"Stupid," she leaned against the wall, pressing her head against it and closing her eyes.

Such a fool. She had always been a fool at love. For love. For men.

Even if she didn't include the horrible mistake that had been Giovanni, Phoebe could point to so many times in her life she had allowed her feelings get away from her.

Being laid off from her job had been partially due to her inability to separate reality from fantasy. Her tendency to develop crushes on male coworkers, even senior members of the company, had become, she was afraid, legendary. She was certain those legends were part of the reason, if not the only reason, she wasn't asked to make the move with the company when they relocated to a new state.

And now Tanner.

Her writing retreat. Her deepest dream of becoming a regency romance author tainted by her feelings for him. Feelings she couldn't control and could barely hide.

Well, no more. She wasn't going to make the same stupid mistake again.

Certain he must have moved on by now, Phoebe risked a quick peek through the curtains out the window. The place where he had paused and looked her way was empty. Even his footprints in the sand had already been washed away by the unrelenting waves.

He was nowhere to be seen and she assumed he was already climbing onto the lifeguard tower, sunglasses reflecting the early morning rays, blonde hair shining, muscles glistening as he greeted the morning.

"Stop it," she wasn't doing herself any favors by obsessing over his looks. She needed to get some writing done and channel the angst she felt into her story.

The best writing was always when the author allowed their emotions, good or bad, to permeate their work. A well written chapter wasn't just a valuable addition to her book as a whole, but a chance to process her pain.

Phoebe did some full body stretching in her room. A replacement of her morning walk for now. She had made a lot of progress on her health since staying at Sol Mate and didn't want to lose ground. She could walk on the beach again the next morning when it was Tanner's day off.

After stretching, she gathered her laptop and printed manuscript to take to the deck and get cracking. When she entered the kitchen she found Violet working at the table. She also noted Bronwyn's manuscript was still laying on the table exactly where Violet had given it to her.

Strange.

Of course, Bronwyn always seemed to be doing something strange in Phoebe's opinion. But ignoring her manuscript wasn't something Phoebe would have expected.

Violet had her earbuds in, blocking out any sound, and a cup of cold coffee at her side. She was typing madly on her laptop. Violet had been so focused on writing both her novel and newspaper articles that she had barely taken her nose out of her computer since they returned from dress shopping days ago.

"Morning," Phoebe said, placing her things down temporarily to fill her own cup of coffee.

Violet looked up, surprised that someone else was there. She pulled out her earbuds. "Hey, Phoebe. How are you this morning?"

"I'm good, how are you? When did you get up?"

Violet pushed stray hairs back from her face and rubbed her cheeks with her hands. "I woke up at three and I decided to get up. I couldn't sleep."

"3 o'clock in the morning?"

Violet nodded, exasperated with her internal clock. "I know. Hopefully I'll get through the first few articles and feel a little less pressure." Her eyes slid to Bronwyn's manuscript. "Do you know if she's looked at that?" she asked.

"I have no clue. It doesn't look like she has," Phoebe answered. When she saw Violet's disappointment she added, "Maybe she will this morning when we do our first writing sprint."

"She's already left," Violet said.

"Where'd she go?" Phoebe wondered for a moment if Bronwyn had gone home to talk to her husband or be with her kids. Ever since they had found out about her marital problems, Phoebe had thought Bronwyn might abandon the whole writing retreat at any moment.

"To get a massage. She asked me if I wanted to go, but I didn't want her to pay for anything else for me and I can't afford massages on my own. Then she said she was going to Tropical Radiance to get some alterations on her pantsuit."

They both smiled.

"The pantsuit," Phoebe said.

Violet laughed, "It is quite a pantsuit, isn't it?"

"It's really high fashion, that's for sure. But if any of us can pull it off it would be Bronwyn," Phoebe said.

They both laughed, knowing that what she had said was both true and funny.

Violet glanced back at the manuscript. "I just hope I didn't offend her or anything by printing that out. It's good. Have you read it?"

Phoebe nodded emphatically. "It is good. Really good. I don't think she's offended. I think Bronwyn is distracted, that's all. She'll get to it when she can."

Phoebe picked up Bronwyn's manuscript and set it in the furthest corner of the kitchen counter, the space behind the refrigerator where it was hidden and safe from general traffic.

"There, it's out of sight and you won't have to think about it anymore," she said with a smile.

"Thanks."

Phoebe was about to ask Violet if she wanted to go for a quick walk to stretch their legs, now that Tanner was safely tucked away at the lifeguard station.

She was interrupted by her cell ringing.

And surprised by the caller.

Tanner.

She looked at Violet with wide eyes and showed her his name flashing on her phone.

"What are you going to do?" Violet asked.

Phoebe couldn't ignore him, not this way. It was one thing to stay out of his way on the beach, but him calling her directly was another thing. Her heart wouldn't allow it.

She accepted the call.

"Hello?"

"Hey, Phoebe, how are you?" Tanner said. His voice in her ear reverberated through her entire body and Phoebe found that she had to sit down to focus.

"I'm good. How are you?" she answered, quickly giving Violet a Why Am I Doing This To Myself face.

"I'm good. I didn't see you on your walk this morning. On the beach. Or yesterday. Are you feeling all right?"

"Oh, yes, yes. I'm fine. I've been, uh, getting a lot of writing in. Staying up late, you know. Sleeping in some." She was rambling. She pressed her lips together to keep from talking.

"That's good. Well, I wanted to ask you something."

"Ask away!" she answered, wincing at the sound of her own enthusiasm.

Tanner chuckled, a warm appealing sound that sent tingles through Phoebe's body. Then he said, "I was wondering if you'd like to go to dinner with me."

Thirty-Four

Bronwyn

Bronwyn was relaxed. So relaxed. An early morning massage had been just the thing she needed to face the day with a smile. Turtle Cove had one high end hotel, the Silver Tide Resort. And that hotel had a magnificent spa, Sparkling Waters Spa.

Sparkling Waters had been perfect. She'd been slathered with oils and kneaded until all of her recent negativity was forced into submission. Then she partook of the Sparkling Waters special rain showers, got a quick makeover with their natural makeup line and had her hair trimmed and blown dry at the hair salon.

After a lovely breakfast of a mango fruit bowl, a delicious croissant, and an espresso at the resort's restaurant, Paradise, Bronwyn gave her compliments to the chef and the hotel management and made her way to Tropical Radiance for her fitting.

"This style suits you, madame," the attendant complimented her as she stood in front of the full length mirrors on a pedestal and allowed their tailor to pin up the places that needed taken in.

"I think you're right," Bronwyn had answered happily. After the alterations it would fit her perfectly. Just what she needed to make her debut as Bronwyn Beck at a swanky fundraiser.

Back in the clothes she had worn into town, a chic pair of white capris, brown sandals and a flirty pink off the shoulder blouse, and fully satiated with luxury and pampering she thought she should probably head back to Sol Mate.

Being the power house of their little writing group she felt obligated to take part in whatever writing exercise Phoebe had put together for the day. If she was being honest, however, she wasn't too thrilled about it. Every decent writer needed some time off to regroup, didn't they? And she, of all people, deserved a little down time.

It was nearly noon when Bronwyn stepped out of Tropical Radiance and headed to where she had parked her convertible for the morning. The sun was angled toward her face and she rummaged through her bag for her sunglasses as she walked briskly down the sidewalk. Just as she had fished them out and bent her head to put them on, someone stepped in front of her and they collided.

"Oof!" Her sunglasses flew out of her hands and skittered across the sidewalk into the street where they were promptly run over by a passing car. Bronwyn cried out at the horrific crunch.

"Excuse me, I didn't see you," a man said. Rationalizing his mistake, just like all men did.

Bronwyn turned on him, her hard earned morning relaxation forgotten as fury boiled up inside of her, ready to unleash on the unsuspecting bumbling idiot who had practically knocked her over.

"Bronwyn?" he said.

Bronwyn, mouth hanging open in yet unspoken rage, stared up into the blue, blue eyes of none other than Bill.

"Are you all right?" he took hold of her elbow, ever so lightly, almost not touching her at all. Warmth from his touch zipped up her arm and into her head, fuzzing up her thoughts.

"Bill?" she asked. Ridiculous question. Of course it was him, she was looking right at him. Yet no other words came to her.

"Are you hurt?" he asked.

Yes, she thought. But that was an answer to a different question.

"No," she said.

"Your glasses," he said, jogging out to the street and picking up the broken pieces. He brought them back in the palm of his hand. "I'm sorry."

Bronwyn looked at her smashed sunglasses in Bill's calloused hand. All of the fury she had felt toward him when she thought he was a stranger was gone, leaving her a little bewildered and unsteady on her feet.

"Don't look now, but I think your sandal broke too," Bill said with dismay.

Bronwyn followed Bill's gaze to her right sandal. The strap on the side had popped off, probably when she was shoved sideways and tried to catch herself.

"My sandal?"

"Unless you were walking around with it like that before," he said, a smile on his lips.

"No," she managed.

Bill's amusement faltered and he took her by the elbow again, more firmly this time. "Maybe you should sit down."

He led her to one of several bistro tables sitting outside a little restaurant. Bronwyn sank into the chair. Her knees were wobbly and she felt a little faint. The after effects of her massage, surely.

"Water," she said.

"Right, coming up," Bill responded. He placed what was left of her sunglasses gently into a pile on the bistro table and hurried into the building.

Dizziness came over her in waves and she put her forehead on the table to keep from falling out of her chair.

"Bronwyn, do you need a doctor?" Bill asked, alarmed, when he returned with two tall glasses of ice water.

While he'd been gone Bronwyn had realized what was happening. All of the symptoms were similar to symptoms she had when she was hung over, and she had drank a lot of wine the night before. The massage and other early morning activities had merely taken their toll on her, shifting what would be her normal hangover into a hangover on steroids.

She raised one hand and shook it back and forth at him, her forehead still on the bistro table. "No, no, I'm fine," she said.

He sat down across from her. "You don't look fine."

Forcing her head up from the table, she rested her elbows on its surface instead and held her head up with her hands.

"Food," she said. "I think I need food."

"What do you want?" Bill asked, obviously hoping to get her back on her feet before carrying on with his day.

"Food," she answered sharply, not capable of giving more specifics.

Without missing a beat, he stood up and went back inside the building. With her peripheral vision, Bronwyn could see several customers scattered among the other bistro tables. Some of them were staring. All of them seemed to be eating hamburgers and French fries. She hoped Bill would bring French fries.

When he placed a basket of French fries in the middle of the table, Bronwyn groaned with pleasure. She groaned again when he slipped a huge juicy hamburger underneath her nose. She grabbed three French fries from the top of the pile and shoved them into her mouth. Sizzling hot and salty. They were perfect.

"You were pretty hungry," he said, amused and relieved that she was at least responsive.

No time to chat, she lifted the burger and bit into it, emitting another moan of satisfaction. She chewed and swallowed. Then bit, chewed and swallowed again. Lifting her glass to her mouth, she washed the burger down with huge gulps of water.

"Maybe you should slow down?" Bill suggested. He was holding a burger that he'd bought for himself, but hadn't taken a bite out of it yet. Bronwyn noticed that her burger was nearly half gone.

She waved away his concern and said, "It's okay. I had a massage." Then she picked up another handful of French fries and went to work on them. Before long her burger was gone and she was picking the last of the French fries out of the basket.

Bill, captivated by watching her consume her food like a lumberjack, had only taken cursory bites of his burger. She realized after she popped the last French fry into her mouth that the basket had been meant for them to share.

"I'm sorry," she said, still chewing on their salty goodness. "Did you want some?"

Bill cracked a smile. "I didn't want to risk sticking my hand in there and pulling out a stub."

Bronwyn rolled her eyes and wiped her hands and mouth on the paper napkins he had brought with the food. "Very funny, a woman nearly passes out after you knock her silly and you're full of jokes."

He grinned. "I am sorry about running into you." His eyes flicked to the pile of broken sunglasses bits. "And about your sunglasses."

Bronwyn leaned back in her chair and sighed contentedly. "That's okay. You made up for it by feeding me."

"Are you full? Do you want some dessert or something else?" Bill asked.

She didn't hear any sarcasm in his tone, but checked his expression just in case. He seemed sincere so she answered, "No, thank you. I think my blood sugar was off. I didn't eat much this morning."

"Glad to help."

"I suppose it's lucky I ran into you. I could have fainted while driving my car." She thought about it a second and corrected herself, "Or, rather, you ran into me." Bronwyn arched her brow at him and smiled.

He grinned again.

The sunshine was nice. It glinted off of the grey in his hair, which actually added to his good looks. Bronwyn had never really thought about being on a date with anyone since she married Ryan. Was this what it would be like? Sunny and comfortable and nice?

"So how have you four ladies been making out at the beach house? Everything going all right?" he asked, finally relaxing enough to make chit chat.

"Four? There's only three of us–" Bronwyn paused mid-sentence. Bill had always thought that Nicole was a different person, not her, she remembered.

"Oh, did one of your group decide not to stay the whole summer?" he asked.

"Um, no, not exactly," she racked her brain for a reasonable explanation for what she'd said. Coming up empty, she changed the subject. "Are you going to that big fundraiser beach party?"

He had to think about her question, she'd switched the subject so fast.

"The fundraiser for Marine Life Rescue," she added. Maybe he needed a clue.

That registered. Bill nodded and said, "Yes, are you?"

"Of course, anything to help the wildlife, right?"

"Right," he gave her a curious look, but didn't say anything else.

"In fact, I was just getting my pantsuit altered for it," she told him.

"Your pantsuit?" His curious expression slid into confusion.

"Don't worry, you'll see it in all of its glory."

He looked at her, deliberating, then gave her a wary smile. "Looking forward to it...I think."

Thirty-Five

Phoebe

P hoebe couldn't decide what to do with her hair and she was running out of time.

Tanner had suggested dinner at seven and it was already almost six o'clock. She had spent far too long searching through her wardrobe for something that wasn't plain old navy blue. After Bronwyn's comment the other day Phoebe had become acutely aware of her monotone clothing, but unfortunately was stuck with mainly navy and black pieces.

"That looks great," Violet said as she paused in Phoebe's bedroom door.

Armed with her best navy sundress and accent pieces donated by her Aphrodite roomies, Phoebe had ended up with a decent first date ensemble. Her sundress worked well with a batik silk wrap in shades of blue and white to drape over her shoulders, borrowed from Violet. And Bronwyn had loaned her some silver bracelets for a little extra bling, as she put it.

"Thanks," Phoebe blew a loose tendril of hair out of her face.

She had been trying to pull her dark locks up into something casual chic, sexy, but done up. It wasn't working.

"Do you need any more help?" Bronwyn asked, poking her head around Violet.

Phoebe's stomach was in knots and her palms were sweating. She needed help, but she didn't know if it was the kind of help the Aphrodites could provide.

She looked at them, distraught. "I don't know what to do with my hair!"

They both came in to assist. Thankfully they had cooler heads and were skilled with different hairstyles, Bronwyn especially. They decided on a bubble braid, where they first braided her thick hair down her back and then used the end of a comb to pull the hair slightly out of place, creating a loose, softer look. Then they pulled some tendrils out around her face and curled them lightly. Finally, they used the comb trick to lift the hair on her crown. The result was pretty and feminine and nothing Phoebe could have done on her own.

"Now you're ready to be swept off your feet," Bronwyn said proudly.

Phoebe laughed nervously. "I am really freaking out about this," she confessed.

"Just remember, he asked you out. You don't have anything to worry about. Just be yourself and try to have a good time," Violet suggested.

Phoebe couldn't help but feel like a teenager going to a dance as she left Sol Mate, waving to Violet and Bronwyn who were watching from the porch. She was meeting Tanner at the Coastline Inn. The same surf and turf place she had first seen him with Layla, on the night Layla had made a scene and abandoned him.

She couldn't wrap her mind around how the tables had turned since that night. After all of her involvement with Tanner, trying to help him get back with Layla, the ruined picnic, everything had brought them to this moment. Phoebe couldn't have been more thrilled.

She calmed her excitement as she drove, not wanting to get into a fender bender because she was so distracted by her new romance.

"Tanner and I...going on a date," She said out loud in the car, trying to make it normal in her ear. "Tanner and I are dating." A happy thrill zipped around her body. She laughed out loud. How long would it be before they were an official couple? Not long if it was up to her. But she needed to give him some time. He had just left a relationship. Still, wouldn't it be fun when they were? "Phoebe and Tanner." She said out loud. "Or Tanner and Phoebe." She pretended she was talking to someone in the passenger seat, "My boyfriend, Tanner."

Her fantasy charades went on until she got to the parking lot. She found a space even though the jitters in her stomach were growing exponentially. When she turned the car off and opened the door to get out, she jerked against her seat belt and fell back into her seat. She had forgotten to unhook it.

"For heaven's sake, Phoebe." She murmured to herself. "Thank goodness Tanner isn't here watching you bumble around." He had already texted and said he was inside at the table. Phoebe took a few seconds to take in some deep breaths. "Calm down. Everything will be fine."

When she managed to extricate herself from her car, Phoebe smoothed her dress and hair and adjusted the silk wrap. Music filtered out of the restaurant into the parking lot. Delicious smells greeted her as she approached. Strings of white globe lights were draped all along the outside of the building, beckoning her to enter.

"Here we go," Phoebe said under her breath when she reached the front door. She pushed it open and all of the sights, sounds, and smells magnified. With the additional sounds of people talking and laughing, and the clinking of plates and silverware, Phoebe thought this was probably the most perfect place to dine on a first date. The most perfect place to start a relationship.

She saw Tanner before he saw her.

His shock of blonde hair stood out in the crowd, as did his incredible good looks. She could tell from her vantage point that he was wearing a shirt she had seen before. It was a decent shirt, but not one he had worn when he was out with Layla. Not one of his nicest. A pinch of disappointment threatened to sour her entrance.

She glanced down at her own outfit wondering if she had overdressed then immediately brushed the thought out of her mind. What man wouldn't want a woman who dressed up a little bit for them?

"How many?" the hostess asked.

"Actually, I'm meeting my date. He's right over there," Phoebe pointed at Tanner, getting a small thrill out of calling him her date.

The hostess showed her to the table and Phoebe's heartbeat quickened with every step. When he finally saw her, Tanner's face broke into a smile that shone so bright Phoebe couldn't see or hear anything else. It was like they were alone in the room.

He stood up. "Wow, Phoebe, you look nice."

She blushed. Happy he was pleased. Overjoyed to be there with him.

"Thanks, you do to," she said as she sat down.

Tanner looked down at his everyday shirt and khaki long shorts. "Not really. If I had known we were dressing up I would have put on something nicer."

The pinch of disappointment again. No matter. There was no need for them to stand on such formalities. It wasn't as if they were strangers.

Phoebe tittered a laugh and picked up her ice water to take a sip. Her mouth was extremely dry.

A puzzled look flashed through Tanner's eyes, but disappeared quickly.

"Do you want a beer or anything? This medium ale is pretty good," Tanner lifted the beer he had already started on and took a sip.

"Um, sure, that would be fine," Phoebe said. Another stab of disappointment. Beer was a little informal. Wine might have been more of an event, but that was okay. She wasn't going to worry about a little thing like that.

Tanner ordered her the same ale that he had and told the waitress they needed a few more minutes to order. Phoebe liked it when a man took over the ordering. She knew it was old fashioned, but it was romantic in a way.

"Unless you're ready to order?" Tanner asked her.

"No, no, I need a few minutes," Phoebe answered. Her stomach was so full of butterflies she didn't know if she would be able to eat at all. She smiled at him, hoping her smile conveyed how special she felt this evening was and how much she looked forward to getting to know him on a more intimate level.

Tanner put his menu down and leaned toward her, a smile in his eyes as well. Phoebe's heart melted. So handsome. So sweet. So sexy.

"You know what?" he asked.

"What," she sighed dreamily.

"I am so happy you could come to dinner with me to celebrate."

"Celebrate what?" She almost tacked 'honey' onto the end of her sentence, but felt it might be too soon for cutesy nicknames.

"It worked!" Tanner announced, leaning back in his chair.

"What worked?" Phoebe didn't understand.

"The picnic date," he said with a laugh.

Phoebe's own smile faded in confusion, but she kept the remnants of it up, hoping she would understand soon. "The picnic date...worked?"

Tanner nodded emphatically. "Yes, can you believe it? That wreck of a date and everything that came out of it? And it still worked. Layla and I are back together!"

Thirty-Six

Phoebe

If Tanner had reached across the table into her chest, took hold of her heart, and yanked it out, Phoebe would have been just as stunned as she was when she heard him speak those words.

And why not? He had, in essence, pulled her heart out of her chest. He didn't know it, but he had.

Her lungs tightened. So hard she could not breathe in or out. Only stare at him as he kept talking about Layla.

"It was crazy, Phoebe. After we finally got her home from the hospital and she shut the door in my face, remember that?"

She did.

"I thought for sure that was it. I thought it was over forever."

So did she.

Tanner laughed again, delighting in telling her the story. Unaware that with every word he was tearing her into pieces.

"It wasn't until the next night that she texted me. Wanted me to call her. We talked. Then we talked yesterday and she asked me to come over and..." Here he dropped his gaze to the table in front of him, not wanting to get into too many details.

He was a gentleman, after all.

"Let's just say it went well and she agreed to be my girlfriend again." He finished his story, looking up at her with those warm brown eyes. So happy. So in love...with someone else.

Phoebe sucked in a breath. The air stung her chest. Her heart. Her soul.

Tanner's eyes grew concerned. "Are you okay?"

All sounds of the restaurant were muffled. The only thing she could see was Tanner's worried face. The only thing she could hear was his voice.

"Phoebe? Phoebe?"

Each time he spoke her name, the dull knife of disappointment embedded deeper and deeper into her stomach.

He stood up. She recognized his expression. It was the same expression he had right before he used the Heimlich maneuver on her in his apartment.

"No!" she shouted, holding up her hand to ward him off. He stopped. As did everyone else in the restaurant. "I'm fine. I'm fine," she said, more quietly, trying to ignore the surprised expressions on all of the nameless faces around them. She picked up her water glass. Her hand was trembling. "I just need a drink of water."

Tanner sat back down, but he was on edge.

She managed a few sips of water and several deep breaths. Pain poked her eyes whenever she looked at him, making her wince over and over again. She trained her gaze on the flickering candle on the table between them to stop.

"You look pale. Are you hungry? Do you want some rolls?" he asked.

No. She did not want any rolls. Her stomach roiled, threatening to reject the few sips of water she had managed to drink.

"Um, I..." her voice was barely there. Tanner had to lean

forward to hear her. He was too close. She couldn't bear it. "I need to go to the bathroom."

She pushed away from the table and found her way to the bathroom through eyes filled with tears.

She shoved the door open, sending it crashing into the wall. An old woman standing at the sink washing her hands cried out in surprise.

"Sorry," Phoebe said. Blinded by tears she pushed on the first stall door. It didn't budge. "Sorry," she said to whoever was inside. Her voice choked. The old lady watched her reflection in the mirror as she went to the second stall and found it also in use.

Out of options, Phoebe covered her face with her hands and leaned on the wall in between the hand dryers. She choked again, trying not to let the sobs out. The pressure of keeping everything contained made her throat ache in agony.

"Oh my goodness, dear, what's the matter?" A thin, kind voice said next to her.

Phoebe peeked between her fingers and saw the outline of the little old lady, blurred by her tears. She tried to say she was okay, but only sobs came out. The little old lady made tsk-tsk sounds and patted her shoulder. Her friendly support only made Phoebe cry harder and now that the spigot was open, she lost complete control.

Another woman came out of one of the stalls and washed her hands before asking, "Man trouble?"

The little old lady answered for Phoebe. "Isn't it always?"

The other woman went back into the stall she had just vacated and came out with a handful of toilet paper, handing it to Phoebe with a sympathetic smile, "Here you go, sweetie. Don't let him get you down. There's a lot of fish in the sea, remember that."

Phoebe laughed. A harsh, caustic sound. Was it that obvious? Was she that cliche?

The sobs subsided and she wiped her eyes and blew her nose, thanking the women for their support.

"We've got to help each other out when we can," the old lady said.

"Amen, sister," the younger woman agreed.

"Are you going to be all right? Do you need a ride home? My Fred will bring the car around straight away for us," the old lady offered.

"No, thank you. It's nothing that bad," Phoebe said. She took a shuddering breath and added, "I'm disappointed. That's all."

Another woman, middle aged, exited the second stall and gave Phoebe a sympathetic smile as she washed her hands and left.

The younger woman shook her head in disgust. "Men."

Yes. Men. Ugh.

Phoebe was beginning to understand Bronwyn's attitude toward the male sex.

The other ladies went back to their dinner, leaving her in the bathroom on her own. She washed her face with cold water and dabbed the mascara that had smudged under her eyes when she was crying. She had left the table in such a hurry she hadn't brought her purse.

Not that it mattered if she fixed her makeup. Nothing about tonight mattered anymore.

She adjusted the silk wrap around her shoulders and scowled at her reflection with her hair pulled up like she was going to a wedding and wearing Bronwyn's silver bracelets. What a fool. What a stupid fool to get all dressed up and come to the restaurant like a giddy teenager.

"No more," she said defiantly to her reflection. Leaning into the mirror she glared into her own blue eyes, puffy and red around the edges from crying. "No more," she commanded, then straightened up. Throwing her shoulders back, Phoebe left the bathroom, ready as she would ever be to face Tanner.

"Everything okay?" he asked when she got back to the table.

Phoebe hesitated. She couldn't bring herself to be cold to him, or angry. But she knew she couldn't stay and keep her sanity.

"I'm not feeling well. I think I need to go home," she said.

Tanner was completely obliging. He hurried to pay the bill for their beers and walked with her out of the restaurant. They passed the little old lady and her husband, Fred, who were seated at a table with their meals in front of them.

The little old lady took a moment to look Tanner over, his height, build, and general over the top attractiveness registering on her face. Then she locked eyes with Phoebe, giving her a knowing look and a sad, but encouraging, smile.

Thirty-Seven

Bronwyn

When Bronwyn heard Phoebe's car pull into the drive she looked up in surprise. Catching Violet's eye, they both stood up from the couch where they had been watching a movie.

"That can't be good," Bronwyn said.

The words had barely escaped her lips when Phoebe came through the front door and spilled into the living room, a blubbering mess.

"What happened?" Violet asked, alarmed.

Bronwyn knew. Deep down in her bones she knew what could cause that kind of emotion, that uncontrollable sadness.

Heartbreak.

"Oh my God, what did he do to you?" Bronwyn took hold of Phoebe's arm and led her weeping form to the couch.

Phoebe slumped into the couch, laying her head back against

the cushions and covering her face with her hands. Sobbing so hard she couldn't answer.

Bronwyn and Violet sat on either side of her. The romantic comedy they had been watching still played. Violet grabbed the remote and put it on pause. She grabbed a box of tissues from the side table and offered them to their broken hearted friend. Phoebe took several and used them to wipe her tears. Her sobs began to subside.

"Phoebe, what is going on? What happened?" Violet asked again. Still, Phoebe couldn't answer.

Bronwyn set her jaw. Furious at Tanner and whatever he had done to put Phoebe in such a state. The poor girl's face was bright red and puffed out from crying, her eyes were swollen, makeup streamed down her face, her body was limp and weak. She had given up on life because of him. His ripped abs and winning smile had crushed Phoebe, a strong and intelligent woman, into a useless pile of emotional goo.

Bronwyn stood abruptly and went to the bathroom. She grabbed a wash cloth from the shelf and ran cold water over it until it was soaked. Then she squeezed the extra water out and brought it back to the living room.

"Here, lay your head back," she said.

Phoebe did as she was told and Bronwyn placed the cool, wet cloth on her forehead. Phoebe closed her eyes again.

"I'll get you some water," Violet said, hurrying away.

To the sounds of ice crunching out of the dispenser in the kitchen, Bronwyn studied Phoebe's despondent face.

She recognized this face. Had seen it countless times in her mirror. In other women she had loved. Her mother. Her sister. Hearts broken, souls crushed, the anguish and defeat of love found and love lost. Bronwyn had only one response, a cold, quiet block of anger in the pit of her stomach.

"Drink this," Violet offered Phoebe a glass of ice water.

Phoebe's sobbing was over. She took the wash cloth off of her forehead and wiped her eyes and cheeks with it, then used the tissues to blow her nose.

She reached out for the ice water. "Thanks," she said, her voice wet and grim. After taking a sip, she sighed and dabbed at her eyes with fresh tissues. Taking in a deep breath, she answered their original questions on the exhale, "Tonight was not a date. He's getting back together with Layla."

Two surprising revelations. Two shocks to Phoebe's system. Delivered by a clueless pretty boy who picked up and shed women as easily as he changed swim trunks, Bronwyn bet.

"Oh, Phoebe, that's terrible," Violet was all tenderness and compassion.

The block of anger in Bronwyn's gut grew harder. Larger. Colder.

Her instinct was to go grab the wine and bring three glasses to the living room so they could help Phoebe drown her sorrows. But she had sworn off liquor for a few days after her near fainting spell with Bill. And when she reconsidered the idea, she realized she didn't really want a strong drink anyway.

She didn't think Phoebe would benefit from one either.

What was required right now was good old fashioned emotional release. For Phoebe, certainly, but also for herself.

"How did he tell you? What did he say?" she asked, hoping Phoebe could talk it out of her system.

Once she started talking, much like when she started crying, Phoebe couldn't stop. She began by describing her entry into the restaurant and the way he was dressed. The light conversation and how she almost called him 'honey'.

Bronwyn and Violet cringed in unison at that little piece of information.

Phoebe went on. Telling them how he told her that the picnic date had surprisingly worked and he and Layla were back together. Her emotional melt down in the women's bathroom. The kind women who helped her. And the drive home where she had to pull off to the side of the road once because she was crying so hard.

"You never told him that you thought it was a date, right?" Bronwyn verified.

"No, I told him I didn't feel good. That's all."

"Good," Bronwyn said.

"Why is that good?" Violet asked.

"Because you don't want him to know all of this," Bronwyn waved the fingers of one hand at Phoebe sitting on the couch. "He shouldn't get that satisfaction."

Phoebe and Violet both looked at her in surprise.

"I don't think he would get any satisfaction out of seeing Phoebe this way," Violet disagreed.

"He didn't know," Phoebe said.

"He didn't know what?" Bronwyn asked defiantly. "That calling up a single woman and asking her out to dinner couldn't be seen as a date? That having a woman help you set up a date for someone else couldn't possibly be overstepping boundaries? That he was using you?"

Phoebe opened her mouth to defend Tanner then closed it again. Her brow knit together in confusion. "Do you really think he knew?"

Violet shot Bronwyn a disapproving look. "You don't know that he knew." She turned back to Phoebe. "He could be thinking of your relationship as a friendship. That's all. I've had close relationships with guys that cross the boundary and get confusing."

Phoebe sniffled. "I don't like to think of him as insincere."

"How about this? Why don't you not think about him at all?" Bronwyn suggested, wishing Phoebe could step up and face life with a little bit more assertiveness. "You are a beautiful, intelligent, wonderful woman, Phoebe. You shouldn't be wasting your time on anyone who can't see that."

"I agree with that one hundred percent," Violet said.

Phoebe smiled weakly at them both. "I am a little tired of thinking about all of it."

"Then let's do something else. How about a movie?" Bronwyn picked up the remote. "But not a romance. This is not a romance kind of night. Something else that will take you somewhere else. Somewhere out of your head." She clicked the romantic comedy off and started flipping through their options.

"I'll make some popcorn. Does that sound good?" Violet asked.

Phoebe nodded. She watched the movies scroll by with Bronwyn.

"Wow," Bronwyn said. "There are a lot of movies with a heavy romantic element."

Phoebe laughed a little at the comment. It was good to know she could laugh already.

"Oh! How about this one?" Bronwyn paused her scrolling.

"Alien?" Phoebe asked.

"Have you seen it?" Bronwyn doubted Phoebe had. She was a little bit too young and very much into regency romances. She had probably seen Pride and Prejudice twenty times, but never Alien.

"I haven't," Phoebe said.

"I haven't either," Violet said, returning to the living room with a huge bowl of hot popcorn and some sodas.

"Do you want to watch it? It's good. And it will definitely take your mind off of everything else," Bronwyn reassured them.

"Sure, why not?" Phoebe answered.

Soon they were settled in with their popcorn and drinks and one of the best sci-fi movies ever made. Bronwyn felt a little bit like a den mother having taken care of her chicks. As they watched Sigourney Weaver play one of the most badass women ever to fly into outer space, Bronwyn couldn't help but smile to herself.

If her Aphrodite friends stuck with her, they could all leave these selfish men behind in the dust.

Thirty-Eight

Phoebe

It was a rainy day in Turtle Cove. Not the normal sunshine good for going to the beach and playing in the water. But a dark stormy day that suited Phoebe just fine. It matched her mood.

Clouds muted the sun and turned the sky, the sand, the sea, even the beach house, varying shades of grey. Phoebe stood at the window overlooking the deck, watching sheets of rain drop, washing away every remaining ounce of joy out of her body.

She hugged her sweater close. Sol Mate may have heat, but they didn't know how to turn it on. They had never thought there might be a need for it over the summer months. The chill from the rain had seeped through the walls of the beach house over night and Phoebe had resorted to putting on a sweatshirt and sweat pants, socks, and a heavy black sweater.

The look suited her mood as well. Frumpy, dumpy, and dark.

She sighed for the umpteenth time that morning and half expected the empty house to echo a response. Violet had left early to help at Marine Life Rescue and Bronwyn had gone to town to pick up her altered pantsuit and grab some groceries. She had said something about feeding them for optimum emotional and physical health before she left, but Phoebe didn't know what that meant exactly.

Both of them had been reluctant to leave her behind and both had asked if she wanted to join them.

"No, thanks, you go ahead," she had answered, each time. And when they hesitated, unsure if they should abandon her in her fragile state Phoebe had reassured them. "I'm fine."

And she was fine. Physically at least.

Her mind was numb, unable to think much about anything. She hadn't gotten out her laptop to write yet and didn't think she would. It would be too hard to come up with words and consider sentence structure. Too hard to think about the Colonel.

Rain drummed on the roof and ran down the windows. Phoebe had cried so much yesterday, finally stopping when she watched the movie with Bronwyn and Violet, but then starting again after she went to bed. Rivers of tears. She was all cried out, but now the sky was crying for her.

She turned away from the window and went to the living room. Soon the rain would be over and there would be no more tears at all. Just emptiness.

She picked up the remote then reconsidered and tossed it aside. She pulled one of the soft fluffy throws from the back of the couch over her body. With the chill warded off and the sound of the rain maybe she could sleep. Drift away into unconsciousness.

And she did drift, for a while. The drumming of the rain grew louder then softer. Louder then softer. Until Phoebe realized it wasn't the sound of rain, but the sound of someone knocking on the door.

Keeping her blanket wrapped around her already bundled up body, Phoebe went to the door and peeked through the peephole.

It was Tanner.

Elation and despair flared through her at the same time.

Beginning at some center point in her core and racing out through every cell and every inch of her skin. With her eye glued to the peephole her breath came shallow and fast and she would have sworn the floor was falling away underneath her feet.

Tanner's distorted image, still perfect in every way, reached up and knocked again.

Phoebe caught her breath in her throat. She was so close to the door that she felt each knock as a tremor in her body. Every muscle was frozen in place. She could not respond.

He raised his arm once more, but did not knock, only let it hang there in the air. Hesitating for a reason unknown to her. She watched. Entranced by her view of him. A view that did not require she look away.

Tanner's hand dropped back to his side. Disappointed? Maybe. But certainly ready to leave.

Fear flashed through her now. Fear that he would turn to go and she wouldn't be able to get the door open fast enough.

She grabbed the handle and pulled, feigning surprise at seeing him.

"Tanner," she said, a little breathless. That was okay. Breathless meant she could have been hurrying to answer the door and not standing on the other side staring at him through the peephole.

"Hey, Phoebe," he said, taking in her bundled appearance, unkempt hair and red swollen eyes and nose. "How are you feeling? I was a little worried after last night."

Last night. Last night came back, blasting through her mind like a sudden destructive wind. But she kept her cool, stepping back to let him in out of the weather.

"I'm okay now. Feeling a lot better," she answered. Though by the look on his face she didn't think he completely believed her.

He stepped into the foyer. His hair damp from the rain. He wore jeans and a hoodie from his EMT school, which were also wet with rain.

"Good, that's good," he said as she shut the door. He rubbed his hands up and down his own arms. "It's kinda cold in here, isn't it?"

"It is, but I think it's just because of the rain."

Tanner didn't agree. "It's colder in here than outside. Is your furnace working?"

Phoebe shrugged. "I don't know. I don't know how to turn it on."

"I can take a look if you want," he offered.

She agreed and Tanner walked into the beach house, scanning the walls. He located the thermostat and leaned down to read it. "58 degrees! No wonder you're wearing a blanket."

Phoebe wondered what he would think if he knew the real reason she was wrapped in a blanket and all of her most comfortable clothes.

"I'm gonna check your pilot light," Tanner told her then disappeared into the basement.

Phoebe stood in the middle of the hallway gripping her blanket with such ferocity a hurricane could not budge it off her shoulders. The way he moved with such ease through the space surrounding her, unaware that everything he did burned a new and more painful memory into her heart, rendered her nearly immobile.

Tanner caring about how she feels. Tanner checking on the furnace. The kinds of things she dreamed he would do because he loved her. But he was only doing them to be polite. A nice guy who had been taught basic manners, blissfully unaware that he was destroying her happiness in the process.

He popped out of the basement, his brow furrowed with concern. "The pilot light is on. I don't know why it's not pushing out warm air." Phoebe didn't know either. "I'll let Bill know for you, if you don't mind."

"Sure," she said. She had almost forgotten Tanner knew their landlord. "Um, do you want something to drink? I could make some hot tea. Ward off the cold."

"No, don't bother. I've got to get going."

"Right, you have class today don't you?" Phoebe cringed at how much she knew about his life. How much she cared.

"I do, but that's later. I'm meeting my aunt for coffee. The one that's a publisher. Did I tell you about her?"

"Yes, I think you did."

"Her and my mom do a coffee thing once a month. Every now and then they make me join them," he smiled sheepishly.

Phoebe needed him to leave. She couldn't be around his politeness, his sweet relationship with his mother, or his dimpled smile any longer.

"Okay, well..." she glanced down the hall toward the front door.

"Right, well, I'm glad you're okay. And stay warm. I'll let Bill know the heat's not pumping correctly."

"Thank you," Phoebe said.

Right before he opened the front door, Tanner turned around and said, "And I still owe you a celebration dinner. When you're feeling up to it."

"Okay," was all Phoebe could say.

Then he left, closing the door to her heart behind him.

Thirty-Nine

Violet

Violet felt a little guilty.

She had spent the morning at Marine Life Rescue with Ben and Bear, and was having so much fun she completely forgot about Phoebe's troubles. She couldn't help but get swept away in the planning of the fundraiser. It was like planning a party for her class of students, but with a lot more money and for adults.

"Look at this," Ben had turned his laptop screen toward her the moment she walked in the door. "It's called Eco Party Time and they've got all the stuff."

By stuff, Ben meant plates and napkins, eating utensils, and other basic decorations. They had already received offers from different local restaurants to provide the food and only had to go over the menu, but they needed party supplies so guests had something to eat the food with.

"And," Ben said with excitement. "Shore is Sweet is donating the cake!"

"That's great, Ben," Violet answered. Shore is Sweet made delicious pastries. She couldn't wait to taste their cake.

Marine Life Rescue had received some cash donations specifically for the party and she and Ben used that to shop at Eco Party Time.

"Look at this palm leaf tableware. It's really neat. Do you think it looks too rustic?" Violet pointed to the images of the plates and bowls that were 100% organic and compostable. Made from dried palm leaves they almost looked like they were made out of wood.

"Let me look," Ben got up from his chair and bent down behind Violet to look over her shoulder. "Those are nice," he said.

"They have bamboo too, and some made from sugar cane, but the palm leaf style have more of a beach-vibe, don't you think?"

"I will let you make the final decisions on how everything looks," Ben said. "I don't have a designing bone in my body."

Violet laughed. "Okay, palm leaf plates and bowls, utensils made from cornstarch, they're completely biodegradable, clear cups made from compostable corn plastic. I've never heard of those before. And what about these plastic free home compostable napkins and table cloths?" She flipped her laptop around this time so he could see it.

"Those look great," he smiled. "I'll be glad if we can do everything eco-friendly. Especially since this year's our biggest yet. It would be kind of stupid to throw a huge fundraiser to save marine life and end up trashing the beach."

Violet nodded, she was studying the options on the website. "Oh look! They have a sea turtle pattern!"

"We have to have those, right?" Ben asked.

"Absolutely," Violet pondered over some of the other decoration options. "We need something to go with the lights."

A few of the boutique shops in Turtle Cove were donating

dozens and dozens of solar powered lights that they would string up over the food tables and the dance floor. But lights alone seemed a little dull for a party.

"Here," Violet pointed at her screen. "We could order some of this tissue tassel garland in beachy colors to string with the lights."

"Sounds great," Ben agreed. "Is that all?"

"I think that will work. Like you said, we don't want to trash the beach."

"And we'll have the bonfire at the far end, plus the bands," Ben reminded her.

Two different bands were donating their performances to the fundraiser. One and a half hour shows each. And they were bringing all of their own equipment and lights. All Marine Life Rescue had to do was put down rugs over the sand where they would be setting up. Ben already had the rugs from previous fundraisers.

"I'll place this order. Then what's next?" Violet asked.

"We need to choose the menu so we can let the restaurants know." Bear barked from underneath the table.

Violet laughed, "Bear agrees."

"Bear agrees with anything to do with food," Ben said.

Bear wasn't wrong to be excited. Each restaurant had sent Ben a list of possible finger food and he was to let them know one main savory choice and a vegetarian to match, and one side. They sat side-by-side and perused the lists.

"Man, this is making me hungry," Ben admitted before they had even finished reading through half of the items.

Before Violet could comment Ben's phone rang.

"Hello? Yes...yes, thank you...okay...oh, wow, that's great," he looked at Violet though he was still talking on the phone. "Hang on, let me check something." He took the phone away from his ear and laid it on the table to muffle their conversation, then turned his dancing eyes to her. "Do you want to go taste cake with me? Shore is Sweet has some samples ready for us."

"Of course!" she answered.

Sensing her excitement, Bear barked from underneath the table again.

Ben drove them to Shore is Sweet in his little truck while Violet read the food choices out loud.

"We've narrowed it down to fish tacos and tofu tacos plus grilled pineapple from Poseidon's," she said.

"Sounds delicious."

"And Cobalt Edge will do crab cakes, cauliflower fritters and single shrimp in a cucumber cup with white cocktail sauce and a sprig of dill."

"Mmm, sounds fancy," Ben said.

Violet giggled. Ben was always full of silly little comments and was so positive about everything. Planning this big event could have been a nightmare, but he made everything easy and enjoyable.

"It will be a little fancy. That's okay for such a special occasion. I'm really excited to see how the cake turns out," Violet said.

Silence fell over them as Ben drove.

He slowed down to turn on the street where Shore Is Sweet was located. Out of nowhere he asked, "They do cake tasting for engaged couples when they're going to order a cake for their wedding, right?"

"Um, yes, I think they do," Violet said.

Ben glanced at her, "Have you ever done that?"

Uncertain what he was asking, she answered his question with a question. "Ordered a cake for a wedding?"

"Or done the whole engaged thing? Not married, or divorced I guess," he awkwardly tried to explain. Violet's surprise and confusion must have shown on her face, because he added quickly, "I'm not asking if you've been married or divorced or whatever. Not to be too personal." His cheeks reddened and Violet realized he must be curious about her personal background.

Her cheeks grew warm, but she was flattered at his interest. She wasn't sure how to take it. She wasn't easily pulled into relationships, she had learned the hard way what can happen when you jump into something. Plus everything she'd learned from watching Phoebe warned her that even though a guy is friendly and attentive doesn't mean he's that into you.

Either way, she didn't like to watch Ben squirm, so she answered his question, "I've never been engaged or married, so not divorced either. But I have known people planning weddings who go to the bakery and taste cake."

They were pulling into Shore Is Sweet and Ben's relief at her answering his odd question with a direct, unemotional response was palpable. Amused at his nervousness, Violet didn't say anything when he gallantly opened the bakery door and stood just behind her to her left once inside, the classic body language of a couple.

"Bonnie," Ben said to the woman behind the counter. "We're here for the cake testing."

Bonnie had dark skin, hair, and eyes and wore deep red lipstick, which only accentuated her warm smile. "Hello, Ben, who is this you have with you?"

"This is Violet, she works with me. For us. For Marine Life Rescue," Ben's awkwardness from the car returned.

"I'm a volunteer," Violet told Bonnie. "I'm helping plan the party."

"Very nice to meet you. I have some cake samples ready for you. Please have a seat," Bonnie said.

Ben guided Violet to a two person table in the window of the bakery and they sat down.

"It's so cute in here," Violet said, looking around at the pink and cream decor.

Ben grunted in agreement, but didn't look around. He didn't look at her either. He stared at the surface of the table. Uneasy. His normal fun and casual demeanor gone.

"Two samples of each of our summer flavors," Bonnie announced as she placed a tray with individual bite sized pieces of cake, each served in a small paper cup made for cupcakes. "There's almond cake with passionfruit filling, lemon cake with lemon curd filling, coconut cake with mango curd filling, vanilla cake with raspberry filling, and chocolate cake with strawberry filling."

Ben finally looked at Violet and his eyes were wide with delight. "I'm in heaven," he said, reaching for the almond with passionfruit sample.

"Wait," Violet said. He paused and watched her search through her purse and pull out a small pad of paper and a pen. "We're going to keep track of what we think of each one. Otherwise we won't remember."

"Good idea," Ben beamed at her, all uneasiness gone.

They tasted each flavor carefully, then rated them from one to ten and wrote the number down. They didn't agree on all of them, but when they were finished there were two clear winners.

"Almond with passionfruit and coconut with mango," Violet announced. "Can we have two flavors?"

"It's going to be a big cake, maybe we can," Ben added.

Bonnie returned to offer them a cup of coffee and check on their taste testing. When they asked her if they could have two flavors she said, "I can do anything you want. Whatever you need to save the dolphins, I'm in."

With the tasting over they relaxed with their coffee. Ben seemed much more himself. Still, the strange fluctuation in his mood still needled at Violet. So much so that she decided to come out and ask him about it.

"You seemed kind of nervous when we first got here," Violet said, carefully watching his reaction. He didn't flinch or frown or look away, so she continued. "Were you?"

Ben looked at her with admiration. "You're very observant, aren't you?"

"If you don't want to talk about it, that's fine. I was just wondering, that's all."

"No, no, no, I can answer your question." He shifted his eyes from hers and looked around the room as if searching for the right words. When he found them he turned his gaze back to her. "I was engaged once. A few years ago."

Violet wasn't sure what she had expected to hear, but that wasn't it.

Ben sucked air through his teeth and dropped his gaze to his coffee cup. "We dated in college and after...and it seemed like the logical next step." He lifted his eyes to hers. "But it wasn't good. It never had been a good relationship and we had to...well, I had to end it. And she didn't take it well." He looked away again. "It was pretty bad."

"I'm sorry," Violet said. She was sorry. Sorry he had gone through a bad breakup and sorry she had brought it up and forced him to talk about something that obviously bothered him.

"All things wedding related kind of get me worked up, you know?" he said, looking at her for understanding.

Violet swallowed. "I can see why."

He held her gaze for a long moment and in that moment Violet understood.

She understood completely.

Ben wasn't interested in being in a relationship. He was a great guy, but a great guy that just wanted to be friends.

Forty

Bronwyn

It seemed to Bronwyn that she returned to Sol Mate just in time. Even though she was laden down with several bags of organic groceries she could still clearly see that Phoebe was barely holding herself together and Violet had returned from volunteering with a sullen face.

"No fear, Aphrodites, I have gotten all of the best for us tonight," Bronwyn declared, waving off their offers of assistance as she lugged the bags to the kitchen and piled them on the island. "No, no, I've got it covered. I know exactly what we need to get us through our current crisis. Modern day comfort food."

To her own delight, if not the others, Bronwyn pulled out each item she had purchased and showed it off. "I've got everything to make spinach quesadillas, shrimp tortellini alfredo, and dark chocolate chip cookies."

Phoebe offered a weak smile. "Sounds good."

Unfazed by the less than robust reaction, Bronwyn continued, "And I went by the deli to get their New England clam chowder with oyster crackers, the fat ones, and a beautiful fruit tart." Bronwyn pulled out the fruit tart piled high with raspberries, blueberries, and strawberries, all enclosed in a clear plastic dome.

Phoebe and Violet were beginning to perk up.

"This is a lot of food," Violet said.

Bronwyn raised her eyebrows and considered the comment. "Okay, not exactly doing cartwheels, but it's something." She continued putting food away, leaving the clam chowder and crackers out on the counter. The rainy day had left the house cold and that would be a perfect first course to get them warmed up. "Oh, I almost forgot!" She looked around for another brown paper sack. Reaching into the sack she grinned and asked, "Guess what else I got?"

Phoebe and Violet exchanged a look then answered in unison, "Wine."

"Very funny. It's not wine." She pulled a box from Shore Is Sweet out of the bag. "Lemon blueberry muffins for breakfast." Folding the bag up to put in the recycle bin, Bronwyn added, "I've decided to cut back on wine for the time being."

Phoebe gave her a genuine smile. "Good for you."

Violet, on the other hand, looked a little ashen.

"I think we could all use some hot food, don't you? It's cold in here," Bronwyn shivered. "I'll just warm this up in–" There was a knock on the door. Phoebe winced at the sound and Violet didn't seem up to greeting a visitor either. "I'll get it. Do you girls want to get this clam chowder warmed up?" She smiled encouragingly at them. just like she would if her boys were having a bad day.

When Bronwyn pulled the door open she was shocked to find Bill on the other side.

"Bill? What are you doing here?"

He smiled, a real smile, not one of his surly half mouth smiles. "Hi Bronwyn, I've come to take a look at the furnace."

"Oh?" Bronwyn looked behind her then back at him. "Is there something wrong with it?"

Bill stepped inside the foyer. He was holding a toolbox and had to maneuver it as he walked past in such a way that their bodies almost grazed. "Yup, Tanner called and said it wasn't blowing heat."

"Tanner?" Bronwyn was baffled. "How would Tanner know?"

Bill shrugged, apparently unaware of any drama surrounding the lifeguard and Phoebe. "I don't know, he just told me so I'm here."

"It is cold in here," she said, but she was only repeating what she had said in the kitchen, because standing with Bill in the foyer, Bronwyn was suddenly warmer.

"That it is," he agreed.

"Hi Bill," Phoebe said from the kitchen, giving him a small wave.

"Hi Phoebe, just here to look at the furnace." Phoebe nodded as if she had been expecting him. He looked at Bronwyn who remained awkwardly poised at the front door. "Do you mind? It shouldn't take long."

Bronwyn shook herself out of the daze that had fallen over her when she saw him. "Of course, do what you need to do." Then as he turned to make his way to the basement she added, "We have soup. Or, actually, chowder." He looked back at her. "If you're hungry."

He grinned. "Thank you, it smells good. I'll check on this first."

The chowder did smell good. New England clam chowder was always one of her favorites. But she found that she couldn't eat much of it while she waited for Bill to come back up from the basement.

"I feel the warm air now," Violet said. She was sitting closest to the vent. "He must have fixed it. It's a wonder you didn't freeze today, Phoebe."

Phoebe was wrapped up in one of the throws from the couch

eating her chowder. "I had this blanket on all day, so it was hard to tell."

Bronwyn fiddled with her spoon and glanced at the basement door every two seconds. She suppressed the urge to yell down the stairs to see when he would be up so she could fix him a bowl of chowder. It was her domestic training to always feed the man in the house, no matter who the man was or what he was doing.

Finally the door opened and Bill appeared. She was unprepared for how she felt when she saw him. His brawny form, the capable way he handled his toolbox, the steady look in his eyes when she caught his attention, all combined and triggered a reaction.

Bronwyn felt safe.

"All done?" Phoebe asked. Her mood had lightened since she started eating. The poor thing hadn't eaten properly since yesterday.

"Yup, should be good now," Bill answered, entering the kitchen. "That furnace has some odd ticks to it, but I can usually fix it right up. If that happens again, don't hesitate to let me know." He peered out the French doors at the sun peeking through clouds just in time for sunset. "I think we're out of the woods on this storm, though. It stopped raining on my way over."

This might have been the most Bronwyn ever heard Bill speak. He had a good voice. Deep and pleasant. When he looked her way she startled. She had been staring at him.

"I'll get you a bowl of chowder," she said, abruptly getting up from her chair.

"No, thanks. I'm not all that hungry right now. I'm gonna do a quick check on those windows upstairs if you don't mind. Because of the rain."

"Of course," Bronwyn answered, though she felt agitated.

With Bill upstairs, they finished their chowder. Bronwyn not quite, but she was done eating. Her stomach was tight.

"That was great, but I'm a little full to eat anything else very soon," Violet said. "Were you planning on making the shrimp tortellini tonight?"

"Let's go to the beach," Bronwyn suggested. "Take a walk."

Phoebe looked surprised. "It's raining."

"It stopped. Look, the clouds are clearing up," Bronwyn motioned out the French doors. "We'll be the only people out there. It will be like our own private island."

"We can wear layers," Violet suggested.

It turned out they didn't need them. The storm had moved on and taken the brisk cold with it. The breeze off the ocean was cool, but not too cool. By the time they had gone ten minutes all three of them had taken off their outer layer to let the ocean breeze cool them.

"This is remarkable," Phoebe looked up and down the beach. "Not a soul in sight."

Bronwyn didn't mention that even the lifeguards were not at their posts. She didn't want to bring up that fresh wound.

"I guess the rain chased everyone away," Violet added. She turned her face toward the sunset. "Look at that. It's magical."

Clouds still lingered in the sky, allowing the setting sun to paint them glorious colors. It was the most brilliant sunset Bronwyn had ever seen.

"Let's swim," she said, excited at the idea.

"I didn't wear my suit, did you?" Violet asked.

Bronwyn had not. Phoebe shook her head 'no'. But Bronwyn had an even better idea.

"We'll skinny dip!" she declared.

"What!?" Phoebe was beyond shocked.

"I don't think–" Violet started to protest, but Bronwyn stopped her.

"There is nobody here. Absolutely nobody." She punctuated her statement by spreading her arms wide and looking up and down the isolated beach. "We're out of sight of Sol Mate and all of the beach houses here." Then she swept her arms toward the sunset. "When in your life are you going to have the chance to swim in the ocean under this sky again?"

Violet screwed her face up, but followed Bronwyn's direction to look at the sky. "It will be dark enough soon. If somebody does come along," she said.

Phoebe looked at them like they were both crazy. "Skinny dipping? Really?"

Bronwyn laughed. "Yes, really!" She dropped the sweater she'd been carrying on the sand and pulled off her shirt. "Once you're in the water nobody can see anything anyway."

Violet laughed nervously, but she started pulling her clothes off as well.

"You two are insane," Phoebe said with disbelief.

Bronwyn and Violet kept stripping, giggling the whole time.

"Come on, Phoebe," Bronwyn urged. She stood in front of Phoebe with only her underwear and bra on. "You've got to ask yourself, what would Aphrodite do?" Then, with a daring smile, she took off the rest of her underthings and ran into the waves.

Violet followed, squealing as the waves hit higher and higher on her body then finally jumping in with abandon. She popped up out of the water near Bronwyn, her face full of joy.

The colors of the sunset reflected on the surface of the water and they were swimming in a sea of pink, gold, orange, and blue. Magical didn't begin to cover it.

"I can't believe I'm doing this. I can't believe I'm doing this. I can't believe I'm doing this," Phoebe's voice carried over the water as she hurriedly took off her clothes.

"Woohoo, Phoebe!" Bronwyn cried out, raising her fists in the air when Phoebe's naked form dove into the waves.

She surfaced and let out a squeal, making Violet and Bronwyn laugh with delight.

"Look at you, you're skinny dipping!" Violet said to Phoebe.

Phoebe laughed, her lips were trembling. Maybe from the cold, but Bronwyn had seen that happen plenty of times on her boys. Not when they were cold, but when they were beyond excited.

"Yes, look at me," Phoebe said with a nervous laugh.

"Look at us!" Bronwyn shouted to the sky. "The Mighty Aphrodites!"

Violet and Phoebe answered together, "The Mighty Aphrodites!"

They swam and laughed in the water shining gold under the sunset. The power of the ocean cradling them as waves buoyed them up and down.

Bronwyn relished the feel of saltwater on her whole body, unencumbered by a swimsuit. Surprising how much different nature felt when it was experienced without clothes.

The sun dipped further down and the golden sheen disappeared, but Bronwyn knew she would never forget what her friends looked like during that swim. Like beautiful mermaids floating on an enchanted sea.

"Look!" Phoebe pointed in alarm at an elderly couple walking on the beach with two dogs running ahead of them.

"Oh no!" Violet cried out.

"We better get our clothes before the dogs find them," Bronwyn said, the idea making her laugh.

They all laughed and squealed as they hurried out of the water and tried to put dry clothes on wet skin. Not a smooth and easy task, made even more difficult by the fact that they were cracking up laughing.

"There, we're safe," Bronwyn declared when they were dressed, taking a look down the beach. The elderly couple weren't too close, but they had almost certainly seen them in their birthday suits. Bronwyn pretended not to notice. She didn't want Phoebe to know.

The sun said its final goodbye as they walked back to Sol Mate.

Phoebe chuckled and said, "Bronwyn, I must say, you are really good at helping someone forget their troubles."

Bronwyn thought that might be the nicest thing anyone had said to her in a while and she almost got choked up, but she didn't want the light mood to break. "There's a reason I was voted PTA Mother of the Month last November," she quipped.

Violet and Phoebe both laughed then Violet asked, "Were you really?"

Bronwyn grinned. "Yes, but it's not what it sounds like. They hand those awards out to almost anybody."

Again, they all laughed. They were still laughing and talking when they rounded the low bluff that hid Sol Mate from their view. The lights were on and Bronwyn was surprised to see a man's form standing on the deck.

It must be Bill.

But as they got closer she could see it wasn't Bill's silhouette. It wasn't Tanner's either, her second guess.

"Who's that?" Phoebe asked just as Bronwyn recognized the slender frame and disappointed hunch in the form's shoulders.

Her stomach sank. Ryan.

Forty-One

Violet

Violet was just as surprised as Phoebe to find Bronwyn's husband waiting for her at Sol Mate. But neither of them were as surprised as Bronwyn herself.

Their friendly conversation as they walked back to the beach house ended abruptly once Bronwyn recognized him. The positive mood Bronwyn had worked so hard to build in all of them dissolved in a matter of seconds.

"That's my husband," Bronwyn said, her voice not much more than a whisper. Not a very Bronwyn-like remark.

Introductions were stilted, conversation was awkward, and as Violet watched Bronwyn and her husband quietly go upstairs to her room together, she had an unshakeable feeling of loss. Something told her the Bronwyn they had grown to know and had started to truly appreciate on their writing retreat was not going to be the same after this night.

"That was rather unpleasant, wasn't it?" Phoebe asked quietly.

"Very," Violet answered. "She definitely wasn't expecting him."

"No," Phoebe glanced up the stairs. "Do you think she's okay?"

"No, but I don't think there's much we can do to help while he's here."

"I wonder how long he'll stay," Phoebe said.

Violet had never had an aversion to the idea of marriage. She had known plenty of married couples who were happy, her parents and other family members included, but Bronwyn's situation was different. She hoped, for her sake, that Ryan wouldn't stay.

"What if he wants to stay a while?" Phoebe asked, a look of dread in her eyes.

"I think we should wait and see what things look like in the morning before we get too concerned," Violet said.

They cleaned up the kitchen together. Still no sign of Bronwyn.

"I think I'm going to go to bed," Phoebe announced. "I'm tired and everything feels a little...strange."

Violet agreed. "I'm pretty wiped out, too. Skinny dipping took a lot of energy," she smiled.

Phoebe chuckled. "Yeah, I'm glad we went though."

"Me, too," Violet said.

Up in her room, the house seemed eerily silent given there was a visitor. Even though she had said she was tired, Violet didn't think she could go to sleep. The expression on Bronwyn's face when she saw her husband, the way they had looked at each other, her wary, him irritated, their silent ascent to Bronwyn's bedroom, Violet couldn't get it out of her head.

She decided to treat herself to a bath with candles and some classical music. Candles lit, earbuds in, she soaked for a while thoroughly washing all of the saltwater off of her skin and out of her hair. When the water turned too cool to be comfortable, she got out and dried herself with a big fluffy towel. Putting on moisturizer and lotion, dressing in her comfortable pajamas, and brushing out her hair, Violet still couldn't shake the sense of sadness Bronwyn's transformation had caused.

What would it be like to be in an unhappy marriage? How miserable does someone need to be before they release themselves from that obligation? Her mind wandered back to her relationship with Toby and Violet knew the answer to that question. Completely miserable. People stayed in unhappy marriages every day.

Of course, she and Toby had never been married, thank goodness. And if she had been older it may have been easier for her to get away from him and out from under his influence, but what would she do if she was ever in Bronwyn's shoes? A cheating husband. Young children. Bronwyn had a lot of hard choices to make.

Violet shuddered at the thought. She didn't want to entertain the idea of having that experience. Propping up all of the pillows so she could sit up in bed, she pulled her laptop onto her lap, still pondering what her fate would be if she were ever to marry and have her husband cheat.

"I would leave him, that's all," she muttered as she lifted the screen. "Or, better yet, never marry someone like that in the first place."

Her documents popped open on her laptop and she was greeted with her most recent article for the newspaper. A piece on dolphins that she had been working on for a few days. It was almost ready.

Violet smiled. The images of the dolphins she had found for inspiration surrounded the text document. She learned so many depressing things about commercial fishing during her research, but there was also inspirational news about attempts to help the dolphin population. She liked to include both the negative and the positive in her articles so people knew there were actions they could take to help. The animals were fascinating to learn about and knowing they existed in the great big world made her happy.

A thought struck her as she settled into finishing up the article so she could send it to the Cove Gazette in the morning. Animals filled her with joy. Seeing them, interacting with them, learning about them, helping them, everything about them lifted her mood whenever she was low. They inspired her to do more. To be more.

Maybe she wasn't cut out to get married and have kids. Being a teacher had made her second guess any previous desire she thought she'd had about raising a family. As much as she tried to connect to her students and failed, after working for Marine Life Rescue and using her writing skills to help animals all summer, she suddenly realized maybe she simply wasn't a people person. Maybe her calling was to work with animals instead.

Her sudden lift in spirits was dulled when she remembered the job waiting for her after this writing retreat was over. She had signed a contract to teach again for the coming school year and she didn't want to let the school down or make them flounder looking for a last minute replacement.

She sighed and zeroed in on one dolphin picture in particular where the dolphin was poking it's head up out of the water and engaging with the photographer. It was almost like the animal was looking directly at her, trying to make her smile again.

"You're right," she said to the image. "I can teach this year and work on making a change in careers. Maybe I could teach biology," she said then immediately made a face. That would mean going back to college. Still, it was a thought.

She clicked on her dolphin article to bring it front and center. None of that had to be decided right now. For the time being she had her marine life articles to work on and, even better, she wasn't dealing with a broken marriage. So, really, Violet did not have any reason to feel glum. In fact, she had a lot going for her and even more on the way.

Bronwyn

"Getting a lot of writing done, are you?" Ryan asked the moment the bedroom door clicked shut behind them.

Bronwyn glared at him. Her hair was still dripping from swimming and her clothes hung in disarray from getting dressed in such a hurry.

"What are you doing here?" she asked.

Ryan scanned the room. Looking for what, she didn't know.

"I wanted to come and see you," he said, still scanning. "See what you've been doing on your summer vacation."

She scowled, but she didn't want to have a fight with Violet and Phoebe so near. "You could have called to let me know."

"I did."

Fury at his glib answer boiled inside her belly, even though she knew he wasn't lying. She didn't have her phone on her. It was still in her purse. And she had been so busy grocery shopping all that afternoon it was entirely likely she had not seen his call. Still, she was angry at his intrusion into her space. Her writing retreat sacred space.

"Who was the guy that was here?" Ryan asked, catching her by surprise.

"What guy?" She knew what guy.

"The guy that was here when I got here," Ryan said evenly, watching her reaction with quiet interest.

Bronwyn felt like a witness being questioned by a cold, calculating lawyer. Except this lawyer happened to be her husband.

"Oh, that was Bill," she said, forcing a nonchalance that she didn't feel.

"You know him?"

"Yes," she answered, pushing past him to get to her dresser. She was going to take a shower before the saltwater dried out her hair.

"He asked me who I was. I told him I was Nicole's husband."

Bronwyn's stomach clenched, but she held the expression of cool disinterest on her face.

"He said he didn't know Nicole."

Bronwyn kept digging through her drawer as if she could not find her pajamas. When Ryan didn't say anything else, she asked, "Oh?"

"You just said you knew him."

Bronwyn looked at him, annoyed. "He's the maintenance guy, Ryan. That's all I know."

Ryan looked around the room again then back at her, his gaze weighted with meaning. "He went up to this room before he left."

"So?"

"Why was he in your room?

Bronwyn had to force herself to keep her voice low so the other Aphrodites wouldn't hear them arguing. "He's the maintenance man. He was probably *maintaining* something."

Ryan grunted, but didn't seem satisfied with her answer. What did she care if he was satisfied? He wasn't even supposed to be here.

"I'm taking a shower and getting ready for bed," she told him.

"Okay," he answered.

He didn't make any moves like he was going to leave. Bronwyn sighed heavily and pushed past him to her bathroom.

Hot water ran over her body, but it wasn't hot enough. There wasn't enough scalding hot water in the building to wash away what she was feeling. Sick. Filthy. She wanted to disappear, let the water dissolve her entire body so she could drain out of the shower and end up in the ocean again. That would be a relief, to never have to leave the bathroom and never have to step back into the bedroom to find him waiting there.

A knot formed in her throat. She tried to swallow, send it back into the pit of her stomach where it came from, but it wouldn't budge. The only way out was to let the tears come. She covered her mouth with both hands to stifle any sound that she might make while she cried and let the tears slide down her face. They mixed with the water and swirled down the drain.

At least her tears would end up in the ocean.

When she could cry no more Bronwyn washed her hair and body and turned off the water. Stepping out of the shower, her skin was pink from the heat. She dried off, put her wet hair up in a towel, and dressed in her pajamas. She had chosen the oldest, baggiest pajamas she had brought to Sol Mate. There was no way she was going to give Ryan any ideas.

Wiping the steam off of the bathroom mirror she was startled at her reflection. Her face was red, not just from the hot water, but from crying too.

She looked old.

She was old.

Regret stabbed her heart. Regret for wasting her youth on the man waiting for her on the other side of the bathroom door. Regret for following him around during college. Regret for working and supporting him through law school. Regret for waiting so long to have children. If they hadn't waited so long, the boys would be almost grown up now and she would be...she would be what? Free?

Bronwyn shook the thought out of her head and wiped her eyes with the edge of her towel before going back into the bedroom.

Ryan was sitting on his side of the bed when she finally emerged from her shower. To her relief he was still dressed. She did not want to have that argument. Not tonight. Not ever.

"Interesting reading," he said, holding up her copy of Ladies of Paradise - Knights of Fortune. "Is this the style of writing you're going for?"

"Sort of," she said, drying her hair with her towel.

"How's that going?"

"What?"

"Your writing. Do you have anything I can read?"

Bronwyn's stomach clenched again. She sat down on her side of the bed with her back to him. "Nothing that's ready for the public yet."

"Is that what I am?" He sounded amused, almost light hearted. Was he trying to flirt? He stretched out on the bed, turning to face her. "The public?"

Bronwyn shot a nasty look at him over her shoulder and stood up, taking her towel to the hamper. When she turned around to face him he was laying on his back, hands laced behind his head, and he had been looking at her rear end.

"What are you doing here, Ryan?" she asked, making sure to keep her voice low.

"I was going to take you to dinner, but I see you have other plans." He let his gaze wander down her baggy pajamas.

"Don't," she warned.

"Don't what?"

She pressed her lips together and leaned forward, reining in what would have been a shout into a hissing whisper. "Don't assume."

He sighed. "All right, all right," he sat up and swung his legs off the side of the bed. "Do you have anything I can eat at least?"

In the kitchen, Bronwyn tried to be as quiet as possible while she fixed him a bowl of clam chowder.

"This is a nice place. Great view," he commented at full volume.

"Shhh," she whispered. "I don't want to disturb the girls."

"It's only 9 o'clock," he said, full volume again. Bronwyn glared at him. He rolled his eyes then whispered, "It's only 9 o'clock."

"It's been a long couple of days. A lot has been going on," she said, handing him a bowl of hot chowder and a spoon.

"Like what?"

This was the most interest Ryan had taken in her life outside of him and the boys in years. She was suspicious of it, and annoyed.

"Girl stuff," she said. That should get him to back off.

He made a show of shuddering to communicate his distaste for the subject and sat down at one of the kitchen island stools to eat.

Bronwyn watched him take one methodical spoonful after another.

"Are there any crackers?" he asked.

She grabbed the oyster crackers out of the cupboard and put them in front of him. As he sprinkled them on his chowder she was struck at how much he looked like Jeremiah and Nathaniel. Or they him.

She was also struck by another thought that was a little more surprising. How much more she would have enjoyed serving Bill a bowl of clam chowder than her actual husband.

Forty-Three

Phoebe

P hoebe couldn't get her head straight.

Bronwyn and her husband were, to her knowledge, still in Bronwyn's room. Violet hadn't gotten up yet, which wasn't normal. And every effort she had put forth to write something, anything, had resulted in absolute zero.

A blank page with a blinking cursor stared back at her and she could think of nothing to fill it.

The only thing she could think of was Tanner. What he was doing. How he was doing. If he was thinking of her at all.

Her previous self would have believed that he might be thinking of her, at least a little, after he stopped by unexpectedly the day before. It was such a caring thing to do. Above and beyond friendship, in Phoebe's opinion.

But she was no longer relying on her opinion.

Phoebe had decided that her take on matters of the heart was not to be trusted. She had been planning on talking to the other

Aphrodites to get their thoughts, but there had been too many distractions.

Bill coming by to fix the furnace. The skinny dipping. Bronwyn's husband showing up. Everything had gotten in the way and Phoebe had felt a little silly bringing Tanner up–again. So she had gone to bed early with the idea to ask the others in the morning.

Except here it was morning and nobody was up. She was alone with her computer and her thoughts about Tanner. Hollowed out, she was dull-witted, with only echoes of Tanner and the way he talked, the way he smiled, the way he made her feel, bouncing around in her mind.

Phoebe's eyes welled up with tears.

"No, dammit," she said harshly, wiping them away with the back of her hand and swallowing hard.

She pushed all thoughts away, put her hands on the keyboard, and typed.

This was the harshest, blackest, meanest day Lady Everton had ever faced. Beyond the day she received word her parents had perished off the coast of Africa. Beyond the day she had been unceremoniously betrothed to the horrible foul smelling ancient Duke of Casterton. For it was today, this day, that Lady Everton knew she had lost the love of her life. The Colonel. He was gone, never to return to her arms again.

Fat tears came again and Phoebe allowed them this time. They flowed in hot streams down her cheeks. As long as she let them flow they did not blur her vision too much to write.

She let the tears come and she let her fingers fly over the keyboard, landing words and phrases and whole sentences that described the anguish she felt. Her heartbreak loaned to the character, Lady Everton, to lay bare to the world in her story.

That's how Phoebe overcame the writer's block and the self-doubt that had plagued her as a writer ever since she told her very first story. Overcame the need to control every syllable so it would be perfect. Perfectly written, perfectly read, and perfectly understood.

In her book the Colonel was torn from the arms of Lady Everton by war, not an ex-girlfriend. Kept away by powerful men who waged wars, not by his own design so he could pursue a relationship with another woman.

The pain was the same.

Phoebe found it easy, cathartic almost, to let the words flow as she brought forth her own feelings for Tanner. And as the words flowed she saw that they were the same words that Lady Everton would have used in her situation.

The pain of love lost was universal.

And so she wrote and she cried, and she wrote and cried some more, until there was nothing left in her to release. Empty of the grief and the longing, the tears stopped coming. As did the words. Phoebe saved her work and closed the laptop, then looked around Sol Mate's quiet living room. She placed her laptop on the coffee table then blew her nose and wiped her eyes with the nearby tissues.

"That's that, then," she said.

The ocean called to her. She hadn't taken a good, solo, soul clearing walk for several days. If there was ever a time she needed one it was now. She put on her red hat and sunglasses and went to the beach.

As she walked she felt lighter. More free.

She walked right along the shoreline where the waves swept onto the sand. Her toes sank into the pristine wet sand then were covered with a new wave. The water pulled the sand out from under her feet as it retreated back into the ocean.

Sea birds called out overhead. The sun glinted off the waves. Children laughed nearby as they splashed in the water. Someone played a radio in the distance, notes floating lightly on the breeze.

Phoebe took in a deep breath of refreshing ocean air.

She had a thousand things to be grateful for, a thousand reasons to be happy. More than anything she had this moment. This summer. This writing retreat to focus on herself and the creative work that she adored.

"You're pretty lucky, Phoebe," she said to herself. "Maybe not in love, but in a thousand other ways."

The upcoming beach party fundraiser for Violet's nonprofit popped into her head. More than ever she was excited to attend. Something had shifted in her, in her writing, she could sense it. The party would be a good way to celebrate that shift. And to celebrate Turtle Cove, the place that had made it all possible.

Later, the Aphrodites sat down for a critique meeting. Violet was distracted by the work she had been doing on her newspaper article. Bronwyn wasn't herself at all. She had been quiet and distracted since her husband had left right after lunch.

Phoebe waited patiently for them to read from her document, making sure not to watch them as they did. There was nothing more excruciating than watching someone read her work. Not sure what to expect, she was satisfied with what she had produced regardless. She knew it probably wouldn't be perfect, but she also knew what they were reading surpassed anything she had written previously.

"Phoebe," Violet said.

Phoebe looked up from her laptop where she had been distracting herself with funny puppy videos while she waited. Both Violet and Bronwyn were staring at her.

"What did you think?" Phoebe asked, a familiar stab of insecurity piercing her newfound confidence.

"Phoebe," Violet said again, putting her hand on her heart. "This is good. Really, really good."

Warmth radiated through Phoebe as she smiled, flattered.

"It's not good," Bronwyn interjected.

"What do you mean?" Violet was shocked, turning toward Bronwyn to argue her point if needed.

"It's not good, Phoebe. It's great. This is the best you've ever written. At least what I've seen," Bronwyn said, her eyes wet. "I cried!"

Phoebe laughed, blushing under the compliment.

"Do you know what this calls for?" Bronwyn asked.

"What?" Violet was laughing too. Delighted that Bronwyn had agreed with her critique. "A toast?"

"Better than toast," Bronwyn grinned, getting up from the table and returning with the box from Shore Is Sweet. "Lemon Blueberry muffins!"

Forty-Four

Violet

Violet barely spoke to Ben on the day of the fundraiser. They had spent so much time together planning the event and had both been involved in every decision down to the last detail, that they were the two who knew the most about what was supposed to happen. So they were the two who were called away, often in separate directions, to assist in the variety of tasks needed to set up the party.

Ben became the go-to guy for the band set up, parking questions, guest list issues and permits. Violet was mainly in charge of decorating and the food and drinks. Several volunteers had stepped forward to help Marine Life Rescue prepare, including Bill and his daughter, Maya, who was visiting from college over the summer.

"I'll help decorate, Dad, maybe you should put up tables?" Maya said to her father with a twinkle in her eyes.

Bill laughed. "I am sure you're better at decorating than I am."

Violet could see right away that the father daughter team had a good time together. It was fun to see Bill relaxed and laughing. He had always been a little reserved and a gruff whenever Violet interacted with him at the beach house. Maybe he had just been trying to maintain an aloof landlord and tenant relationship.

"I'm sure you're better at decorating than I am, too," Violet added. She held up a ball of string lights that she was trying to untangle.

Violet enjoyed the banter that went on during set up and was glad for the help. She also learned more about Ben. Not that she was snooping, but he was the face of Marine Life Rescue and the volunteers naturally talked about him.

"Ben sure is doing better these days, isn't he?" Maya asked her father as he footed a ladder so she could start hanging the light strings that Violet handed up to her.

"Yes, he is. He's done a lot with the conservatory. I'm real glad he took over the reins on this thing and built it up," Bill answered.

Violet refrained from asking Maya what she meant about 'these days' and added, "He loves this work, that's for sure."

Maya nodded. "He always has." They all glanced over at Ben who was helping the first band carry in their gear, laughing and joking with them as he did. Maya added, "I'm glad he's moved on from all the problems with Amber."

Bill grunted his approval, but didn't say anything else. Violet took his silence as a cue that he didn't want to gossip. Violet would normally agree with him, but she couldn't help but wonder about the details of Ben's previous relationship. For him to still have such a strong reaction to the memory of his ex like he did when they visited Shore Is Sweet, the end of their engagement must have been awful.

It wasn't until later when Violet was alone with Maya dressing the tables with the sustainably sourced and recyclable dinnerware that Violet broached the subject again.

"The Amber you mentioned before, would that be Ben's ex-fiance?" Violet asked.

"You've heard of her?" Maya asked.

"He's mentioned her, that's all," Violet answered, already feeling too nosy.

Maya nodded as she organized the cornstarch utensils into pretty designs on the sea turtle tablecloth. "Yes, she wasn't from around here. I guess they met at college? Anyway, she went off the deep end or something when they broke up."

"That's too bad." Feeling guilty for asking in the first place, Violet didn't want to push for any more of the story.

With Maya, it seemed, one didn't need to push.

"She was, like, violent about it, you know? Which sucked for Ben especially."

"Why especially?"

Maya stopped organizing and looked for Ben at the other side of the party area. He was going over some paperwork with the security service that provided assistance at the beach.

"He's just so nice. Always has been. He was one of my first surfing instructors. Well, besides my dad. Anyway, Ben is Turtle Cove's biggest softy and it was such a bummer to watch him get all messed up by that...that..." Maya didn't say the word, but she mouthed it.

Violet nodded her understanding. Glancing Ben's way she agreed, "That is too bad."

"I've heard him say he's done with relationships forever. He said he's never trusting another woman again. He's just gonna focus on saving sea turtles and that kind of thing," Maya added. She had finished laying out the utensils and the napkins. "How does that look?" she asked Violet.

Violet, still distracted by the news that Ben had sworn women off forever, took a second to respond. She couldn't tear her eyes away from Ben as he joked with the security team, Bear running happily around his feet.

"Violet? Do you think it's okay?" Maya asked again.

"Um, yes, yes it looks wonderful," Violet finally answered.

When the set up was done and all they had to do was wait for the caterer to arrive with the food and Bonnie to bring the cake from Shore Is Sweet, Violet decided to make her escape and get changed.

"Hey," Ben greeted her with a huge smile as she approached. The first band, a Bossa Nova style band from Brazil, was testing out the sound equipment and smooth jazzy notes added a sense of anticipation to the late afternoon. "Everything looks great," he said.

"Thanks," she said, but she had a hard time returning his smile. Ever since Maya had shared what she thought about Ben's past love life, Violet had a strange sensation in her body. An emptiness she didn't understand.

Ben's brow furrowed in concern. "Is everything all right?"

"Yes, it's fine," Violet said, wondering how in the world he could tell so quickly that she felt a little off. She should have never poked around in Ben's business by asking Maya questions whose answers could bug her so much.

Bear hopped up and licked her hand. "Hi, Bear," she said, rubbing the dog's black furry head.

"I'm sorry, Violet, I shouldn't have let you work so hard," Ben said, his concern deepening. "You've worn yourself out with all of this," he swept his long arm toward the decorated party area.

"I had plenty of help," Violet said. "I think I'm going to go home and get changed though. If you don't need anything else?"

Ben looked down at his own shorts and T-shirt, reminded of what he was wearing. "Right, absolutely. I almost forgot we're actually going to be at the party instead of just setting it up," he laughed. "Yes, you go home and rest up and take all the time you need. You've done more than your share of work here. Tonight's for you to enjoy and nothing else," he insisted.

"Thank you, Ben. It was my pleasure to help," she said, smiling up at him.

Part of her wished she was attending tonight's event with him as his date, but that wasn't reality. He was in charge of Marine Life Rescue and she was a volunteer. That was all there was to their relationship and, according to those who knew Ben better than she did, that was probably all it could ever be.

She did as he suggested and took her time showering and getting dressed at Sol Mate. When she returned to the party, the food and the cake had already arrived. The lights were shining and the band was playing Bossa Nova music that drifted across the sand and into the approaching sunset.

Violet had brought the other Aphrodites with her and when all three of them strolled into the party, Ben, Bill and several other men took notice.

Violet attributed the attention to Bronwyn, whose pantsuit was what Violet's mother used to call a show stopper. The palm frond pattern, the strapless bodice, the perfect fit, the flamboyant cape hanging off the back, Bronwyn's pantsuit almost had a life of its own. Violet was wearing a literal rainbow dress and almost felt invisible standing next to her.

"Good evening, Violet, ladies," Ben was the first to greet them, nodding first at Violet then Bronwyn and Phoebe.

Violet was certain it had taken him great effort to greet her first instead of zeroing in on Bronwyn and her pantsuit. She also noted he was looking particularly handsome in a pair of off white slacks and a sea green long sleeved shirt that matched the color of his eyes.

"Good evening," Violet said. "I don't think you've met my friends, Ben."

"I have not had the pleasure," Ben responded, his eyes twinkling as he spoke, making her smile at the formality of it all.

"This is Bronwyn Beck and Phoebe Collins, they're my writer friends," Violet continued.

After giving them each their due, Ben turned his attention back to Violet. Taking one step back he made a show of admiring her dress.

"And may I say you are looking exceptionally lovely this evening, Violet," he said, again with the twinkle in his eyes.

Violet felt her cheeks warming and she avoided eye contact with Bronwyn and Phoebe, who were both admiring Ben's particular brand of tall good looks.

"I wonder," Ben turned to look as the band started a new song, cool and smooth, complete with the rattle-like sounds of a cabasa. He turned back to her and held out his hand. "Would you like to dance?"

Violet had not expected the question. She thought he was going to ask her opinion on the band placement or if they needed to put up more lights.

"Dance?" she repeated.

There was a pause, which Violet realized was too long for comfort, but she could not make herself formulate an answer. She didn't know if dancing with him was appropriate.

Ben waited, but not without some hesitation on his own part. As if he was also second guessing his request.

"Well go on," Bronwyn finally broke the awkward pause. "Dance with the man, Violet. You're at a party after all."

Violet felt her blush deepen, but she took Ben's hand and let him lead her toward the music. The light fabric of her dress swished around her feet as Ben, his hand warm and gentle, guided her onto the dance floor.

"Ready?" he asked, putting one hand on her waist and lifting the other hand into the air.

The song had a nice beat, not too slow, but not too fast either. Violet followed Ben's lead around the dance floor as the clouds started to turn orange and pink on the horizon.

"It's beautiful," she said, observing the party which had filled with people since she left to change.

"And so are you," Ben said, turning them quickly and making her dress flutter prettily.

She laughed, flattered, but not convinced he meant it as a serious compliment.

"It's been great working with you this summer," he said.

"Thank you, it's been great working with you, too," she answered politely. "It's going to be harder to go home in August than I thought it would be," she added, a twinge of melancholy in her heart.

His steps slowed even though the rhythm of the music stayed the same. "It's too bad you have to leave Turtle Cove."

"Yes, it is too bad," she said wistfully as he turned her again and she felt her rainbow dress twirl up against her ankles.

They danced without speaking for a while, letting the music and the sound of the waves on the shore take over their thoughts and their bodies.

Violet liked how it felt to dance with Ben. The way he his hands lightly touched her body, yet he was able to move her whatever direction he wanted with the slightest pressure. He didn't dance too fast or too slow or too close or too far away. He was about as perfect as she had ever had, as far as dance partners go.

"Would you want to stay, if you could?" Ben asked.

Violet's mind had been wandering and the question took her by surprise. "In Turtle Cove?"

"Yes, do you like it enough to stay?" He searched her eyes then added, "If you could?"

He didn't understand her situation or he wouldn't have asked. Violet couldn't even entertain the idea. She had too many obligations back home.

She shook her head sadly, but with resignation. "It's out of the question, really. I couldn't make that kind of change."

He nodded. He understood, certainly. Violet couldn't make gigantic life decisions like that during one dance.

The question basically settled, they finished the song in silence.

Forty-Five

Bronwyn

B ronwyn needed the beach party.

The days after Ryan's surprise visit and their incompatible night sleeping on the same bed, Ryan on top of the covers and Bronwyn underneath, had been rough. Having him in her Aphrodite space had thrown her existence at the writing retreat into a free fall.

Every morning she had to force herself out of bed and go through the motions of being alive. And always under the watchful eyes of Phoebe and Violet. It was excruciating.

She didn't want them to know how Ryan's mere presence had single handedly crushed her dream of becoming Bronwyn Beck in the real world. She didn't want them to know how fragile that dream had been.

On top of everything else she had openly sworn off alcohol, so she didn't even have that small comfort. Not that she wanted to get drunk to block off all of her emotions anymore. Not exactly.

What she wanted was an escape from her thoughts. From her life as Nicole Speer.

Violet's fundraiser provided her with that escape.

When Bronwyn had pulled on her pantsuit after primping and preening her face, hair, and body into perfection, she looked in the mirror and smiled.

"Hello, Bronwyn," she said to her reflection. "You look about as perfect as possible."

She hadn't been exaggerating to build her confidence either. Bronwyn knew how people reacted to perfect beauty, having been blessed with a shapely form and pretty face. She knew what it felt like to receive an approving look from a stranger, even if those looks had come less and less as she grew older.

In her pantsuit, however, with her long dark hair straightened and the careful application of expensive makeup, she saw that look on Phoebe and Violet's stunned faces when she came downstairs ready to go. And she saw it on the faces of men and women in the crowd of party goers who watched her approach the beach party.

"This is gorgeous, Violet. What a great party!" Phoebe exclaimed upon seeing the decorations and the attractive people mingling on the sand.

Bronwyn agreed, it was a nice setup for a party. The beach at sunset. Music and dancing. Violet could hardly have gotten it wrong.

"Are you ready, Aphrodites?" Bronwyn asked. "Are you ready to show them what we've got?"

Violet and Phoebe only laughed. They weren't exactly taking her seriously.

Bronwyn was serious, though. Serious about making this the night she came out into the world as Bronwyn Beck.

Not simpering Nicole Speer who fed her cheating husband soup and let him sleep in her room all night then cooked him breakfast. Not pathetic Nicole who couldn't even keep her weaselly back room lawyer husband interested in her sexually, or any other way, during their long boring marriage. Not shy Nicole, hiding away in a beach house.

Bronwyn Beck was front and center now and she was going to make a splash.

The first person they ran into was Ben, the tall and tasty director of the non-profit where Violet had been working all summer.

"No wonder she's been so excited to save the sea turtles," Bronwyn said slyly to Phoebe after Ben whisked Violet away to the dance floor.

Phoebe smiled quietly. It seemed she had gotten over the worst of the whole Tanner fiasco and was more her old self. Spending most of her time since that wretched night writing her Lady and the Colonel story, which was really quite good, Bronwyn thought.

"Good evening, ladies," a man's voice came from behind them.

"Hi Bill, I didn't know you would be here," Phoebe said. "Full transparency, I wouldn't know who would be here tonight, because I don't know anybody involved! Except for Violet," She laughed at her own lame joke. Definitely on the mend. Phoebe was out to have a good time tonight, which was excellent news.

"Hi, Bronwyn," Bill said. His eyes lingered on hers and Bronwyn became fully aware of how his long sleeved white dress shirt fit against his muscled chest. He had on a pair of faded blue jeans. The shirt was untucked, the top buttons unbuttoned, and the sleeves rolled up, but the casual chic thing worked on him. He was tan and rugged and the white shirt brought out the blue in his eyes.

"Bill," she answered. The corners of her mouth tugged up into a coquettish smile and Bill reacted with a mischievous gleam in his eyes.

"I hope you're feeling well these days?" he said.

"Yes, of course. I'm all better," she said. Bronwyn was pleased to see Bill struggle to keep his eyes on hers instead of letting them wander down the form fitting bodice of her pantsuit.

"You're a friend of Marine Life Rescue?" Bronwyn asked.

Bill nodded and took a sip of the drink he held in one hand, scanning the party before returning his gaze to lock eyes with Bronwyn. "You could say that."

The most delicious shiver tickled her bare neck and back as she looked into Bill's eyes. He seemed amused and she would have sworn he knew that his presence was giving her chills.

"This band is amazing," Phoebe declared. She was enthralled with their surroundings.

Bronwyn was enthralled with Bill.

"They are, they're from around here. We have a lot of talented people in Turtle Cove," Bill said with pride. "Would you ladies care for a drink?" he asked. "They have some killer Sangria punch."

Phoebe hesitated and looked to Bronwyn. How sweet, she remembered that Bronwyn had declared she was done drinking for the summer.

Bronwyn gave Phoebe a reassuring smile. "Why not? It's a party, isn't it?"

Bill grinned and pointed at her with his glass. "Don't move. I'll be right back."

"Everybody looks so different when they're dressed up at a party, don't they?" Phoebe mused after Bill stepped away.

"They do," Bronwyn agreed as she watched Bill's blue jeaned back side disappear into the crowd.

Violet returned, looking a little wan. She wasn't as flush with the joys of recently dancing with a hottie as Bronwyn would have expected. Ben did not return with her. Bronwyn could only speculate about what had happened between them on the dance floor, because Phoebe had her own ideas.

"Is that a cake?" Phoebe pointed at a tall blue and white tiered cake on the other side of the dance floor where the food and booze were.

Violet nodded, "It's from Shore Is Sweet. She told us it was going to be elaborate, but I haven't seen it yet. It was delivered after I left this afternoon."

"I want to take a picture of it before it gets cut up," Phoebe said.

"Let's go see," Violet agreed.

Phoebe looked at Bronwyn. "Do you mind staying here so Bill knows we didn't abandon him?"

"Sure," Bronwyn said nonchalantly.

Mind? She preferred.

Let the children go look at the fancy cake. The grownups had other things on their minds.

For the next minute or so Bronwyn ran her fingers through her straightened hair and pulled it forward to better frame her face. Posing her body to show off her assets and all of the flattering aspects of her pantsuit, she waited for Bill to reappear.

When he walked through the crowd carrying three glasses of Sangria punch it was like he was moving in slow motion toward her. Bronwyn's heart raced faster and faster the closer he came. His eyes were fixed on hers then moved down her body, roaming down every inch of her well fitted pantsuit, a gleam in them the whole time.

Bronwyn didn't shy away from his gaze. She didn't turn aside or hide from him.

She let him look. Wanted him to look. Wished he would do more than look.

When he reached her he noticed Phoebe wasn't there, raising the third glass of Sangria in a silent question.

Bronwyn wrapped her hand around his and took the cup from him, never breaking eye contact.

"I'll drink hers," she said, raising the glass to her lips and taking a seductive sip of the red liquid inside.

"You want both of them?" Bill asked.

"Why not, Bill. It's a party isn't it?"

He gave her a rakish smile, handed her the second glass, and said, "That it is. That it is."

She giggled and took another sip. The punch was delicious and she could feel its heat moving down her throat already.

Something caught Bill's attention from somewhere behind Bronwyn. "Sorry, I've got to go take care of something. You'll be here for a while?" he asked.

"I'm not going anywhere," Bronwyn reassured him.

He grinned again. "Good, I'll find you."

He'll find her. A hot flash of attraction shot through Bronwyn's body when she heard those words.

She took another sip of Sangria punch number one and giggled. She hadn't wanted to be found this badly in a long time.

Phoebe

Phoebe was curious about Violet's mood. She had expected Violet to be upbeat and enjoying herself at the fundraiser. From the looks of it the party was a big success and Violet had worked hard on making it so. But she didn't seem happy or even pleased. To Phoebe's eye, Violet looked nothing but sad.

"So...that was Ben?" Phoebe asked when she went with Violet to look at the cake.

Bronwyn was far enough away so she wouldn't hear. She was not the gentle nudger of their group. Phoebe preferred to broach the subject of Ben out of Bronwyn's earshot.

Violet did not break into a shy smile like she normally did when she talked about Ben. She pressed her lips together grimly and nodded, avoiding eye contact with Phoebe.

"Is everything okay between you two? You seem a little down..." Phoebe waited. She didn't want to be pushy, but Violet did not seem okay.

Violet finally looked at her. "Everything's fine. I think I let my feelings for him get away from me, that's all." She gazed dismally at Ben who was speaking to a well put together couple near the entrance. "He's a great guy, but we're on two separate paths."

Phoebe empathized. Her relationship with Tanner wasn't exactly the same, but had yielded similar results.

She put her arm around Violet's shoulder and gave her a side hug. "I'm sorry, that's a bummer."

"Let's not focus on the negative tonight," Violet said, forcing a bright smile. "Like Bronwyn said, we're at a party after all!"

Phoebe laughed, "She is ready for a party tonight, isn't she?"

"Who's ready for a party?" Tanner asked, appearing out of nowhere and looking handsome in a pair of khaki slacks and a black short sleeve dress shirt.

Surprise didn't quite cover how Phoebe felt. Her heart did somersaults. She sucked in her breath and held it. Her mouth almost dropped open, but she managed to stop that from happening. Though she couldn't get any intelligible words to come out.

"Hi, Tanner, how are you?" Violet answered, filling the empty awkward pause.

He moved next to Phoebe, completely comfortable in her company, with no idea his presence ripped her apart inside.

"Good, I'm good. It looks like a great turnout tonight," he gestured to the growing crowd filling up the space they had allotted for the party.

"Yes, a lot of people. Hopefully it raises awareness and some money," Violet said, making conversation easily while she glanced occasionally at Phoebe to see how she was handling the situation.

Phoebe focused on not passing out. Breathing in then out and making sure her knees were slightly bent to prevent dizziness.

Tanner turned his attention to her, taking in her new dress and her hair, which the other Aphrodites had done up in soft braids. Almost exactly the way they had done it when Phoebe thought she was on a date with him.

"You look beautiful, Phoebe," he said.

Did she detect a softer tone in his voice? His smile reached all the way into his eyes. Phoebe still couldn't answer, but managed an embarrassed smile.

After looking at her for a long moment, Tanner turned back to Violet and said, "You both look very nice tonight."

"Thank you," Violet said, again covering for Phoebe's conversational inadequacies.

Time stood still for Phoebe. Tanner made more small talk with Violet and she couldn't even listen to the words. His body had moved ever so slightly closer to hers and their arms touched.

Tanner didn't move away. Neither did she.

All she could hear were the deep warm tones of his voice, but as if she was listening to him under water. Everybody around him became a blur. The only thing she could feel was the warmth of his arm on her skin. She had to look at the ground and close her eyes so nobody could read the emotion on her face.

Maybe she shouldn't have come.

Violet had told her he was on the guest list. Maybe part of her had wanted to see him again. But she hadn't expected him to stand by her, touch her, look at her with that twinkle he always had in his eyes.

"What do you think?" Tanner's voice penetrated her thoughts.

She looked up. What had she missed? Violet was watching her with wide eyes full of fear and joy.

"I'm sorry, what did you say?" Phoebe finally formed words and spoke them.

"Do you want to dance?" Tanner asked.

Shock. Again. God she needed to get herself together.

Her voice came out as a squeak, "Sure."

Tanner put his hand under her arm and walked her to the dance floor. The music was a nice easy song, not too fast and not too slow. But as soon as they stepped out to dance the song ended.

The lead singer picked up a guitar and started playing slow, sad notes.

Phoebe froze. This was every nightmare she had ever had about a high school dance. A boy being forced to slow dance with her when he didn't want to.

Couples streamed onto the dance floor hand in hand while others who were less inclined to a slow dance left. Phoebe wanted to sink into the ground. She knew Tanner didn't mean to slow dance with her, but she didn't know what she would do if he led her back off the dance floor.

Shatter into a million pieces, that's what.

Tanner looked at her, his eyes questioning. He held his hand out and she took it, fully expecting him to lead her away and back into her miserable, lonely life.

He pulled her to him, placing his other hand carefully on her waist. A tremor moved through her, but amazingly she stayed steady on her feet.

The song began and she had been right, it wasn't just a slow song. It was a sad slow song.

Tanner gazed at his hand holding hers for a long moment then gently laced their fingers together. He let his eyes move down her arm, onto her bare shoulder, up her neck and to her eyes where he stopped.

Phoebe held her breath.

The music played and they stood, not moving, ready to dance, but somehow uncertain.

Tanner searched her eyes. As if he wanted her to tell him what was happening. What she was feeling. What he was feeling.

But Phoebe didn't have an answer.

As the other couples moved past them, the song grew louder, more intense. Tanner looked at the singer for a moment, like he was coming out of a dream. When he switched his eyes back to hers there was a smile in them. He squeezed her hand gently and pulled her close.

"It's not Have You Ever Seen the Rain, but it'll do," he said. Then they danced and he stole what was left of her heart.

Bronwyn

Without anyone else to talk to, Bronwyn searched the cake table area for Phoebe and Violet. Spotting them she made her way there, downing Sangria punch number one before she walked through the crowd. She didn't want to look like a lush holding two drinks.

By the time she arrived at the cake, Phoebe was gone.

"Did you see what happened?" Violet asked.

Bronwyn took a sip of Sangria punch number two. "No, what happened?"

"Look," Violet used her eyes to direct Bronwyn's attention to the dance floor where none other than Phoebe and Tanner were about to dance.

"Oh, no," Bronwyn said, frowning.

Surprised at her reaction, Violet asked, "You don't think that's sweet?"

The song switched to a slow song and Bronwyn watched along with Violet as Tanner took Phoebe in his arms.

Bronwyn groaned. "This is bad."

"It is? I thought maybe it was a good thing?"

"Of course it's not good, Violet. The man is playing with her. He has a girlfriend, doesn't he? Where is this girlfriend? Why isn't he dancing with her?"

Bronwyn took another slug of Sangria punch. Noticing the table where the drinks were being dispersed she motioned Violet to follow her there.

"I'll have another," she stuck her empty cup in front of the adorable young man they had pouring drinks with a sly wink. "I can use my cup again, can't I?"

"Yes, ma'am," he said politely, filling her cup to the top.

Bronwyn grunted. "Ma'am," she muttered, turning back to Violet. She zeroed in on Phoebe and Tanner slow dancing again and made a tsk-tsk-tsk sound. "See? Not good. See how she's looking at him? This is bad." She shook her head in dismay.

Violet watched them dance with growing concern. "You should have seen how he looked at her when he first showed up. I thought he was really taken with her."

"I'm sure he was. She's beautiful and smart and sweet. But men are taken with women all the time, Violet." She tried her new Sangria punch and was pleased to find it was just as delicious as the first two. "The problem is they can't pick only one. They're *taken* by a brand new woman every day. Sometimes more than one!"

Bronwyn chuckled dryly at her little piece of wisdom, fully aware it was deeply unfunny. She took another hefty sip of her drink, enjoying the way the Sangria punch was warming her muscles from the inside out.

That's when she saw him.

Bill.

Bill, in his sexy blue jeans and even sexier untucked white shirt. Bill, who had promised to come find her. Bill, who wanted to find her for an unknown reason, but still had made a promise.

Bill, who was standing next to the band and yucking it up with a gorgeous young thing who couldn't be more than 21 years old if she was a day.

All the air left her lungs. She couldn't take in a new breath, as if she had fallen down and had the wind knocked out of her.

Bill took hold of the young woman's hand and turned her. No, *twirled* her. She laughed and pushed him on the chest. He took the opportunity to pull her into a hug.

They were obviously on intimate terms.

More intimate than Bronwyn was with him.

More intimate than Bronwyn was with anyone.

Forcing herself to look away, she stared at her feet. She could breathe when she wasn't looking at him. Suck in oxygen and not have to see what was happening between him and his young love after they hugged.

Between all of the Sangria punch she had consumed in a short period of time and staring intensely at her feet, Bronwyn got dizzy. She threw her head back and was hit with a major head rush.

"Whoa there!" She grabbed for Violet to steady herself.

"What is it?" Violet asked, eyeing the drink in Bronwyn's hand.

"No, no, no you don't," Bronwyn moved her Sangria out of Violet's reach and waved her finger at her. "Don't blame the Sangria, which is excellent, by the way." She knew she was slurring her words the teensiest bit. But she refused to feel bad. It was a party, after all.

"Do you need to sit down?" Violet took hold of Bronwyn's arm and was leading her toward an area set up with cocktail tables and chairs.

"I'm all right," Bronwyn wrenched her arm away from Violet, only spilling a few drops of Sangria onto the sand at her feet. She steadied herself without Violet's help and smoothed her hair down with one hand. "I'm all right, Violet. I don't want to sit down yet." Bronwyn looked in the direction she'd last seen Bill. He was gone. "I have a few things to talk to Bill about," she added.

"You're looking for me?" Bill sidled up next to her, sly as a fox. Foxy as a fox as well, but too sly for Bronwyn's taste.

Her tongue was thick, making it hard to say everything that came to mind when she saw him. She wished she hadn't drank those two glasses of Sangria so fast. Or was it three?

Bronwyn turned to face Bill and caught a glimpse of Phoebe and Tanner returning from the dance floor out of the corner of her eye. Good. Phoebe should hear what she had to say to Bill, because it went for Tanner, too.

Both of them needed to learn a few things about being gentlemen. About leading women on and playing with their hearts. About trading in older women for younger ones like they were cars.

She pointed at Bill with her free hand and only then did she notice that he had the little floozy on his arm. He had brought his too young, ridiculously firm beauty over to flaunt in her face. Show her that he could get someone better than her at the snap of his fingers.

She glowered at him.

"I'd like you to meet Maya," Bill said, just as casual as could be, as if he hadn't just been flirting with Bronwyn a few short minutes before he hooked up with the little sex pot. "She's my–"

"Hello, Maya, I'm Nicole," Bronwyn shot her hand out to Maya. She wasn't going to let anyone know how much it bothered her that Bill had Maya on his arm. Least of all Maya. "Nice to meet you."

"Nicole?" Bill asked.

Bronwyn froze.

Bill looked at the other two Aphrodites who were both gawking at Bronwyn, mildly horrified. When his gaze returned to hers, he was puzzled.

For a split second she thought about trying to cover up her slip of the tongue. Pretend he had heard her incorrectly. Pretend everyone had heard her incorrectly.

But, why? This was never going to work anyway. She had nobody to impress.

"Yes, I'm Nicole. Okay?" She said. "Nicole Speer. Not Bronwyn Beck. Are you happy? "

Still bewildered, Bill asked, "You're Nicole?"

"Yep, that's me. Good ol' Nicole. Is that what you want to know? That I made up my name and my life? That I'm not really Bronwyn and I'm not really an author?" She took a big drink of her punch.

Through his confusion she could almost see Bill's mind working. "Then that was your husband I met?"

"Yes! That was my husband," Bronwyn threw her hands up in the air and laughed. The punch in her cup sloshed over the edge and splashed onto her toes. "Ryan, my husband, who wanted to leave me for some–some–" she pointed her cup at Maya. "Someone just like her."

"Bronwyn," Phoebe was on her right hand side. "Come on, let's go get you something to eat."

Violet had slipped in on her left. She was being handled. She laughed again, a joyless sound.

"Excuse us," Violet said to Bill and his little girlfriend, and everyone else in their vicinity who had turned to look at the commotion.

Halfway to the food table Bronwyn said, "I can't eat. I think I might be sick."

Phoebe and Violet looked at each other, alarmed. Bronwyn almost laughed at their expressions. Except she couldn't laugh too hard, because the beach fundraiser party where she was going to break into to the world as Bronwyn Beck was spinning out of control.

Forty-Eight

Phoebe

A t least Bronwyn hadn't thrown up in the middle of the party. Of course, the night was young.

Phoebe and Violet rode out Bronwyn's bout with the spins on the beach, just far enough for the waves not to hit them, as the sun went down. Violet fretting over Bronwyn and the party. Phoebe fretting over Violet and Tanner.

"I don't think anybody really noticed," Phoebe told Violet.

They had sat Bronwyn down carefully on dry sand to keep her pantsuit as clean as possible and stood, one on either side, making sure she didn't fall over.

Violet glanced back at the party, an oasis of lights and music and laughter on the nearly deserted and darkening beach.

"I hope you're right," Violet said. Switching her attention to Bronwyn, she added, "I didn't know the punch would be that strong."

"She must have drank it too fast," Phoebe said.

"Can we please stop talking about the punch?" Bronwyn moaned.

Phoebe held back a laugh. She and Violet shared a this-is-absurd look and Phoebe sighed, turning her face toward the cool evening breeze coming off the ocean.

Her dress fluttered around her arms and ankles, reminding her of the dance she had shared with Tanner only minutes before. His touch, his body moving with hers, the look in his eyes, everything had been perfect, felt perfect. When they stepped off the dance floor Phoebe experienced a calm contentment she had not expected.

When it was just the two of them she felt so peaceful. So assured that everything was going to be all right. She felt loved.

"I would ask you how your dance was, but I think I know," Violet said.

Phoebe smiled, unable to contain the joy in her heart. Still, she didn't want to assume. She had done enough assuming. "It was nice," she admitted. "But I don't know if it means anything."

Violet's eyebrows raised as she looked past Phoebe in the direction of the party.

"Don't look now, but I think someone else found your dance nice," she said.

Phoebe turned to see Tanner walking their way in the golden light of the sunset, carrying several bottles of water.

"Anyone want some water?" he asked when he got close.

Ignoring Bronwyn moaning in protest at their feet, Violet pointed down at the top of her head.

"We have a taker, thank you," Violet said.

"I don't want anything," Bronwyn complained.

"I also brought these," Tanner showed them two bread rolls wrapped in a napkin. He squatted down in front of Bronwyn. "How are you feeling?"

"I'm fine, I'm fine, just fine, fine," Bronwyn answered.

"I want you to try one of these rolls for me, okay? Here's some water, too." He spoke kindly, but with authority. His emergency medical training kicking in.

Bronwyn made a face like she was going to argue.

Violet sat down next to her and took over coaxing. "You'll feel better and we can go back to the party."

Tanner stood and smiled at Phoebe over the loud opposition that followed. Violet, friend that she was, stayed seated next to Bronwyn and got her to drink and eat a little, leaving Tanner and Phoebe to talk.

"That was sweet of you, thanks," Phoebe said.

"No problem. It will help her hydrate. Maybe feel better until the alcohol has a chance to leave her system."

Phoebe nodded, not sure what else to talk about. She didn't want to rehash Bronwyn's strange behavior with Bill and she didn't know what to say about their dance.

"Beautiful, isn't it?" Tanner asked, looking out over the water at the setting sun.

"It is," Phoebe agreed, happy to have something to look at, but wishing she didn't have to look away from him.

Music from the party drifted over the sand and met the sound of the waves, creating a space of perfect limbo around them as if they were part of each world, but in a world all their own. Phoebe allowed the sensation of standing next to Tanner settle into her soul. The sun kissed the horizon and sent the last glimmers of light across the water to them and only them.

"Phoebe..." Tanner's voice was quiet, deep.

She looked at him and found he had turned away from the sunset and was facing her. He looked down into her eyes with the same questioning expression she had seen right before they danced.

She faced him, wanting to ask him what he was thinking, but she didn't get the chance. A voice interrupted them. Not from Bronwyn or Violet, which Phoebe might have expected. A voice carrying over the sand from the party. Layla's voice.

"Tanner!" Layla yelled. Then more forceful, more high pitched, "Tanner!"

Tanner didn't look away from Phoebe immediately. His previous questioning gaze became apologetic before he turned to Layla and waved, letting her know he had heard her shout.

Much to Phoebe's surprise, he didn't leave. He crouched down next to Violet and Bronwyn again, checking in.

"I've eaten almost a whole roll, doctor," Bronwyn announced, holding up the end of a roll so he could see.

"Great, do you feel any better?" he asked.

As Tanner talked to Bronwyn, Phoebe watched Layla grow more and more frustrated at the party's edge. Finally, she threw her hands up in the air and stomped across the sand in their direction. As much as a person could stomp on sand.

"Tanner!" she shouted when she was about halfway to them.

He looked up. "Hang on, I'll be there in a minute."

Layla did not like that. Not at all. She stopped short, holding up her sea blue silk dress so the bottom wouldn't touch the sand. She muttered to herself, but was too far away for Phoebe to hear her words. She was close enough, however, for Phoebe to see the hot flashing anger in her eyes.

"Tanner!" This time she screamed his name.

All of them stopped and looked at her. Even Bronwyn, who hadn't been paying any attention to anybody for a while.

Tanner stood up slowly, his eyes trained on Layla. "I said I'll be there in a minute."

Layla's normally beautiful face grew beet red. "I told you I would be at the entrance at 8 o'clock. You weren't there! What are you doing with them?" She cast a nasty look at Bronwyn and Violet then let it land on Phoebe. "And her!"

Tanner raised his hand for her to stop. "Hang on, you need to calm down."

Phoebe and Violet shared an 'uh-oh' look.

"Calm down?" Layla shrieked. She was so mad she was shaking. "Calm down!?"

"What is your problem?" Bronwyn asked, pushing herself up off the sand, still holding her uneaten piece of roll. She moved pretty smoothly for someone in her condition.

"My problem?" Layla looked Bronwyn up and down. "What's your problem, lady?"

Bronwyn raised one eyebrow and coughed out a laugh. "I think I'm looking at her."

"Okay," Tanner stepped in front of Layla, blocking her from Bronwyn's view. "Let's go." Grim faced, he gestured for Layla to walk ahead of him.

With a final sniff of disdain, Layla turned her back on Phoebe and the others, allowing Tanner to escort her back to the party. As she walked, however, she continued to complain and her voice carried over the sand.

"I can't believe this, Tanner. I told you what I wanted you to do and you're down here babysitting some drunk lady. I've warned you a thousand times and you keep screwing up..."

Her horrible whining grew dimmer and absorbed into the music of the party. Finally.

"Sheesh," Bronwyn said, brushing sand off the back side of her pantsuit. "She's awful."

Violet had stood also. She looked at Phoebe. "Wow. I kind of feel sorry for him, don't you?"

Speechless from everything she had just witnessed, Phoebe watched Tanner and Layla at the edge of the party. Just before he stepped into the crowd to follow Layla wherever she wanted to go, Tanner looked back. But the sun had gone down and the beach was dark. There was no way he could see that Phoebe was watching him go.

Forty-Nine

Violet

Violet was glad the party was over, but she wished she had gone home with Phoebe and Bronwyn. They had left earlier than expected, big surprise. Violet, however, remained, because she had signed up to help break down the party after it was all said and done.

It was too much, really. She should have realized that setting up and breaking down a party that went into the middle of the night was a lot of work. But when she was planning it all she had been so excited. And she hadn't had any idea of the drama that would unfold.

"The cake was delicious and beautiful," she told Bonnie who was there to help pack up whatever was left.

The four tier cake had been frosted in beautiful shades of blue and cream, decorated in fondant shells and fish, and given a final touch of hundreds of round pastel candies that looked like bubbles. There wasn't much left of the beautiful cake to pack up.

"I'm glad everyone liked it," Bonnie said happily.

"More than liked, they loved it," Ben added as he joined them.

Violet tried to think of something to say that didn't have anything to do with Bronwyn or Layla. She didn't know how much their dramatic interactions had interrupted the flow of the party and she really didn't want to find out.

"Wow, Violet, I feel like I haven't seen you all night," Ben said. "I didn't mean to ignore you. Every time I turned around there was another person wanting to talk to me about the conservatory or donations." He raised his eyebrows high, excited to convey this information.

"That's great, Ben," Violet smiled. She was truly happy for him. "That was the point of the whole evening, wasn't it?"

"Don't tell me you didn't dance with this lovely woman?" Bonnie teased Ben. "Look at her in that dress. That's a dancing dress if I've ever seen one."

Violet's cheeks burned under Bonnie's compliment. She continued grabbing used plates and utensils and tossing them in the compost bag.

"I managed to get one dance in," Ben said. "Wish it could have been more."

Violet suddenly felt uncomfortable. Exposed. The excitement she had experienced earlier in the evening when she and Ben danced was gone. She was picking up garbage, not twirling around a dance floor. The writing was already on the wall, she wasn't Cinderella and Ben wasn't her Prince Charming.

"Maybe next time," she said politely. That ended Ben's flirty conversation.

"We picked up all of the trash from that section and the table-cloths and tassel garland," Maya announced.

She and Bill had also volunteered to clean up. Violet wondered if some of her mood had to do with them being nearby and the unnerving feeling of waiting for the other shoe to drop.

"That's great, thank you," Ben said. "I think we'll leave the lights up tonight and I'll come and get them in the morning. Otherwise we'll be working in the dark out here."

"Good idea," Bill said to Ben, but he was looking at Violet.

She continued to toss used plates into the compost bag. One of the guys from the second band waved to Ben to get his attention and he excused himself to go take care of last minute business with them. This left Maya helping Bonnie with the remains of the cake and Bill watching Violet.

"Can I ask you a question, Violet?" Bill asked.

She looked up. They were virtually alone since Maya and Bonnie were in a lively conversation of their own.

"Sure," Violet smiled, hoping he wasn't going to bring up Bronwyn. Or Nicole.

"Have I somehow offended...Bronwyn?" he used her name of choice with obvious uncertainty.

She had been dreading this.

Violet studied Bill's face. He seemed sincere and more than a little confused. She couldn't blame him. Bronwyn confused the heck out of her, too.

"I don't think you did anything to offend her," Violet said. "Though I can't really say if she is offended or not. She can be a somewhat up and down about things."

Bill smiled. "Yes, I get that from her."

Glad he was being friendly about the whole incident, Violet felt compelled to explain a little more about her fellow Aphrodite. "And the whole name thing is, I guess, a little weird from the outside looking in. But Bronwyn Beck is her pen name and we're on our summer long writing retreat so I understand why she wants to go by it. Using the pen name makes the writing goals seem that much more attainable."

He nodded. "Right. So she is both? She's Nicole and Bronwyn?"

"Yes."

He paused, thinking, then cleared his throat and asked, "And she's married?"

A spike of happiness shot through Violet for Bronwyn's sake at his question. Also a twinge of disappointment for Bill's sake. Bronwyn had acted less than married on a few occasions and she could see why he might be confused. It was sweet that he wanted to clarify.

Hesitant, because she felt like she was delivering bad news, she answered, "Yes, she is." She wanted to add that perhaps Bronwyn wouldn't be married for too much longer, but she didn't know that for certain and it really wasn't her place to say. Plus she wasn't comfortable gossiping.

"I see," Bill said, a clear flash of disappointment in his eyes. Then he smiled, pushed that conversation to the side, and started a new one. "I read your article in the Cove Gazette. It was very good."

The unexpected compliment shifted the weird negativity she'd been holding in her stomach since early in the party.

"Oh, thank you," she said.

"Ben said you're going to be a regular contributor to the paper?"

"Yes, well, for the summer at least. They were kind enough to request a few more articles while I'm here."

Bill nodded, thinking again. "It's important information you're conveying and you have a real knack for making it interesting."

"I appreciate you saying that."

Bill chuckled. "I'm not just saying it as a compliment. I have an ulterior motive. There are a lot of little newspapers in other cities and towns up and down the coast that could use someone like you. Someone who can get the message out."

"Oh?" Violet wasn't sure what he was proposing.

"I know a few editors of some of those smaller newspapers. Would you mind if I gave them your information?"

Shocked into silence, it took Violet a few moments to respond. Finally, in a stammering, unprofessional, and almost gushing voice, she managed to answer, "No, I don't mind at all."

"Great, does Ben have your phone number? I don't keep my cell on me all the time. I can get it from him?"

She said he could and as the rest of the cleanup came to an end, Violet found her thoughts in a completely different place than they had been at the beginning of the party.

No longer was she concerned about how the party would turn out or how she looked in her dress. No longer was dancing with Ben the biggest thrill of her evening or Bronwyn's outburst weighing on her mind.

No, Violet had something else occupying her headspace. Her writing career. And it was exhilarating.

Phoebe

After the previous night's events, Phoebe was happy to be alone. Both Bronwyn and Violet were still asleep, but Phoebe could not stay in her room any longer.

Moved by what she had seen and felt at the fundraiser party, with Tanner, with Layla, with Bronwyn, she had woke with the pressing urge to write it all down. Experience all of it through her characters. Put it into words before the entire night disappeared from her memory or she had too much time to rationalize it away.

Head bent over her keyboard at the kitchen table, nothing more than coffee to keep her going, Phoebe was typing feverishly before the sun came up.

She didn't hold back.

All of the emotions from the beach party came alive again in her story of Lady Everton and the Colonel. The bitter angst emanating from Bronwyn, the sense of failure and betrayal with which she had lashed out at Bill. The anger and jealousy of Layla and the quiet resignation of Tanner when he went to be by her side. The gentle sensuality of Phoebe and Tanner's dance. The spark of electricity between them as they moved across the floor, hand in hand, body to body, gazing into each other's eyes.

Phoebe couldn't type fast enough. Her fingers flew across the keyboard and with each word she relived the moments, allowing them to sink deep into her soul so she could articulate them clearly and weave them into her story.

Minutes turned into hours and before she knew it the sun was up. Birds sang their morning greeting, grabbing Phoebe's attention. She looked up. It was almost 8 o'clock. She had been up for several hours writing. When she checked her document file she saw that she had written enough for two, possibly three, chapters.

"Wow," Phoebe leaned back in the kitchen chair. Her shoulders were a little tight, but overall she felt amazing. Surprising given much of what she had been writing was the decline of Lady Everton's relationship with the Colonel. But somehow writing it all out was healing for her, the author.

"The author," Phoebe smiled as she said the words out loud. As many times as she had told herself she was allowed to refer to herself as an author, doing so had always taken some effort, some pushing to overcome internal conflict and insecurities.

The thought that had just came to her, that she was the author, had needed no such inner dialogue. It had come freely, without coercion.

She looked around at Sol Mate's kitchen, in wonder of the moment. The normality of it all. Her first unencumbered thought of being an honest to goodness author with no apologies or excuses hadn't come to her in the middle of a critique group or in a beautifully designed home office or even at a meeting with a publisher. It had come to her humbly, honestly. At the kitchen table, sleep deprived and suffering through one of the deepest experiences with heartache of her life.

Phoebe laughed to herself. "Figures," she said, reaching for her coffee. It was ice cold. As was the whole pot. She had neglected it for so long the burner had turned off.

Just as well, she deserved a fresh pot anyway. Plus the others would be up soon and would want coffee. Especially Bronwyn.

As she made a fresh pot her mind wandered to Tanner. Her feelings toward him had not changed, but the raw wound he had left on her heart seemed less sore now. After putting her all into Lady Everton and the Colonel, Phoebe didn't exactly feel empty, but she did feel more in her body. Not pining away for some future that would never be, but being present in her own skin and allowing the thrill of their dance the night before to fill her heart.

At least they had that dance. She would always remember it as one of the highlights of her summer in Turtle Cove.

A knock on the door brought her out of her reverie.

Still in her state of calm and not wanting any noise to wake the others before they were ready, Phoebe hurried to the door and opened it.

"Tanner," she said, the sight of him wrapping around her heart.

For a moment she wondered if she was imagining him. Manifesting his image because she had been thinking about him all morning. But a bird sang nearby and a breeze came through the door and he smiled at her and she knew it was real.

"Hey," Tanner, looking like he had also gotten up before dawn, gave her an apologetic smile. "Sorry to bother you so early."

Phoebe realized she was still in her pajamas and probably looked like she had just rolled out of bed. "It's okay, I've been up a while." She stepped back and let him in, adding. "The others are still asleep though. We won't wake them if we're in the kitchen."

As he followed her down the hallway to the kitchen Phoebe marveled at how normal his presence felt. Their relationship had brought them together in so many places for many different reasons. Having him with her in the kitchen while everyone else still slept didn't feel too out of the ordinary, and that by itself was extraordinary in a way.

"Coffee?" she asked.

"Sure, thanks," he said, leaning casually against the kitchen island. "It smells good."

"Bronwyn bought it at Salty Java I think. It is good. We've been drinking it like crazy here."

Tanner glanced over his shoulder at the stairs that led from the hallway to the second floor. He turned back to Phoebe and asked quietly, "Is Bronwyn here?"

Just as quietly, Phoebe answered, "Yes, she's sleeping though." She dumped the cold coffee out of her mug and poured fresh into it and a new mug for Tanner. "Why?"

He took the coffee and looked down at it, deciding what to say. Phoebe had an idea he wanted to talk about Bronwyn's performance at the party, but she didn't want to put words in his mouth. Maybe he had come by for a completely different reason.

"It's about last night," he began.

Or maybe not.

Phoebe winced at what was coming, but remained quiet.

"I came by because, well, I wanted to apologize," he said.

"Apologize? What do have to apologize for?"

He looked into her eyes. "I wanted to apologize to you for how Layla acted last night."

Taken aback, Phoebe could only stare at him in mute surprise.

Determined to get his point across, Tanner continued, "I don't condone her acting like..." he searched for the word. "Like a spoiled child, but screaming like that and taking out her frustration with me onto you was completely wrong. Totally uncalled for."

"Oh, well, I didn't think too much of it," Phoebe said, only half lying. In truth, she had been more upset that Tanner left to be with Layla than by what Layla said. She tried to laugh the whole incident off. "I actually thought she was being more rude to you than to me."

"See? You're so caring and sweet, you would think that. You would gloss over how mean she was being to you and to Bronwyn and be more worried about how she was acting to me." As he spoke Tanner moved restlessly around the kitchen, unable to get comfortable in any one place.

Phoebe tried to take him calling her caring and sweet in stride by focusing on other aspects of what he had said. "If it makes you feel any better I don't think Bronwyn was upset. She may not even remember most of what happened anyway," she joked.

Tanner chuckled wryly. "I don't know. It was all so ugly." He sighed. "I don't know why she always has to do that kind of thing."

Phoebe assumed he was talking about Layla, not Bronwyn. He hadn't been privy to many of Bronwyn's outbursts when she was drinking.

She wanted to tell him that he shouldn't put up with the way Layla treated him. That some woman, maybe not her, but some other lucky woman out there would treat him the way he deserved, with love and respect. That he should seek out that kind of woman.

Before she had a chance to put any of those thoughts together, Tanner changed the subject. Sort of.

"But that's not what I wanted to talk to you about," he said.

"It's not?"

"Not exactly. I had a thought the other day when I was talking to my aunt. You remember my aunt that I told you about? The publisher?"

"Yes, I remember."

"My Aunt Brenda, that's her name, well, I told her about you and that you're a writer and...well, she wants to read your book."

Phoebe thought she must have misheard him. Her early morning wake up and too much coffee must have made her delirious or something.

"What?" she asked.

With a hopeful smile he repeated. "My Aunt Brenda, the publisher, wants to read your book." When Phoebe didn't respond again he looked at her carefully. "I hope you don't mind I told her about you. You don't already have a publisher, do you?"

"No, I don't," she said quickly.

"She said she would like to take a look. Maybe she would be interested in it and, you know, you could get it published," Tanner said, excited at the prospect.

"I don't know, I mean, it's not done," Phoebe stammered a little bit as she spoke.

"I'm sure she would take that into account. If she likes it maybe that would be even more reason to finish it."

The possibility of a publisher reading her work and liking it boggled Phoebe's mind. What if she liked it enough to publish it? Or even offer her a contract to pay her to finish it?

"Tanner, I'm overwhelmed. That's so nice of you and of her."

Tanner smiled, pleased at her reaction. "I'm happy to do something for you after all you've done for me this summer."

As Phoebe's mind raced with everything this could mean for her writing career she was struck by a new thought. A devastating thought.

What if Tanner's Aunt Brenda read her manuscript and realized she was basically writing about Tanner? The way he looked, spoke, and moved, not to mention the feelings he stirred inside of her. Deep, private feelings that she assigned to Lady Everton, but a publisher would very likely know that the writer was the one actually having those feelings.

Worse than that, what if Tanner read some of it before handing it off to his aunt?

She froze, her smile fading. The elation that had filled her body just moments before curdled and turned sour, leaving a sick feeling in the pit of her stomach.

"It's settled then," Tanner said, beaming. "Do you have a hard copy of it that I can take to her?"

Phoebe's heart was torn. She couldn't disappoint Tanner after he offered to do something so nice for her. But she couldn't give him her writing either.

She dropped her gaze, avoiding eye contact to buy time so she could figure out what to say. Panic rose in her chest.

That's when her eyes fell on Bronwyn's manuscript that she had tucked away next to the refrigerator. Bronwyn's manuscript was printed out and had nothing about Tanner in its pages.

She grabbed it and showed it to him with a smile. "Luckily, I have a copy right here."

"Great," Tanner held out his hand to take it.

Phoebe glanced down at the first page. Thank goodness Violet had not printed out a title page with their names on the hard copies. The first page was only the first page of the first chapter.

Phoebe's heart was pounding a mile a minute. She did not practice deception often, but the thought of Tanner or his aunt seeing what she had written about him was too much for her to handle.

She could give Bronwyn's manuscript to Tanner and tell him later that she gave him the wrong one. That would give her time to figure out a good excuse to not give him a copy of her novel. She just needed to see him on his way before the others woke up and messed up her plan.

Stomach churning, palms sweating, Phoebe handed Bronwyn's manuscript to Tanner so she could hurry him out the door with a final reminder, "Remember, tell your aunt it's not finished."

Bronwyn

Bronwyn woke up with a splitting headache. Again.

She opened one eye and groaned, closing it against the morning light streaming in her window.

"No..." she mumbled.

Another hangover. And she didn't even remember having that much fun at the party. In fact, she specifically remembered having a miserable time.

She groaned again and rolled over onto her stomach. No reason to get up. Nothing to look forward to but being nauseated and a throbbing pain in her head. She may as well stay in her room and remain dead to the world for as long as possible.

Thoughts of the previous night rolled through her head, adding to her misery.

First the memory of Tanner's snotty girlfriend showing up as Bronwyn was recuperating from too much punch. She didn't quite remember what she had said to her, but she remembered how angry the girl was. That might have been Tanner's fault, though. She did recall him telling the girl to calm down, which usually only adds fuel to the fire of an infuriated woman.

Then there was Bill.

How he had ditched her for the much younger – much, much younger – woman. How she had gone off on him and, for reasons that escaped her now, told him she was Nicole. That Nicole and her were the same person.

"God..." Bronwyn flopped miserably onto her back. What had possessed her to admit that to anyone? Let alone Bill?

Excited voices from downstairs filtered through her door. She sighed. Maybe it would be better to get up and be distracted rather than relive all of her glorious mistakes from last night. Either way she would have a headache.

When she finally walked into the kitchen she found Phoebe and Violet in lively conversation.

"Good, you're up!" Violet greeted her.

Squinting to keep incoming light at a minimum, Bronwyn put her finger to her lips. "Maybe just a little quieter?"

"Here's some coffee," Phoebe placed a steaming hot cup on the island in front of her.

"Thanks," Bronwyn's voice was still a little croaky, but sipping the hot coffee would help. She lifted the coffee to her lips, noting how Phoebe and Violet were both gawking at her like happy puppies. "What's all the excitement about?"

"You're never going to believe what happened," Violet began. "Phoebe's afraid you might be mad, but I think it could turn out to be a great opportunity for both of you."

Bronwyn sipped, swallowed, winced at the stab of pain just over her right eye, then looked at Phoebe. "I feel too awful to be mad. What's going on?"

Relieved at that, Phoebe explained. "Tanner was here earlier–"

"Oh, Tanner," Bronwyn controlled an eye roll and took another sip of coffee.

"No, it's not what you think," Violet defended Phoebe, then urged her to go on.

"He came by, first of all, to apologize for the way Layla acted last night with us, with you." Phoebe gave Bronwyn a pointed look.

Bronwyn dipped her head in a slight bow. "Very gentlemanly of him."

"Anyway, he was also here to tell me that his Aunt Brenda, who's a publisher, was interested in reading my book."

"Really?" Bronwyn had not expected that category of news. She was surprised. Surprised and glad for Phoebe. She was a good writer and maybe this would be a stepping stone into an actual career. Of course, a small stab of jealousy interrupted her flow of good vibes for Phoebe, but she managed to squelch it pretty quickly and put on a happy face, or as happy as her face could get while hungover. "This could be your big break, couldn't it?"

Phoebe cringed and glanced nervously at Violet while she answered, "There's more to the story."

Violet, exasperated at Phoebe's hesitancy, said, "Just say it, Phoebe. I'm telling you, I think what you did could mean big things for both of you."

Utterly confused, Bronwyn looked back and forth between her two Aphrodite friends. "Both of us? What are you talking about?"

"I couldn't give him my manuscript. I couldn't do it." Phoebe's eyes were round and pleading for understanding. "You know how much of Tanner I wrote into my story, don't you?"

Bronwyn nodded. "You used him as your inspiration, yes. But what does that have to do with me?"

"I gave him your manuscript instead of mine!" Phoebe blurted out, immediately covering her mouth with both hands.

All of the blood rushed out of Bronwyn's face and hands. She put the mug carefully down on the kitchen island, Phoebe's words reverberating through her aching head.

Phoebe and Violet kept talking in excited voices that sounded like chipmunk gibberish in Bronwyn's ears. She felt like she was moving in slow motion as she watched the two of them chatter happily. A heavy thudding, slow and rhythmic, filled her ears. She realized it was the sound of her heartbeat sinking into despair.

"You see? So it could totally work out that both of you get your work read by a real live publisher. Isn't that amazing!?" Violet asked.

"My–" Bronwyn's throat was almost too dry to speak. She placed her hand on her chest and tried again. "My manuscript?"

Phoebe's face fell when she saw Bronwyn's reaction. "I wasn't trying to steal your work or anything. I was going to call him and tell him I gave it to him by accident and then come up with an excuse why I couldn't give him mine."

"I told her she should give him hers anyway, because it's good," Violet said with authority. "And then I thought what if we wait until his aunt reads yours," she pointed at Bronwyn, who stared at her pointing finger in stunned silence. "Then tell him he gave the wrong one to his aunt and give him Phoebe's? Then you both get read by a publisher!"

Bronwyn's slow motion panic sped up, rising through her body with the power of a volcano about to blow.

"N–n–no," she stammered, stood up and put her hands on her pounding forehead. "No, no, no, you cannot give my manuscript to a publisher!"

Violet's positivity would not be damped. "But it's so good, Bronwyn. And if Tanner's Aunt Brenda actually reads it, even because of a mistake, you might have a chance at getting it published."

Bronwyn thought she might be sick. Her actions last night and hangover this morning paled in comparison to this problem.

Phoebe watched her carefully, beginning to grasp that perhaps there was something about the situation she and Violet did not fully understand.

"What is it?" Phoebe asked. "Why can't a publisher read it?"

Bronwyn's panic reached full crescendo. Her face was hot, probably bright red, every nerve in her body crackled with alarm.

She turned to Phoebe and Violet, wholly distraught. They leaned back with wide eyes as she shouted, "Because it's not mine! I didn't write it!"

Fifty-Two

Phoebe

Bewildered by Bronwyn's confession and astonished at her reaction, Phoebe didn't know what to do. She had been afraid Bronwyn may not approve of what she had done, but she had no idea her fellow Aphrodite would become so distressed.

Violet was the first to try to get a grasp on the facts. "The printout I gave you was not yours? I don't understand. I printed it off of your shared document."

Bronwyn leaned over the island and collapsed her upper body on top of it, her arms covering her head.

"This isn't happening. This isn't happening," she repeated over and over between short wails of misery.

Phoebe couldn't stand by and watch this breakdown. She leaned over so her face was even with Bronwyn's face on the island and said, "I'm so sorry. I didn't think it would hurt anything."

Bronwyn was almost beyond tears. And it was all Phoebe's fault. Her heart twisted at the sight of her friend. She put her arm over Bronwyn's back for comfort, though she doubted it would make much difference.

Bronwyn's face was contorted with anguish. She wailed again, "What am I going to do?"

"Bronwyn," Violet spoke with authority, her teaching training coming to the forefront. "Bronwyn," more firmly.

Bronwyn stopped wailing and rolled her head to one side to look at Violet. Strands of her dark hair stuck to her face.

"You need to tell us exactly what the problem is so we can fix it. What do you mean when you say you didn't write it?" Violet asked.

Bronwyn took a few shuddering breaths then said, "I'm not a real author. I was c-co-copying!" Another wail, this one long and loud that led directly into sobs.

Phoebe stood up. Bronwyn's distress was too much to take. She had been worried about taking liberties with Bronwyn's manuscript, but now her guilty conscious took over. Confused tears trickled down her cheeks as she mumbled, "I'm sorry. I'm so sorry."

Violet took Phoebe by the shoulders and looked her directly in the eye. "She's working herself into a frenzy. Get a cold damp wash cloth. I'll move her to the sofa."

Having a task to do helped control Phoebe's crying. She hurried to the bathroom and brought the cold damp wash cloth into the living room, finding Violet had successfully seated Bronwyn in the middle of the sofa. She was not wailing or crying anymore, but she looked awful. Violet was sitting on one side of her, she motioned to Phoebe to sit on the other.

"Okay, lay your head back and we're going to put this on your forehead," Violet instructed.

Bronwyn did as she was told and Phoebe gently placed the wash cloth on her, just like Bronwyn had done when she was melting down about Tanner only a few weeks before. A few weeks that felt like forever.

"Is that better?" Violet asked, still very much being the teacher.

Bronwyn croaked out, "Yes."

Violet reached up and rubbed Bronwyn's shoulder. "That's good. Can you talk about it now?"

Two tears squeezed out of Bronwyn's closed eyes, but that was all. She let out a heavy sigh and sniffled. Phoebe handed her the box of tissues.

"Thanks," Bronwyn said, wiping her face and nose with a tissue. Keeping her head tilted back so the wash cloth wouldn't fall off, Bronwyn looked sideways at Phoebe. "I don't blame you, just in case you're worried about that."

Hot tears pressed anew on the back of Phoebe's eyes, but she kept them under control. Nodding her understanding, she put her hand on Bronwyn's knee.

Looking back at the ceiling, Bronwyn continued her confession, "It's nobody's fault but my own. I...I've been copying a book instead of writing. An old romance novel that I found in my nightstand."

Phoebe was shocked. She could tell Violet was, too, though Violet kept her stoic, stable teacher face on for Bronwyn's sake.

"But, why?" Phoebe asked before a horrible idea entered her mind and she gasped. "You haven't been doing that the whole time in writing group, have you?"

Bronwyn sat forward, the damp wash cloth plopping into her lap. "No, I haven't. Ever since I joined the Mighty Aphrodite Writing Society I never plagiarized anything. Ever. Until now."

"Why now?" Violet asked.

With a frustrated groan, Bronwyn slumped back into the cushion. "I haven't been able to focus. I sit down to write and my mind is, like, running with...everything. And even if I can get it quiet and calm I can't think of anything to write. When I'm quiet and calm I just get depressed."

Her lower lip trembled slightly, but she cleared her throat and kept the tears from flowing.

Phoebe filled with remorse as she watched Bronwyn's struggle.

"I didn't know you were having such a hard time writing. I thought it was helping you to focus on something besides Ryan," Phoebe said. Sadness that Bronwyn had been covering up all of her pain momentarily overrode Phoebe's pangs of guilt for not asking permission to hand over her manuscript.

Violet's stern teacher countenance cracked and she gave Bronwyn a sideways shoulder hug. "I'm so sorry. I didn't know either. I wish you would have felt more comfortable telling us what was going on."

Bronwyn tilted her head to the side so it rested on the top of Violet's head while she hugged her.

"I'm sorry I didn't tell you. I was embarrassed. Here we were, the Mighty Aphrodites, finally at our writing retreat. And you two were always tapping away. I just felt so useless. And I was only using the copying as kind of an exercise to get my fingers used to writing words, you know? Get in the flow."

Phoebe and Violet both nodded. They knew exactly what she was talking about.

"I never planned on sending it out as my own work to a publisher," Bronwyn added. "You guys know that, don't you? I would never do anything like that."

The pangs of guilt returned and Phoebe slumped back on the cushion next to Bronwyn. "You didn't have to. I did it for you!" She pressed her palms to her forehead. "I can't believe I gave Tanner your manuscript without talking to you first. It was presumptuous of me. I'm sorry."

Bronwyn looked at her with surprisingly kind eyes. Phoebe was used to the brash Bronwyn, the one who wasn't afraid to ask questions or speak her mind. She had far less experience with a forgiving Bronwyn.

"I really thought I could hand it to him as a decoy then figure out what to do later," Phoebe reiterated.

"I know you didn't mean anything by it," Bronwyn said. She

sighed, resigned to her fate. "Maybe Tanner's aunt won't read past the first paragraph. Maybe she'll hate it. Problem solved."

"That could happen," Phoebe agreed hopefully. "Even if she does like it and is interested in publishing it you can just say no. Or, I guess, I would say no? She thinks it's mine anyway."

"But what if she searches it online. Is a search like that standard for publishers?" Bronwyn wondered.

Phoebe's stomach sank. "If she does a search and finds it then she'll think I plagiarized it. That can't be good for a writer's reputation."

"We need to be proactive. We can fix this," Violet said.

Phoebe and Bronwyn turned to her, a little amazed at the strength in her voice.

Violet, who had started the summer fairly soft spoken and submissive, seemed changed in the moment. Lately, she had appeared physically different after spending the summer on the beach. Phoebe had noticed her healthy tan and even thought her hair seemed thicker and curlier. But this crisis was doing something more for Violet, there was a feistiness in her brown eyes that was new.

"How can we fix it?" Bronwyn asked.

"I don't know right off the top of my head, but I think we can figure it out. We're intelligent, we're creative, we can come up with a solution," Violet answered.

Bronwyn smiled, the despair she had been suffering only a few minutes before seemed to be dissipating. She looked at Phoebe, jerked a thumb toward Violet and said, "I like this one's attitude."

"Me too," Phoebe said, the glimmer of hope she felt inside reflected in her voice. "So where do we start?"

Phoebe's phone buzzed and she pulled it out of her pocket. She froze then looked up at the others. "It's Tanner."

Making the first definitive decision of their creative solution, Violet answered, "Don't answer it."

Violet

"We need to come up with what we're going to say before you talk to Tanner," Violet explained as Phoebe stared helplessly at her buzzing cell phone.

Watching Phoebe and Bronwyn flop around madly in emotional turmoil had inspired Violet to take charge. She wasn't the type to push herself into a leadership position, but she wasn't going to shrink away when necessary. She had received plenty of training in managing other people in college. Of course, the people in question were elementary school students and these were grown women. Still, there were similarities.

In the end Phoebe and Bronwyn's predicaments were just problems to be solved. Tanner's aunt having the plagiarized manuscript wasn't the end of the world, but she understood the anxiety the situation was causing her friends. If she was in their place, she would have been a wreck.

But it wasn't her and since she was the only one not directly involved, she had to think clearly for the other two Aphrodites.

Bronwyn's mental health was a concern. Violet didn't understand why she had chosen to basically deceive them the whole summer, but obviously she was struggling and needed their support. At the moment, however, Phoebe's problem was the most pressing.

"Phoebe," she said, grabbing both of the other women's attention. "You need to review what you've written since I printed everything out. It's your best work so far and I think it should be included in what we give to Tanner's aunt."

Phoebe started to protest, "But I don't want–"

"I know you're worried about Tanner seeing himself in your writing, but you need to think about yourself and your career. This is an amazing opportunity to get a publisher's eyes on your work. Period. You need to forget about everything else," Violet said, all business.

Phoebe hesitated. Her phone buzzed once more then, thankfully, Tanner went to voicemail.

"She's right," Bronwyn said. Her face and eyes still puffy from crying. "This might be your chance. Forget what Tanner thinks. All that matters is what his publisher aunt thinks."

Violet added, "Tanner may not even read it. Or, if he does read it, he may not see the similarities between him and your main character."

"Maybe," Phoebe said.

"He's a man, Phoebe, he's oblivious," Bronwyn added.

"It shouldn't matter either way. Think of it this way, you need to get your best work in front of a publisher and this is an excellent opportunity for you," Violet stated with her best no nonsense voice.

The worry that Phoebe had been wearing all morning began to fall away, replaced by a spark of something else. Something bold and brave. A Phoebe full of potential instead of insecurity and regret. Not attached to Tanner or what Tanner thought about her, but what she felt about herself.

"Okay, I'll do it," Phoebe announced.

"Yes!" Bronwyn cheered.

"Great! Once you make sure your online document is put together the way you want it, I'll print it out at the conservatory," Violet said. "That's the first step."

Phoebe's cell beeped. "It's Tanner's voicemail." She hit play and put it on speaker so they could all hear.

"Hey, Phoebe, it's Tanner," the recording played. "So I took your book to my Aunt Brenda, but she was on her way out of town. I didn't know she was leaving for vacation. She goes to this off grid wellness yoga thing in Mexico for two weeks every year." Violet's hopes lifted. He hadn't given the manuscript to anyone yet. She gave a thumbs up to Phoebe, which quickly turned into a thumbs down as Tanner's message kept going. "But, good news is, since she won't be here she gave your book to her assistant. And her assistant's gonna give it to her boss to read. So you're going straight to the top!" Here Tanner gave a little laugh, then continued, "That's all. I just thought you'd want to know. Talk to you later."

Phoebe looked sick. "His aunt's boss? Who could that be?"

"We've got to switch that manuscript out with your real one," Bronwyn said. "We can't let the big boss find out it's plagiarized."

"Let's tell Tanner what happened and see if he can get it back from his aunt's assistant before it gets to the boss," Violet suggested.

"Tell him?" Phoebe asked, surprised and alarmed.

"You don't have to explain exactly what happened." Violet wanted to lay out their plan quickly before Phoebe lost her nerve. "Text him. Tell him you grabbed the wrong manuscript. The one he gave his aunt was a copy of an already published book we were using for...for..."

"A writing example?" Phoebe said, still sounding uncertain.

"Yes, perfect. That sounds fine," Violet encouraged.

"Text is a good idea. He won't be able to hear any nervousness in your voice. It's perfect for unwanted communication,"

339

Bronwyn agreed. "Then he can get mine back and we can give him your new one."

Violet was glad Bronwyn was onboard. Keeping Phoebe psyched to stand up for her own interests would be easier as a team.

"Okay, I'll text him." Phoebe bent over her phone and texted the message to Tanner. After several minutes of texting back and forth with him she received the final update. She read it silently at first, then out loud. "I asked her assistant. Already gave it to the boss. She's not sure about asking for it back. Says boss is pretty uptight and doesn't like mistakes."

"That's not good, is it?" Bronwyn asked.

Phoebe's face drained of color and Violet knew she had to think of something to keep her focused on the positive.

"Phoebe, why don't you get your laptop and put your document together so I can print it," she suggested.

Phoebe followed the directions like a zombie, going through the motions, but a little brain dead.

"How are we going to get mine back from the boss?" Bronwyn asked Violet in a low voice when Phoebe went into the kitchen.

"I don't know. We might need to do it ourselves," Violet answered.

"How would we do that? We don't even know where Tanner's aunt works."

That's when Violet had an excellent idea. She looked at Bronwyn. "We get Tanner to help us." She checked to make sure Phoebe was still in the kitchen. "But we don't have time to try and convince Phoebe. The sooner we get those manuscripts switched out the better." Violet picked up Phoebe's cell phone that she had left on the coffee table.

"What are you doing?" Bronwyn asked in a whisper.

"I'm doing this for Phoebe and her future," Violet replied, quickly typing in a text and hitting send.

Fifty-Four

Phoebe

"You did what!?" Phoebe couldn't believe what Violet had just told her.

"I asked him to come over. I didn't say exactly why," Violet answered, semi-apologetically. "We don't have time for you to build up the nerve to talk to him about this, Phoebe. Your reputation as an author could be at stake and the only person we know who can get us in to see the publisher is Tanner."

Phoebe's heart was pounding and nerves bubbled in her stomach. Even though everything Violet was saying sounded reasonable, every muscle in her body was tight, like she was about to run away as fast as she could.

"God, why am I so afraid of him?" she asked, more to herself than Violet or Bronwyn.

Bronwyn spoke up, "He broke your heart. It's self-preservation to be cautious, even ultra-cautious."

Phoebe sat down to try and relax. Maybe Bronwyn was right.

She was overreacting to protect herself from Tanner, afraid interacting with him would cause her more pain.

"But this is your career." Violet's eyes beseeched her to listen to what she was saying. "You're an incredibly talented writer. This is a big break. Who knows, it might be the biggest break you ever get. We never know what the future holds for us. I am begging you not to let your emotional attachment to Tanner get in the way of your goals and dreams, Phoebe. I'm afraid if they do you might regret it forever."

Bronwyn nodded fervently. "She's right. She's so right, Phoebe."

Phoebe's nerves bubbled harder until they were boiling. But she realized part of her reaction might have nothing to do with Tanner. What Violet was saying could be true. This could be a huge break in her writing career. The career she had dreamed of for so, so long. Maybe she was afraid of being successful even more than she was afraid of being around Tanner.

She nodded firmly, looking Violet evenly in the eyes. "Okay, let's do it. What should I tell him when he gets here? What are we going to do?"

"He needs to understand the urgency," Violet said.

"You need to ask him if he can get us into the office somehow to switch out the manuscripts," Bronwyn added.

"Okay, that doesn't sound so bad. But if it's not so bad then why am I shaking?" Phoebe raised her hands level so the other two could see them trembling.

Violet gestured to the laptop she had brought in from the kitchen. "Why don't you focus on getting your document organized so I can go print it out. I'm sure Tanner won't be here for a little while."

"I'll fix us some breakfast. This could turn out to be a long day. I know I, for one, could use some bacon and eggs," Bronwyn said.

By the time breakfast was ready Phoebe had reviewed her

latest chapters, put everything in order on her shared document and made sure it all looked as cleaned up and correct as possible.

She walked into the kitchen, her case of the nerves under control. "I'm done."

"Good, so's the bacon." Bronwyn put a plate full of crisp hot bacon on the kitchen island and pushed it toward Phoebe. "Eat up, we'll–"

A knock on the front door interrupted her.

Phoebe's stomach did a familiar flip-flop, the same thing it always did when she was about to see Tanner. She ignored the feeling and smiled confidently at Bronwyn and Violet. "I'll get the door."

She managed to keep up her confident smile as she opened the door and ushered Tanner in.

"Sorry this is so complicated," he said as he followed her to the kitchen. "I didn't know my aunt was going out of town." He nodded at Violet and Bronwyn when he saw them. "Good morning, ladies."

"Good morning," Violet answered.

"Morning, want some bacon?" Bronwyn asked.

"Sure, thanks." He grabbed a piece and munched on it. As he chewed he looked from Phoebe to Violet to Bronwyn and realized they were all watching him. He swallowed. "What is it?"

The other Aphrodites looked to Phoebe to answer. She took a deep breath and started, hoping her voice didn't shake.

"I want to get the wrong manuscript back before your aunt's boss sees it and replace it with mine. Can you help me do that?"

He considered her question and said, "Diane, that's my aunt's assistant, didn't seem to think that was going to be possible. Plus it's the weekend, I'm not sure we could even get into the office..." his voice trailed off as he took in their determined faces. He zeroed in on Phoebe. "You want to get it back that bad?"

She nodded. "I do. It's important to me that I get the correct manuscript to a publisher. I know it was my mistake, but it's unprofessional to make that kind of mistake and I don't want them thinking I'm unprofessional."

Tanner nodded, accepting the seriousness in her tone. "Okay, I'm in. How do you suggest we do this?"

Within two hours Phoebe and Tanner were standing in the upscale lobby of Giant Publishing waiting for Diane to arrive with the keys to the office.

Violet had printed the real manuscript at Marine Life Rescue while Phoebe fixed her hair and got dressed. Tanner convinced Diane to let them into the office to make the switch, promising they would be quick and leaning heavily on how much his aunt would appreciate her helping them while she was gone. Since it was the weekend they hoped there would be very few, if any, people there. Especially his aunt's boss.

When they were putting together their plan, Tanner had explained to the Aphrodites that Giant Publishing wasn't in Turtle Cove. The company was located in the nearby city of Whitmer, in the upper class business area. They had all agreed just Tanner and Phoebe would go. Fewer people meant less hassle and less chance of anything going wrong.

"You need to dress like a famous published author," Bronwyn had instructed Phoebe. "You'll command authority that way and nobody will question you if there is someone in the office."

Following that advice, Phoebe had put on a simple, but elegant, black sundress, her wide brimmed red hat, sunglasses and red lipstick.

"You look nice," Tanner told her as they waited in the lobby.

"Thank you," Phoebe answered, quietly thrilled that he took notice, but too nervous about switching the manuscript to think about it for too long.

Diane arrived and Tanner turned his attention to her, smoothing over any concerns she might have about letting them in.

"We really appreciate this, Diane. I'm sorry I didn't get this corrected before Aunt Brenda left," he said.

Diane was an older woman with short brown hair sprinkled with grey, and wearing what Phoebe guessed was her weekend clothes, a pair of white capris and a flamingo pink cotton blouse. She looked somewhat more annoyed than suspicious as she led them past the front desk and used her key card to access the elevator.

"I know your aunt would want me to help you," Diane said as they rode up the elevator. "If we can't find it immediately in Mr. Randolph's office then I'm afraid we will need to wait until Monday and ask him." She looked sideways at Phoebe. "I don't feel comfortable searching through his paperwork."

"Right, of course," Tanner agreed.

Phoebe kept what she hoped was a trustworthy smile on her face and removed her sunglasses so she didn't appear to be hiding anything.

Once off the elevator, Diane led them past a gleaming reception area and down a hushed hallway with lush carpet and framed images of famous book covers tastefully displayed on the walls.

Phoebe couldn't believe she was in a real publishing office, however clandestine the reason. The whole space oozed knowledge, power, and success. She wondered how many real authors had walked down this same hallway and the thought made her skin tingle. Giddiness threatened to take over, and she had to concentrate on quietly following Diane.

Tanner stayed close to her side and caught her eye when he was sure Diane wasn't looking. He grinned playfully. He was having fun, too. There was an espionage vibe to the whole experience, which she was pretty sure he was enjoying as much as her.

"Here we are," Diane announced, using a gold key she had on the end of a laniard to open an impressive mahogany door.

"Whoa," Tanner said what Phoebe was thinking when they entered the office.

It was a huge corner office with windows on two walls. A massive desk almost the size of a conference table was centered in front of a wall of bookshelves full of expensive looking hard cover books. Completing the look, behind the desk, was an impressive black leather office chair. Mr. Randolph's chair.

Phoebe was stunned at the sight. Butterflies multiplied in her stomach as she realized the man who sat in that chair would be reading her manuscript. Her palms started to sweat.

"Here we are." Diane had gone to a thick leather binder sitting on the desk and opened it. Several printouts lay pristinely inside. She looked up at Phoebe. "Which one is yours?"

Phoebe couldn't move. Her feet were stuck to the luxurious carpet as uncertainty filled her heart. She caught Tanner's questioning eyes and held them, unable to speak.

Sensing she was struggling, Tanner jumped into action. "Let me see," he said, walking to the desk and looking through the manuscripts with Diane. "Here it is." He held up the plagiarized print out for Phoebe to see.

Summoning all of her inner strength, Phoebe forced her feet to move across the carpet and joined him at the desk.

"This is the wrong one, correct?" Tanner asked.

She nodded and managed to croak out a feeble, "Yes." She took it from him and handed him the correct manuscript. Her manuscript. The manuscript that he had inspired.

"And this is the correct one," he said, slipping it into the leather binder. He gave her an encouraging smile. "All good?"

"All good," she answered. She still had a bundle of nerves rolling around in the pit of her stomach, but they weren't from anxiety or fear. They were pure excitement.

Bronwyn

Bronwyn couldn't remember being so pleased. Watching Phoebe and Tanner return from their successful adventure at Giant Publishing filled her with satisfaction.

As the two relayed how their trip to switch out manuscripts played out, they laughed and finished each other's sentences and generally appeared tickled to be in each other's company. She hadn't realized how much she wanted, or needed, to witness what a happy couple could look like.

Not that Phoebe and Tanner were a couple...yet.

But Bronwyn had a feeling an intimate relationship might be in store for the two of them. She knew all about Tanner's girlfriend and the fact that Phoebe was leaving Turtle Cove in just a few weeks at the end of the summer, but she couldn't shake the feeling that there was something big going on between them.

Phoebe practically glowed in his presence and when Tanner watched her tell her side of the manuscript switching story his eyes shone with pleasure, and something even more important, in Bronwyn's opinion. Pride.

Bronwyn couldn't recall a time when Ryan had ever been openly proud of her...proud to be with her. If he ever had, she hadn't noticed.

"I'm so glad everything worked out." Violet beamed with her own sense of victory, which Bronwyn agreed she deserved. She had really turned around the despair from that morning and pressed Phoebe to do what was best for her career.

"Bravo to all of you," Bronwyn declared. "I feel like we should celebrate! Why don't we grab a late lunch at the Silver Tide? My treat."

They all agreed and soon she was sitting with Violet, Phoebe, and Tanner at a patio table with a marvelous view of the ocean. The Silver Tide was resort dining at its best and she knew the other three weren't quite as financially flush as she was, which made treating them even more enjoyable.

Her day was turning into quite the feel good day.

"This view is magnificent, isn't it?" Bronwyn asked the trio.

They all agreed. Especially Tanner.

"The only other restaurant with a view like this is Cobalt Edge out on the dock. I haven't eaten here at the resort for a while. I think the last time was a graduation party for one of my cousins," Tanner informed them.

"Are you from here?" Violet asked him.

"Yes, born and raised in the suburbs just inland of Turtle Cove. But this is my home now. Right on the beach."

"It is beautiful," Phoebe said.

He looked at Phoebe with that same special gleam in his eye that Bronwyn had noticed earlier. "If you get your book published at Giant Publishing, would you move here?"

Bronwyn almost gasped. She caught Violet's eye and knew they were thinking the same thing. What an interesting question for Tanner to ask their friend.

Phoebe blushed under his gaze and stammered out an answer.

"I don't think they're really going to publish my book. It's not even done yet."

"Don't think negative. You've got to think positive. They might really love it," he answered.

"That's right, Phoebe. It's all in the hands of the writing gods now," Violet said.

"May Mighty Aphrodite bless your romance novel with publication," Bronwyn added.

Phoebe laughed, her eyes shining at the idea of being published and from Tanner's special attention. "If I do get published I can't think of a more beautiful place to be than Turtle Cove."

"We would be lucky to have you." Tanner gave Phoebe a genuine smile.

Bronwyn could see why Phoebe had a thing for him. He was good looking and sweet, but also disarming. Bronwyn may have misjudged him slightly in the past. He wasn't overtly flirting, he was just a super nice, super hot guy. It would have been difficult for any woman to be around that combination for too long without giving away a piece of her heart.

Tanner turned his attention to her and Violet. "What about you ladies? Are you planning on staying here when summer's over?"

Bronwyn held her breath. This was not a question she wanted to think about, hadn't allowed herself to think about all summer. What was her life going to look like when the Mighty Aphrodite retreat was over? Dread seeped into her good mood and she couldn't come up with any kind of witty remark.

Luckily, Violet had an answer for him. "It's absolutely gorgeous here, but I have a contract with my school to teach another year. So I'll have to put moving to Turtle Cove off at least until next summer." She giggled at her own joke.

"Will you be publishing any of your writing while you're teaching?" Tanner asked.

It was Violet's turn to be flattered by his attention. "Actually, I will. I have several articles commissioned by the Cove Gazette and a couple more newspapers interested as well. I'm thinking I'll be working on writing more articles and see if I can get some kind of syndication."

Bronwyn was surprised. "Violet, I had no idea you were making bigger plans for your ecological writing. That's wonderful!"

Violet shrugged. "I've been mulling it all over in my mind for a few days. I don't know much about newspaper syndication, but I think I can learn. I'm looking forward to figuring out how it works."

"That's a great idea, you could get your own column!" Phoebe was just as happy for Violet as Bronwyn.

But a seed of darkness had sprouted inside Bronwyn when she thought about the end of their writing retreat, and it grew inside of her as they chatted about Violet and Phoebe's career possibilities.

She had nothing to show for their summer of writing. The summer they had all three planned on becoming the writers they had always dreamed of being was almost over. And Bronwyn had spent the whole time building a facade. She hadn't written a word of her own, had failed at using her pen name for anything but being a laughing stock, and was facing a painful divorce followed by emptiness when she left Turtle Cove.

Phoebe and Violet knew she had not accomplished anything to crow about during their time at Sol Mate, and they were tactfully not asking her about her post summer plans. But Tanner didn't know and Bronwyn grew more and more uncomfortable at their table thinking that at any minute he might turn to her and ask about her future plans.

As if she had willed it, her cell phone rang inside of her purse. Thank goodness, a viable reason to step away from their lunch party.

Bronwyn stood and grabbed her purse. "If you'll excuse me a minute, I'm going to answer this."

She dug her phone out of her purse, determined to answer it even if it was one of those scam numbers, just so she could stay away from the table. When she saw who was calling, however, her stomach sank and the darkness inside of her bloomed.

Violet

iolet went to work at Marine Life Rescue after finishing lunch at the Silver Tide. She had scheduled the time with Ben several weeks before, and was surprised to find for the first time since starting as a volunteer, she didn't really want to go.

Since leaving the fundraiser party, which admittedly she had hoped might be a catalyst to building her relationship with Ben, everything about volunteering at Marine Life Rescue felt off.

The thought of walking into the shabby little building that was the conservatory made her uncomfortable. It was as if her time there was up, that any possibility of her involvement with the conservatory being anything more than a one time summer vacation pastime had only ever been a fantasy.

And Violet wasn't in the mood for fantasies.

Her pep talk to Phoebe about doing whatever she could to move her writing career forward had come from Violet's heart. As she told Phoebe that she would regret not choosing to follow her dreams because of her feelings for Tanner, Violet had realized she needed to heed that warning as much as Phoebe did.

It was time Violet took a hard look at what she was doing to achieve her goals and follow her dreams. And when she did take that look there was one thing that became crystal clear.

Violet hated teaching.

She wished nothing but goodness to teachers everywhere, but knew now more than ever that teaching was not her calling. After her experiences writing over the summer, especially getting paid for her newspaper articles, Violet was sure what she wanted out of life.

She wanted to be a writer. And since shifting her thinking to include non-fiction writing and journalism as acceptable writing careers, not just fiction, everything seemed to be falling into place.

The Cove Gazette had already requested more articles from her. Articles that she would be writing up through the coming fall months. After talking to Bill about his newspaper contacts, Violet concluded she could happily spend her time researching and writing about nature, climate change, and sustainability. With hard work and a little luck, it was entirely possible for her to carve out a career.

If she only had the nerve.

When she opened the door to the conservatory, Bear greeted her first. The floppy furry dog hopped around her feet and licked at the air until she bent down and pet the sides of his face with both hands. Neither Bear nor Ben had been there earlier in the morning when Violet came to use the printer for Phoebe's manuscript.

"Hi, Bear, how are you today?"

"He's been wondering if you were going to take the day off after so much hard work at the fundraiser," Ben said jovially.

Ben stood behind the long counter and Violet was struck by how perfectly he was suited to the setting. She couldn't imagine him working anywhere else other than Marine Life Rescue. She at once admired and envied the perfect fit he had found.

"Last night seems like such a long time ago," she said.

"Does it?" Ben put aside the paperwork he had in front of him and gave her a quizzical look. "What's happened?"

Violet didn't know where to begin. Ben and Marine Life Rescue were the reason she had started writing about nature and the reason The Cove Gazette had picked up her articles. She owed Ben a great debt, but she needed to move on.

Unable to articulate any of her thoughts, Violet merely looked at Ben, sorrow growing in her heart.

"Hey, hey, hey." Ben read the sadness on her face and came out from behind the counter. "What's wrong? Has something bad happened?"

"No, nothing's happened," she sniffled, fighting back an urge to cry. "Nothing terrible anyway."

"Come sit down." Ben gestured to the table where they always sat together to work on various projects. "We can talk about it."

Violet shook her head 'no'. "I can't, Ben. But I've realized something that I need to tell you."

He turned to her with worry in his eyes. His lanky arms and legs made him seem more awkward than normal. "Okay, you can tell me anything you need to tell me, Violet."

Hearing him say her name sent a pang of grief through her heart. Violet closed her eyes to gather her thoughts. No grief over a loss of a nonexistent relationship between her and Ben could be worse than the grief she would feel if she didn't do her best to become the person she wanted to become.

She would not allow regret to be her destiny.

Still, it was difficult to communicate her thoughts to Ben without feeling like she was closing a door. Then again, maybe she was closing a door. Maybe she was supposed to close one door so she could go through another door to a brighter future.

"I can't do any more volunteer work here this summer," she finally spoke. "I've been offered some more writing jobs for the Cove Gazette and I need to get those done plus pursue sales in other newspapers." There, she had said it.

Ben didn't answer immediately, but the worry in his eyes lessened.

"I just don't have time," Violet added, wishing he would answer.

"Oh, right, sure...of course," Ben let out a half-laugh and relaxed, though the awkwardness remained. Looking around the room, he seemed to be searching for something to offer her, some reason to stay. "Yeah, this place can really burn up your energy. I get that."

Violet's heart ached for him. "No, it's not like that, Ben. I've enjoyed all of the time I spent here."

He turned back to her, rubbing his chin and nodding slightly. "I'm glad to know that."

Surprised to feel a hard knot in her throat threatening to turn into tears, Violet swallowed hard and continued, "It's just that I'm running out of time here."

He held her gaze for a long moment. Long enough for everything they were leaving unspoken to hang in the air between them.

Then, with all the amiable warmth he had shown when they first met, Ben shoved both of his hands in his pockets and smiled. "You've helped so much, Violet. I can't thank you enough for everything you've done, but I understand. This was never going to be full time nor forever, was it?"

Again, the tears reached her throat. At the risk of losing control of them, Violet managed to answer, "No, it wasn't."

And that was that.

Bronwyn

"Mom! Mom!" Jeremiah waved both arms at her. "Watch this!" He ran as fast as he could into an oncoming wave. When the water hit his midsection, he dove in, surfacing several feet out and looking immediately for her reaction.

Bronwyn raised her hands so he could see them and clapped. She was sitting on a beach towel surrounded by the remains of their picnic lunch watching her boys show off. Any other time in her life this outing to the beach would have been a welcome diversion from her everyday existence. A family getaway where she would celebrate by taking pictures to share on social media and commemorate the event.

She didn't feel much like celebrating today.

Ever since Ryan had called and interrupted her lunch at the Silver Tide to suggest he bring the boys to Turtle Cove for a visit, Bronwyn had been dreading their arrival. Not her boys. Waiting to see them and then watching as they scrambled out of the car and ran up the front steps of Sol Mate had filled her heart with joy. But sharing that moment, and the moments since, with Ryan had been hard.

"Nicole," Ryan called to her from the water. He had picked up Nathaniel who was squealing with delight. "Watch this!" Ryan tossed her youngest in the air and he splashed happily down into the water.

As soon as Nathaniel poked his head out of the water he looked for her response, she raised her hands and clapped for them, too. A genuine smile touched her lips. She had missed the rowdiness that having little boys brought to her life. So much energy, ready to take on anything and everything.

She picked up their used paper plates and napkins and put them in a bag inside of the picnic basket, the same picnic basket Bill had gotten down from the attic for Phoebe to loan to Tanner. Bronwyn paused, her hand running along the edge of the vintage basket that had been beautifully crafted and was still in perfect condition.

Her mind wandered to Bill as it had so many times over the past few months. She glanced down the beach where she could just see the roof of Sol Mate, Bill's beach house. She couldn't help but wonder what he thought of her and her erratic behavior.

Shaking her head to try and rid herself of any more thoughts of Bill, Bronwyn murmured, "Get a grip."

Right on cue, Ryan left the boys, who had started building a sand castle in the wet sand near the water, and headed her way. Bronwyn busied herself picking up the rest of the trash and straightening the blanket.

Ryan flopped down next to her, his swim trunks and hair still wet with salt water. Resting on his back, he laced his fingers behind his head and closed his eyes, soaking in the sun. He let out a sigh of satisfaction. "I can see why you've gotten more fit over the summer."

"I have?" Surprised at the unexpected compliment, she looked down at her stomach and legs. She had worn her black bikini, which was her most flattering suit.

Ryan squinted one eye open. "Yes, you look really good. Tan and fit."

"Thank you," she answered with a touch of suspicion. "I guess it's just life on the beach."

He lifted himself onto his elbows and looked up and down the beach where several other families were playing with their children in the sand and surf. His gaze stuck on their boys carrying a bucket full of ocean water to their sand castle building site.

"I've missed this," he said.

His words grabbed her heart. She didn't respond. Couldn't respond.

Ryan rolled onto his side to face her. "I've missed us."

Bronwyn looked at him. Her husband. He seemed sincere. There was no slight sarcasm or haughty lawyer attitude coming off of him. The pressure around her heart turned into an ache.

Tilting his head, he held her gaze with his. "Have you missed us this summer? Have you missed me?"

She blinked back tears. "I don't know how to answer that, Ryan. I've had a hard time this summer."

He cast his eyes down and stared at the space on the blanket between them. "I know. That was my fault."

Something about the way he was acting made Bronwyn want to sink into the blanket next to him, talk to him, forget everything he had done.

"I haven't accomplished anything either. The whole summer is almost gone and I don't feel any better than..." she let her voice trail off.

He raised his eyes to hers. "Than when?"

"Than when you told me about her." The words came out quiet, choked.

Ryan groaned and moved into a sitting position right next to her so their hips and thighs were touching. Bronwyn didn't move away.

"I can't tell you how awful I feel about everything," he admitted.

Tears filled her eyes. "Not as awful as I feel."

"No, I'm sure you're right." He squinted at the boys playing. "Though it has been hard at home without you."

Bronwyn scoffed. "Right, that's about all I'm good for, cooking and cleaning the house."

"That's not what I meant."

She sniffled and wiped her eyes with a spare napkin. "It's not just the situation with us." She paused, wondering if she should confide in him. Finally, with a heavy sigh, she confessed, "It's my writing."

"What about your writing?"

Bronwyn tilted her head back and looked up at the brilliant blue sky, letting out a groan of her own. "I didn't write my book, Ryan. I wanted to come to the beach and write my masterpiece and I didn't do it. My whole life is a joke. I'm a dud. I haven't been able to create anything."

Ryan watched her carefully. For once in his life he didn't immediately try to diminish her feelings. Bronwyn was surprised. She stared at him, waiting for a thoughtless comment or an eye roll.

None of that came. Instead he took a moment to watch the boys. They had finished the first layer of their castle and were digging a mote.

Without taking his eyes off of them, he said, "You have created something amazing, Nicole. Just look."

Bronwyn drew her breath in sharply at his words, switching her eyes to Jeremiah and Nathaniel. Her heart swelling.

Her boys.

It was true. She had created them. She had created a family and a home. She thought she had created a marriage. Her eyes fell back to Ryan who was still watching their boys. She wondered if there was anything of that marriage still remaining.

He turned to her again, his face full of contrition. "I know I've done a terrible thing and I can't tell you how sorry I am."

Bronwyn's eyes filled with tears again. This time she didn't try to hold them back. Even though Ryan's face was blurred from her crying, she could hear the remorse in his voice.

"I hurt you and the boys. I threw away what we had. I can't change what I did, Nicole."

Her throat burned as she tried her best not to break down in the middle of the beach.

"But I want to try again. If you'll have me."

Bronwyn covered her face with her hands. Even if she could speak, she wouldn't know what to say. What had happened to Bronwyn Beck's brash declarations of freedom at the beginning of the summer? Where was her fortitude and independence?

In the trash can with the manuscript she had copied from Lacy Spencer, that's where.

She sucked in her breath to stop the tears from flowing and wiped them from her eyes and cheeks. Taking a shuddering breath, she looked Ryan dead in the eyes. "What about the divorce?"

Stunned, but only for a second, Ryan answered, "I didn't file for divorce. Did you?"

"No."

"Then we're still married. We're still a family."

He was half right. They were still married, but she wasn't sure if they were still a family.

Phoebe

It had been several days since Tanner helped her switch the manuscripts at his aunt's office. And what mighty days they had been.

Phoebe smiled to herself at the word 'mighty'. When she had named the Mighty Aphrodite Writing Society she had planned to empower herself and other writers with that word. Almost none of the ways she had imagined that empowerment might happen had come true.

Yet here she was, proudly striding down the beach on her morning walk, full of a sense of purpose and ability like she had never before experienced in her life.

All three of the Mighty Aphrodites had changed in unexpected ways. They had all started out with the goal of writing their first novel and propelling themselves into the world of their dreams to become professional authors. Yet circumstances and their personal choices had shifted each of their dreams in wildly different directions.

Bronwyn had struggled. With her marriage on the rocks she had spent much of her time on the writing retreat drinking away her pain, processing her emotions, and copying another author to try to rekindle her love of writing. With her husband and sons visiting Sol Mate, Phoebe had glimpsed what Bronwyn's life had been as Nicole. She wondered what her friend would choose to do when their time in Turtle Cove came to an end.

Violet had already chosen, it seemed. After pulling back on volunteering at Marine Life Rescue, she had kept her head down researching and writing newspaper articles. Phoebe had seen a side of Violet she had never known existed. She was driven, sharply intelligent, and motivated to expand her writing career, just not in fiction. Who could have guessed that would happen?

"And what about you, Phoebe?" Phoebe asked the wind.

She was walking along the shoreline, as had been her habit all summer. This time, however, she had driven to another beautiful beach in Turtle Cove, because she wanted to avoid seeing Tanner. Not that she couldn't handle seeing him, but she really needed to spend more time alone with her thoughts.

Phoebe knew that she would always carry tender feelings for Tanner. Love never truly went away, did it? But she also knew that she didn't need to let those feelings interfere with her future. Especially since she and Tanner were not a couple, never would be a couple, and would probably never see each other after she left Turtle Cove.

She sighed, looking out over the pink morning light reflected on endless blue water. Small waves peaked, creating slivers of white foam that rolled closer and closer until washing up on the sand at her bare feet. Beautiful. Hypnotizing.

"I wish I could stay here," she said to the waves. The lonely sound of a single seagull cried out as if in answer to her request.

She smiled. Though she would love to stay, she was grateful to have had the summer in Turtle Cove and the experiences which had reinforced her strongest desires.

Writing all summer and learning that her work was enhanced

when she allowed her inner most emotions to flow had only intensified her dream of being a full time author. Walking into the publisher's office had been inspiring as well. But the final ingredient in her metamorphosis into a woman obsessed with being a writer, was seeing her own words printed out and placed neatly in Mr. Randolph's leather binder.

That moment had dramatically changed her perspective. The dream she had always thought was far away and out of reach, suddenly wasn't. Her words, no matter how good they were or how they got there, were going to be read by a senior editor at a publishing company. From that point forward, Phoebe realized, she was hooked forever.

Of course, she had a few things to work out. When she left Turtle Cove in a few weeks she didn't have a place to live or a job. Thankfully, her parents had offered to let her stay at their house while she was looking for work. And there was always her Aunt Scarlet, who would love for her to visit for a while. And after she was settled in with one of her relatives, she had decided the best approach to her bigger goal of becoming a writer.

Phoebe had come up with a simple, yet doable plan. She would get the easiest job she could find and the cheapest place she could rent. Then she could spend every waking hour that she wasn't working to survive, writing her book.

"And the summer's not over yet," she reminded herself.

There were a little over two weeks left of the Mighty Aphrodite Writing Society writing retreat and Phoebe was going to fill every moment working to complete her Lady Everton novel. Just in case Tanner's aunt, or Mr. Randolph, wanted to see the rest of it.

Bronwyn

Bronwyn got up earlier than the others, which was a first, and made scrambled eggs and buttermilk biscuits using her mother's biscuit recipe. The delicious smells mingled with the scent of freshly brewed coffee and drew Phoebe and Violet downstairs.

"To what do we owe this pleasure?" Violet asked as she sat down to the steaming hot breakfast.

"Oh, I don't know. I'm feeling domestic," Bronwyn answered. Ryan and the boys had gone home the day before and she was still in Mom mode. It felt good, which she had not expected at all.

"How did everything go with Ryan?" Phoebe asked.

Bronwyn took a cleansing breath. "I am feeling cautiously optimistic."

"Really?" Violet's eyes flew open and she put her hand on Bronwyn's arm. "Are you serious?"

Bronwyn nodded, a smile growing on her lips. "I am."

Phoebe's smile stiffened. "You're getting back together with him?"

"I know what you're both thinking, but it's not like that. I'm not going to ignore everything he's done. But we're not getting divorced. At least not right now."

"So a trial separation or something like that?" Violet asked, biting into a fluffy buttermilk biscuit. Before Bronwyn could answer, Violet's shoulders dropped and she put her non-biscuit holding hand on her chest. She spoke with her mouth full, "Oh my God, these are delicious."

Bronwyn chuckled. "I'm glad you like them, they're my mother's biscuits."

As Violet swallowed she made a variety of delighted moans. "So good! You could have a restaurant."

Amused at how much Violet was enjoying her breakfast, Bronwyn grinned.

"Back to the whole no divorce thing," Phoebe interjected. "If you're not separating, what are you going to do?"

"We're going to go to counseling. He wants to try again," Bronwyn answered.

"Is that what you want?" Violet slathered butter and jelly onto one side of her biscuit.

"What I want is for it to never have happened at all. But that's not possible. Second best would be if my kids didn't have to grow up in a broken home and Ryan and I could find a way to be happy together."

There was a pause as her words sank in, then Phoebe straightened her shoulders and nodded. "If you want to try to work things out then counseling is a good idea."

Violet followed her lead. "I can understand wanting to explore all possible options before getting divorced."

Bronwyn knew this wasn't a full endorsement of her plans, but she appreciated Phoebe and Violet trying to be positive. It wasn't her dream life, but working on her relationship and keeping her family together was a start. Her famous author persona was going to have to wait a while longer.

As if reading her mind, Phoebe asked, "You won't be giving up on Bronwyn Beck, will you?"

Bronwyn scoffed. "Absolutely not! I may be Nicole in the suburbs, but here with my Mighty Aphrodites I will always be Bronwyn Beck."

Violet finished the last bite of her biscuit and reached for another one. "Will you always make these biscuits for us, too, please?"

"Of course! In fact, I was thinking we need a special dinner. A kind of end of the writing retreat shindig."

"Yes," Phoebe nodded whole heartedly. "What should we do?"

Bronwyn was a little uncertain about what she had in mind. "I would like to cook for you two."

"But that's so much work," Violet said.

"It won't be that bad. Besides, I like to cook. I haven't done enough of it this summer. Plus I'll have a lot more free time than you two."

"Why is that?" Phoebe was puzzled.

"Because I'm not going to write any more on the retreat." Bronwyn looked back and forth at both of them. They were shocked. "I wasn't really writing my own stuff anyway, as you know. And all I can handle at the moment is writing in my journal, which won't take up hours of my day."

"But–" Violet started to protest.

Bronwyn held up her hand for her to stop. "I won't hear any more about it. You have your articles to work on and Phoebe needs to finish her novel. What if Giant Publishing wants to see the finished product? No, you're not going to help me. You're both busy, which I'm fine with, I promise. I want to cook the goodbye dinner. It will make me feel good."

In the end, Bronwyn got her way and she left Phoebe and Violet tapping happily away on their keyboards while she went out on her own to do menu planning and peruse the different grocery stores and markets for supplies.

At the Salty Java she got an iced latte and set about planning the menu. She liked doing those types of tasks at coffee shops. Also she needed to pick up more of their bagged coffee, which was delicious and they were almost out.

Under an orange umbrella at a turquoise blue table on the patio of the Salty Java overlooking one of Turtle Cove's quaintest streets, Bronwyn searched her laptop for her best recipes. She had digital copies of all of the favorite show stoppers she had cooked over the years, organized by food type and cross referenced under categories like holidays, time of year, formal or informal, as well as the standard breakfast, lunch, dinner and desserts.

For the goodbye dinner she wanted to do something quintessentially beach house. Casual chic, filling but not heavy, and something that would wow Phoebe and Violet. May as well go out with a bang for her cooking since her writing hadn't panned out.

She didn't normally begin with desserts, but she had been thinking about making mini lime tarts for a while, which would be yummy. And, for a bit more of a challenge, she would do a chocolate strawberry pavlova that she had done once for a dinner party. Bronwyn was scribbling her choices on a pad of paper when she heard a familiar voice. She turned to find Bill smiling politely down at her.

"Good morning," he said.

She noted he did not use her name. How could he? He didn't know which one she was using today.

Fighting the urge to shrink away from him, she managed a too bright smile. "And a good morning to you, too, Bill." That wasn't cringy at all. What was she, a leprechaun? Seeing he carried a fresh cup of coffee and to prove she wasn't embarrassed, she blurted out, "Would you care to join me?"

Bill hesitated for an instant, a flicker of what might be amusement crossing his face, before he answered, "I'd love to. As long as you aren't going to pass out on me."

Bronwyn barked out a laugh, an over the top laugh, but managed to get it together enough to look him in the eye when he sat down across from her. She gripped her pen tightly as he glanced down at the scribbles on her pad of paper.

"Are those menu ideas?" he asked.

A little surprised he could tell from such a cursory glance, she gave him a light smile. "Why, yes, they are. I'm making a sort of celebratory goodbye dinner for our retreat."

"Nice." He leaned closer and peeked at what she had on her list. "Pavlova?"

"Yes, do you like Pavlova?"

He thought about the question. "Isn't that like merengue?"

"Very good, I'm impressed. Do you cook?"

"A little," he admitted. Then with a twinkle in his eye, "I do like to eat, however."

Bronwyn laughed.

"When is this dinner? Maybe I should find a reason to come by and fix something on the house," he teased.

Disarmed, she relaxed a little bit and found that she wanted to make amends for her behavior at the fundraiser party. Tapping her pen lightly on the table she lifted her eyes to his.

"Bill, I would like to apologize."

"For what?" He took a sip of his coffee.

"The other night at the fundraiser. I kind of went off on you for no good reason." He kept his reaction neutral. Smart man. "I'd had a little bit too much to drink and, well, I know I've told you conflicting information since we met, like..."

"Your name?" The corners of his mouth twitched into an almost smile and he took another drink of coffee.

Heat rushed into her cheeks. "Yes, my name for one."

He pressed his lips together as he swallowed then let out a satisfied breath. "Ah, well, Violet explained to me about how you were using your pen name for the summer. No big deal."

Lifting her eyebrows, she nodded her head as if she wasn't surprised at all to hear that he had spoken about her to Violet. "Right, well, I've been having some, um, I guess you could call them *issues* with my husband since I've been here. And when I saw you with your girlfriend the whole May-December relationship thing sort of pushed the wrong buttons in my psyche and, I'll admit, sent me over the edge a teeny weeny bit."

When she paused to take a breath Bronwyn saw the confusion in Bill's eyes.

"My girlfriend?"

"Yes, your beautiful young girlfriend. At the party."

"I, uh, I don't have a girlfriend."

He looked stumped. Just as stumped as Bronwyn felt.

"The beautiful young thing you introduced me to. What was her name? It started with an 'M'."

Bill's face tensed. "Maya."

"That's right, Maya." She could see that he was not pleased at her mention of the girl. Maybe they weren't an item. "I don't mean to pry or anything. It's really none of my business. I'm just saying that seeing you two together made me think of...of other things going on in my life that I haven't exactly–"

"Maya's my daughter."

Bronwyn stopped talking and stared at him. She blinked several times before asking, "Your daughter?"

"Yes, my daughter." He let out a dry laugh. She didn't know if he was amused or offended.

"Oh, I...I didn't realize." Her body sunk slightly in her chair from a heaviness she didn't understand.

"Obviously," he laughed again, this one came out as more of a snort. He looked away then back at her in disbelief. "You really do take the cake, Bronwyn."

A nervous smile played on her lips and she swept one side of her hair back, tucking it behind her ear. "I'm going to take that as a compliment, if you don't mind."

He chuckled and shook his head slightly, but didn't respond.

He merely lifted his cup to his mouth and took a sip, watching her over the edge as he did.

Sensing a chance to move on with the conversation, she continued her explanation, "I've been a little on edge all summer, is what I'm trying to say."

"Problems with the husband?"

She nodded, sliding her eyes to her coffee cup to avoid his direct gaze.

"May I ask you something?" He folded his hands on the table in front of him.

"Sure." She cupped her coffee mug with both hands.

"What are you doing when summer's over? When your time is up at Sol Mate?"

A weight hung in the air between them. Bronwyn's breathing slowed. She ran one thumb up and down the side of her mug.

When she looked up at him, he was watching her, but there was distance in his eyes.

"I'm going back home. We, my husband and I, are going to counseling."

Bill didn't move. His expression didn't change. She swore she saw a flash of pain in his eyes, but it was gone so fast she couldn't be sure. Nothing but wishful thinking.

Finally, he cleared his throat and nodded. "I wish you all the best, Bronwyn. I really do."

Her heart twisted in her chest. Maybe because he had become so stiff and formal, or maybe because he was calling her Bronwyn, the name she had chosen for her new life. The life that was no more.

There was nothing to be done about any of it. All things must come to an end, sometimes before they even begin.

Sixty

Phoebe

Phoebe couldn't believe their time at Turtle Cove was almost over. The last several days had flown by and they were already sitting down to the writing retreat goodbye dinner that Bronwyn had painstakingly prepared.

Since they were checking out of Sol Mate on a Thursday morning, they had opted to have their goodbye celebration the Friday of the weekend before.

"Because if we wait until the night before we leave we'll get busy packing and planning to travel and we won't have time to really enjoy each other," Bronwyn had insisted.

Phoebe could see the logic in that. She was already processing her exit from Turtle Cove back into the real world. Having this one last big Friday night at the beach house had sounded like a good idea.

"Everything smells delicious," Violet stood next to Bronwyn at the grill on the deck, sipping a Bahama Mama.

"These are really good, too," Phoebe took another sip of her coconut rum and pineapple juice Bahama Mama.

"I figured we needed a festive cocktail. Though I'm only having one!" Bronwyn laughed.

Phoebe admired the table Bronwyn had set with Sol Mate's coral and white dishes, blue starfish cloth napkins, and coordinating coral and blue candles. "Where did you find these napkins?"

"I picked those up at Oceanfront Market. I got these at Poseidon's." Bronwyn held up one of the skewers of shrimp she was turning on the grill. There were several already sizzling and next to the skewers loaded with fat spiced shrimp were skewers with chunks of marinated steak, cherry tomatoes, and bell peppers. "These are the margarita shrimp and these are garlic butter steak kabobs."

"Delicious," Phoebe said. "Anything else I can do to help?"

"You can bring out the salad and the rolls."

Phoebe went inside to grab those items. Pausing at the kitchen window, she looked out at Violet and Bronwyn who were laughing and talking over the grill. The late afternoon sun shone in a brilliant blue sky creating the perfect backdrop for her two friends.

Unseen by them, Phoebe watched, taken in by their beauty.

Bronwyn's smile was bright and genuine as she said something to Violet. Apparently it was a joke, because Violet bent forward laughing, her cheeks flushed from her cocktail and the fun conversation.

Phoebe was struck at how changed they were from when they had arrived at the retreat. Besides having healthy glowing skin and that special beach hair look that only happens by spending a lot of time in and near salt water, they both appeared...happy.

Smiling softly, Phoebe wondered if she appeared the same to them. She certainly felt different since she had first arrived at Sol Mate. Even though not everything had turned out the way they had each wanted, they had shared some memorable experiences and were all changed, she hoped, for the better.

Grabbing the asparagus salad from the fridge and the basket of French rolls Bronwyn had made from scratch, she joined them on the deck.

"I'll open the wine," Violet announced, picking up a bottle of Rioja that waited on the table.

"Good, these will be done in just a minute. Pick your seat!" Bronwyn attended to the grill while Phoebe and Violet sat down.

When the steak and shrimp were on the table and they were all seated, Bronwyn raised her wine glass. "A toast to the Mighty Aphrodite summer! And what a summer it was."

Phoebe and Violet laughed and raised their glasses, too.

"You've really outdone yourself," Phoebe told Bronwyn as they dug into the food.

Violet finished her first shrimp. "Seriously, this is better than the lunch we had at Silver Tide."

"It really is, Bronwyn. And that's the fanciest restaurant in Turtle Cove!" Phoebe added.

Bronwyn shook her head demurely and sat back in her chair with her wine, watching them enjoy her food. "That's very kind, but I doubt it's that good. Also, I think Cobalt Edge is the fanciest restaurant in Turtle Cove," she added with a laugh.

"Oh, that's right. I meant to go there to eat before the summer was over, but I got distracted by everything," Phoebe said, disappointed.

"We still have time, don't we?" Violet asked.

"I wish we did. It's a reservation only kind of place. And you need to have them weeks in advance I hear." Phoebe gave her a sad smile.

"Maybe we can go next time." Bronwyn lifted her eyebrows at them expectantly as she scooped asparagus salad onto her plate. "What do you ladies say? Shall we do this again next year?"

Phoebe's pulse quickened at the suggestion.

"That would be wonderful," Violet said, her eyes shining for a moment before dropping briefly to her lap. "But I don't know if I'll be able to afford it."

"I'm in the same boat," Phoebe confessed, her own excitement ebbing. "I don't know how literally anything in my life is going to work out after we leave. I would love to do this again next summer, though."

Bronwyn nodded somberly. "I know what you mean. I guess I don't know what's going to be happening next summer with me either." Her eyes shone with tears. "But I don't want to lose you two after we go back to our lives."

Tears sprung up in Phoebe's eyes as well. "We won't lose each other," she promised.

"We'll still have our online Aphrodite writing meetings, won't we?" Violet seemed alarmed at the idea that they might not.

"But what if I'm not writing?" Bronwyn asked.

"If you're not writing then you can fill us in on how everything's going with you and Ryan." Phoebe suggested. "And once we all figure out a few details in our lives we can book Sol Mate again. Although I doubt we'll have time to set aside the whole summer. I'm sure Bill will fit us in where he can."

The sound of knocking drifted to them from the inside of the house.

"Speaking of Bill, he threatened to come by when I was cooking." Bronwyn chuckled at the thought, then added, "But I didn't tell him our goodbye dinner was tonight."

Interested in when that conversation had taken place, Phoebe started to ask Bronwyn to give them details when Tanner came around the outside corner of the house.

"Hey, ladies," he said.

The sight of him put a silly grin on Phoebe's face, which she found difficult to suppress. Ignoring the look Bronwyn and Violet were giving one another at her reaction, she asked, "Tanner, what's going on?"

Easily hopping over the deck railing, he approached the spread of food on the table with a low whistle. "You do it up here at the beach house, don't you?"

"Are you hungry? We have plenty." Bronwyn began to stand in order to set a place for him.

He held up his hand to stop her. "No, thank you, I don't want to intrude on your nice dinner."

All three of the Mighty Aphrodites protested, but he refused politely.

"I'm only here because I have big news for you." He turned to Phoebe, his eyes dancing with a secret.

The buzz she felt inside her stomach just from being in his presence increased tenfold. Phoebe's eyes widened. No. He couldn't mean...

Unable to contain himself for any more chit chat, Tanner bent down and put both hands on her arm. "My Aunt Brenda wants to see the rest of your book!"

Phoebe's mouth fell open.

Violet and Bronwyn both gasped then erupted into squeals of excitement.

Tanner squeezed her arm, his eyes still shining. "She was checking messages on her yoga vacation and said Mr. Randolph called to tell her that he loved it. They want to see more." He gave her arm a congratulatory shake before releasing it. "You did it, Phoebe!"

Phoebe sat perfectly still, her heart and mind racing too fast to respond.

"Oh my God, Phoebe!" Violet jumped out of her chair and came to Phoebe's side, leaning down to hug her shoulders.

"Well done, Phoebe," Bronwyn rocked back and forth in her chair and clapped, her eyes full of delight.

Phoebe's insides vibrated as she tried to find words, tried to find her breath. The laughter and excited chatter of the others buzzed in her ears.

Tanner crouched down next to her, his face bright. "What do you think? Are you excited?"

"She's in shock is what she is," Bronwyn said.

Anchored next to her, Tanner reached over and took her hand. "I'm so excited for you. Are you happy about it?"

Phoebe managed to lift her eyes to his. Those deep brown eyes. That brilliant smile. Her hand in his. Her book on the desk of a publisher who was interested to see more. Phoebe could hardly ask for more in life.

"I can barely believe it." Her words came out in a whisper.

"Well, believe it, Phoebe Collins," he said. "You're gonna go far in life. You should get used to it."

"Tanner you should eat with us," Violet said.

"No, you ladies go ahead with your dinner," he insisted. Catching Phoebe's eye again, he added, "I do want to take you out to celebrate, though. I still owe you a thank you dinner, you know."

Phoebe's heart twirled in her chest. She hoped he thought she was only excited about his news, not at the prospect of going out with him.

"You don't have to–" she started.

"I'm not taking no for an answer. Does tomorrow night work for you?"

Phoebe looked to Bronwyn and Violet, uncertain how to answer. They were both beaming and nodding–vigorously.

With her heart feeling as if it had been tied to a balloon and was about to be let go into the atmosphere, Phoebe answered, "Okay. Tomorrow night sounds good."

Sixty-One

Violet

After a full night of celebrating their Mighty Aphrodite retreat and Phoebe's good news, Violet woke in the morning with a slight heaviness in her chest. She slipped out of bed and went to her private balcony.

Sunlight barely lit the early morning sky, but the birds were already announcing its arrival. Surprised at the coolness in the air, Violet grabbed a light sweater and pulled it on as she sat in the chair to look out over the landscaping.

Her favorite flowering Bougainvillea was still going strong. She swore the giant climbing plant covered with hot pink blooms had grown several feet since the beginning of the summer. Along its base, the Bougainvillea was complimented by gorgeous Cape Honeysuckles with orange blooms and another one of her favorites, Hibiscus, whose showy red flowers reminded her that she was in a tropical paradise.

Violet took in a deep slow breath, the sweet scent of the flowers mixed with the fresh salty breeze coming off of the ocean and refreshed her...for a moment. She hugged her sweater closer to her body, thinking about what was to come.

In a matter of days she would return to her real life. Her condo, her job. That was it, she realized. There was nothing else. No boyfriend or husband or children. No pets. She did have her family, she supposed. But she had moved a whole state away from them when she took her teaching job so many years ago and had grown accustomed to the distance.

There were her friends, of course. Her co-workers, actually. Fellow teachers slugging it out in the education system that held equal parts joy and grief. And for her the joys didn't outweigh the grief. She didn't share their passion for bringing knowledge to the youth of the world. She admired the passion, certainly, but didn't share it.

As she pondered the life she had created, Violet realized she had never spent an evening talking and laughing with her fellow teachers. She had never worked through difficult moments with any of them. Not like she had with the Mighty Aphrodites this past summer.

She wondered what her life would have turned into if she had tried to become a writer sooner. Really tried. If she hadn't let the world tell her she wasn't as smart and inspiring as Virginia Woolf or Jane Austen, what might her life have looked like?

"The world will never know," Violet said to herself.

Watching Phoebe react to Tanner's news the night before had been bittersweet for Violet. The joy she felt for her friend's success in impressing the senior editor and potentially becoming a published author was genuine. But she couldn't deny a twinge of sadness in her heart when acknowledging that success would never be one she shared with Phoebe.

She couldn't envision that kind of future for herself, but couldn't deny the ache it left in her soul. Seemed like a shame that she had squandered any chance of it ever happening in her life.

Violet Brown even sounded like a classic literature author's name, she had always thought. But that dream was in the past. As were a lot of things. As would be her summer as an Aphrodite on the beaches of Turtle Cove soon enough.

Violet cleared her throat to stop the lump threatening to form and sat up straighter in her chair. "No reason to dwell on the past. I've got work to do."

If she started right away she could get a few good paragraphs in on her latest article about the amount of plastics found in sea animals globally. Quick answer, too much. But she had found some resources to expand on that thought, give real numbers, and provide plausible solutions.

She went inside to her small desk to get her laptop, which she had left charging all night. When she flipped it open there was a warning on her screen that the battery was almost dead.

"Shoot," she muttered, inspecting the charger to make sure she had plugged it into the wall. She had. Next she plugged it back into the laptop, but there was no juice. She wiggled the connection. Still nothing. "Well, great."

Violet dug through the laptop bag for her backup charger. Nothing. After a quick search of the desk drawers and her purse, she remembered where she had left it. At Ben's.

Going back by Marine Life Rescue and seeing Ben again wasn't high on her list of things she wanted to do that day. But she needed her charger and she supposed it wouldn't be terrible to see him one last time. It wasn't like they had been dating and she broke up with him or anything quite that dramatic.

Walking into the conservatory and seeing Ben studying his own laptop at the work table they had shared so many times pricked Violet's heart, but she managed a friendly smile when he looked up.

"Violet." It took a few moments for her presence to register, then he smiled warmly and reached out an open hand in her direction. "To what do I owe this pleasure?"

"Hey," she waved awkwardly, her body feeling a little too wobbly to respond to his greeting properly. Looking for something to say, she suddenly noticed Bear wasn't at her feet greeting her with sloppy kisses. "Where's Bear?"

Ben stood and came around the table, closer to where she stood. "He's at the groomer's. He'll be bummed that he missed you."

Violet lowered her head briefly as she chuckled.

Ben's smile grew wider. He turned and pulled out a chair for her. "Please, sit down and tell me what I can do for you today."

Violet sat down, straightening her peach cotton sundress. "Nothing big. I forgot my charger here, that's all."

"Your charger!" Ben put one hand on his chest and feigned surprise making Violet laugh again. Then he went to the drawer underneath the printer on the counter and pulled it out. "This charger?"

"That's the one."

He sat down in the chair opposite her and pushed the charger across the table, but when Violet reached to pick it up he snatched it back.

"Wait, I have a proposal for you." Ben's eyes twinkled.

Violet's eyebrows lifted and heat rushed through her body. The moisture in her mouth dried up. Shocked at her reaction, she squeaked out, "Oh?"

Excited, Ben leaned forward. "I've been working out the numbers all morning just to be sure."

Violet managed to swallow. "Be sure about what?"

"We received so many more donations than we ever have before at the fundraiser. Thanks in no small part to you and all of your hard work."

Violet kept her eyes locked on Ben's, not sure where he was going with this line of thought.

"I know, get to the point, Ben," he laughed nervously. "The thing is, we have enough to hire an administrative assistant. It's not the best pay in the world, but it's not bad. Right now I still have to get it approved by the board, which I don't think will be a problem. But we have the money and it means the conservatory can grow. We can do more for the marine life and get the word out, and really, the sky's the limit if we can continue this level of fundraising in the future."

He stopped to take a breath. Violet didn't think he knew how fast he had been talking, but her head was spinning with his news. Her involvement had increased donations so much he could hire someone to help?

"That's fantastic news, Ben!"

"Wait, I'm not done yet." He reached across the table with both palms facing her, entreating her to pause all comments.

"What other news is there?" She couldn't imagine anything more exciting.

"I want you to be the administrative assistant," he said, his eyes big and hopeful.

Violet blinked several times, his words not quite sinking in.

"If you're interested, that is. If it's something you would like to do. I know it's kind of sudden, I just got the numbers worked out," he added, his hope dimming at her lack of reaction.

"I don't know what to say," Violet said quietly.

"I was hoping you would say yes." Ben's hands went limp and he drug them across the table as he leaned back in his chair. "You don't want to, do you?"

"No, no, it's not that I don't want to. I don't think I can." As she spoke the words she knew that it was true. She couldn't give up her benefits and pension at her teaching position until she had something more lucrative set up. Something that was more in line with what she wanted to be. A writer.

Shoulders dropping, he tilted his head down and frowned at his hands. "That's disappointing."

"I'm sorry, Ben. It's a great offer. If I didn't have my teaching contract I would consider it."

"You would?" He looked up at her with a wince in his eyes, questioning her truthfulness.

"I would. Of course I would."

Ben shifted in his chair, offering her a weak smile. "Can't say

I'm not bummed, but I understand. Too bad, we could have made a good team."

She nodded, her voice threatening to tremble. "Maybe," she said, but she couldn't say anything more. Her heart was shrinking inside of her chest and all she could do was sit there and hope it wouldn't disappear altogether.

Sixty-Two

Phoebe

N *ot casual.*

That's what Tanner had answered when Phoebe texted him about what to wear to dinner. He refused to tell her where they were going to eat, insisting that it was a surprise. All she was allowed to ask was what she should wear.

"Not casual is what he said. That would mean it's someplace nice, right?" she asked Violet and Bronwyn who were, once again, doing her hair for the big night.

"I would say yes," Bronwyn answered as she brushed out Phoebe's long dark locks so they could be curled and braided into an impressive do.

"Why don't you wear this?" Violet pulled the plum dress she had worn to the beach party fundraiser out of the closet.

Phoebe balked at the idea. "That's too much, isn't it?"

"There's no such thing," Bronwyn quipped.

Violet held the dress out to study it. "Technically it's not a formal gown, is it?"

"Nope," Bronwyn answered.

Phoebe squinted at the dress and wrinkled her nose. "You don't think it will make me look...desperate?"

"Are you desperate?" Bronwyn asked.

"Good question." Phoebe had been wondering that very thing all day and had not come to a conclusion. "I'm not sure."

"You're not desperate." Violet held the dress in front of her and showed it off to Phoebe. "How is it desperate to accept an invitation to dinner and wear a nice dress?"

Bronwyn caught Phoebe's eye in the mirror. "You're not desperate, Phoebe. You're a strong, beautiful woman who should wear whatever she damn well pleases to dinner."

Decision made. Phoebe ended up answering the door to Tanner a few hours later in her flowing, fluttering, flirty fundraiser dress.

When he saw her he put his hand on his heart like he had been shot with an arrow. As if looking at her was causing him exquisite pain, his posture loosened for a second then he caught himself and stood tall again. "Wow, you're beautiful."

If Phoebe could have responded, she would have, but she was equally taken aback by him. Tanner was not dressed in his standard shorts and polo shirt. Nor was he dressed in his slightly more fancy khaki pants and silky dress shirt. No, he was all decked out in a pair of navy slacks, white dress shirt and a cream colored blazer. She didn't know he owned a blazer.

Her shock was complete when Tanner presented her with a white rose. She took it, blushing, and tried to ignore the gasps and giggles coming from Violet and Bronwyn who were watching from down the hall.

"Thank you."

"Shall we?" Tanner offered her his arm.

She took it and allowed him to lead her to his car, repeating one phrase over and over in her mind – we're only friends, we're only friends, we're only friends.

In the car there were two Phoebes. One sat normally in the

passenger seat, talking and laughing with Tanner easily. The second one, not so much.

Phoebe Two was completely quiet, observing Tanner as he drove. Drinking in the way he looked, the sound of his voice, the scent of his cologne. Phoebe Two couldn't move past the surreal sensation she was having that this man, this gorgeous, kind, intelligent, funny man, was taking her to dinner. Phoebe Two's fingers trembled as she held the white rose in her lap.

There was something so dreamy about his presence in the car. His dashing good looks and easy smile seemed to Phoebe Two to be right out of a movie. Intended to make women across the world swoon, not meant for her sole enjoyment.

Phoebe One told Phoebe Two to stop being so ridiculous. She wasn't a schoolgirl with a crush. She was a grown woman who didn't need to freak out about riding in a car with a gorgeous man.

As Phoebe wrestled with her two personas so she could enjoy the evening without gawking at Tanner like a rock star groupie, she realized she had not been paying attention to where he was driving.

Looking out the window she saw sand and water and Turtle Cove's pier. "We're eating on the beach?"

"Not exactly."

A few minutes later they were strolling down the pier, Phoebe still wondering what he had up his sleeve, but too wrapped up in enjoying the moment to care when or where they ate. An early evening sun shone softly down as the ocean's deep blue stretched out to forever around them. As the end of the pier grew nearer, delicious smells from the exclusive restaurant, Cobalt Edge, increased her appetite.

They encountered more and more well dressed couples out for an evening of fine dining. Glad they had both dressed up, Phoebe's heart swelled when Tanner once again offered her his arm and she took it. Certain she was the luckiest woman on that pier, Phoebe wished they could stay in the moment indefinitely.

Suspended above the magnificent ocean, away from the beach, under a brilliant sky that promised anything was possible.

To her surprise Tanner didn't veer away from the slow flow of people approaching Cobalt Edge's door. Still, it took far too long for Phoebe to connect the dots. When it finally dawned on her where they were going for dinner she stopped short.

"Are we having dinner here!?"

Tanner nodded, putting his hand over hers on his arm. "Yes, we are."

Phoebe gasped and covered her mouth with one hand. "I can't believe it!"

"Well, believe it."

"How did you get reservations?"

He tilted his head and squinted one eye. "It's kind of a long story. I'll tell you over dinner."

Cobalt Edge did not disappoint. Travertine floors, tongue and groove ceilings, black rattan chairs and tables, set with white table cloths and shimmering dinnerware, the restaurant boasted nearly 360 degree views of the ocean. The brilliant blue of sky and water were reflected in the blue glass centerpieces that graced each table and blue and white flower arrangements placed strategically around the dining area.

After talking about the beautiful decor and ordering, Phoebe asked, "So, how did you get a reservation?"

Tanner grinned and wiggled his eyebrows up and down. "I called and gave them my name."

"That's not all, is it?" Phoebe glanced around at their elegant surroundings. "I was told you needed to call weeks and weeks in advance to get in here."

"I did," he said lightly.

"You made this reservation weeks ago?"

He nodded, but before she could press him for more information the waiter brought their appetizer, char-grilled octopus. An unpleasant thought came to Phoebe. If Tanner had made the reservation weeks ago, it was probably to take Layla to Cobalt

Edge and for some reason she couldn't make it. Phoebe was merely taking the other woman's place for the night.

"This smells amazing," Tanner rubbed his hands together.

Phoebe nodded and offered a thin smile. Some of the fun had been sucked out of the room by her realization. She watched Tanner as he dished up a portion of octopus onto her small appetizer plate then took one for himself.

She dropped her gaze into her lap for a moment and gathered her emotions. She didn't need to obsess over his girlfriend. They were here together tonight enjoying a lovely evening and what promised to be some delicious food and she wanted to be grateful for the moment. Stop pining for a future that would never be.

Tanner moaned in ecstasy as he chewed the octopus. He pointed his fork at Phoebe's plate and swallowed. "You've got to try this."

Phoebe picked up her fork, it was smooth and heavy in her hand. She stabbed a chunk of octopus and put it in her mouth then closed her eyes as the flavors overtook everything else on her mind.

"Wow," she murmured, still chewing.

"Yeah, wow," Tanner agreed. He readied another bite. Right before putting it in his mouth he continued their pre-octopus conversation. "I made this reservation the day after you got sick at Coastline Inn and had to go home."

Phoebe cocked her head. "You did?" She looked around at all of the dating couples nearby. "I would have thought you'd want to bring Layla here."

Head down chewing, Tanner's eyes shot up at her at the mention of Layla's name. He shook his head as he swallowed. "I made the reservation to bring you here. Because we never got to eat dinner that night."

"Oh," Phoebe was surprised. Trying to stay nonchalant she took another bite.

"Of course, I didn't know at the time that we would have your book to celebrate also."

She smiled brightly and chewed happily on the rather large piece of octopus in her mouth, nodding.

Tanner put his fork down, wiping his mouth with his napkin. He leveled his gaze at her and cleared his throat. "I also didn't know..." he hesitated and took a quick drink of water, clearing his throat again.

Phoebe continued to chew, watching him with interest. If she didn't know better she might think he was nervous.

He looked at her again, this time not breaking away. "I also didn't know that I was going to break up with Layla."

Phoebe stopped chewing.

Tanner watched her reaction.

Staring at him in shock, she tried to think of something to say, then remembered she had a mouth full of grilled octopus. The flavors seeped down the back of her throat, threatening to make her cough. Terrified of repeating her choking and subsequent Heimlich maneuver incident with Tanner, she grabbed her own water and took a swallow large enough to force the entire mouthful down.

Wiping her mouth with her napkin she leaned back in her chair, attempting a look of calm observance. "You broke up with Layla?"

Tanner nodded. He picked up a roll from the basket and tore off a piece. "Yep."

"Wh–" Phoebe's voice cracked and she covered her mouth with her napkin to cough before continuing, "When did that happen?"

Tanner scrunched his eyes together, feigning memory loss. When she thought she couldn't take it any more he grinned and said, "The day after the party."

Phoebe's mind ticked back. "The day you took my manuscript to your aunt?"

He nodded, refilling his plate with more grilled octopus.

"I'm sorry, Tanner. I was so wrapped up in my stuff I didn't even notice that you were going through a break up."

He lifted one shoulder and let it drop in a half shrug, but Phoebe was filled with sympathy. How could she have been so selfish to not see his pain?

"How are you doing now?" she asked with a sad frown.

Tanner chuckled. "I broke up with her, Phoebe. I'm completely fine." He held eye contact with her, a gleam of amusement glittering in his big brown eyes. "Better than fine."

Sweet warmth filled her body and she had to avert her eyes from his to keep from giggling.

"Enough about that," Tanner announced. "What I want to know is what your book is about. What's got my Aunt Brenda and her boss all excited?"

Intoxicated by his presence and their surroundings and the freedom she suddenly felt knowing it was just her and Tanner with nobody else involved, Phoebe described her book. Without letting him in on the fact that she had used him to model the Colonel, he was still intrigued by the story.

Dinner came. Tanner had lobster risotto. Phoebe had crispy salmon. The conversation flowed as they dined. They easily shared stories and dreams, laughter and something more. Something flitting in the air between them, which Phoebe thought she might be misinterpreting, but felt a lot like flirtation.

After sharing a slice of heavenly cheesecake, Tanner paid the check and they made their way back out onto the pier. The sun was beginning its descent on the horizon, the first pinks and oranges of the coming sunset kissed white puffy clouds.

Phoebe could relate to the clouds. Light and fluffy, content to be exactly where they were, reveling in the glorious beauty of the sun. She smiled at Tanner who was even more handsome than normal in the glow of the pending sunset and after the two glasses of wine she had at dinner.

He guided her smoothly to the railing so they could lean on it and look out over the water. "Did you enjoy yourself?" he asked.

"Yes! This has been really lovely, Tanner."

He nodded, smiling down at her. He turned to face her,

leaning ever so sexily on the railing, and cocked his head. "Would you like to do it again?"

Phoebe's flowing mood stuttered. She glanced at the restaurant behind him, confused. "Eat again?"

"Not tonight. I mean another time. I was hoping you would want to go out to dinner with me again."

Stunned into silence, she turned to face him, not sure what he was asking.

When the pause went on too long, he made a funny cringe face. "Is that a maybe?"

Still in shock, but exhilarated by his words, she pointed a finger at him that just so happened to touch his chest. A jolt of excitement pulsed through her body. She tried to act normal. "Are you teasing? I'm going home this week you know."

He sighed and dropped his big brown eyes to her finger, which was lingering on his chest. "Yeah, about that. I'm not sure of the specifics, but I think we can work that out."

She started to laugh until he wrapped her finger and the rest of her hand in his and lifted his eyes to meet hers. Phoebe held perfectly still, not breathing, not sure what was about to happen until it happened. The most unbelievable, unimaginable, perfectly exquisite thing happened.

Tanner bent down and kissed her lips.

Tenderly, sweetly, he pressed his mouth to hers, holding her hand against his warm muscled chest. Hesitant at first, then not so much, Phoebe found it remarkably easy to kiss him back. Her free hand wandered up to his neck and touched his jaw. Tanner pulled her closer, the kiss deepening. Her heart gave away, releasing a torrent of passion through her body.

When he pulled back from her, he did not release her hand on his chest, but reached up with his free hand and pushed one of the curls Bronwyn had so painstakingly put in her hair away from her face.

"I realized something at the fundraiser," he said.

"That Layla wasn't for you?"

"No, that it was you I wanted to see that night. You I wanted to dance with. You I wanted to talk to. It had nothing to do with Layla, but everything to do with you." He searched her eyes for a response then headed her concerns off at the pass. "Long distance dating is not unheard of. And, who knows, you might be a famous author soon and you can live anywhere you want. Even Turtle Cove. What do you say, Phoebe?"

Phoebe wasn't standing there staring dreamily up into the eyes of her muse, she was floating. No longer part of reality, because her dream man was in front of her asking her to be his.

"I say yes," she answered blissfully.

Tanner smiled and kissed her again, both of them more confident this time. The sound of whinnying came to them over the water. Tanner pulled away. "There's one more thing."

He led her to the opposite side of the pier and pointed to the beach where a young man stood holding two saddled horses. One shining black and one pure white. Tanner waved at the young man who waved back.

"What!?" Phoebe laughed with delight. "What is that about?"

"I've learned a thing or two from you. Romance is important. But even more important is *who* you romance. C'mon, wanna go for a ride?"

That was how, Phoebe Collins, aspiring author, Mighty Aphrodite, came to be flying down the beach on the back of a steed as dark as night. Her hair flowing, her dress billowing behind her, living out a fantasy with the man of her dreams – quite literally the man of her dreams – by her side.

Sixty-Three

Phoebe

It was with tears in her eyes that Phoebe hugged Violet and Bronwyn goodbye the following Thursday morning. Both of them were heading back to their lives. Her plans were still pending.

Pending a job. Pending a new boyfriend. Pending a book getting published. Pending a brand new life.

Not that any of that was bad. All of the possibilities waiting for Phoebe on the horizon were the best things she had ever had pending in her life.

With no job to return home to and every reason to stay in Turtle Cove, Phoebe had taken Violet's suggestion and talked to Ben about the new administrative assistant job at Marine Life Rescue.

"You have all of the qualifications and a great reference in Violet," Ben had told her. "I'm waiting for approval from the board on the salary so the position won't begin until September. Will that work for you?"

Thrilled beyond measure, Phoebe had answered, "Yes, September will be just fine."

With no place to live and her new job in Turtle Cove not starting for a few weeks, Tanner had gone with Phoebe to talk to Bill about staying on at Sol Mate until she found a permanent place.

Bill smiled approvingly as he listened to Tanner describe Phoebe's predicament, as if he could tell Tanner's protectiveness over her was more than just friendly.

"I planned to do a little fixing up on the place. Do you mind if I get some of that done while you're there?" Bill asked Phoebe.

"Oh, no, I don't mind at all."

"Then you can stay for a while longer. That's not a problem."

"Thank you, Bill," Phoebe said. "Would it be okay if I pay you the rent once I get paid from Marine Life Rescue?"

Bill waved her suggestion away. "I'm not gonna charge you rent to stay in a house under repair. Don't worry about it." He gave Phoebe a knowing look and a quick wink, which made her smile. There was no doubt in her mind that Bill knew she and Tanner were dating. She was going to have to get used to that feeling.

As for her book and Giant Publishing, she had turned in all but the last five chapters to Tanner's Aunt Brenda. Those had yet to be written, but she had a few weeks to finish them before her new job started. She wanted to make them the best that they could be.

And then? Who knew? But the potential boggled her mind daily.

As for the Mighty Aphrodites, their last morning together was laced with sadness and laughter.

"Well, Phoebe, you're on your way," Bronwyn announced after she loaded her bags into the trunk of her convertible. "And you're going to have such a great time."

Phoebe smiled sadly. "I don't know. It's going to be so lonely here without you two."

BEACH RETREAT AT TURTLE COVE

"Lucky for you, you'll have Tanner around to keep you company," Bronwyn teased.

Violet joined them with her suitcase wearing her floppy blue Mighty Aphrodite hat.

"Oh, let's get one last picture with our hats." Bronwyn hurried to her trunk and took out her yellow hat. "Do you have yours, Phoebe?"

Phoebe retrieved her red hat from the front hall closet. Joining the other two on the front porch steps, they all posed several times. Enough so they could get a series of selfies on each of their phones. When they were done, it was time for Bronwyn and Violet to go.

Bronwyn sighed, looking up at the great big beach house then back to Phoebe. "You'll take care of the place for us, won't you?"

"Sure," Phoebe smiled, a pang of grief in her heart knowing they wouldn't all be staying there together for a long time, if ever.

"And you'll let us know right away what you hear from Giant Publishing? Promise." Violet asked.

"Yes, I promise. And you guys drive safe and don't forget we have our next online Aphrodite meeting in two weeks."

They promised not to forget. They hugged. They waved to her as they drove away. And then they were gone.

Lost in thought, Phoebe watched the empty driveway. The ocean breeze seemed cool and she hugged her arms to her chest. A seagull cried out on the other side of Sol Mate, stirring her out of her reverie.

She turned and went up the front steps, running her hand thoughtfully along the painted railing. How odd that she wasn't leaving with Bronwyn and Violet. What a strange and wonderful turn her life had taken.

Pausing at the door, Phoebe looked at the sign she had tacked up at the beginning of the summer.

The Mighty Aphrodite Writing Society Summer Retreat!

A little battered around the edges from being exposed to the outside weather, the sign was still remarkably bright and cheery.

She smiled and pulled the tacks out so she could take the sign inside. She wanted to keep it, this souvenir of the summer that changed her life forever. Maybe she would start a scrapbook or frame it. She didn't know.

What she did know was it was time to write. She had a new life to get on with and a novel to finish. Not to mention all of the other novels that were inside of her just waiting to be written.

The End

* * *

We hope you enjoyed *Beach Retreat at Turtle Cove*! Find out what happens next with the Mighty Aphrodites - look for the next book in this series, *Beach Wedding at Turtle Cove*...(yes, a *wedding!!*)

Also by Darci Balogh

Dream Come True Series

1. Her Scottish Keep

2. Her British Bard

3. Her Sheltered Cove

Lady Billionaire Series

1. Ms. Money Bags

2. Ms. Perfect

3. Ms. Know it All

Sweet Holiday Romance Series (Box Set - great value!)

Want a quick escape over the holidays? These feel-good romances will get you in the spirit for Halloween, Thanksgiving, Christmas and a brand New Year!

1. Enchanting Eve

2. Love is at the Table

3. Mistletoe Madness

4. New Year in Paradise

Sugar Plum Series

Christmas, cooking, and chefs falling in love!

1. Charlotte's Christmas Charade

2. Bella's Christmas Blunder

Love & Marriage Series (Box Set - best bang for your buck!)

Steamy, emotional, relatable characters, these older woman, younger man novels are both racy and romantic.

1. The Quiet of Spring

2. For Love & For Money

3. Stars in the Sand

About the Author

Darci Balogh is an author and filmmaker who spent much of her life living both in and near the majestic Rocky Mountains of Colorado.

She now resides in the beautiful state of Michigan near Lake Huron. She has two amazing grown daughters, too many dogs, and an aversion to dusting.

Her fiction is a blend of women's fiction and romance (mostly sweet) with strong female characters and charming leading men. She has been a writer since she was a child and enjoys crafting stories into novels and screenplays.

Big surprise, some of her favorite pastimes are reading and watching movies. Classic British TV is high on her 'Like' list, along with quietly depressing detective series all while sipping coffee with heavy cream.